FADED LUCK

TWISTED LUCK SERIES
BOOK SIX

MEL TODD

BAD ASH PUBLISHING

THOUGHTS

To all of those who have believed in me, thank you. I promise there are more stories to come.

Copyright © 2022 by Melisa Todd

Cover by Covers by Ampersand

All rights reserved. No part of this publication may be reproduced, distributed or transmitted in any form or by any means, without prior written permission.

Bad Ash Publishing

86 Desmond Court

Powder Springs, GA 30127

www.badashpublishing.com

Publisher's Note: This is a work of fiction. Names, characters, places, and incidents are a product of the author's imagination. Locales and public names are sometimes used for atmospheric purposes. Any resemblance to actual people, living or dead, or to businesses, companies, events, institutions, or locales is completely coincidental.

Cover by Ampersand Books

Faded Luck/ Mel Todd -- 1st ed.

Paper 5x8 ISBN 978-1-950287-22-2

Hardback 6x9 ISBN 978-1-950287-23-9

Audio ISBN 978-1-950287-30-7

CHAPTER

ONE

While some familiars exhibit above animal intelligence, and the monsters that live in the realms occasionally talk to people, for the most part what evidence we have is they are barbaric, possibly nomadic, with minimal social structure and no formal higher education. It is possible there is an apprenticeship structure in place, but that is only a theory. ~History of Magic.

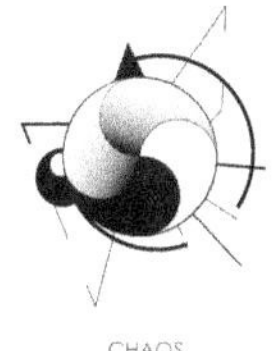

CHAOS

"Tiantang, I don't care what Cixi wants, I can't and won't move to China." The exasperation in my voice must have finally registered because Tiantang sagged. Even his whisker tendrils and yellow neck ruffles drooped. The Dragon of China rarely looked depressed but right now he looked wilted.

~But you'd be treated like royalty. And I'd have someone to talk to,~ he whined.

I glared at him. "A hundred and fifty-year-old being should not be whining. You can talk to and visit Carelian whenever you want. You know how to find and visit your family. Which means you are being ridiculous." I crossed my arms, not taking my eyes off him. He had to quit doing this.

~She is correct. It is most unbecoming of a dragon to beg, especially to a human.~ Zmaug's voice rang in my head.

"Thanks, Zmaug." I managed to keep my voice level and I didn't glare at the dragon, much. Her help always left me feeling even smaller than I usually did around the dragons.

We were standing in one of the many dragon pocket realms, this area they had altered to make it tolerable for humans, what with our weak skin and puny lungs—a direct quote from Zmaug. It was a mountainous area with peaks that reached above the clouds, the air crisp and cold, and part of me wanted to go for a hike. There was the sense of adventure waiting just out of sight. The rest of me wanted to go home. I had work in the morning and being here meant I wasn't helping Jo and Sable with dinner.

~Cixi values your input. She has figured out the medal to give you and everything. The ceremony will be extravagant.~

The obvious sop to my ego didn't help and I glared at Tiantang. "I've told her, I don't need a medal and she has advisors and family and other mages. While I know less than nothing about Chinese politics. The unrest is settled. She needs to make friends and contacts in China." It had taken a full year for the obvious infighting to settle down and for the government to accept Cixi as the empress. There were still some social issues going on, but as far as the rest of the world knew, China accepted their new ruler.

I, on the other hand, got hit with Tiantang whining, Carelian bouncing over to hang with him, and a lonely woman who I couldn't even talk to without my familiar. My Mandarin was less than nonexistent.

~I know,~ Tiantang sighed. ~But she expects traitors everywhere. It makes it hard for her to trust even when I tell her the person is trustworthy. She needs to show how much you saved us.~

"I saved my people too. She will learn." I didn't mean to be unkind, but really, calling me every time his mage had issues was ridiculous. Besides, Cixi was a decade older than me. Then there was the medal business. China, well more accurately Cixi, and the US State Department had been fighting for ages to agree. It took months to get the medal they wanted to give me approved through Congress, then Cixi got in on the medal idea and she wanted a big joint awards ceremony in Bejing. I just hoped that if they kept arguing about who was going to host the ceremony, eventually it would all go away.

~I guess.~ If anything Tiantang looked even more dispirited and I had to resist giving in to his desires.

Carelian had been exploring the area, ignoring us, which told me I was as safe as I could be. Granted, with dragons that didn't mean much. They were very capable of killing me by patting me on the back.

~Go home, Tiantang. Teach your chosen to be as strong as Carelian.~ Zmaug shooed her son with her wing. He moped, but left a minute later. I took a deep breath, forcing a smile, then looked up at Zmaug.

"I take it you wanted to talk to me," I said looking at the dragon. Zmaug didn't do subtle or at least the human version of subtle.

~I do enjoy humans who know how to think. There is a request for you to visit the Council of Lords later this turning. I want you to come.~

"The council of what?" I blinked at her, feeling off balance. That wasn't anything I had expected. I'd never had anything to do with the realms or the lords, besides the weird friendship we had.

If you could call it that. "Why would anyone want me at anything involving the Lords? That is Esmere and Tirsane stuff. It makes no sense for me to go. Do you?"

Zmaug shifted a bit. ~Onyx usually goes. I find them boring. But the Lords want to talk to you, something about needing human input. I think. Or was it about the magic Tirsane is still getting from your people?~ She wiggled her wings. ~Or maybe they just want to see her pet human.~

"I'm not her pet human," I growled. I still didn't know if that had been my most brilliant idea ever or the worst in the history of the world. Caught in a situation where a disabled girl was about to be killed, I'd leveraged the favor Tirsane had gifted me and asked her to drain the magic from the girl. Because of how I'd phrased it, she'd taken the magic from everyone who couldn't use it appropriately according to our laws. It had been a lot of magic and Tirsane, a lord of Spirit, had been drunk on magic for months afterwards. Salistra, her equal for Order, still wasn't speaking to me and it had been almost two years. That part I didn't mind so much. But I still didn't know what the tattoo Esmere gifted me with meant. And I still owed Salistra three favors for making an assumption.

Thinking about the complexity of these relationships had me rubbing my left forearm where a snake, a unicorn horn–with three of the four sections of the horn empty, waiting for me to fulfill a favor–and a cat nose with whiskers tattoos gleamed back at me. Brands, warnings, promises, they were all of that and more.

"I don't know what they want me to say. I didn't know she'd do that. I just was trying to save one girl." The fact that it had probably saved thousands meant no one was complaining. Plus, Charles had mentioned to me that they had seen an overall drop in crime rates, at least in the US. No data was available as to why, but it had sharply dropped off starting days after Tirsane absorbed the magic. Was it causation or correlation? I didn't know. And I wasn't going to worry about it. That was way out of my scope of responsibility.

~They are concerned that she is still getting the occasional magic boost.~

"Huh?" I swear I sounded like an idiot in half of my conversations with denizens from the other realms. But there was never any logic as to where the conversation would twist to, hence I was always playing catch up.

~You didn't know?~ Zmaug sounded intrigued, twisting her head almost upside down looking at me. It made my back hurt thinking about my spine mimicking her movements.

"Nope. No clue. But I'm not sure what they think I can do."

Zmaug straightened up her head. "That is why they want you to come to the council meeting."

I groaned and looked at my watch. Three hours had passed since Tiantang had begged me to come. "When is it?" Maybe I'd be lucky and it would be at a time I couldn't possibly attend.

"At your convenience. They are setting up an area now. Any time in the next Earth year would be acceptable."

I groaned and nodded. "Fine. Try to make it a weekend." At her tilted head I groaned. "The sixth and seventh day of our week. Check with Carelian. He knows the days." I didn't want to get any more involved in things with the realms, but it looked like I wasn't going to be given a choice.

"Excellent. I will let them know." She lifted her head. "Now I believe I shall hunt. Until we meet again, Herald."

I groaned and ducked as she beat her wings, sending up clouds of dust into my face. I pulled on Air, countering her effects as she flew away from me.

"You ready to go Carelian?"

~This place is nice. The scents are sharp. But yes. The egos around here are exhausting.~

Snorting in amusement, I sidestepped back to the house in Albany, only to be greeted by the discordant notes of my phone ringing. "Dang it." I dove for my phone.

We didn't want my easy sidestepping to be obvious, so my phone number was a voice over internet number that Charles routed around for us. He had a server in his house and used it to host various websites, but he also set up encrypted VPNs that all of our calls went through. And since it rang via the net you'd have to know what cell tower to look at to find my data usage. I also made sure my phone was in airplane mode every time I sidestepped. But if I was going into the realms, I just left it behind.

The screen listed two missed calls as I answered. "Munroe," I said not sure who was calling me.

"About time. We needed you in New Mexico two hours ago. A plane is waiting for you at the Dekalb-Peachtree airport. Can you be there in thirty?" Naomi Towers, my boss, snapped out. I didn't apologize or protest; if they were calling me it was bad. What I had to figure out was if I could realistically get to the airport that fast.

The Draft had placed me with a special activities group. Some days I was in the lab trying to figure out where a bacteria came from, the next I was helping hunt down an escaped criminal. I might be doing Search and Rescue, or I might be combing through reams of data to figure out how someone was laundering money. We caught all the cases that they didn't know where to dump, or that were too weird to make sense. It wasn't medicine but I enjoyed it, especially as it gave me access to all the libraries. I never knew when a bit of research might give me a clue about Stevie and that kept me from stressing over when Kristos would turn eighteen.

Jo Guzman, Sable Lancet, and I had moved into the Albany house a few months after Jo finished her draft. They were my partners and my best friends. But the Draft Board had placed my central location in Atlanta. We kept a small studio apartment in Atlanta that I crashed at occasionally, and it gave me a safe place for sidestepping. Jo and Sable used it when they wanted to spend some time closer to Jo's family. We missed being able to go see the Guzmans easily. But Carelian helped with that, acting as a shuttle service when needed.

Jo and Sable had found local jobs here, and we loved the house and Hamiada the dryad that was part of the house. We were happier here than in Atlanta, which meant juggling my need to commute, sometimes at the last second. Hamiada's excitement after we moved in had kept the house filled with a sense of effervescence. Somehow, James and Jeorgaz had grafted her tree as part of the house. This had the effect of making the house Hamiada's physical body and made it alive. She acted like our protector and was almost a friend. Though in some ways, she was more inhuman than Esmere or Tirsane.

"Can you have a car pick me up at the apartment?" I still didn't enjoy driving, didn't own a car, and I usually took public transportation—or rode a bike–but if time was of the essence, then that wasn't really feasible.

"Yes, it will be there in five," she snapped out and then hung up.

"Come on, Carelian." I changed clothes, twisted my braids into a thick tail down my back, then grabbed my go bag and Carelian's kit. "I'll get your harness on you in the plane." He was by my side as I raced down to where Jo and Sable probably were. Sure enough, they were curled up in the sitting room, though Jo swore it should be called the living room. Jo was reading the gossip tabloid *Daily Magical News*, mostly for the ridiculous things they put in there.

"Hey, Cori you're back," Sable blurted, sitting up straighter. "We wanted to talk to you for a bit."

"Sorry, no time. Stopped by to tell you I'm running to work. They have an emergency and are picking me up outside the Atlanta apartment in, oh, two minutes. I've got my phone and you can ping Carelian. Love you both, bye." Sidestepping, I turned before they could say anything. I landed, then darted out the door of the apartment running down the stairs.

Carelian loped beside me. ~Do you know where we are going?~

"Not yet. I figure we'll find out in the car or on the plane."

~Planes are uncomfortable and just wrong. I may meet you

there.~ We had let my boss know that he could step through the planes to find me, but never mentioned people could come with him or that he could take me to a place he had found. Most people still forgot he was a person in his own right, treating his ability to come to me as a cute trick rather than thinking about what it actually meant.

I was more than willing to let people underestimate him. It made life easier. Those few who suspected what he could do didn't say much to me. Even though I sidestepped probably more than I should, most people didn't question me or even wonder. Everyone "knew" I lived in Atlanta and that was the end of it. As long as I didn't force them to figure out a conflict, they accepted what they thought of as true. The Draft seemed happy with me in this job and mostly ignored me. Maybe I'd been lucky and they had more important problems to focus on.

I made it to the sidewalk, tugging on my official hoodie, dark blue with the word Agent on it and our logo in the corner. My id badge was in the pocket of my cargo pants, and everything else was in my bag. Carelian's harness, water bowls, food, and booties were in his kit bag. If they were flying me out somewhere, it was a place that needed my on-the-ground abilities, not my research skills, so I'd dressed accordingly.

A car, the ubiquitous black which always amused me, pulled up and a man rolled down the passenger window and looked at me. "Agent Munroe and Calin?" he asked, eyes lingering on Carelian who yawned.

"Carelian, but yes." I already had the door open as we spoke and Carelian leapt in first.

"Okay, buckle up, this is going to be a fast ride." He nodded once at both of us, flipping on the lights and siren before taking off.

Carelian sank his claws into the seats as I gripped the handles. The driver wasn't kidding when he'd said fast ride. I gave up and closed my eyes, otherwise I'd have a heart attack before we got to the airport.

~This is why I prefer transporting myself,~ Carelian snarled in my mind.

I silently agreed with him, but didn't say anything, though a sigh of relief slipped out of my lips as we jerked to a stop at the tarmac. They must have had the gates open waiting for us. My life was rarely this exciting.

"They are waiting for you," the driver said as I gathered my stuff.

"They?"

"The boss."

That would be interesting. I didn't think Naomi had tagged along for quite a while.

"You staying or traveling alone?" I said in a low voice as I trudged to the stairs into the plane.

Carelian lifted his head and examined it, ears laid back. ~I will meet you there. Maybe there will be a hunt. I need to practice my skills.~

I snickered and rolled my eyes, climbing the stairs to the plane to find out what the mission was.

CHAPTER
TWO

Cori Munroe made the news again today with the violent apprehension of a suspect. The man, wanted for questioning in a child trafficking ring, was delivered maimed and screaming. She had no comment when asked. The monster at her side had been observed licking blood off its claws. Later she was seen petting and praising it. Should the stance on familiars be revisited? Are they safe to be roaming around? Do we want to be rewarding attacks on humans? ~ Daily Magical News

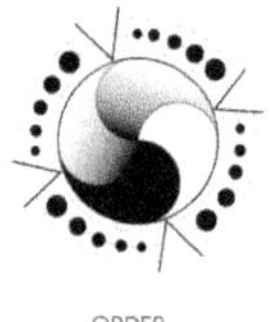

The airplane delivered me to Atlanta late two days later, and the same driver brought me back to the apartment. I was too tired even to talk to him. I trudged up the stairs in the muggy fall heat that was somehow worse than the dry heat of the Arizona desert. I slipped into the apartment and the air conditioning slapped me like an ice-cold fuzzy lint rag. I shivered, the temperature difference too great to make it comfortable

"Ugh. This is when I envy you the fact that you don't have to wear clothes," I muttered. Carelian sprawled out on the cool floor of the tiny kitchen, content. I sighed and started to strip. I was exhausted but needed a shower. Half-naked, I repacked the bag, making a note of what I needed to restock. The assignment had been interesting, but they'd grabbed me more for Carelian than my skills.

While most didn't regard him as human-intelligent, they had no doubt he could understand them. The tracking of a fugitive pedophile across the open desert had been exhilarating, if exhausting for me.

~I enjoyed that,~ he said while licking his claws. His muzzle pulled back making a face. ~But the stuff they clean off blood with is disgusting. Blood has a good flavor; you destroy it with that awful stuff.~

"Huh. I'll ask them to skip the acetone, but most people don't like the idea of animals licking up human blood. It worries them." I sent a text to Naomi asking that next time Carelian be cleaned off with water not chemicals. I doubted she'd argue with me too much. He still cowed people when he yawned.

~I'm not an animal, I am a Cath. And humans put too much crap into their bodies to ever be my first choice, but the spice of fear is delicious.~ He was laughing at me. I picked up my sweaty undershirt and threw it at him. ~Mmm, scent of a strong quean, my favorite.~ He stopped his grooming to roll in my shirt.

"You are such a cat." I headed to the shower and tried to wash off as much grime as possible. Jo and Sable knew what I did, but they both got oddly upset when it looked like I'd been doing dangerous activities. More so in the last few months than before. It was easier to shower and go home looking sedate rather than dangerous. Carelian always looked himself though; before we sidestepped back I always double checked to make sure there wasn't any blood on him. Blood got everyone upset and Hamiada hated it.

The mail hadn't been checked for a while, but I shrugged. All the bills were paid and it was almost always junk mail. It would wait. With a sigh of relief, I stepped home and felt Hamiada's warmth wrap around me. My house, or our roommate depending on how you wanted to look at it, made sure the house was the right temperature and always smelled delicious. But that could also be Jo's cooking.

"I'm home," I called as I stepped away from the sidestep area. We'd cordoned off a small corner that we never put anything into just so I had a safe sidestepping place. Hamiada had decorated the walls in that corner with a mural of her glade, the flowers and trees creating a unique area. All in all, my life was pretty good and it finally felt like all my dreams were coming true.

It was dinner time and walking in, I moaned at the smell of Jo's cooking, my mouth already watering. Jo and Sable sat at the kitchen counter arguing over something, the remnants of dinner pushed away.

"Ooh, anything left? Sorry, it was a busy day."

They both looked tired but Jo nodded. "Yep, plate in the oven for you."

~And me?~ Carelian managed to whine and look hopeful at the same time.

Jo grinned and some of the stress left her shoulders. "Yes, I have some for you too." She stood and grabbed a bowl with meat and some grains in it. He didn't each much grain but occasionally liked it for the texture. "Heart fresh from the butcher. He ground it especially for you."

~Excellent. Heart and liver are the best parts of any animal.~

I shuddered while Jo just looked amused, setting it down for him. Carelian tended to eat big meals like that twice a week, otherwise just nibbling on our food along with the kibble we stored in a jar if he wanted it. He told me once the kibble was like fiber was for us, good but not something you really looked forward to.

As if he could read my thoughts, he went up on his hind legs and grabbed the kibble off the counter, opened the jar, and sprinkled some on the heart. ~It adds a bit of crunch and the chase wore me out.~

"Chase?" Jo and Sable snapped their attention to me at that. I pulled my dinner out and we all transferred to the dining room. The bar worked great to talk to someone cooking or if there were just two of us in the kitchen. But with three of us, being able to see faces made talking easier.

"Yeah, you knew they flew me to Arizona." I'd sent them the bare details but not much more than a "I'm here and alive". But they needed details. "I needed to track a fugitive from an illegal border crossing. Turns out he was a pedophile. We had to race across the desert. Their dogs couldn't keep up with the motorcycle he had and he knew the canyons out there well enough to stay out of the way of the helicopters. So Carelian got to play hide and seek."

I was downplaying it a lot, not mentioning the cave system and him taking potshots at anyone who came into his line of sight. I also didn't mention the crazy request from some unidentified officers to let him escape. That bit of information was never mentioned to Carelian. Naomi could deal with interagency bullcrap. I'd had fun tromping through the desert and caves. Sometimes magic wasn't as good as a keen nose and the ability to make intelligent decisions.

~It was fun. And this is suitable recompense as I did not get to eat him.~ Carelian had blood on his muzzle and I mock gagged at the sight.

"One of these days I'm going to let you eat someone and then laugh when they taste horrible and you get indigestion," Sable teased.

~Who says I haven't already?~ He delicately picked up a kibble and popped it in his mouth.

"I hear nothing. I don't want to know," I said turning to my food, pot roast and some bread. "So, what is going on with you two? You both look like you're discussing something heavy, but I know, or at least think, work is going fine and you would have told me if there were any medical issues." I took a bite, watching as they glanced at each other.

They looked at each other again, then Sable reached out to hold Jo's hand. "You know we want to have kids, right?" Jo asked, an oddly beseeching look on her face.

"Sure. You've always wanted that. I've joked that I'll be the aunt that spoils them and hands them back." I kept eating, confused by this conversation.

Jo cleared her throat. "You remember the SEC game?"

"I'm pretty sure I'll never forget it," I said dryly. It was the first time I met Tirsane. "Watching almost 20,000 people die tends to stick in your memory."

"Yeah, well. Even with Carelian, a normal offering wasn't enough." At this point I paused, my throat tightening. "I would have offered my life to save everyone, especially Sanchez and Sable." Her hand clutched harder on Sable's. "But normal offerings weren't enough. To break the bonds I had to offer all of my eggs and the lining in my uterus. Even if I had an embryo placed inside me, I couldn't carry it." The grief on her face made me want to spring across the table and pull her into a hug, but the stiffness in her body held me in place.

"Jo, I am so sorry. Why, why didn't you say anything?" I asked setting my fork down, suddenly not very hungry.

She shrugged mustering up a fake smile. "What good would it have done? It was over and it couldn't be changed and I don't regret the offering. And while I was a bit sad I figured my partner could have the kid and we'd work something out. I didn't know if

Sable was the one or not." Jo laughed. "It was our first date, remember."

I nodded slowly the but the lump didn't go away.

Sable started this time, her smile a pale version of her normal joy. "We were still taking it slow, even if we had moved in together, then Esmere fixed my pancreas. We didn't think anything about it until the last month or so, when we started talking seriously about children. We figured I'd get artificially inseminated and no problem."

This time Sable took a deep breath. I wanted to throw up. Something bad was coming, I just knew it.

"We thought we'd run the idea by Esmere, just in case. And she let us know that because of how magic changed my pancreas to work, insulin won't work on me. And the odds are the weight gain from being pregnant would slip me into brittle diabetes and insulin wouldn't be able to counter it. Very likely it would kill me and any child I was carrying."

"Oh Merlin," I murmured, my heart breaking for the two of them. "I am so sorry. I don't know what to say." I could see their dreams breaking in their eyes.

"We've been looking at options, but we don't have many," Jo said, her voice hesitant. "We're well paid but paying someone is really expensive."

"Plus it just feels wrong," Sable added.

"Since there is no way we can carry a child, we were hoping maybe…" Jo trailed off and I glared at her.

"Jo, spit it out. What are you talking about?" A pool of nerves swarmed my stomach. Jo rarely got nervous talking to me. I'd never seen her hem and haw so much over anything.

"Can I ask? I know. I want to ask." Hamiada appeared in the entrance to the kitchen bubbling up and down, her toes hitting the floor with ballet like taps.

~Anything to stop this. You are both acting like timid baby goats,~ Carelian said, his attention on finishing the last drops of food in the bowl.

"Don't you dare, Hamiada," Sable gasped glaring at her. "We need to ask. It has to be right."

"Humans. You fret so much over spawning. Just let your seeds go like I do. Yours will grow and be strong." Hamiada danced, spinning around with flowers sprouting. I was distracted as bits of leaves and flowers scattered around the room.

"Hamiada are you... coming all over the floors?" I asked, looking at what could only be pollen dusted over a chair.

"I am not coming anywhere, I am here." She looked at me confused while Sable and Jo were turning red trying not to laugh. Hamiada was very sensitive to laughter and didn't understand the difference between laughing at and with.

I managed to find the right words. "Is that pollen you just dusted over the kitchen."

She peered down at it then nodded. "Yes, but it isn't fertile. Dryads don't spawn like that. The house has seeds and I shoot them down the gutters so they can find someplace to grow. But I don't think any of them have yet," she said, an odd sadness in her. "Earth isn't very habitable to my kind."

Sable looked up from where she'd had her head on her arms trying to get control of herself. "Hamiada, do you want to have a child?"

Hamiada tilted her head like an owl, eliciting a shudder from the three of us. "I had not thought about it. But here it is too dangerous?"

The fact that she questioned it made me curious. "Why would it be dangerous? We could plant it in back with the other trees and it would be safe here."

"Yes, but when you die others come in. It takes decades for a child of mine to fruit."

I wasn't a hundred percent sure what that meant. "Maybe, but there are things we can do."

"I will think. It is something I did not think I could do." She floated, her head still looking at us like a twisted owl. "But that is a theme here. Are you going to ask her? Otherwise I will. I wish for this. Children make laughter. Laughter makes magic."

There were too many meanings in those sentences for me to parse out. I grabbed the lowest branch. "Laughter doesn't give fairies wings, does it?" The phrase from a children's story where a bunch of children lived in the Spirit realm having adventures flicked through my head.

"There are no fairies. How would they get wings anyhow? No; laughter is just beauty in sound, especially from children. Now say yes," she demanded.

"To what?" At this point I'd given up eating. No idea what was going on with anything.

"To their request," Hamiada exclaimed stomping one foot and flinging an arm at Jo and Sable, who had paled and looked like they were trying to form words.

"They haven't asked me –" I started but Jo blurted in.

"Hamiada. Stop. Let us ask, okay? You can listen if you want." It came out in a rush and sounded like bribery to me. But who was I to judge?

"Ooh, yes!"

I swear she sounded like she was about to get the best gossip in the world. With a sigh I turned to Jo and Sable. "So ask me what? This is getting silly."

Jo looked like she might pass out, so I was relieved when Sable squeezed her hand. "I'll ask." Jo sagged a bit, but nodded.

"Cori," Sable started, and I swear the whole house creaked and leaned in to listen. "Will you carry our child for us?"

THREE

Mages get pregnant all the time, just like all other women. While some report less exhaustion than their non-magical friends, there seems to be no significant difference in how the gestation proceeds. Remember to use your magic while you're pregnant. It will help keep you in touch with your abilities. ~ The Pregnant Mage

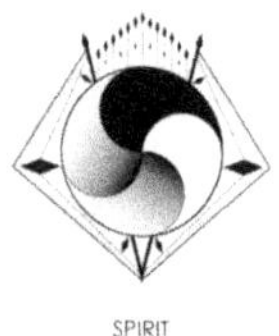

SPIRIT

I choked, eyes wide, looking at them. Even Carelian seemed a bit stunned. "Wait, what?" I stared at my best friends, my partners, and Jo had the audacity to smirk.

"Is magic killing your ability to hear too?"

I blinked trying to process the request. "Explain why you

would want me to carry a child? I don't even have sex. Sex sounds completely unpleasant. Why ask me?" I didn't know how to explain my confusion.

"We've been talking about this for days. We want children. But we don't want a stranger and while we can adopt, we want to try this first." Jo reached her hand out to me. "Will you be part of this with us? Carry our children? Be their mother in both fact and name?"

How was I supposed to answer that? I'd never even considered being pregnant before. It didn't sound horrible, but at the same time it didn't sound fun.

"Who would the father be?" I needed more information to figure out the correct answer to this. I needed all the information.

Jo shrugged, an odd expression on her face. Sable, on the other hand, laughed. "We talked about this a little before we realized I couldn't have children either. We kind of want to keep it in the family. I'd feel weird about a stranger. I said we should ask Sanchez."

"Stinky?" I blurted, then laughed at myself. It might have been a bit hysterical. "You want to ask your brother Sanchez to be your sperm donor?"

"I know. It sounds ridiculous. But Sanchez is a good man and is the only one of my brothers not seriously involved with anyone. The one girl we thought he might stay with got tired of his refusal to commit." Jo shrugged. "We'd need to discuss it with him, and normally I don't think parents of parents should have much say so in this, but I think my parents should know. It would be their grandchild from their son and daughter after all." She smirked at both of us, sitting up straighter, her tone of voice changing to smugness. "Besides, we Guzman's have good genes."

Sable groaned and yanked her hand away. "With comments like that, I might change my mind."

"Nah. You love my family," Jo countered, still grinning.

"Yes, I do. I guess I'll just have to put up with you." Sable leaned over and kissed Jo on the mouth and a minute later I cleared my throat as they were still kissing.

"If I want porn, I'll pay for it, thank you." My voice was sarcastic, but still I loved their passion. I just had never felt any of it.

"Sorry. So?" Jo asked, looking anxious.

My mouth went dry as I looked at their hopeful faces. "I need to think about it. I've just never really considered it before." When their faces fell, I held up my hand. "I'm not saying no, but this is like finding out I'm a mage. I need to think about it first. Okay?"

Sable nodded, even though Jo looked sad. "That makes sense. In all honesty, I might have worried you felt pressured if you just said yes."

"Is there any time pressure?" I looked at both of them.

Jo shrugged and looked at Sable, who grinned. "Before you're forty might be smart. Under thirty would be preferable." Sable winked at me. "My eggs have a decade or so before we need to worry about viability, but sometime this year would be great."

I threw my napkin at her. "And here I was worried you needed the answer today or tomorrow."

"Nah," Jo said as she leaned back in her chair. "While I might have hoped you'd scream yes and start bawling in joy, this makes more sense. Besides, Sable is right. If you'd just said yes, I would have worried. This is more you. Tell us when you decide and we'll go from there."

I nodded, my thoughts turning inward as I ate and considered this new wrinkle in my life. Children. They would be mine, but not mine. Could I handle that? Did I want to be pregnant? There were so many things to consider that I felt a bit overwhelmed. I spent the evening doing internet searches about being a surrogate.

In retrospect that was a huge mistake. The horror stories that abounded terrified me. They made me want to flee to a mountain top and never come down again. The pregnancy stories weren't much better. By the time I was done, I'd decided I'd never be pregnant. Who would want to go through that?

My panic lasted through the rest of the week. Work kept me

busy with samples from random scenes that I needed to test, and I sank into my science brain as a way to distract myself.

"Cori?" I looked up at Naomi'svoice through the lab intercom. "The investigators are here about the Arizona incident. They requested to meet with you and Carelian."

I sighed. "Let me finish this and I'll be up. Twenty minutes?"

"Got it. Conference room 3C." She clicked off. I finished the titration, recorded the results, saved them, then I headed out. I stripped off my lab coat, shoving it in a locker, then looked at Carelian.

"Come on. They want to ask more questions."

He lounged in a dog bed I'd gotten for him and placed outside the lab between the entry doors and the doors to the break room and bathrooms. He said it let him monitor who was coming and going, but kept him out of the lab where everyone agreed he didn't need to be. Even him. Labs reeked of chemicals to his sensitive nose.

~They want to praise me again? It was a beautiful takedown.~ He stretched as he got up. The location of his bed was also the perfect temperature and out of the way. I figured he slept more than monitored anyone, but with cats you never could tell.

"No clue. Probably just a pro forma thing." I headed for the stairs, taking every opportunity to exercise as I hated working out. Carelian and I needed to go for a hike somewhere. Jo over the years had dropped down to one yoga class a week, though she and Sable went on walks regularly. I figured she'd start a garden in Albany while looking longingly at the Tudor house. There was something else to consider if I carried their child. Would they want more than one?

Any time I stopped focusing on something intently, all the questions rose back up in my mind and they started to spin around. Even being faced with interrogators was better than this quagmire of questions without answers.

I trotted up to the third floor. The labs were in the basement, reception and conference rooms were on the first floor, with offices on the second through fourth floors. I had a nice little office, nothing fancy and no windows, but big enough for a desk, a flat spot for Carelian, a mini fridge, and a bookcase. I grabbed a water, poured some out for Carelian in his bowl, then drank the rest. The lab always dried me out.

My mind still was more focused on pregnancy ideas than anything else when I walked into the conference room. That came to a screeching halt as two men whirled, staring at me as I walked in.

One was dark, almost swarthy, with a bushy mustache that wouldn't have looked out of place as a toupee. Though I got a Hispanic vibe from him, not European. He had a badge that I recognized as the Border Patrol. The other was more fireplug than anything, with a barrel chest that made the door look too narrow. The fact that he didn't have a badge told me he was probably Homeland Security. What I didn't have was a clue about was why they were here. The lack of any agenda or even a formal request just screamed that interagency politics was about to slam into me, again.

I hate this macho crap.

"Merlin Munroe, why did you order your pet to savage that man! Ricardo Martinez was under Witness Protection." It should have been a question but the bellow from the Border Patrol agent made it come out like an accusation. The level of embarrassment his agency must be feeling and the amount of shit flowing from up above was obvious in his tone. Five years ago I would have quailed and stammered and tried to reassure them. Now I had a lot more confidence in myself and those around me.

I glanced at Carelian. "Did I order you to attack anyone?"

Carelian looked at me, jumped up on the conference room table and sprawled out almost covering it. It wasn't that big of a table and he was a big cat. His claws came out as he licked them. ~No. He was in danger of escaping. That creature,~ he managed to hiss out the word implying Martinez wasn't a man, ~had information about the location of three human children, all under the age of six. Children are to be protected.~

Both men paled at Carelian's voice in their minds, as I saw the step back they took.

"You do know that Carelian is an agent as well, with full choice as to which orders he wishes to follow and which ones he doesn't," I said as I sat down near Carelian's head. "And as a side note, we were never notified that our suspect was in WitSec, nor were we given any instructions other than he needed to be apprehended for questioning."

"And why was a star like you sent after him? That is an egregious display of exceeding the authority of your agency. Had we been properly consulted we would have taken care of this before it became an issue." This came from the Homeland Security man, his gruff voice and red hair making him look like the movie stereotype of an Irishman.

"A star? I'm a draftee who happens to be excellent at my job. The fact that given my power I can go up against almost anyone and I have a partner who is faster than a horse, we tend to get tagged when people suspected of horrendous crimes try to run. This Martinez, as you call him, fired a gun at me, then was going to jump on a motorcycle and flee. Carelian doesn't like people shooting at me. I believe the notes from the doctors were that he accurately hamstrung our witness. An instantly incapacitating injury, yet not immediately deadly. And I'm not responsible for notifying other agencies. You have an issue with how we did stuff, talk to my boss. I'm sure she'd love to hear your opinion." Naomi would chew them up and spit them out.

They both ground their teeth, and I wondered what the man wasn't going to be able to do because he'd been crippled. I didn't really care. He had talked after Carelian detailed exactly what else he could do to a human body. I just verified it was the truth. Terror worked wonders and Carelian could be scary as all get out. Amazing what seeing a few dead kids will do to your moral compass. As far as I knew he'd spilled everything he knew.

"You damaged someone who was going to lead us to the ring, and potentially have delayed numerous ongoing cases. We had assumed that your boss would offer you up as a sacrificial lamb for your agency. But it appears we're going to have to take this up to a directorate level," the fireplug snarled.

I shrugged. "Go for it. Again it is her problem, not mine, and you should have kept closer watch on him and made sure he wasn't hurting anyone. Besides, if you check the notes I provided, you'll see I pulled out every bit of information he had on his contacts. We are done here." I turned and walked out, hearing Carelian's claws scrabble on the table behind me.

"Bitch. Can you imagine what her kids would be like?"

I couldn't tell who muttered that, but the snarl from Carelian had me turning and looking back at them. "Powerful, smart, loved, and feistier than a Cath. I can't wait to meet them." With a smirk I continued down the hall, my anger once again driving me to a possibly rash choice. But their comment had made me realize the idea of little Jo's and Sable's sounded wonderful. Nieces and nephews I could spoil and love and never have to worry about their parents abandoning them.

The men stopping by my office and accusing me of things had been odd. But there were still a lot of people in law enforcement who treated me with caution after the incident with China and how close those bombs came to detonating in Washington, D.C. How close we came to dying and D.C. turning into a nuclear wasteland still burned in my mind with crystal clarity. All of that meant I wasn't sure about anything anymore, much less my own decision-making ability.

I needed another opinion.

CHAPTER

FOUR

Relations with Japan have improved greatly over the last year. The new ruler of China has met multiple times with the Emperor of Japan and there is talk of even closer ties. All discussions of trouble between the US and Japan has faded. There is still an air of mystery over what happened at DC regarding nuclear bombs, but no trace of nuclear radiation has been found. The investigation has been classified, restricting access to it for at least a decade. ~ House of Emrys Newsletter

CHAOS

ou wanted to talk to me?~ Esmere's tail swayed back and forth like a green snake, her fur as always a shade of emerald green that would put gems to shame. Esmere was Carelian's mother, or *malkin*. She was the size of a Shetland pony and screamed regal attitude.

"You are one of two mothers I know. And as much as I'd like to talk to Marisol, I don't feel it is fair to get her hopes up until I've made a decision." We were in Esmere's realm, a place I'd been a few times before. Whereas the glade Baneyarl, my griffin teacher, called home was trees and breezes. Jeorgaz, my phoenix friend, had one of flames, fruit, and trees. But Esmere did it differently. Hers was a long wide savannah, with stones to perch on to see the land and a few large trees that created circles of shade. I could see creatures that looked like deer in the distance and birds darted from branch to branch in the trees.

We were sitting under a tree, me on a blanket, her lounging like the ruler of the area. Carelian watched some ground rodents that kept poking their heads out of their dens, then back down. His tail lashed back and forth, ears flicking between our conversation and his prey.

~While I have no issue talking about my pregnancy or the acts both before and after, I do not believe I can provide you with much information. A Cath carries kits much differently than a human.~ She sounded bemused, and I thought often that she tolerated us for her son, but she and Marisol still had regular teas. After the fourth time Laurel, the police chief, had been called about the monster at Marisol's house, she started joining in the teas. It must have been an interesting discussion. And the idea of those three conspiring on anything made my skin twitch.

"I know that. And I figure I'll talk to the doctors and then Marisol if I agree."

Esmere snorted at that, but I ignored her and kept talking. "I wanted to know about giving children away. Or maybe losing them? Carelian came to me so young and I know you lost many of your kits. How did you do that without, I don't know, pulling him back?"

~Ah.~ Her eyes pierced me and shifted uncomfortably. ~I think you are worrying about nothing.~

"I am?" I blinked at her. "Why?"

~Cori, I have watched you around children, both human and animal. You find the animals cute and the humans puzzling. You are a kind and loving person who puts the needs of others before your own all too often. Yet you have zero tolerance for the needs of a child. I suspect you will nurse a babe for the first month or two, but more than gladly turn it over to your partners. You are not maternal for all that you are loyal and committed. This child will be a part of all three of you, and if I had to guess, your love and interest will grow as the child does.~

"Oh." I thought about that. The other grandchildren of the Guzman's I'd watched from being born to the ages they were now. And Esmere was correct. I liked them. Didn't mind them, but I'd never cooed over the babies or demanded to hold them. They were much more fun now that they were older. In many ways, Carelian had more maternal feelings than I did. "And letting Carelian go?"

Esmere laughed, a rough coughing purr in my mind and in my ears. ~You think I could have stopped him? But remember, a six-week-old Cath is about the equivalent of your five or six-year-old, more than old enough to let someone else take care of him. Though you may not have been aware of it, I checked in on him regularly. He is my son, after all, and one of the few mages I have birthed. If you had not treated him well, there would have been consequences.~ The words were idle, but I instantly had the desire to see if any mages disappeared after emergence where they gained a familiar.

"I would never—"

~I know. You chose your clan well. Your mates are family to

you, this child will be family as well. Do you really think there will be more than a day that you are not part of their life? I suspect you will be more than willing to hand off the child to those you love and who you know would protect that child with their lives.~

I stared at my toes. "In other words, I'm being an idiot."

~You are being a fussy woman faced with a choice that forces changes to your body and creates a life. I would think less of you if you did not think about this fully. But you made your decision ages ago. This is you resisting what your heart decided in the first second.~

Trying to hide my smile, I narrowed my eyes at her. "Really?"

~You would never refuse your loves anything, though it cost you your life. And this is what they want more than anything. A child for them to love.~

She was right. Even as I stressed, I had been wondering if I could do it, not if I would. So many things could go wrong. But I wouldn't be alone.

"Let's go home, Carelian." I rose and scratched Esmere's ear. All the Cath seemed to feel scratches were acceptable payment for their attention.

~I will get those rodents someday,~ he murmured looking back at the meerkats peeking their heads up. ~Then I shall have a fine snack.~ He muttered as he rose, following me back to the house in Albany. A thought and a step and I was home. Jo hummed in the kitchen while Sable was in the dining room. She'd been playing with painting and using her Water abilities. So far it was interesting.

Leaning against the doorway jamb, I watched them for a bit, trying to see them as a stranger might. Luminous dark skin, muscles and curves with a touch of age starting to soften them. Hair twisted in braids and held in buns to stay out of the way. Both wore tank tops and shorts, humming and bopping their heads to the music playing in the house courtesy of Hamiada's speaker system.

"Yes." I pitched my voice loud enough to be heard over the music, watching them with amusement and so much love.

Sable's head jerked up, her dark eyes locked on me. "Jo. Kill the music."

Jo turned, her face lighting up when she saw me. A frown crossed her face as Sable waved her hand. "Fine." A quick two steps and Jo killed the stereo her phone was connected to. The music playlist paused mid note. "What's up?"

"What did you say?" Sable asked, straightening up and walking towards me a bit.

A smile crossed my face. "Yes."

Jo glanced between the two of us, then her eyes locked on mine. "Yes to the question? Yes to the baby?" Her voice rising in pitch and talking faster as she stood frozen in a strange mix of hope and fear.

"That would be the yes. I'll carry the baby."

"YEESSS!" Jo's yell made the music earlier seem quiet. She did her happy hip dance, but Sable flowed around the boxes and grabbed me in a hug so tight I feared for my ribs. But I didn't mind. I hugged her back, just as excited.

"Thank you. Thank you," she murmured in my ear and I felt wetness drop on my shoulder.

I pulled back and kissed her forehead. "I love you both. Did you really think I'd say no?"

By this time, Jo had made her way out of the kitchen and added her arms to the mix.

"Think?" said Sable. "Maybe not. Feared? Oh yes. And I didn't want a stranger. I wanted my partner. My joined." Her voice remained soft as she wrapped her other arm around Jo. "We're going to have a baby."

"Yes, we are!" Jo's arms squeezed us tight.

I laughed, joy bubbling up in my heart. "I'm making lots of assumptions, mainly that you two have researched this until you can quote numbers and figures."

Sable broke our hug and gave me an affronted glare. "Of

course I have. This is important. I have all the information saved and collated."

That sounded like the Sable I loved. "Given that we can't do this the old-fashioned way," I said waving at the three of us, "what is the next step?"

"Steps. There are so many steps. While magic makes some of them easier and more expensive, the first one is your parents," Sable directed this comment to Jo, "and Sanchez."

Jo sighed. "Asking Stinky for this favor is going to be a pain."

"You know there isn't anyone else to ask. And if he's going to be the donor for our baby, don't you think maybe we should stop calling him the nickname he earned when he was twelve?" Sable countered, smiling at her wife.

"Point. I'll try to remember. I'm still having a hard time believing he's all grown up and responsible and stuff," Jo muttered, pulling out her phone.

"You? I'm having a hard time believing we are," I said, laughing.

"Cori, you were always a grown up and you know it." Jo made a funny face at me while she called her mother. "Mami, can we come over for dinner? We need to talk to everyone."

I couldn't hear the other side of the conversation, but I had no doubt Marisol was ecstatic. She understood why we moved to Albany. Living rent and mortgage free was a huge benefit. But she hated us being so far away. I think the only thing that kept her from fretting more was Carelian being willing to move her through the realms to visit us when we asked. No one liked me sidestepping them for anything less than a true emergency. I still didn't understand why it felt so different for me versus my passenger.

"Yeah, we'll be up there by five. Can you ask Stin- Sanchez if he's free? We wanted to talk to him too." A pause. "No, Mami. We just need to ask him for a favor." Jo had that mischievous smile that I loved. "Si. See you in a while."

She hung up and looked at me "Thank you. This is going to be the best thing ever. Even better than my workshop." Her smile was so bright and wide it hurt my heart.

"I hope so, you love that workshop." I grinned. Hamiada had helped Jo extend the garage so she could keep her motorcycle there and work on it a bit. It wasn't a full workshop like she wanted, however her job doing mechanical part creation for some pretty impressive machines soothed her creation bug. I still expected her to quit and start her own machine shop, but so far she'd been pretty quiet about what she wanted to do down the road.

I went back up to my room to change.

"You coming with us to let the Guzman's know?" Carelian was stretched out on my bed.

~Of course. She saves the good stuff for me. Though maybe you should take the queans there with sidestepping. If you do they will not be as interested in eating and I will get more.~

I threw my shirt at him. "You are a greedy jerk."

~Smart. Marisol has excellent food.~ He purred and stretched out further.

I met them down in the kitchen, all of us dressed up and ready to go. "Parents. Think we'll be good ones?" Jo asked as she leaned against Sable.

"I think the three of us will be the best ones." Sable kissed Jo softly. "I know it."

A few days ago I might have protested that, but now I just smiled. The idea of having kids was slowly making more sense in my soul.

Sable moved over and took my hand and I looked at her, a bit surprised. They were affectionate with me and I with them, but this seemed more serious.

"Cori, I'm going to repeat this as many times as I need until you believe me, well us." Jo draped an arm over Sable's shoulder smiling at me. "They will be our children. We are joined, which means your children are ours. And vice versa. I know this was never anything you thought about, but there isn't anyone else I'd ever want as our third."

I managed not to cry, but her words and the look of love on Jo's face sat in my mind as we walked into Marisol and Henri's house.

CHAPTER

FIVE

The draft is slavery! Revolt now. Quit giving up years of your life to the government for nothing. Demand equal rights as citizens! You are taxpayers also. Why should you be punished? Give up your magic and quit the draft! ~ Freedom from Magic

---

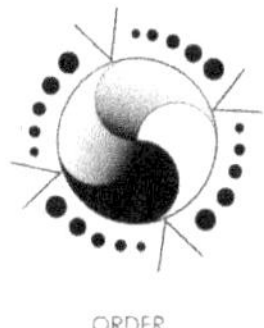

ORDER

J o led the way into the house, opening the door to the aroma of cumin, tomatoes, and chilies. I smiled as we traipsed in. While I was sure of my choice, I had expectations of great entertainment at her family's reaction. Being the only daughter meant Jo had always been expected to have kids—I think that was the one thing that had disappointed her parents about her preferring women. This should delight them, but it was the conversation with Sanchez I was looking forward to. Carelian followed us in his nose high in the air.

"*Mami*, we're home!" Jo sang out as we entered. The table was set and Marisol stepped out of the kitchen, smiling.

"My girls," she exclaimed, coming over and giving us all hugs and kisses on the cheek. "Come, food is ready. Henri and Sanchez will be here shortly." She reached down and scratched Carelian. "How is my gorgeous boy? I saved some shrimp and sausage just for you."

"That cat is so spoiled," I muttered.

~As is right. I am the glorious focus of not only one mage, but three. It is right I am rewarded for my superior choices.~ He leaned into Marisol's touch, before slipping out to the living room. He knew better than to be underfoot while she was in the kitchen. That resulted in stepped on tails, dropped dishes, and a pissed off cook.

"How is his business going?" I asked, curious. Sanchez had started his own towing company, giving preference to the Guzman's shop and lowered rates if you wanted to be taken there. Last I heard, he had three trucks and even an office attached to the Guzman's. In other words, like the rest of us, he had grown up.

Marisol's smile lit up her face, and the red of her Fire tattoo seemed to shine with extra joy. "Really well. He might open up another location. Last we talked he was still trying to figure out the logistics. He doesn't want to take out a loan."

I poked a bit, still worried about the request we were about to make. "No love life at the moment?"

"Pfft. That boy wouldn't know settling down if it bit him. Why can't he follow in Marco or Paolo's footsteps? No. He is still all social butterfly." Marisol's voice held love and exasperation. But with three grandkids, two girls and a boy, she didn't have much to complain about.

Laughter drifted in from the dining room where Jo and Sable were putting food on the table. They both seemed a bit manic to my eyes, and from the glance towards that room from Marisol, I think she sensed something too.

"Your son has arrived!" Sanchez bellowed from the garage door.

That comment was followed by Henri, in a much lower voice, "We are home, *mi corazon*." He emerged from the hallway and came into the kitchen, boots in hand, and overalls covered in grease and dirt. Henri's eyes were for his wife and he leaned over and kissed her, making sure only his lips touched her. "Let me shower and I'll be out."

Marisol looked at Henri the same way Jo looked at Sable, and I watched, feeling almost voyeuristic.

"And this is why I haven't settled down," Sanchez muttered in my ear. "I'm not settling for anything less than that."

I laughed as I turned and gave him a hug. He returned the hug, squeezing me tightly. From the skinny kid annoying his sister to a teenager who would rather game, he'd become a strong young man. A few years older than Jo, he had the dark Hispanic coloring, but a stronger and sharper face than his father, plus three inches.

"So, what is the occasion that you three ladies needed my presence?" Sanchez raised the question after we'd sat down and plates had been filled. Dinner tonight was paella with shrimp, sausage, and lots of peppers. All the Guzman's had added more jalapeno's to theirs. I kept to my much lower levels of spice. Carelian had his own seat at the table and was busy inhaling the shrimp that he dipped in hot sauce first. That cat made no sense.

Jo and Sable exchanged looks, then glanced at me. I shrugged. It was their story to tell in the manner they wanted to tell it.

Just that interaction was enough to cause a slowdown in the clanking dinner sounds.

"Is something wrong?" Marisol asked, a groove of worry creasing her forehead.

Jo shook her head. "No, just trying to figure out where to start and how to explain." She wet her lips and sat up a bit straighter.

~She wants to use Sanchez's seed to create a child for Cori to carry. Though apparently without the enjoyable part of procreation.~ Carelian didn't even look up from his shrimp as everyone whipped their heads to stare at him, Jo and Sable horrified, the rest just confused.

"I should have locked him in the trunk," I muttered.

~And I would have left. Do you think I would miss delicacies such as this for any reason?~ He held up one of the shrimp before tossing it in his mouth and purring as he ate.

"My seed? Wait, you want me to father my sister's baby?" Sanchez sounded horrified and stunned at the same time.

"Carelian!" Sable hissed out the word and then covered her face. "We were going to ease into it, explain everything. Not drop a bomb."

~Humans overcomplicate. It is progeny. That is always good. Though sex is more fun than this healer guided fertilization you talk about.~ He grabbed another shrimp. ~But either way, children are good.~

"I think I'd like some explanations?" Marisol said weakly. Both hands flat on the table as if the world was spinning on her.

That started the explanation why Jo couldn't have a child. A firestorm of horror and shock followed as she explained. Even Sanchez looked stunned.

"Jo, I am so sorry. It never occurred to me. What you gave up for me, for all of us." Sanchez's voice shook, he'd been there that day. He had almost died.

"Guys, it has been, what, almost seven years?" Jo had to count for a minute. "At that time it wasn't even a choice. And do you really think I'd keep my ability to have kids at the risk of twenty thousand people dying? At least I think that was how many I would not have been able to reach if I hadn't used everything in my offering. It wasn't even a question then and something I've known for a long time. So being upset about it now is a bit ridiculous."

It took a minute, but everyone settled down and they

explained Sable's risk if she carried a child, and then the logical decision to ask me to be their surrogate. I'd spent the time during all this eating the delicious food and listening. The Guzman's turned to me, their gazes searching. "Cori? You are okay with carrying a child for them?" Marisol said hesitantly. "Pregnancy can be rough and I don't know that you've ever talked about having kids."

"I know. But it would be their kids. Our kids. And why not? Who else would they ask?" At the end of the day that was what it boiled down to. Who else would I ever want to do this for?

Marisol stared at her plate; the food having grown cold as we all talked. She heated it up with her magic, and I smiled. "You've been using magic more," I said.

"I realized you are right. We get conditioned to not use it. Well, I have all this hair. Why not use it for things to make my life easier?" She nodded at the shrimp. "Being able to parboil shrimp on the plate is rather nice."

Sanchez was rubbing his face. "Let me get this right. My sperm, Sable's eggs, and Cori's uterus." He gave us all a wary look. "And I wouldn't be the child's father, just his uncle?"

"Or her uncle." Jo grinned at him while she spoke. "But yes. I mean, I have no desire to hide that, but you don't want to be a father yet, and this is for us. This child will have three people doting on her. I don't think feeling unloved will be an issue."

~And two Caths. I believe Esmere is excited at the idea of watching a human kit grow up.~

"Esmere knows?" Marisol asked, an odd note of hurt in her voice.

"That would be me. I wanted to talk to another mother, but you and Esmere are the ones I know best and I didn't want to get your hopes up. Esmere has a different viewpoint on having children." I studied my food. "At that point, I still didn't know if I was going to say yes or no. It was a bit of a shock when they asked me."

"Ah. That does make sense. And you are correct. My hopes

would have skyrocketed. But there is no guarantee this will work, you know." Marisol had an uncharacteristic look of worry on her face. "The embryos may not take or worse, you may miscarry." I knew she'd had miscarriages and my heart clenched at that idea. Maybe being a mage would make it easier to keep the baby healthy.

Sable nodded. "We are assuming my eggs are good, and that Sanchez has healthy sperm. We want to get a genetic test on both and make sure there aren't any hidden time bombs. But this all depends on Sanchez saying yes. If you don't, well, we will need to go back and think about how we want to handle this." She looked at him, a sad smile on her face. "If you turn us down, we have a lot of decisions to make."

Sanchez nodded slowly. "I'm still shocked, but I guess I don't have a reason to say no. It also keeps the child genetically a Guzman." He had a questioning look on his face as he gazed at his parents, then back to Jo and Sable.

"Which was part of why we asked you," Sable said with a smile, her hand touching Sanchez. "This way the child will really be your grandchild." She looked at Marisol and Henri as she said that.

Marisol looked at Henri, then back to Sanchez, and her head bobbed up and down in a quick little gesture.

"Okay. Then the answer is yes. I guess I'm going to be an uncle-daddy? Daddy-uncle? Whatever, I'll do it." His good cheer sounded a bit forced, and I wanted to tell him it would all be okay. "Now what?"

Jo and Sable squealed, and I mean loud enough that I winced and Carelian's ears laid flat.

~Why must you hit such an unpleasant pitch? I understand young ones doing that. You are not young.~ He spat the words as he looked mournfully at his empty plate. ~I thank you for the excellent vittles, Malkin Marisol. Now I shall go nap while those two talk about overly complicated things.~ His tail brushed

Marisol's hand and then he left the table to stare out the sliding glass doors to the back yard and groom.

Everyone watched him go, and Henri sighed. "If any of you kids had an ego like that, I would have paddled your butt until you couldn't sit. And then your real punishment would begin."

~I heard that,~ Carelian said while cleaning his muzzle. The late evening sun shone off his red coat, and he looked like a regal being, not the spoiled overgrown house cat that he was.

We giggled and like that, the tension vanished.

"So now what?" Marisol asked, and Jo and Sable began to gush. Much of it I had no idea of. They had put a lot of work into this. There was an Invitro Fertility specialist here in Atlanta they wanted to work with, but they had found a mage OB/GYN, Anna Lobdell, in New York, near Albany, and had verified she was taking new patients. When we decided to start the process, there would be drugs for Sable to get her eggs, then drugs for me to ensure implantation and so much other stuff that it seemed overwhelming.

I closed my eyes and reminded myself that I trusted them. After all, women gave birth every day. How hard could it be?

My phone rang and I let them talk, taking it out back to answer it. "Cori Munroe." The number wasn't in my contact list and hadn't been flagged as spam.

"Yes, this is Gloria Atkins. I'm calling from the Department of State about the medal award ceremony?"

"Oh. Yes?" I rolled my eyes and leaned against the wall.

"We wanted to discuss the plan. We are still trying to confirm the dates and coordinate it with all parties involved."

I rubbed my head. "That sounds great, but can we do this all via email? It allows me to make sure I have dates right, and this way everything is in writing so there is no misunderstanding."

"Of course. That would work out well. If you provide your email I'll forward you all the details."

I rattled off my email address and said goodbye. With a smile, I walked back into the house and the discussion about the process and the doctors they had researched. By the time we left, they had my life planned, appointments made to start the process, and I tried not to panic again at this idea, but the joy on everyone's faces ensured that I would do this. I'd faced down dragons, I could give birth.

~You will be a fine malkin, and an even better pack member. You worry too much.~

I glanced at Carelian out of the corner of my eye. ~Just wait until I'm in labor. It's your tail I'm holding onto.~

CHAPTER
SIX

In the last two years, the survival rate of mages making it through the draft has increased by almost fifty percent. The reason for this is unknown, but it provides more resources to be called upon down the road. Don't forget that previously drafted mages are usually used to making money and can be seduced into jobs that will necessitate large offerings and help private sector research. ~ Internal OMO memo

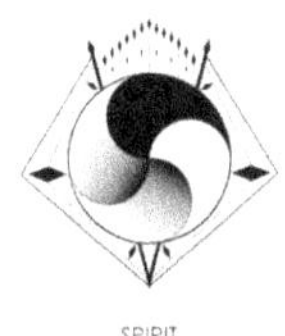

Work distracted me from my decisions. Sable and Jo went to the first appointment to collect eggs and fertilize them. Sanchez had already done his part and

the genetic tests came back clean. My appointment was scheduled a few days after that. They had given Sable some drugs to help her ovulate. I theoretically understood the process, but it was somehow different when it was someone I loved.

Part of me was excited, part terrified, so I focused on work. My work week was mostly lab testing, which allowed me to leave work at a realistic time. Before, it gave Carelian and me time to hike, explore the area in Albany. Now it gave me time to walk and try to work through my feelings and fears. I wanted to do this, but there were still a lot of emotions wrapped up inside me.

Days blended together and I swung between being completely focused on work or staring off into space. Before I knew it, the week of implantation had arrived.

I stretched, the quiet of the lab soothing. I tended to focus on biological and chemical samples. Most of the time the samples were from cold cases, where they didn't think I'd find anything. Often I didn't, but there were enough wins under my belt for them to keep handing them to me. The multiple issues with chemicals had made me go back and take more chemistry classes. I could probably qualify for a secondary degree in chemistry at this point, but the knowledge rather than the paper was the important part.

"Munroe. I need you." Naomi's voice snapped through the intercom.

"Okay. I'll be up in a bit."

I saved what I'd been working on. A group of bacteria samples that had caused widespread food poisoning but wasn't a familiar strand of Listeria. Three people died from the poisoning. Five were still in the hospital. Multiple groups had samples, and while no one expected me to figure it out first, I still needed to play with vectors and other aspects regarding the growth patterns. Needless to say, lab safety protocol was more important than rushing up there.

Ten minutes later, I knocked on the door to Naomi's office. "You needed me?" Carelian followed me up and almost instantly flopped down to lay against the wall. He'd been busy chasing squirrels in Albany in the evenings while I read or worked on learning to knit. It wasn't going well so far, but I was determined to knit a baby blanket. It gave me motivation.

"Come on in." She looked up at me and smiled as she said it. I'd seen her mad and happy, and this was her business neutral. I took a seat, the door still open, as I waited for her.

"I've got a few things. First, I'm officially reprimanding you." My temper bubbled as she raised her hand, waving her finger at me. "Cori, don't have your cat help bring in dangerous felons again, if you know they are in witness protection and might have ties to a larger ring. You might upset pretentious jerks and that would be horrible." Her voice was stern, but her rolled eyes killed any resentment rising inside me. By the time she finished I was fighting to keep my face straight. "Now that you've been reprimanded, here is your official thank you from the FBI regarding the information you pulled out of his skull. They shut down three rings and have evidence to make over forty arrests." Naomi slid an envelope across the desk to me. "This I've noted in your file. The reprimand, for some reason, didn't get saved."

I snorted. Naomi had no patience for fools, and these guys qualified. "All that just to tell me this?"

"And to officially reprimand you," she reminded me with a grin. It faded as she continued. "But no. I've got a case and you've been requested," she said, frowning at her computer.

"I have?" That was rare. Usually, I was sent with a team or as a general help request and Naomi decided who was best suited for that.

"Any issue heading to Quantico and working with a Steven Alixant?"

My laughter answered her question before she could finish. "No, he and his partner are my mentors. Technically, I still owe him assistance with research and what not. Sounds fun."

~Good people, if overly emotional.~ Carelian didn't stop making sure his tail was perfect.

"Ah, then this will work. Anything going on next week?"

"Ack. Yes, I need Tuesday off. I've got a doctor's appointment."

She nodded and typed it into the system. "So noted. How much longer to finish your tests with the bacteria?"

"Mmm, another week. But mostly it is a variant of Listeria. Just different enough the tests aren't picking it up."

"That sounds good. Then work here Monday, Tuesday you are off, and on Wednesday head to Quantico? If you know him, he can tell you where to meet him."

I nodded at each part of her sentence, adding things in my phone to keep me on schedule. "Will do. Any idea what this is about?"

"No. He asked if you were available to assist with an odd case." She shrugged. "Normally I'd press for more, but since you seem fine with the request and it has been quiet, I don't have an issue with you going."

"Sounds good. I'll ping him this weekend."

"Excellent. Let me know if he wants you to exceed your authority. Remember you can stick your nose into things, but anything else you call for the people in charge in that area."

"So, more pretentious jerks?"

"Exactly," she said with a grin.

We laughed, and I headed out. It was close enough to the end of the day that I just went home. I grabbed my bag and made sure I swiped out of the building before turning down an alley. When it was clear, I sidestepped to the house in Albany.

Once home I looked at the mess of my bedroom. I'd been so busy with everything, it had been easier to leave stuff in piles. But now it was starting to annoy me. My wardrobe had clothes shoved in it, and a laundry basket sat next to it with more clothes. I was an adult, why was I still living like I was in college? I needed a better closet layout.

"Hamiada, can you help me for a minute?" I said out loud. Carelian was out back, enjoying the coolness of the shade under the trees. Or chasing things. There was much in my life I didn't need or want to know.

A swirl of gray-green appeared in the room next to me, and Hamiada took shape. With a figure resembling a waif girl of sixteen, her round green teeth, slanted eyes, and leafy hair screamed she wasn't human.

"Cori," Hamiada said as she finished materializing. She rotated slowly, examining my bedroom. Trying to see it from her perspective I saw a room with pale cream walls, the baseboards painted a slate gray, and a bed with rich burgundy covers. The pictures on the walls popped in blue and green, while copper was the main metal accent in the room. Then there was the neon yellow and brown dog bed Carelian loved. I tried to cover it with a dark blue blanket, or a gray throw, but he pulled them off. The clash of neon yellow and his ruby red fur always made my head hurt, but he loved it. He either dragged it under the bed or out into the middle of the room. At least when he wasn't sleeping on my bed.

"Do you like?" Most of the furniture was what James had left, but I needed a better closet and it was all built-in. We'd learned that all the built-in shelves and drawers were a part of her. It explained the beautiful details that encompassed the house. Rather than pulling them out, we just asked her to change them. It created less damage and greater control. It had taken me months to do what decorating I'd managed.

"It is colorful. It reminds me of Jeorgaz and his feathers," she said.

I looked around after her comment and nodded. "With all the various colors I can see the resemblance. I'll have to ask his opinion next time he's over. Are you willing to change how the closet is laid out?"

"You do not like?" She seemed almost hurt.

"It is excellent for a guy. I have a few more clothes and need a different structure." One lesson learned early on by all of us, was that her feelings and ego had to be appealed to at all times. It didn't bug me. I was criticizing her body, after all. I'd want people to be nice about critiquing me too.

"Ah. Yes. That makes sense. What would you like to change?" Her hurt disappeared, and she lit up at the idea of having something to create.

I gave her my list, a few more drawers, some shelves for sweaters, and doubled clothing rods to hang things on. Then I stepped back and watched in awe. None of the rules of magic I'd learned in college or from experience made sense for what Hamiada could do, but it didn't matter. She did what she did and within her sphere of power she all but ruled supreme.

Wood sank back into the wall until the whole space was empty of everything. "Can you make it bigger?" I injected a hopeful tone into my voice. I might not be the clothes horse Jo was, but still I needed more than a tiny closet from the early 1900s. A bit more room for my clothes would make my life easier.

Hamiada tilted her head one way, then the other. "In real space, no. But I can extend it into my space and provide extra room." She paused, her face pulling down into a sour look no human face could have duplicated. "I do not know what you need."

I started to say never mind, but the idea of a large closet, the kind you see in magazines, sparked an idea in me. The worst that would happen was nothing. "Give me a minute." I dug out my laptop and in a minute had the image of a drool worthy closet. It had drawers and shelves, hangers and racks for shoes. I liked it because it had enough space for me to organize search and rescue gear and set up a workspace to make sure I could reload my kits. Even if it wasn't an S&R job, I still traveled with a kit. It had prevented some serious complications.

"Can you do this?" I showed her the picture.

The sour look brightened like a flower unfolding. "Interesting. It might take me a while."

"No hurry. I still have lots of work to do." And I did. Journals to read, a baby blanket to fight with, and apparently a baby to plan for. That still took me by surprise.

She nodded and faded away. I looked around and shrugged. I had plenty to do. My clothes were stacked in tubs next to the too small closet with the S&R gear that I desperately needed to organize and my med supplies. It was one of the reasons I'd hesitated about agreeing to the pregnancy. I hated the idea of not being available to work. But hopefully it would only be about four months that I would be restricted from field work. I needed to research the pregnancy stuff more, but right now I had too much to do.

"It's ready." Hamiada's voice right behind my ear had me squeaking in surprise as Carelian laughed in my mind. While I could feel her approach if I concentrated, I'd been in the middle of wrestling boxes down to the recycle pile. Jo might be able to use air to levitate, but every time I tried, they just flew around and created even more work for me to pick up. Carrying was easier.

"Oh great. Give me a minute?" I got the boxes down to the curb, then headed back up. Carelian deigned to rise up and follow me. He'd found all our possessions amusing, though he'd growled when I suggested we could dump his brushes. The Cath was a hedonist and his stuff was the only important stuff.

She waited for me, doing her weird float, one pointy foot supporting her. "Does this work?"

I stuck my head in the opening and my jaw dropped. Not only was there everything I had daydreamed about, she provided a bench to sit on and remove shoes, a place for all of Carelian's toys and brushes, and space for more clothes than I'd ever own.

"Oh wow. This is incredible. Jo and Sable will be so envious." The joy on her face made me smile. "Yes, I love it. You up for doing more?"

"Yes. This is fun. I like the pictures. Can you show me more?"

I might have created a remodeling monster, but I wasn't sure I cared.

"You know we are planning on having a baby. We will need a

nursery," I suggested softly. Flowers bloomed down her arms and she spun in a whirlwind.

"A child!" Her voice lilted with joy.

I laughed and called for Jo and Sable. This would all work out. I just knew it.

SEVEN

The wall that went up around Japan lasted for three weeks. The death toll has not been verified but at least five mages are rumored to have died from offering too much. Research is requested as to how to minimize the cost and implement on a smaller scale. Multiple companies are interested in this level of magic for security reasons. Bonuses will be offered. ~ Tomes of Wonder

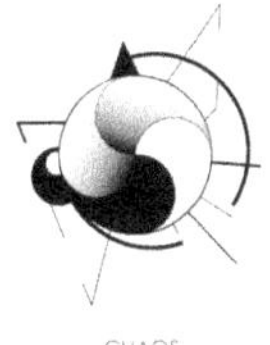

Tuesday morning I paced in my bedroom. The implantation was today, and I was about to crawl out of my skin. Jo and Sable were crashing at the apartment. The best IVR place was in Atlanta, even if the obstetrician they

wanted was in Albany. Sable's eggs had been extracted, and the clinic was ready to implant them. I'd been taking the drugs they prescribed to help ensure implantation.

To make me pregnant.

The idea was causing me to panic, and I needed to get ahold of it before I sidestepped to Jo and Sable. That was one thing I'd checked with Esmere, that me sidestepping didn't affect the embryo or baby. She'd assured me life didn't have any issues with magic of that type, only advanced technology. I made a mental note to never need a pacemaker. I liked sidestepping. It meant I really never needed to drive.

"I got this. Women get pregnant daily. They give birth daily. You can do this. It's normal and part of being a woman." I took a deep breath. "You have magic, friends who love you, an invitro specialist who is a mage, an obstetrician who is a mage, and you've survived everything else. It will be fine."

~You are worrying over nothing. My queans will produce glorious children. You are my quean. You won't fail at anything.~ Carelian pressed against me purring and I rubbed his ears.

"You are biased."

~Accurate. But we should go.~

He was right, as usual. I took a deep breath. I could do this. I stepped over to the apartment to find Jo and Sable sitting at the table, their hands wrapped around coffee. They looked as tense as I did and a part of me unwound. Together we had this.

I walked over and dropped a kiss on both of their heads, rare for me, but my heart felt ready to burst. "We have this. We are going to be parents."

"That we are." Jo shot up, the chair screeching as it slid back. "Which means we better go get pregnant."

"That just sounds wrong," Sable muttered as she rose. She'd gotten the eggs extracted fine, but the drugs to increase ovulation had made her nauseous for the last few days and she was just now getting it under control. "Though if I react this way to this little part, I'm glad I'm not going to be pregnant."

"Are you trying to freak me out? Because that is the way to do it," I said as we headed down to the street. The rideshare waited for us and we piled in, rattling off the address. Nerves jangled as the ride took an eternity and a few minutes. Carelian purred loud enough we could hear him over the car engine. The driver had paled when he saw Carelian but didn't protest. That was better than most reactions.

Getting out at the office building it all seemed surreal; I'd go in there just me, and come out pregnant, responsible for another life. I swallowed down my doubts and fears and focused on knowing I was loved and I'd be bringing a child into the world who would be smothered in love and never abandoned.

The waiting room was done in cool blues and greens, and the feeling of odd serenity made my skin crawl. I closed my eyes and repeated my mantra, "I can do this." We walked forward and I let Jo and Sable take the lead. My hand stayed on Carelian's head as an anchor and support.

"Guzman. We have an appointment," Jo said, her voice a forced lightness that I knew covered nerves.

The receptionist didn't take her eyes off Carelian, who seemed a gleaming ember with his ruby fur in the midst of all the serenity. "Okay, one minute. Are all of you going in?" She glanced down at the computer, then back up. "It is supposed to be a sterile environment." Her words stuttered out.

~Why does everyone assume I am dirty?~ Carelian growled, and I thought the girl might have a heart attack or pass out as she paled to the point her ivory blouse looked dark compared to her skin.

"They don't furball; they assume you're covered in fur. Stay out here. Really, it will be weird human stuff." Jo scratched his ear as she spoke.

His tail lashed, but he sank down in the middle of the room. ~Very well. I shall wait and listen. If you call I will be there, fur or no fur.~

"I know." I rubbed his head and then turned. My body tensed. "We ready?"

The receptionist nodded at the door as it opened and a nurse forced a smile at us. "Come on. I'll help you get ready."

She led us to a small room. "You are receiving the embryos?" She looked at me and I nodded, my throat suddenly tight and refusing to make sounds. "Excellent. Here is your gown and sit on the table here. The doctor will be in shortly. Are these two ladies staying?"

"Yes," they both said in stereo and I bobbed my head, glad I wouldn't have to talk.

"The doctor will be here shortly." She left me with a last spooked glance at us before shutting the door.

Jo shook her head. "I swear, some people have dogs the size of small horses as a familiar. You'd think a cat the size of a dog wouldn't be that big of a deal."

"Cori? You okay?" Sable wrapped her arm around me, her eyes dark. "You don't have to do this."

I almost grabbed at that. The need to run back to my uncomplicated unpregnant existence was strong, but equally strong was the desire to have their children be a part of us, not a stranger. Everyone got pregnant unprepared the first time. I could do this.

"I'm good." I stripped quickly into the stupid hospital gown, then sat there on the table, feeling stupid and exposed. Jo held my right hand and Sable my left. From the strength of their grips, I knew they were as tense as I was.

Doctor Singh came in and nodded at us. He was middle aged, East Indian, with gray hair at his temples pulled back into a long tail at the nape of his neck, and his mage tattoo gleaming in silver and yellow on his temple. I'd met him before when we had our first meeting and he explained the process.

"Ladies. I am happy to tell you that we have five viable embryos. With IVF there is always a strong chance of the embryos not implanting, so you need to decide how many you want to try now and how many you want to hold back for later."

"I am NOT having quintuplets." My voice was adamant. That was not an option.

Jo snorted. "That isn't my preference, either. What do you recommend?"

"Three implanted usually means about a 15% chance at twins, 5% chance of triplets, and a 65% chance of a healthy baby."

"And a 15% chance of failure?" I asked, worry gripping me.

"Normally yes. Pregnancy isn't a sure thing, but I can help up the odds." He tapped the side of his head where the Order tattoo sat. "I can encourage the implanting, but still, your body is the one that is going to decide."

I chewed my lip. Triplets sounded exhausting, but then we'd have all the children at once. That didn't sound so bad. And it meant we'd probably get one. If I didn't hate being pregnant, then we could try again? All the possibilities swirled around in my mind.

"Three?" Sable asked, looking at me.

I swallowed hard. The odds were it would be one. Three though would be doable, if awkward. I nodded my head in a jerky manner, the whole thing feeling insane.

"Three," I said, my voice cracking the tiniest bit as I squeezed their hands.

"Excellent choice." He gave us a big smile. "You've been taking the meds for the last few days?" He directed this question to me and I nodded, my hands gripping Jo's and Sable's so hard I was vaguely surprised they weren't protesting. Dr. Singh nodded, giving me a hard look. "You are sure about this? Normally I don't work with surrogates who haven't already had at least one pregnancy, but you aren't exactly a surrogate, are you? Though I am worried about your lack of sexual experience."

Oddly, the question made me relax, and I heard the sighs of relief as my hands loosened on theirs. My nose wrinkled. "Thank you, but no. It doesn't even interest me. But this will be our child and women get pregnant all the time. I can do this."

He looked at me a long time, and for a moment I wondered if

he wasn't a Soul mage as opposed to Order. "Yes, I believe you can." He clapped his hands together and stuck his head out the door, saying something. He turned to wash his hands and put on gloves as a nurse came in carrying a tray with medical equipment on it, and, I suspected, the embryos. "This is going to be a bit tight with all of us in here, but this is how it will go. Jo and Sable, you should be able to stand in that corner and see the ultrasound. Nurse Pine will be helping guide me with the ultrasound while I implant them. It will feel a little uncomfortable, like a rough Pap smear. But we will be able to verify the implantation. Once that is done, we'll snap pictures, your first ones, then you need to lie here for about fifteen minutes to give your body a bit of time to adjust. After that, you will officially be pregnant." He talked as he got ready and helped me lay back.

My hand felt cold as Jo and Sable had to move away, and I slipped my feet into the stirrups for the process. I wanted to close my eyes and ignore it all, but I also wanted to know every step. So I forced my head to turn and watched the ultrasound. I could see the baster, I knew that wasn't the name but still, nudging the side of my uterus. He frowned and I could sense an offering being made.

"Why did you offer?" I asked, curious.

"Healing. It is a Pattern aspect. They teach it to you in med school." His voice was distracted, as he didn't take his eyes off the monitor. "All mages get a full semester of how to use your magic with healing. Some of the best surgeons in the world are mages. I'm helping the cells adhere to the lining in your womb. It looks like it is at the perfect thickness for implantation."

The room fell silent as we watched. Then he pulled back, pulling the tool out of me. "Done. Congratulations, you are pregnant."

Jo and Sable squealed a bit as the nurse printed off pictures of the blob on the screen. I lay there in the room, listening to the sounds around me, and placed my hands over my stomach, wondering that it was so easy to change the world.

"Now it might take a day or two for your body to realize, so don't go running any marathons. Remember, you may see some bloody discharge. If you have severe cramping come back and see me. I've done what I can to ensure a successful implant, but your body still has a mind of its own. Any questions?"

I had a million, but none that I could figure out how to ask. I mutely shook my head, and he left. Jo and Sable held my hands, babbling at me in excitement and worry. The words washed over me like a wave of love and support and I reached out to Carelian.

~I'm pregnant.~

~You will be an excellent malkin. I have faith in your magnificence.~ His voice came back in an approving rumble and I started to laugh, sharing his comment with Jo and Sable.

Jo grinned and kissed my forehead. "He is right, as usual. You are magnificent."

Maybe, maybe not, but either way, my life was going to be drastically different. I couldn't wait.

CHAPTER

EIGHT

Yet another airplane crash was reported of the Bering 777's this week. This plane was crossing from the China Sea to Australia and disappeared after a short mayday. The investigation is still continuing, but no survivors have been found. In other news, the newest fashion for mages is brilliant blue hair. It has been confirmed that dye doesn't affect genetic offerings at all. ~Daily News

---

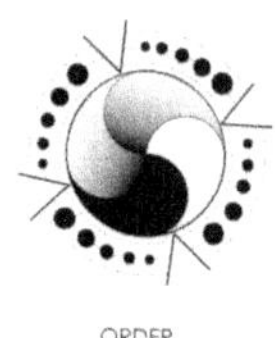

ORDER

We talked late into the night Tuesday. We decided to not tell my job about the possible pregnancy until we were past the first trimester and I was showing. If it didn't work, we didn't want to have to explain to anyone, not even Jo's parents. Stinky didn't know when we would try, so we'd just keep it to ourselves until then.

That also meant not telling Indira or Steven.

Wednesday morning I showed up at Steven's office dressed in simple black slacks, a knit top and a large shirt, as well as my messenger bag. The last year or so, I'd settled into my style and it almost felt like me. At this point, they could deal with my style or not.

I walked into the office, approaching the security guard, Carelian by my side. As usual, Carelian got a second glance and widening of the eyes. "Cori Munroe, here to see Agent Alixant." Technically, I could say I was an agent too, but mostly it was fun to hold that back until I needed it. My badge was tucked away in my bag near my phone. I could grab it easily.

"One minute."

I turned and looked at the area outside the lobby windows. The rideshare had checked with me twice before bringing me here. I didn't have any place to sidestep to near the FBI. Besides, they tended to get upset when people got into their secure locations without ID. I'd stepped to a place near the State Department and paid the outrageous fare to get taken here.

"Cori, good to see you." I turned to see Steven approaching and smiled. Part of me wanted to blurt out the change in my status, but the fear of jinxing it stopped me. It also made me check to see if there was a Murphy's Cloak on me. The last thing I needed was to make my own life worse.

"Steven," I said, as I gave him a hug.

"Carelian," he said with a nod. Carelian flipped a tail, stalking next to me. He'd been odd since it was official, but had, as far as I knew, not told even his mother about my pregnancy.

We chatted about inconsequential items and promised to get to dinner more often now that I lived in Albany. Not that distance really was an issue, but it meant we could get there easier with Jo and Sable.

He ushered me to an office that had bookshelves full of books about investigations, true crime, and FBI manuals. He didn't rate a window but the four large screen tv's all showing different scenery made it almost not matter. He had a small table with two chairs, a desk, and two other tables. With a wave, he pointed me to the chair at the table and grabbed a coffee pot and mugs from a place behind his desk.

"I figured you'd want coffee."

"Thank you." I'd had some before I left, but not enough to make me happy. He pushed the mug to me and I added my cream and sugar. He did the same, though his was black with a touch of sugar, and he settled into the other chair.

"I'm guessing you didn't want me here just for coffee? Not that I'm complaining. Kona Blue?" Carelian had sprawled against the door, ensuring no one would be able to push the door open if he didn't move. Glancing at him, you'd be sure he was moments from falling asleep instead of listening intently.

"I'd not dare serve you anything less." His smile had a teasing aspect to it and I grinned.

"Smart man. So spill, what is all the cloak and dagger about?"

Steven settled in, holding the coffee close to his nose. "What is your background in virology?"

That had me pausing for a minute before I took a sip of my steaming coffee. Enjoying the rich flavor gave me a moment to think. "Standard I would think. I can identify viruses with the use of a microscope, or sense them if I know which one I'm looking for. Think of it like call mineral. But searching for a virus isn't as easy as for gold. Why?"

He stood up and grabbed a folder from the desk. "This isn't a case yet. But it might be. The CDC notified me that they thought there might be either a weapons lab or someone who has some of the missing samples."

"Samples?" I asked, my brow arching. Even if it was of something innocuous like the common cold, it could be deadly.

He gave a bitter smile. "Were you aware that since 1972, at least thirty samples of various diseases have disappeared from storage? They figure most of them were just put away in the wrong place, but not all. Getting samples of other diseases like Ebola or vole pox or even SARS isn't that hard."

I set my coffee down, blinking. "Really?" I had to resist the urge to cover my stomach where that tiny life or lives might be growing or dying even now. "And this is normal?"

He shrugged. "That was my question. They said most of the epidemiological community knew about it, but there wasn't a reason to make it public. It would just scare people."

"Yeah. Because it scares me." I pulled out my phone and started to pull up the shapes and structures of these viruses. And I'd need to practice in the lab on how to identify and break them. Breaking a virus didn't work the same way as breaking a molecular structure.

"So that is why I asked for you."

I lifted my head from the website I was on and looked at him. "No, I have no clue why you asked for me."

"You are strong enough to go in and find the source. You received the smallpox vaccine as part of your medical tests prior to the draft. You also have him." Steven jerked his thumb at Carelian. "I don't believe he is susceptible to most Earth diseases, has a much better nose than any of us, and can react as needed. Anyone else I'd send in would be a huge team and the person would have time to shut down, destroy the lab, or go full mad scientist. The odds are you can arrive as a visitor and just not create much notice."

I gave Steven an incredulous look. "Did you miss the Cath that is almost my weight and bright red?"

He started to laugh. Carelian ignored both of us, still pretending to sleep. "I grant you that. But it means you are so obvious no one is going to expect that you are investigating anything. I can't force you, because we don't have a valid case yet. Five weird infections with one death aren't enough to start a true investigation, but I know Naomi and she trusts me. Your department has a lot of leeway and frankly, you're one of the most level-headed people I know. Your skills just make you even more perfect for the job."

Part of me lit up with excitement. Another part, a new part, thought about the life growing inside me.

Stop it. Women get pregnant every day. They don't go into confinement. I'll be fine.

"When would I need to leave?"

"I was hoping by Saturday. You'll need to fly out and get a place to stay that can act as your home base for a while. It won't make sense to people if you don't stay anywhere." He handed me the folder with a shrug. "People get snippy."

I gave a grunt of acknowledgment as I opened the folder. It had the notes from a local doctor and some geographical information. "This isn't much," I pointed out. "And where is this?"

"You're right, it isn't much. It's a small town in Nebraska. The county coroner is the one who reported it, but it's a bit more complicated. I think there is something going on, and these are just the slip ups, not the actual attack. I would prefer to stop it before there is an actual attack."

I shot him a glance from under my lashes. The frown and darkness in his eyes were heavier than normal.

He's really worried.

"If Naomi doesn't care and I'm not paying for our flights, sure."

"No. I'll be paying for everything out of a discretionary budget. I'm hoping you find nothing, just a weird coincidence, otherwise I'll deal when you let me know what is there."

I nodded and closed the folder. "I'll have to take the time to sit and really read this. There's a lot of information here. But I'd rather do it back in the office."

Steven sighed. "That makes sense. I'll wait. Maybe it is nothing but random chance. It can happen, but right now the CDC is facing major budget shortages and until an investigation is declared, they won't step in. But your office can act in absentia for them, so I'm hoping with your skill set it will be enough to prevent a major issue."

I nodded at that. We worked with the CDC, the Centers for Disease Control, often. We had people experienced with dangerous situations and could react to seal down areas if needed. The CDC tended more towards lab nerds than people like me. Naomi had ensured I was sent through basic weapons and law enforcement training, making sure I would only shoot what I wanted to shoot, though I only carried my weapon if on a specific job. With Carelian and my mage abilities, a gun didn't make me more lethal.

"Trust me, I find anything actively going on like a new disease breeding ground or worse, a bunch of animals that are spreading a disease, I'll be locking it down and calling the CDC. I'm good at chasing small things to find a clue, not managing a major outbreak."

Steven nodded, his eyes not lightening up. "I know. I'm really hoping it's a rare animal that got infected. There is still the occasional rodent that carries the black plague in the Southwest, so that isn't impossible." He rubbed his face with his hands, just adding to his exhaustion. "Of course, then there is Carelian."

At that, Carelian lifted his head to look at the two of us. ~What about me? I do not carry diseases.~ He sounded affronted at the very idea.

"No. I know that. But do you know if you are susceptible to any of them? Can they mutate and affect other denizens?" Most of my friends had taken up my name for the beings from the various realms. It sounded better than calling them creatures.

Carelian yawned, but I sensed it was mostly for show than a real yawn. ~I am unsure. I shall ask. But I must point out that I have never heard of it.~

"True. But how many familiars are there and how often do they stay in contact with other denizens?" Steven had his body shifted towards Carelian, paying close attention.

~Hmm... not many. Familiars require a very unusual set of desires. We are usually very young or very old. I am an example of the young being but a kit when I chose. Arachena is the other extreme. She was hatched when your country was being founded. I have asked, but do not expect an answer fast. The realms are not as consistent as your world is. And many familiars may only be known to magic.~ He rolled over in a stretch that had his tail touching one wall and his front paws the other, then he sprawled out on his back, eyes closed.

"How many familiars are recorded by the OMO?" The Office of Magical Oversight had records on the majority of mages in the world. While not required to report familiars, only because of their rarity, most mages had it noted in their files. I could go look it up, but I had no doubt Steven already knew the answer.

"Worldwide? About 462,000. As far as we know, it is about 1 out of 5000 mages who have one."

I tilted my head, thinking about it. That was barely any compared to the mage population, much less the human population. But still, it was more than I expected. At this point I'd met easily three hundred mages in my life and five had familiars, including myself. Though it was six if I included James. His familiar, the phoenix Jeorgaz, was still around, but an independent entity.

I flicked my hands away. "That is a problem for another time. Though I doubt they are susceptible to Earth diseases and for the most part, they've never talked about sickness in their realms. It has always been poisons or venoms. I'll assume not unless he gets information otherwise."

It looked like Steven was going to argue, then his shoulders sagged. "Thank you. Let me know."

"Anything else?" I asked, still watching him. Something didn't seem right.

"No. I'll file the request. Naomi will approve it as a fact-finding mission. Let's hope I'm becoming paranoid in my old age."

"Please. You're what, forty? That isn't old."

He laughed. "Thank you, I think. But I'm forty-eight, or almost. Remember, I've already done my draft, then worked for the FBI for another twenty. A few more years and I'll be able to retire." Something I couldn't catch flickered across his face. "Either way, this was a good excuse to see you. Please remember to leave the gate before you teleport back," he said with a smile in his voice, even if his face was stoic.

"Lesson learned. But I will see if I can find a good location to teleport to. I get the feeling this won't be my last trip here."

"Probably not." He rose and when I did also, he pulled me into a hug. I returned it with interest.

"Why don't you and Indira come up for a long weekend. Next month?" I figured by then we might be ready to start sharing the information about the pregnancy, at least to close friends.

"I'd like that. I'll check with Indira." We talked for another few minutes, settling on a date in late October. One more hug and he escorted me out of the building. I walked to the gate, then a bit further, looking for a suitable location outside of the gates to memorize as a good sidestepping spot. It took me a few minutes. Manmade structures were better than plants, those tended to change too much. Finally I found one, shaded from view, and I memorized it before stepping home.

CHAPTER

NINE

The Bureau of Indian Affairs still sends out mages to try and communicate with the American Indian Nation. The only known portal has a door that looks like it was taken from a castle. There is a bell on it, but up to this point no official has gotten anyone to open the door. The wall separating the AIN from the rest of the world is still impossible to breach. ~ OMO Internal Memo

SPIRIT

I hit the office first thing the next morning. The file needed to be revised, travel requests needed to be made, and I wanted to think about what I was walking into. Naomi swung by my desk as I was trying to find a hotel to stay at. There weren't many options and if this was supposed to be subtle, a rental might be better. That meant more paperwork.

"You meet with the FBI yesterday?"

I nodded, looking up from the numbers on diseases listed in the report. "Yes. I'm going to head out Saturday, but I need to get a booster shot for some of the diseases the coroner reported. I didn't realize smallpox was still an issue."

"Smallpox?" Naomi arched an eyebrow, tilting her head a bit. "Interesting. It is considered an extinct disease, but it does crop up very occasionally. Go ahead, get the full booster today. You'll need tomorrow to recover. Some of those shots pack a wallop."

I sighed but sent a note making an appointment for right after lunch. "I'll keep you updated, but for now I'm just digging into the file." I didn't mention I had an appointment in two weeks. We were waiting for that long before my first obstetrician appointment, a doctor Jo and Sable promised I would like.

Naomi pursed her lips, then nodded. "Working with the FBI is always questionable, but if you think he's trustworthy."

"He is. It's probably nothing, but I'll bring the gear I need in case it is something. Permission to requisition that gear?" I meant a full hazmat suit. In theory I could create a vacuum around me with Air, but why trust my abilities when I could be doubly safe with a suit and only use my magic if needed or as extra protection.

"Ugh. Yes. But if you don't use it, please check it back in. Those things are expensive."

"Will do." I typed as I spoke, entering in more forms. Naomi waved and headed to her office while I continued to dig into the report. My contact there would be a coroner by the name of Adam Walsh.

Carelian grumbled in his sleep, rolled over, thudding into the desk, and went back to snoring softly. I went back to reading the file Steven had given me. Adam Walsh had been called in to consult on three cases at the local hospital—it had a whole fifty beds in it. He'd been surprised to see a pox that wasn't chicken pox. And he'd only recognized it because he'd been a military doctor back in his thirties. They had better infectious disease symposiums. He actually noted this. The victim was isolated and treated with anti-virals and they made a full recovery. He had sent samples to the CDC of the three victims, but they were backed up for months on running samples. The fourth victim died. The notes weren't clear, but if I interpreted them correctly, the fourth victim was found already dead and only came into town occasionally. So there was no reason to believe he had spread it, though it was always possible.

The bottom line of the report, with the autopsy notes, was that he thought they were three different poxes, but without a microscope that could see the virus shape and a catalog to compare them to, he couldn't be sure which ones they were. But his gut told him the old man died from smallpox.

I sat there staring at the file. Smallpox was taught as the scary civilization ender. But it hadn't been seen widely since magic rippled across the world. Magic helped to create the vaccines for it and many others, so why would it be in Nebraska, of all places. I didn't find any CDC labs near Genoa, but that didn't mean there weren't smaller labs, and remote locations were better for some research.

It could be nothing, or it could be a ticking time bomb. I filled out the requisitions for a suit and sample collection cases, then I headed down to get my shots.

I walked in and bared my arm for the shots. "Are you pregnant?" the tech asked.

My body froze as did my mind. "Maybe? Does it matter?" I managed to stammer out the question

The tech paused. "Let me check." She reread some notes. "No. If you were in your last trimester, we would advise you to wait, but they are safe. Though you need to wait for fifteen minutes to make sure you don't have any reactions."

I let a sigh of relief out as she jabbed me in both arms. Anthrax and smallpox. I was up to date on the more common ones, and I'd already had my flu shot for the year.

Dutifully, I sat there the fifteen minutes, setting up plane flights for Saturday afternoon out of ATL. It was just easier as we still had the apartment to leave from that airport, as opposed to JFK. The tech decided I hadn't died and let me go, with both arms already aching. I left, stopped at the apartment to do a quick clean, then, even though it was early, I headed back to the house. I needed to pack, let Jo and Sable know I was headed out, and work on that blanket. Knitting was annoying, but maybe I was getting better. I stepped into the house and into the middle of an argument.

"I say the nursery needs to be near Cori's room. She'll need to nurse the baby for at least six months." Sable was glaring at Jo, her arms wrapped around her stomach and lower lip out.

"And then what? Are you going to go upstairs every time the baby cries? How would you even hear it? We can get bottles and bottle feed at night. Cori will probably be more than glad to not have to get up in the middle of the night." Jo glared back.

Off to the side, watching both of them, was Hamiada with an odd expression on her face.

"I don't need to guess as to the argument," I said mildly, hefting my bag on my shoulder.

"Cori!" They both spun on me, relief and vindication clear on their faces.

"Tell her," they said in unison, pointing at each other.

"I'm right. It should be upstairs." Sable waved above her head where my bedroom would be.

"Downstairs," Jo jabbed at their bedroom.

I held up my hand. "First, we have nine months, if I'm actually pregnant."

"Which is why we have to decide now, before we need the nursery," Jo groaned. "If we wait, the kid will be sleeping in a cradle in our rooms for most of its life."

"And what, exactly, is wrong with that? That was how Dad

raised me." Sable had a dangerous, almost mutinous look on her face and I sensed an explosion coming.

The need to interject rose off of Hamiada like steam in the morning, but she waited as both women had fiery tempers when they got riled up.

"So, have you thought about talking to or listening to the dryad that is all but bouncing over there?" I spoke loud enough that my voice acted like a gong in the tense room.

"Who? Why? You can help us settle this," Jo said focusing on me.

"Oh no. Not a chance. Again, ask the dryad." I had an inkling that she had a solution after I'd seen my closet and her joy at the idea of a child.

"What?" Sable turned to look at Hamiada. "Oh. I am so sorry. Jo and I were so busy that we didn't really notice you. I am sorry. What did you want to tell us?"

Jo blushed and rubbed her face. I had no doubt that if they had been alone, the fight would have culminated with them in bed, then talking it out and coming to a compromise. Both of them were all fire and fury, little actual anger. I'd accused them once of this being their foreplay, silly arguments that they ended up in bed over. They'd changed the topic.

"I show?" Hamiada asked, green leaves sprouting out on her face like a line of feathers. "I know you have started making the baby. New life is always good. So I made a room?" Her leaves turned red-orange as her eyes darted between the three of us.

Jo opened her mouth, but before she could say anything, Sable slapped her hand over Jo's mouth. "I would love that, Hamiada," Sable said with a big grin. "Please show us." She pulled her hand away with a muttered ouch. "Biting is unfair."

Jo grinned at her, then gave a soft bow to Hamiada, her body relaxing. "Lead on, Hamiada. You know we love your home."

The leaves along her cheeks brightened back to green and sprouted down her arms. She did her toe float walk, which made me wonder once again how much of her was here versus still in the realm, and headed into Jo and Sable's bedroom. They'd grabbed the room on the first floor mainly because of the huge walk-in shower. It was a decent sized bedroom, but I liked the view from my second floor, plus the little balcony near the study.

Last time I'd paid attention to the room, it had an armoire, then the bathroom with the walk-in shower. The room seemed a bit smaller, and I realized a closet had been created along the wall that had previously supported the armoire.

"Oh, that's nice. You did that?" I asked Hamiada.

"The three of us. Turns out if we buy the drywall, she can pull it into her and build. It's kinda nice." Jo had a funny smile on her face, and I rolled my eyes.

"You mean you were worried you wouldn't have any place to put all your clothes," I retorted with Sable nodding up and down behind Jo.

"Hey. I just have good taste and a body to display it," she replied with a mock pout. She turned and frowned. "But that's new. There're two doors."

Where before there had been one door to the bathroom, now there were two.

CHAPTER

TEN

CHAOS

This morning the door had been roughly in the center of the wall. Now it was four feet from the center, with the other door barely a foot from the hallway wall.

Sable pursed her lips as she shot a confused look at Hamiada. Still frowning, Sable opened the door near the outer wall. It opened to reveal the same bathroom that had always been there, though the door was now closer to the sinks. We all looked at Hamiada, who bounced up and down on her toes like a giddy child.

Sable 's smile as Hamiada's joy spread through the house like a wave of bubbles, was unmistakable. She stepped over and opened the other door. It swung open to a room done in tones of spring green, about eight feet by ten feet. She stepped in and Jo and I followed. Our curiosity was so strong I could taste it. Inside the room, the ceiling provided the illusion that you were looking up into the sky from a clearing in the forest. The brown trunks of trees sprouted up from the corners of the room. The three doors in the room were created from solid wood and adorned with carvings of nymphs, dryads, and other forest creatures. The baseboards looked like roots about to burst into the room. The room would have been at home in a fairy tale.

A cradle in gleaming, honey-toned wood rocked in one corner. The wall without doors housed a long dresser with a built-in changing table. On the side near the bathroom there was a door, and another one on the wall across from us. Logically that door should have led into the hall powder room

An inkling of what I would find led me over to the door. I pulled the door open and stepped into my bedroom with a soft laugh.

"How? What? That isn't possible," Jo protested. She stood in the middle of the room, looking at her bedroom through the open door we'd come through and me standing in my room.

"Magic house, remember?" I teased. I turned to Hamiada and with true sincerity spoke. "Hamiada, this is wonderful. It is exactly what we needed. And you did an incredible job decorating it."

Little flowers burst out in her hair, peeking out around her leaves as if shy.

"How or where are the lights?" Sable stood next to the wall where a switch sat. It was one of the slider ones that I didn't think were anyplace else in the house. Her finger ran down the slider and the room slowly dimmed, going from high noon, to late summer sun, to dusk, to midnight with a full moon, to the dark of the moon. As we stood there, eyes flicked open in the trees. They watched us, but it made you feel safe, protected, as an owl hooted. "This is incredible," Sable's voice was hushed as she moved the light back up to noon.

"It is the light in most of the realms. We have a sun, but not as you think. It is pure magic and lights the realms going through a cycle similar to your sun." Hamiada spun in a circle, leaves dropping from her. "But I'm so glad you like."

I gave a wide-eyed look to Jo and Sable, who both sported dumbfounded looks on their faces. It was Jo who spoke first.

"Like? Hamiada, this is incredible. Like doesn't begin to express it. I hoped for a room a bit bigger than a closet. This? This is glorious." Jo waved her hand to encompass everything. "How can we thank you? Because I, we, never expected anything this amazing."

Hamiada spun in a circle, then paused. "Can I get some more nitrogen?" She meant for her roots, which were intertwined into the foundation of the house in the basement. Her branches weaved through everything and formed the structure of house.

"Hamiada, you ever need anything like that, you just ask. No favors, it is your food. You tell us what you need." I said these words very firmly, catching her glance. "Just like I would get Carelian food or medicine, we will always get you what you need."

Her body sprouted tiny red flowers up and down her arms and legs. "Okay." She spun once more and disappeared.

"That definitely resolved the argument, though not the way I expected," Sable murmured, moving over to Jo's side. Jo instantly wrapped her arms around Sable, pulling her close.

"Get over here, Cori. You deserve this hug, too," Jo ordered. I moved over and Jo pulled me into the hug. The three of us stood there looking at the wonder that was the nursery. "A baby. We're going to have a baby."

There was a muffled squee from the two of them. I just smiled. It didn't feel real yet.

"We have an appointment in six weeks. Even if we know you are pregnant, that doesn't mean you still will be." Sable shot me an urgent glance. "You will tell us if you bleed or miscarry, right?"

I hugged them both tighter. "The second I start to cramp. But I'm going to remain positive. This will work out. You will have a child I get to spoil royally and hand back to you."

Tears might have glimmered in eyes, but if they were there, we didn't mention it. I luxuriated in the hug for another minute, then pulled back. "Where's Carelian?"

~The kit of my litter is in the tree.~ Esmere spoke in my mind and she sounded exasperated.

"What?" Jo turned to glance at Esmere. We'd all given up being surprised when she appeared.

~Up.~ Her emerald green fur looked so right in the soft green room, you might have thought it had been made to highlight her beauty. She tilted her head up, and I followed her gaze. There, up in what I had thought were painted on branches, sat Carelian. His tail waved back and forth as his eyes tracked motion in the trees.

"Carelian, I swear to the gods, if you ever drop down from there and scare me or the baby, I will have a new fur rug for the nursery." The snarl in Sable's voice was impressive.

~I like her. And I'd help. You should know that disturbing mothers, especially new ones, is unwise.~ Esmere had sat down, tail drifting back and forth.

~I would not do that.~ He had a note of offense in his voice as he crossed down the branch, and as I watched, it went from real to two dimensional. It made me want to ask Hamiada what else she could do.

Maybe I can see the stars at night?

I pushed the thought away. There were other things to pay attention to right now. "Esmere?" She turned to look at me even as Carelian lay on the floor, sulking and ignoring all of us. "Are you here to talk about the disease question?"

~Yes,~ she said simply as she looked around the room. ~Hamiada did an excellent job creating a micro realm here. Did she point out you could use it as a fortress room?~

"Micro realm?" Jo asked while Sable burst out with "Fortress room?"

Esmere shook her head. ~If I know that dryad, she didn't mention anything practical, just showed off the pretty stuff like the lights and the trees.~

"No. She didn't. Would you?" Sable stood in front of Esmere, who, sitting up with her tail wrapped around her, had her head at the same level as Sable.

~This is a realm, keyed to you and this house. If you came in here and shut the doors, no one could open them besides you. It would defeat anyone except maybe Tirsane, Bob or Salistra.~ Those were the names of the Demi-gods for Spirit, Chaos and Order. None of them were beings you wanted to upset. ~It is a wonderful gift and as the years go by will be very useful. She could even make it so only you can see this room; no intruder could ever find it.~

Sable and Jo looked around again, and I could almost feel them thinking.

"Stop it, both of you," I ordered. "Worry about other things down the road and you know you will always have a home here."

Jo shrugged. "I was just wondering if we do decide to move to the Tudor house, if there was a dryad that might want to live with us."

Esmere bristled, and I cringed. "I would be very careful about how you ask that. Apparently, James trapped her here. It wasn't anything she chose." My voice was soft, this was more information I'd found out via his journals.

~Yes. It upset her greatly. But she likes you.~ A low grumble came out of Esmere, not a purr yet not a growl. ~I will say, if I find a damaged dryad who would like to live on Earth, I will offer, stressing that you would cherish and protect her. That might be the tipping point. Many of the dryads live in fear of their tree being chopped down. Houses are much better protected."

Jo had a stricken look on her face, while Sable looked around, frowning. "Should we set her free? I never thought about it." Jo came over and wrapped an arm around Sable's shoulders as they both watched Esmere.

~No. She is the house. The only way to free her is to destroy her. She is happier now than I suspect she has been in centuries. You bring life, laughter, and love where you go.~

For a moment I thought she was going to say something more about that. But instead she tilted her head to face me. ~The answer to you, Cori, is no. At least mostly no.~

Jo and Sable had been whispering to each other, but the look on their faces told me they decided to not follow up on the comments. "And the question is?" Sable asked instead as she walked around the room, her hand invisibly measuring things.

I shrugged, trying to downplay everything. "Trying to figure out if human or Earth diseases can affect Carelian, or really any realm denizen." I shifted my attention back to Esmere, who sat picture perfect. When she started to pose, it worried me. She rarely cared enough to pose. "What did you mean, mostly no?"

She shifted her amber eyes over to me and I swear her whiskers twitched with amusement, but it was gone so fast I couldn't prove anything. ~Your viruses will not harm us. So the diseases that wrack your world find us unfathomable. However, your fungi and spores do not care about their host. They can cause issues, but only if we are very lax in monitoring our bodies.~

"And bacteria?"

Her head tilted and her tailed twitched. It must have meant more than I thought because Carelian rose up to come over and rub his face against hers.

~That is more questionable. Some will, most will not. Our internal digestive systems are less conducive to your bacteria, but that is not to say that they are unable to hurt us. Overall, it is deemed unlikely. Our inherent magic tends to destroy their small life forms.~ Her tail flicked. ~There is nothing else. Now,~ she paused and sniffed me. ~I thought you were pregnant. You do not smell pregnant.~

Jo and Sable froze like two deer caught in the path of an oncoming meteor. I just shrugged. "That doesn't really surprise me. I was only implanted yesterday. Even with the drugs, I don't think my body has caught up with what is going on yet." I kept my tone light and amused, even if I was trying to fight down panic that maybe this was over before it even began.

~Ah. Yes. Normally after a few days, the body starts to change, but not yet. I shall be back tomorrow.~

"Sure. But I'm leaving Friday night, so if you want to sniff me, you'll need to find Carelian first."

"Where are you going?" Jo asked as she and Sable unwound a little.

"You know, if you two are going to be this jumpy, having a kid is going to make you both have heart attacks," I teased.

"And you are deflecting," Jo countered.

"Yep. Because I'm headed out to Nebraska for work. It's that thing I do?"

They looked at each other, then Sable opened her mouth. I cut her off. "No. I still have a job, you know that. With the draft I can't even skip out or take a sabbatical. I will be careful, Carelian will be with me, and I can always sidestep home if I need to. Take deep breaths and let it go."

Again that silent conversation, then Jo nodded. "Point. But Cori, you be careful. We couldn't live with losing you."

~You will not lose her. I will always be there to guard her and the child.~ Carelian huffed as he walked around me, his tail wrapping around me like a furry lasso.

~Bah. You all worry too much. She is the herald. She will be fine and bear strong children.~ With that comment, Esmere turned and slipped back out the way she had come, and we went to make dinner.

ELEVEN

Pregnancy Fact: The sensitivity of the nose sharply increasing is one of the first signs that you might be pregnant. Previously mild odors can register as strong and unappealing. The reverse can happen also; smells may be all but invisible to a pregnant woman.~ The Pregnant Mage

---

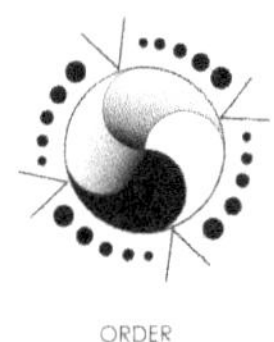

ORDER

Jo and Sable gave me tight hugs on Friday, well before I sidestepped to the apartment, then headed to the airport. I hugged them back, assured them they were worrying over nothing, and headed to Genoa, Nebraska.

The flight was exactly as I expected: long, boring, and claustrophobic. The government didn't pay for business class, though at least I was reimbursed for checking my bags. With the hazmat suit and the sample kit, there was no way to travel with only a carry on. I spent the flight reading up on pregnancy and wondering when my scent would change. The warm fuzzy feeling at the idea of being pregnant made me roll my eyes at myself. I didn't know if I wanted or didn't want maternal feelings. Either way, I'd find out.

There was no major airport at Genoa or Columbus, so I was forced to land in Omaha and rent a car. I still didn't like driving. If I had my way, I'd sidestep everywhere or drive a rig. Driving the ambulance never made me nervous, maybe because of the two tons of steel around me.

I got the car, a sedan that seemed way too small to offer reliable protection, and put my bags in the trunk. I'd specified I needed a car with a GPS system. I loaded up the location of the rental I'd be staying in, checking the travel time. The only accommodation I'd been able to find was a vacation rental that slept sixteen. It meant I'd rattle around in the house, but better that than an hour plus drive back and forth to Columbus.

I headed out, relaxing once I was on the highway. At a gas station that was both well-lit and empty, I let Carelian know where I was. A momentary flash of pain as the rip opened, and he was there.

~I do not like you being away from me for so long where there is no access to you.~ His grousing warmed my heart as I petted him.

"It wasn't that bad, and you know you don't like flights. This is easy enough."

His ears were back as he jumped into the car, careful not to extend his claws. He had shredded the leather in my first rental car. I was not happy about paying for those damages and let him know. Plus I'd made him apologize. He hated apologizing. Since then he'd been much more careful.

~You might have needed me,~ he muttered, letting me buckle the seatbelt into his harness. It freaked people out to see him sitting in the car as we drove down the road, but it made me feel better to have him buckled in even if he'd never let himself be caught in an accident.

"And if I did, were you going to step into an airplane in the sky? We've talked about this."

He didn't look at me, but his tail lashed. I let him be. He was always like this when he couldn't easily reach me and airplanes were difficult. Not only couldn't he accurately sense me, he couldn't come if I called.

The drive was endless. Nebraska is nothing but land and the occasional farmhouse. I think I saw more animals than people as I drove into town. The rental had mentioned getting groceries, and I wanted to find a safe local place to sidestep to before I started on my investigation.

I pulled into the local grocery store, a small one called Rae Valley Market. I gave Carelian a hard look. "You going to behave yourself and act cuddly? Or should I just leave you here?" He'd finally chilled out an hour into the drive.

~I want to stretch,~ he admitted. I clicked the leash to his collar. It was totally for show, but until I had a chance to know people, I wasn't going to freak them out more than necessary. Looping the leash around my arm implied control. Most days, he thought it meant he could control me. I laughed to myself. The vagaries of having a familiar. Maybe it was like having a child and a husband all wrapped into one.

That thought caught me and I paused, looking at him stretching out, the familiar ass and tail in the air as those long limbs stretched in a way the human body could never hope to.

"You know I love you, right? And that I couldn't imagine my life without you."

He froze mid-stretch, glancing over his shoulder at me. ~Of course you do. I am beyond par. I chose you and will always know I made the best selection in my quean. She was just smart enough to acknowledge the wisdom of my choosing and choose two other incredible queans.~ He finished his stretch and rubbed his face across my hip.

"You just like making me smell like you," I teased, knowing it was the only way he could respond to my emotion laden statement. Most denizens seemed to be more than a bit bewildered by the facets of human emotions. It was okay. I knew he'd kill for me, and what more could anyone ask for?

~Of course. Everyone should know you are mine.~

"That statement coming from a human would worry me greatly."

~You wear a ring symbolizing possession. Why do you not want others to know you are cherished?~

I didn't answer. There was a world of discussion there I wasn't going to get into in the parking lot of a small-town grocery store.

We headed through the sliding glass doors into the store and I grabbed a cart. One of the employees near the door froze as we walked through, mouth open and eyes wide. I headed to the vegetables and produce, trying to grab a few things so I didn't have to eat out constantly. When I turned around, some apples and salad in my cart, there were five people watching us, all with looks of fascinated terror.

"Hi," I said to them with a small smile and headed to the meat section.

~Salmon,~ Carelian said, and I glanced at him.

There were still people following us at a distance, so I opted to mind speak instead of out loud. No reason to really freak people out. ~This is about as far from the ocean as we can get in this country. Beef or pork or chicken. Because I'm not paying those prices.~

He heaved a sigh that would have made you think I'd told him he would be eating salad for a week. ~Fine, chicken or beef.~

I grabbed two meals' worth of beef and chicken. Then I finished up the shopping. The cart was full with various items and I smiled as I approached the checkout. I got to expense all of this. Feeding Carelian was expensive.

"Mm..ma'am," the checkout person stammered as I put things on the conveyor. "Is that your pet?" His voice squeaked on the word pet.

"No. It's my familiar." I tapped my temple, pointing to my merlin tattoo.

"Oh," he said, his eyes locked on Carelian, who played it up, sitting up and yawning. Around us people were staring and even the music overhead had been cut off.

I ignored them all and let the man scan my groceries as I bagged. I'd paid with the agency card, and was wheeling my purchases to the car when the first cop showed up.

So much for a low profile.

They didn't have lights or sirens on, but the car jerked to a hard stop as I stepped out. My gun was in the car and I wasn't going to do anything to make them more freaked out than they were.

I rolled my eyes, then scratched Carelian's ears. "You are more trouble than you're worth occasionally. Don't be a jerk and scare them. This is a work assignment. Be professional."

~You're no fun. I bet I could have gotten them to pee in terror,~ he said in a mock whine.

"And shoot you? Only if you want to deal with the wound," I countered, popping open the trunk and loading the food, the leash still looped around my hand.

The sound of another vehicle approaching, then the opening of car doors, had me turning as I shut the trunk. The food would be fine until I got to the rental.

It had been a while since I'd been in the more rural parts of America, and the few times I had, it was with a government group and Carelian had his official harness on that made people assume he was the equivalent of a K-9 or something like that. Now he had on a basic harness that didn't do anything besides look pretty. If I yanked on the leash, it would snap and was meant to. But it also meant he looked like an exotic pet, which most jurisdictions frowned on.

If only they knew how exotic.

Two police cars were in the lot behind me, each with a uniformed person standing next to the door, hands on their guns, but not drawn, which was a bonus.

"Hello officers," I said, my voice calm as I leaned against the trunk of the car.

"Is this your animal, ma'am?" the officer asked, his voice wary. He was older, about fifty, with a receding hair line that made his forehead seem huge. He didn't have the belly I expected, but instead a body that looked like it could use a bit more exercise and fewer pot roasts. The other officer surprised me for some reason. A woman, my height, but with long straight black hair that hit her waist in a mass of braids. She had the tiny frame the Japanese side of Sable's family had. A glint of color at her temple reinforced the fact she was a mage, though too far away for me to tell what type.

"Not exactly. This is Carelian, my familiar." I waved my hand at Carelian, who, to my relief, was acting like a good guard animal. Even in my thoughts I was smart enough to not think of him as a dog.

A tiny bit of tension bled out of them, though hands did not drop away from their guns.

"You passing through?" This was the female police officer.

"Staying here for a while. Taking a break from the hectic life, you know?" I tried to be light and amused, but their wariness worried me.

Slowly they came closer, and I sucked in a breath at how breathtakingly beautiful the female officer was. Her eyes were green, and she had beautiful skin and a heart-shaped face. They both had their eyes locked on Carelian.

"That thing going to be out and about without a leash?" the man asked, his voice one that I used to hear from Steven Alixant all the time. The cop voice.

~I am not a thing, I am Carelian, and the leash would not stop me from anything I wanted to do,~ Carelian replied, his voice icy.

I wanted to face palm as both officers paled and took a step back.

"He also has an attitude." I smiled as I said that. I'd strangle him later.

The woman glanced at the man and he nodded once. "Have a good day, ma'am. Sergeant, call me if you need me." He gave one more long, searching look at Carelian and me, then turned and headed back to his vehicle. A minute later, the car was pulling out.

The woman's hand had fallen off her gun as she walked over to me. "You must be Cori Munroe."

I arched a brow at her. "Was there a BOLO put out on me?" The police life had sunk into me more than I realized when I was using police acronyms for "be on the lookout for".

She smiled and her face lit up. "No. But my husband is a merlin and gets the House of Emrys monthly newsletter. You're talked about. The cat is rather hard to miss." She nodded at Carelian.

~I am a Cath, not a cat. Like I would deign to be a pampered house cat.~ Somehow he managed to sound affronted and snooty at the same time.

The Sergeant's mouth twitched. "Sergeant Amy Johansen." She held out a card, and I took it. "We got calls about a lady with a scary lion as a pet." Her eyes traced over Carelian. "While I've never yet seen a red lion, the size isn't that far off."

"Trust me, when he decides he wants lap time, you'd think he weighed as much as one," I replied as I slipped the card into my wallet.

She laughed, and I blinked again, my own preconceptions being shattered again. I wasn't expecting friendly amusement. Oh well, Steven had asked for low profile, not no profile. "I was wondering. I'm supposed to meet with the town coroner. Any chance you could point out his office?"

Her face slipped into a beautiful mask and all of me went tense. "Ah, so that's why you're here. I think you and the captain should talk."

CHAPTER

TWELVE

The incident at the SEC game in Atlanta is still a topic of discussion for magical historians and researchers. While agents Alixant and his team have all been interviewed, it has been determined that they were under the effects of some localized magic that distorted their perception of events. It is ludicrous to think that a unicorn and an undefined blob could have a rational conversation. The gorgon might have low level human intelligence, but mostly they are powerful monsters that mimic human expectations well. ~ Portal Incident Reporting

SPIRIT

She followed me back to the house I'd rented, or more accurately, I followed her after I took two wrong turns. The directions and the reality of the location did not match up. She even helped me get the groceries in and Carelian got a stretch in, then I followed her to the police station.

Police station might have been a misnomer.

It was a small suite of offices in the city offices building. No jail, no tough sergeant manning the counter, just two officers talking over something on a computer and two private offices.

"I told him you were coming. Second office." She meant that literally, the offices had Office 1 and Office 2 stenciled on them. The two officers had fallen silent as we entered and upon seeing Carelian, their hands drifted to their guns. I really couldn't blame them, regardless of how much it annoyed me. I mean, who in their right mind was calm when faced with a hundred- and fifty-pound cat with a long tail and eyes that saw way too much?

I gave a nod and a smile as I moved to the door indicated. Carelian stayed behind me, his silent paw steps betrayed only by his low warning rumble.

I could say something, but that would dismiss both the officers' valid reactions and Carelian's, so I just knocked on the door.

"It's open," a man called out. I turned the knob and stepped in. Carelian brushed by me. I swept my gaze over the room, taking in bland beige walls, industrial style desk, and a man with sharp blue eyes and black hair staring back at me. The blue eyes didn't surprise me, the copper hued skin and hawk nose typical of the few American Indian images I'd seen did.

The American Indian Nation had pulled away from the United states back in the late eighteen hundreds. I don't think outside of the occasional picture I'd ever seen one. From what I knew, they rarely left their reservations. James Wells had made notes about the wall that let animals and weather through, but that no human could touch. He'd wanted to explore it more, but Jeorgaz refused saying, "They are protected by their own. Let them be."

His blue eyes scanned me once, and he nodded. "Corisande Munroe. Double merlin. Familiar is a Cath. Highly intelligent and anti-establishment. Works decently in a team. Thinks outside the box." His voice had the soft lilt of the mid-west, but his eyes reminded me of a raptor, hard and sharp.

"Are you describing me or Carelian with that?" I asked as I sat down in the only chair in the office. The door swung shut behind me. In a move that struck me as unusual, Carelian sat next to me, watching the man behind the desk.

"The report was unclear. John Taliance, Sheriff for Platte County." My eyes narrowed as I looked at him.

"Not to be rude, but what is an AIN member doing out here? And this doesn't look much like a Sheriff's Office."

He shrugged. "Working. Staging point for the county, main office is in Columbus. So why exactly are you here?"

Two could play at this game, though I wondered if he was a mage. There were no tattoos at his temple, but from what little I knew the AIN didn't mark mages that way. I pushed that to the side. While interesting, it didn't have anything to do with my mission here.

"I suspect you know, or you wouldn't have had one of your officers pull in a poor mage out on vacation."

"You must be desperate if you are vacationing in Nebraska. But I'm guessing it has something to do with what Lizzie Reardon found."

I shrugged. "FBI asked me to follow up as a favor. One dead means probably nothing. But if it leads to a lot dead, better to figure that out sooner."

His shoulder twitched as I watched, but other than that, I had no idea what he was thinking.

"In my experience, Lizzie doesn't overreact. But then, as you say, one death doesn't mean much. It's when there are lots who die that it is too late."

"That's why I'm here," I said, my voice mild. "To see if there is an issue before it's too late."

He looked at me, then moved his gaze over to Carelian, eyes narrowing.

~Yes, she knows who and what I am. Directed mind speak to bypass someone else is rude. It is the equivalent of speaking another language in front of them.~ Carelian's voice surprised me, and I glanced back at him. His ears were canted back and eyes dilated as he stared at the sheriff.

John pulled back as if shocked. I gave in and laughed softly. "I'm impressed you can mindspeak, but don't expect Carelian to be like other familiars." I tilted my head, my own curiosity aroused. "You are familiar with realm denizens?"

His eyes flicked to me and I had no idea what he was thinking behind those shuttered, dark orbs. "Realm denizens. Interesting name." He paused and gave me a sharp nod. "You'll do. I hope you find absolutely nothing but a weird set of coincidences." The sheriff scribbled something on a notepad on his desk. "Here's the directions to where Doc Reardon's got a small lab. Don't expect much. We don't have all the fancy money out here."

I took the piece of paper he handed me and stood. Curiosity nagged, so I asked a very rude question. "Are you a mage?"

He looked at me, face impassive. "I'm Arapaho. I hope you find absolutely nothing that is cause for concern."

I recognized a clear dismissal and turned, Carelian already standing by the door, and headed out. The three officers out in the small area nodded at me, but their attention remained on Carelian.

Idiots. I could kill them quicker than Carelian could.

It never ceased to amaze me how much people downplayed the things mages could do. Even now, having been a practicing mage for almost a decade, most of the mages I knew only used their magic at work or when it was needed. Something else to think about, though I knew a lot of the answers.

We got outside, the useless leash in my hand and the cold spring day blooming around us. "Might as well go talk to the doc and see if there is any information for us to read." I didn't know if people were listening in, but from the curiosity of the sheriff's deputies, I'd be more surprised if they weren't.

Carelian flicked his tail as we headed back to the car, all too aware of many sets of eyes on us. I got the feeling that by the time this case was over, I'd be very ready to get back to a more urban setting where no one blinked an eye at Carelian.

Or everyone had heard about him.

Over the years, there had been various feature articles about him in the paper and news, and he even had his own social media page. Sable ran that, not me. She enjoyed posting his silly pictures, and Carelian was both proud of the number of followers and horrified at humans fawning. It really depended on the day. In some ways Carelian, Tiantang, and the Phoenix of France—whose name was Flora—were the most well-known of all the familiars.

I brushed aside my rambling thoughts as I started up the car after getting him in. The directions were straight forward and the lab was only ten minutes away, but a single building with the words Platte County Courthouse on it wasn't what I was expecting.

Small town. Have to remember this isn't Atlanta or New York.

I sighed and got ready to go through the whole rigmarole again. Maybe it was a good thing I didn't wear a weapon. If I had a gun, the temptation to use it might just be too much.

We walked in, Carelian next to me, pretending to be a meek animal, at least in his words. The security guard looked up as we stepped inside.

"Merlin Munroe?" he asked before the door had even closed.

I held back a sigh and nodded. "Yes. I'm here to see the coroner?"

"Yes, ma'am. The sheriff sends his apologies. He'd called to make sure you and Carelian here were cleared, but Dr. Reardon had already left for the day. The sheriff said he didn't have your number to let you know. Reardon will be here tomorrow morning about nine a.m."

I glanced at my watch and to my surprise, it was after four.

The day had taken longer than I realized. It registered that I was hungry and tired.

"Thank you. I'll be back tomorrow."

I turned and headed back out the door, waiting until we were both secured in the car. "How does dinner sound?"

~Excellent. And you smell pregnant.~

CHAPTER

THIRTEEN

The changes taking place in China are upsetting decade-long policies and traditional ways of dealing with that country. Empress Cixi has already turned her court upside down. Many traditions are being cast aside and the impression that the Dragon of China is her primary advisor has many people worried. Is this a good change or will the shift occurring in China signal global changes? ~ Magic and Politics

---

CHAOS

arelian's comment ensured I wasn't surprised when Esmere popped in as I was pulling steaks out of the refrigerator.

~Ah. Yes. Now you smell like you carry a child.~ Her words

drifted into my mind, and I turned around to find her peering into the small kitchen.

"Hello, Esmere. Staying for dinner?" I held up the steaks. It had originally been enough for leftovers, but if she ate, it would just barely be enough.

~No. I found something tasty earlier. Though I might remember this area to go hunting.~

I cringed. "Please remember to hunt the wild animals, not the domesticated."

~All animals are wild at heart, no matter the circumstances of their current existence,~ she replied, looking around the house. ~You will live here?~ There was a touch of concern to her thoughts, and I shook my head.

"No. This is just for me to stay while on this case. Albany will be my home for many years."

Her tail stopped lashing and I could see her relax. ~That is good. This is not the proper place for a child or you. Those who court the tribes pay close attention to these lands. Ah. It matters not. Deal with your human needs. I shall be back later to check on you. A human child. This shall be fun.~

She was gone before I could follow up on any of it. "Carelian, what did she mean by the tribes?"

He answered, though he still lay on the deck. ~The tribes.~

"That tells me nothing. What are they?" I got the steaks ready to cook and found some vegetables to steam, something I was pretty sure I couldn't screw up.

~The tribes. They are the tribes like the sky is the sky.~ Exasperation was in his tone and I let it go. There were some questions that without a specific frame of reference, it seemed like we were talking two different languages.

To my relief, I didn't burn the steaks, nothing happened that evening, and by nine the next morning, I was pulling up to the county office buildings. I knew the county seat was in Columbus, but apparently they had extra offices to make trips not so long? I wasn't sure and got out. Sidestepping had spoiled me. In the last two days I'd done more driving than I had in the last three months put together.

With Carelian's leash in my hand, I went into the building. The same security guard as yesterday nodded at me. "Ma'am. I told the doc you were coming. Doc said fine. If you turn to your left and go all the way down, the satellite morgue is at the very end, past the pressure doors."

"Thank you." I passed through the metal detector, then collected the accouterments I'd removed to get through and headed down the hallway. I only passed three people on the way there. Two of them gasped and pressed against the wall, acting like a rogue lion was walking down the hall.

The third, a woman with short spiked hair in red, purple, and blue, turned to look at us. "I totally need to try that color of red. The hair colors always go to blue or orange. Merlin Munroe, I'm Dr. Elizabeth Reardon, but call me Lizzie."

There are days when I wonder if someone moves me about on a chessboard, throwing me into situations just to see how I react. Lizzie Reardon was about my height with a chunkier, more muscled build, and eyes that told me she had an old soul. She couldn't have been older than forty, but if I found out she was sixty, it wouldn't have surprised me. Her temple was empty of a tattoo, but then I might have been more surprised if she had been a mage.

"Cori, please. Though I have to admit I thought you were a man? And a lot older."

She grinned at me. "I do that on purpose. Dad was the coroner for about five counties here until oh, six years ago. Edward Reardon. I sign everything E. Reardon and make them guess. It amuses me." She angled her eyes back at Carelian, who stood there, bored with human small talk.

I grinned at her mischief. "This is Carelian, my familiar."

"Huh. Not what I expected when I forwarded my report to the FBI and the CDC. Come on." She pivoted and strode down the hall, moving fast. I increased my speed and kept up with her as she went through the double doors and then turned almost immediately into a small office. "Take a seat. I'll show you what I've got. The patient has already been cremated, so nothing for you to see there. But I've got my samples."

She flung herself into the chair behind the desk and began typing on the keyboard like she had a need to crush the keys. I settled into the one chair. Carelian stuck his head in and snorted.

~I'll wait out here. If I tried to squeeze in there, either my tail would get stepped on or something would get shredded because my claws caught it.~ He was exaggerating, but only because he had exquisite control over where his claws ended up. But the office was that small.

Lizzie's head jerked up, and she narrowed brown eyes at Carelian who stretched out across the doorway, acting like he'd already fallen asleep.

"I thought familiars didn't talk to other people. I also didn't realize they were that intelligent."

I shrugged. "He's the equivalent of a cat attitude-wise, however he creates and follows his own rules. And yes, he is very intelligent." I didn't say anything about the others I knew. That wasn't something most people needed to know. In many ways, it was safer for most to think about them as animals.

"Huh." She gave Carelian a long speculative look, then shook her head, focusing on her computer screen. "I really don't have much more than what I sent the CDC. Patient Miles Herman, died of complications from cowpox, something I've never seen in a human before. Lived alone in a shack outside of Genoa."

I interrupted. "Isn't Genoa in a different county?" I'd scanned the maps while on the plane here. Genoa was in Nance while Monroe and Columbus were in Platte.

"Yeah. But the coroner there is ready to retire, doesn't like weird, so he tosses them over to me." Her face lit up with a quick grin. "And I am more than happy to take those on. In exchange, he picks up any of the nursing home deaths in the area. They all know him better anyhow. They don't resent him coming in, while

I'm still a young whippersnapper." The humor in her face made me snicker.

"Got it. So cowpox? I mean, I did some research on the way here, but how likely is that to kill someone here?" A viral or epidemiology expert I wasn't. Maybe I could become one with time, but for now I knew the basics and what I could find to read up on.

"Not very. I had to go research it. The last death was to a fetus when the mother was infected and that was twelve years ago. There are dairy farms here, but I checked with the Department of Agriculture and they don't have any records of breakouts anywhere for more than fifty years."

I leaned back, frowning. "So you're saying it's odd."

"Odder than a flying pig. There were three people hospitalized between Monroe and Genoa, but nothing in Columbus or anywhere else." She hit a button on her computer and something started to print outside the door. "One had a mild case of mouse pox, the other a case of chicken pox after being fully vaccinated, and the third"—she snorted but kept talking—"has exactly three infections. He freaked out, thinking it was shingles, but instead he had camel pox. I have no idea where any of them came from. The chickenpox is at least possible if you don't get vaccinated fast enough, or get hit with a stronger strain. But the rest? I had to get the virus images uploaded to the CDC to figure out what they were."

I sat back in my chair, thinking. "How close to each other are these viruses?"

Lizzie sighed, running her fingers through her short hair, making it stand up even more. "Well, smallpox, monkeypox, and cowpox are all orthopoxviruses. And camel pox is closely related, so close? He barely had any symptoms and as far as I can tell, he's the first human victim. It makes no sense. That's why you're here. I'm not an epidemiologist. I was hoping you would be."

I laughed. "Nope. I'm a draftee who goes to all the shitty jobs and tries not to screw up."

She glanced at my temple, then at Carelian laying in the door. "Uh, huh. Well, that is all the information I have. Addresses of the infected people and the one who died. But what little worry I could get anyone to muster is fading as it's been four weeks with no more infections. An epidemic doesn't go quiet like that."

"Without human intervention," I said softly.

"Exactly. Hence my worry." She stood, and I followed suit, mainly because she couldn't get out of her office if I didn't move first.

"Move fuzzbutt. I'm not stepping over you. We've been down that path before."

Carelian cracked open one eye, heaved a sigh, and rose, moving out of our way.

"Nice to know size doesn't change attitude. He's still a cat."

"In all ways." I took the sheaf of papers she handed me. "Anyone going to get their nose out of joint if I go talk to people?"

"Nah. John knows you're here. How much luck you'll have talking to people really depends on you. People around here can be super friendly or super closed off. Depends on the day and how you approach them." She shrugged. "And they are still working on accepting me."

"That's where Carelian can help or hurt. Do you expect me to find a rogue mage in his lair?"

Lizzie snorted. "Oh, I hope not. It never ends well for the plucky medical discoverer in those movies. They always die a horrible death, gasping out the final clue. What I expect is maybe a stash of samples that disappeared years ago that have decayed and maybe some animals are spreading them. Or worst case, a newly emerged mage being a blasted idiot because they are eighteen and immortal. Or this is just the weirdest coincidence ever and I'm crying wolf."

The sheaf of papers in my hands felt very real and not like someone trying to get attention.

"Okay. I'll let you know. Thanks."

"It's me who should be thanking you. Be careful. Even mages

still die from disease," Lizzie said, her voice serious. "But I've got two accidents to autopsy to make sure they were from sheer stupidity and not murder. News flash—it was the twenty beers they had first."

I left laughing, wondering exactly how the two dead bodies she had waiting for her had died. Carelian followed in his low prowl and the hallway was conspicuously empty as I left.

~I like her.~

"Me too. Let's go see if we can figure out what's going on."

I went to the hospital but they couldn't give me any more information due to HIPAA issues. That left me investigating. I could have driven out to the dead patient's home immediately, but instead I swung by a gas station and bought three maps, one of the state, one of the surrounding cities, and one of Platte and Nance counties. Then I mapped out each of the addresses for the victims. Only the one who died had lived in Genoa and that was barely. It was in a house as far from the little town as you could get and still be part of Genoa. The others were scattered about.

I checked and on the surface and per social media, the extent of anything they had in common was two had kids in high school. The locations didn't form a perfect circle, or a pentagram, or anything else scattered. One lived in Monroe, the others outside. It looked random. Which it might be.

I'd dressed in my hiking boots and cargo pants, and had a windbreaker in the car, along with all my other supplies.

"Ready to go exploring?"

FOURTEEN

Seductive, isn't it? The ability to change things with a thought. To whisper something in the wind and have it happen. Magic corrupts you from the inside out. Resist. The only way to truly be free is if we all turn away from this addiction. Say no before you succumb. ~Freedom from Magic

---

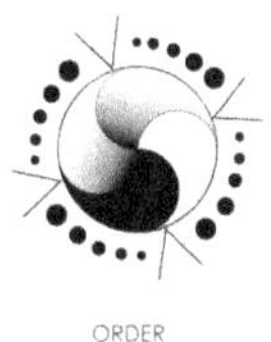

ORDER

There was still police tape on the door, but it had been broken since it was taped there. I looked the area over, but all I saw was a house that looked on its last legs. "Carelian, you stay out here and watch. I don't want to risk you coming in."

He shot me a look but stretched. ~It is wise. There are much

more interesting things to watch here. When this is done, I wish to go hiking and hunting. It has been boring of late.~

"That's only because you have been laying out back and being lazy. Or bouncing back and forth between here and China," I pointed out as I stood on the porch wincing at every creak of the wood. The house, made of logs and a dirty brown substance, could have starred in any number of horror movies.

~Cath need rest and relaxation. Jumping between countries can be exhausting.~

"Oh? You can always say no," I teased. He enjoyed seeing Tiantang and freaking out Cixi's court. I pulled an air shield around me to make sure everything except gasses were pushed away from me. It was a neat trick they taught you in the high-level science labs. I frowned as the offering Air required was almost twice what I would have normally expected, but the lure of discovering what clues might be inside distracted me.

~Why would I want to stay here? I did mention I've been bored?~ he asked as he prowled around the outside of the house. ~If you did more exciting things I would be here more often.~ He exaggerated how often he left. Most of the time it was while I slept as it worked out well with time zones.

"I'm sorry there are not enough life and death chases for you," I said with a laugh as I stepped in. While I couldn't smell anything via my shield, the house hadn't been well kept up even before he died and now, from the bugs and scurrying things with tails I saw, it wasn't going to get much better. "I can ask Hamiada to dump you into some of the more interesting realms when you sleep?"

Carelian ignored that comment. No one was stupid enough to enrage Hamiada. Seeing what she could do when she liked you raised nightmares, in my mind at least, of what was possible if she hated you.

The house was a one-bedroom place with a small bathroom, a kitchen/living area and that was it. Definitely not a laboratory. There hadn't been a basement or even a root cellar. I walked around, not touching anything, just taking in what information I could. I knew that forensics had been through here, but per the report, they hadn't found anything of interest.

"Where did you go to get sick?" I murmured as I turned slowly in a circle. There was a pile of mail on the desk and I looked out the window. No mailbox. Walking over, I saw all of it was to a PO Box. Curious, I put a piece of obvious junk mail in my pocket, after running the tiniest bit of static electricity over it and frowning again as it took almost a full two inches from three strands of hair.

That confused me, but I finished my perusal around, then walked out. Carelian met me on the steps into the house. I rubbed his ears. "You find anything odd?"

He leaned into the caress, tilting his head so I would get his chin. ~No.~

I snickered and scratched his brow between his eyes. "I might have an idea. Come on." I didn't say anything more until I reached the car and sure enough, two of the three other victims had PO Boxes. "Let's go to the post office."

~I'm going to nap. There is nothing to chase or hunt.~ He curled up in the back seat and I let him be, though I drove extra carefully. Both because I didn't want him hurt, but also the idea of all that weight and claws coming flying at me in a panic did not sound fun.

I pulled up to the post office and looked around. It was small, a bit dingy, but serviceable. I walked in and convinced someone by dint of using my ID card and the sheriff's name to show me where the boxes for the three people were. They weren't next to each other or anything, but in a post office this small, I didn't really think it mattered.

Outside the post office, the scenery stayed the same, rolling land, buildings, cows. I stopped. Cows. I pulled up the Department of Agriculture website and called. As I waited I leaned against the car and stared at the cows and the smallish barn in the distance. It took me twenty minutes to get the right person on the phone who pulled up records for the area.

"There are no reported cases of any diseases in animals in the State of Nebraska." Even over the phone, I could hear the official capitalization. "However, for normally treated diseases, you will need to check with the local veterinarians to see if there have been any outbreaks that needed to be dealt with. Only large outbreaks are reported, though any farm selling to consumers has to have a certificate of health on file with us. Are there any more questions?" The person sounded exasperated and annoyed.

I didn't care.

"One more. Which diseases are required to be reported immediately?"

From the sigh on the other end, you would have thought I was asking a teenager to clean their room. "The NLRAD, National List of Reportable Animal Diseases is available on the website." They rattled it off and I noted it, only because www.aphis.usda.gov was relatively easy to remember.

"That's it. Thanks." I disconnected and tracked where I could drive up to the barn in the distance. I could do it today, but I needed to file a report, review the diseases, let the sheriff know what little I'd found, and I was starving.

"Where do you want to go hunting at?" I asked Carelian as I started to drive back to the house. "And remember, you only have a license for a deer. No bringing down an elk or bison. I'm not wasting that much meat." No matter how much he wanted to eat, ten pounds of meat tended to fill him up and then he'd not eat for two to three days. When he ate daily it was about double a serving of what I'd eat and be happy. Mostly meat. Though he had a soft spot for the weirdest foods: pasta and hot sauce topped the list.

~You are cruel. Think how delicious an elk would taste.~

I was driving, so I couldn't turn around to stare at him. "Have you ever seen me dress or butcher an animal? Do you think I have any idea how to? Do you think I want to know how to? If you get a deer, I expect you to take it to share with your mother or even your siblings."

He didn't deign to answer me, but I figured my point was made. Normally when he hunted with me, he might catch something small. But he couldn't eat a whole deer. My familiar was being arrogant and wasteful.

Ten minutes later, we were driving up the road to my rental house, while I was still thinking about the idea of a farm being the epicenter. I waited until I had made some food. I really needed to quit skipping meals. I sat out on the deck while Carelian was busy terrorizing the wildlife. Once I'd eaten enough to take the edge off my hunger, I called the sheriff.

"Yes, Merlin Munroe," he said after I identified myself.

"Sheriff Taliance, I believe you wanted to be kept up to date with what I've found."

I heard him shift as he replied, "Yes." He didn't say anything else, and I sighed.

"I didn't find much. I have more research to do, but I had a question about the small farm, a bit run down, near the post office."

"The Jensen's. Old place. Son, Billy Jensen, stayed to take care of it, but isn't making any money. Meat isn't high enough quality, and he has too many issues with the locals for them to be willing to help." His answer was fast, but the tone didn't tell me anything.

"Issues?"

"Mother died when he was a freshman in high school. She was a magician, did her service, and married someone with no magic. Still not sure why she died. The autopsy didn't show anything. Billy started having problems in high school. At first little things, truancy, fighting, then it escalated to shoplifting and drugs. Nothing bad enough to get more than a slap on the wrist, but enough that he doesn't have many friends. His dad wasn't the friendliest either. They might live here, but few would regard them as members of the community."

"Mages?" I put another bite of chicken ala king in my mouth and chewed as I listened.

"No. Or at least not tattooed. If either emerged they didn't reach past hedge or they didn't get tested."

The way he said that made me wonder how common it was. I knew anyone who was AIN didn't have to be tested. It had to do with the treaty they signed back in the late 1800s. But there was some level of control, wasn't there? And how did an AIN get to be sheriff? More questions I'd probably never get the answers to.

"Good to know. Any issue with me visiting out there tomorrow?"

"Bring the Cath. It should keep them polite."

The fact that he named Carelian as a Cath surprised me. Most people assumed I had said cat, and I hadn't told him what Carelian was, had I? "Will do. Any other advice?"

"Don't get killed. I dislike the paperwork." He hung up, and I laughed. Alixant and he seemed to be cut from the same mold.

I got up to grab my laptop and a water, then went back to the deck, listening to the quiet as I pulled up the USDA website. There were some pox variations on the list, but interestingly, not cowpox. The list wasn't as large as I had somehow expected, yet more comprehensive at the same time. So many diseases and I had no idea how many could kill people—some, most? Epidemiology had never excited me too much, so anything I learned was outside the basics.

Nothing jumped out at me as to what might be causing this. I filed a report for Naomi and copied Steven. It didn't say much besides that I had arrived, met with local authorities and had a few things to check out.

Then I closed my laptop and stared out at the landscape. It was so different from Georgia or Upper New York. My hand drifted down to the life in my stomach. The idea still amazed me. The idea that I could carry another life inside me. How did women do this?

~Cori?~ Carelian's voice filtered in and I looked up, searching for him. Nothing looked like him on the grassy plain, and I thought I might be able to see his red coat if nothing else.

"Yes?"

~I think you should come see this.~ He sounded odd. Not glutted from a hunt or sated. Just odd.

~Where is here?~ I asked, standing up and looking around.

He sent an image of where he was standing, and I went to sidestep, and shuddered as magic fought me. I stumbled, coming out of the step, the price two inches of hair.

"Why by Merlin?" I gasped, shuddering. I'd been sidestepping for so long I barely even thought about it anymore. This startled me.

~Cori?~ Before the word faded from my mind, Carelian was pressed up next to me. ~What happened?~

"I don't know." I placed my hand over my stomach, not that I could sense anything. I knew I could sense magic being used if I tried, but I still just felt like me. "It was like I had to fight to come here and the offering was high. Way high."

~Hmm… that might be because of this.~ He turned and pointed to something a few yards away from us.

I turned and stared. There were plants growing in a riotous manner around a gap in the trees. None of them looked like anything I had seen before in the United States. The colors of the plants might have looked at home in a jungle, but not in a small grove of trees. But that wasn't what really caught my attention. I was riveted on the small rip that hung there. When Indira had been teaching me, she opened small rips about an inch or two long and I would close them. I knew there were detectors for rips, but I'd never thought about how big they had to be for detection to register.

Lips pursed, I pulled out my phone—luckily it had been in my pocket—and texted Indira. *How big does a rip have to be for the detectors to catch it?*

I stared at the phone, willing her to respond. The typing buttons appeared, much to my relief. *At least two feet in diameter, three is always caught. Why?*

I hadn't realized they could get that big without detection. *Found one. Was curious about why it hadn't been closed.*

She sent me a shrugging emoji. *It happens. Close it and let the OMO know. Those tend to be small enough that not much can slip through, so no one worries about them, we just deal with them when they are found. Be careful though, even small things can be dangerous.*

Got it. Thanks!

I slipped the phone back into my pocket and, with a bit more trepidation than I would have had ten minutes ago, I reached out with my magic to close the rip. It resisted, which I expected, but I closed it. Again it required a much larger offering than I'd ever experienced before.

"Should I destroy those plants?" I asked, not moving any closer. They looked like they could have been extras in a horror movie.

~Probably. Chaos things are a bit too aggressive for Earth.~

I reached for Fire, Jo's magic. We'd never let slip that since the joining I could use her and Sable's branches at the same level they could. There was enough heat in the area and in the ground around me, I didn't need to cheat with a lighter. Maybe I should have.

To my surprise, Fire spouted. Coming to me only after I offered ten times what I had offered when I was null in that branch in college. But at that offering, it kept up around the plants and inhaled them, giggling away as it devoured all of them.

"What in the world is wrong with my magic?" I burst out, confused and more than a bit worried. Was it fading away?

Carelian gave me a sidelong glance, his tail lashing. ~I do not know. But I am not happy about my quean having problems with her magic.~

CHAPTER
FIFTEEN

Our favorite mage is in the news today. Steven Alixant was seen with his long-time lover Indira Humbert leaving a five-star restaurant tonight. Will they ever marry? Rumor is more than one eligible merlin would be ready to snatch her up. ~ Daily Magic News

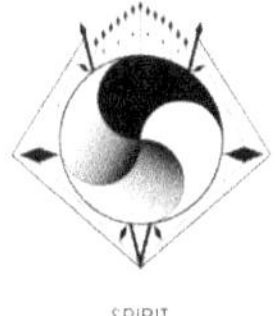

SPIRIT

Given the weirdness of my magic I decided to walk back to the house. It was only a mile, and the exercise did me good. We did get a few double takes as we walked the last bit up the road to the driveway for the house, but mostly it gave me time to think and enjoy the different scenery.

None of this made sense. The real world didn't have mad

scientists, did it? Something Steven Alixant had said to me years ago popped back into my mind. He had pointed out the government didn't allow stories of rogue mages to remain active news very long. No one wanted people scared of what mages could do.

If I accepted that as fact, and I had seen it happen more than once, then were there people like from a bad thriller lurking in the corners? I'd seen killers, abusers, drug traffickers, and worse. Why couldn't there be people who were mad scientists?

The knowledge that I was bringing a kid into a world that seemed to get a bit darker every day made me shudder. I fell asleep that night with my hand over my stomach and promising I'd do everything to make this world a better place.

My phone woke me before six a.m. "Hey Naomi," I said through a yawn as I staggered into the unfamiliar kitchen. I missed knowing where everything was.

"You're sleeping late," she said with a slightly arch tone.

"It's only six here. I was enjoying the extra sleep." I started the coffee.

"Oh. Well you're up now. Find anything?" She sounded way too awake.

I glared at my phone, only half awake. "I filed a report yesterday. I've only been here a day and a half. Not really. Though I have a few things I need to check out."

"When do you expect to be back?" She sounded exasperated and I wanted to throw something at her.

"When did I get clairvoyant abilities? I don't have a clue. I have no idea if there is an issue here or what it might be. So I'll be back when I wrap it up here." I snapped that out a bit less politely than maybe I should have, but I was cranky.

She sighed. "You can't blame me for wanting the double merlin to have solved all the problems in half the time of any other agent. Anything I should be worried about?"

I yawned my way through my answer. "Not really. Found a rip, closed it. But that isn't your department, more an OMO matter."

"Yes. I'm not interested in managing magical issues. Having mages is bad enough."

I snorted and poured some coffee. "Please. You like our abilities."

"Yes, but the ego gets annoying." Her voice was acerbic, and I laughed.

"Are you implying I have an ego?" I sipped the coffee, smiling as the bitter heat cut through my exhaustion.

"Actually no. You might have a cat with one, but you don't. It's refreshing. Just be warned, I think I'm going to have an investigation coming up with some aspects that will be right up your alley."

"And that would be?"

"Human traffickers and drug mules. We think they are using magic to transform the outside of the drugs so they aren't easily detected. Granted, it's lowering the overdose counts, but it's making it much more difficult to stop."

I nodded as I looked out the window. "I can see that. Okay. I'll try to see if there is anything I can do and wrap it up in a few days."

"See you then." She hung up, and I headed to the shower. I wanted to hit that farm first thing this morning. If you had animals you were up early to feed them. At least that was the impression Carelian gave me.

Thirty minutes later, with Carelian complaining the entire time about having to get up and get moving without morning treats, we were on our way. Driving through farmland and seeing houses in the distance was almost relaxing, and nothing like driving in Atlanta or Albany. To be honest, if driving was like this all the time, I'd probably own a car.

I took the road to the dairy farm, then the long driveway up to the house. I got out and Carelian didn't bother to wait, leaping out the car window. "You could have opened the door," I pointed out.

~Where would the fun be in that?~

I shook my head. The Cath was a menace that I dearly loved. I knew without a shadow of a doubt our child would be the most protected kid in the world. Part of me couldn't wait to see Carelian around a human baby. I suspected that I could create an entire video channel off of his cuteness. I'd have to shoot that idea to Sable. She'd love it.

Up close, the farm seemed even more run down than it had yesterday from the post office. The cows were in the field, and they looked mostly healthy, but then they could have been on the verge of death. I might not have realized it.

"Carelian, can you tell if they are healthy?" I figured the hunter would have a better idea than I would. I preferred my meat from the grocery store.

He stood looking at the wandering bovines and flicked his tail. ~I would eat them.~

I took that at face value. He'd eaten things before that I wouldn't touch if you paid me. Our taste buds and what was deemed edible differed greatly.

I looked around, but I had no knowledge of what would seem right or wrong on a farm. I tried to think about the paint on my parents' house, but they'd had siding, so maybe flaking paint was normal? The number of things I didn't know annoyed me. The barn was off to one side, while a small house was to my right.

Being polite rarely hurt. I headed toward the house, looking around as I went. It all looked normal if a bit run down. But then, most people didn't have a living house that made sure she and the grounds always looked perfect.

I knocked on the door and stood there, listening carefully. Other than the echo of my knocks, I heard nothing. There was a standalone garage, but the door was down. The barn, the pastures, and an abandoned chicken coop, and another open building that had a tractor and a lawn mower parked in it. I didn't see anything else.

I shrugged and headed to the barn. It was similar to a lot of others in the area, two stories, wings on either side, and a small silo attached to the back. It wasn't red, but white and gray, with an opening on the side I'd driven up on that I believed was for hay. Though my knowledge was mostly from the westerns I'd watched as a kid, so very likely to be wrong.

Mostly it looked big, messy, and smelled like cow. Or cow manure, to be more exact. I headed to the smaller door on the side of the barn, not the huge double doors to the main part of the building. I wasn't sneaking exactly, but I didn't have a warrant or a valid reason to be here other than curiosity and a nagging feeling.

That feeling sharpened as I pushed open the door. "There's a rip around here somewhere," I said to Carelian, my voice swallowed by the barn.

He lifted his head looking around, but if he saw anything besides the feeding and milking stations, stacks of feed and other equipment, I had no idea. Down at the end, there were a few big rooms with doors. Maybe someone was in there.

The only experience I had with dairy farms was seeing them on the occasional show, and they weren't things I'd paid a lot of attention to. If there was anything off in this place I'd never know. If there was, part of me really hoped it had neon letters over it saying, "BAD STUFF HERE". It never worked like that.

I headed towards the doors, glancing at the cleanish stations. The milking apparatus had me imagining it attached to my breasts. Ugh. Hopefully the ones for babies weren't as creepy as that.

I'll have to pump.

That idea had me stumbling to a halt as my mind spiraled out of control. What had I gotten myself into?

Women worldwide do this daily. You can handle it.

I repeated the mantra in my head over and over again. This wasn't worth freaking out about. I could pump milk. Women did it all the time. I fought to swallow and dragged my mind back to the job. People getting sick. Odd viruses and something that was twanging off my senses. Where was that rip?

I moved towards the doors, listening for anyone, though Carelian would hear it well before I did. The first room I entered was a parts room, with a small desk in it, mostly covered with paper. I just shut the door and moved to the next one. A quick peek let me know it was a bathroom, and I didn't bother going any further. Toilets were mostly the same everywhere.

The last door opened smoothly, without a hint of resistance. Fear and the feeling of a rip ate at my hindbrain. I peered into a room with tables against two of the walls and equipment that would have looked right at home in our lab. Except that where ours was pristine, clean, everything carefully put away and wiped down, this place looked like a dorm room for jocks.

There was a refrigerator against the other wall and what looked like a small wine fridge. And in the far corner, above the tables, was a rip. It wasn't very big, only about a foot long and six inches wide, but even through that small little gap, I could see things moving that made me jerk my eyes away.

"Chaos?"

~Yes,~ Carelian confirmed. He sounded as worried as I felt. I pulled up my air shield.

"Do you want me to shield you?"

He paused, looking around. ~Let me go to the other side. I want to see what area of Chaos this is.~ His tail twitched as he looked around. ~Be careful.~

His tail stroked the back of my hand, then he pulled open a rip and stepped through. It closed, unlike the one hanging in the air in the corner. I could close it, but I'd wait to see what Carelian found there. He could walk in the realms without an issue. I wasn't about to step over without someone else maintaining the pocket realm I was stepping into. The realms could be dangerous, even if you were a double merlin. And I really preferred not to be in situations where I needed to rapidly grab magic. I did better if I could plan out my actions.

The offering for the air shield had been really high, and I frowned. Never before had I needed to worry about the amount magic would cost, but a half inch of hair for a shield? That didn't make sense. I triple checked that it only let in air molecules, something I'd trained myself to visualize exactly, then moved into the room. It was significantly cooler than it had been outside and I looked around again, finally spotting a small portable AC that vented to the outside.

The ramifications of that made me shudder. If it was venting air and anything was loose in here, then that might explain the contamination. But I was jumping to conclusions. For all I knew this was a common set up in dairy farms, though I doubted that. I worked my way around the room, looking at but not touching the equipment. Microscopes, a small tablet computer, and lots of petri dishes and lab slides that seemed to be everywhere.

I glared at the tablet but it didn't turn on; and without a hazmat suit, which was still in my car trunk, I wasn't touching anything. The knowledge that I should go get the suit popped up in my brain, but I didn't want to take the time. I wanted to verify there were deadly viruses here, get out and call in the authorities. While I might be one of them, I definitely wasn't the right authority for this job.

I could call for a full hazmat team, but if they got out here and it turned out all this was just for validating milk quality or something, I'd look like an absolute idiot. Even though I'd been working for Naomi for almost two years at this point, I was still the most junior person and I made some bad mistakes. For all the awesome I did, there was also the stupid.

I stood in the middle of the small lab and wrestled with myself.

"Just a quick look around, verify that there are viruses here, then get out and call the cavalry." My voice sounded muffled in the air shield. The petri dishes all looked the same, gunk in them, but nothing that meant anything to me. I kept moving around to look at everything, but without peering in microscopes I couldn't tell anything.

I crept around the corner with the rip. The need to close it clawed at me but I waited. If this was as bad as I thought, I needed to leave it there as evidence. The AC wasn't on at the moment so I kept walking around looking for papers or something else I could glean information from, but regardless of the mess, there wasn't much lying around I could snoop through.

The refrigerator sat there, mocking me. I spun slowly and my eyes landed on a box of gloves. Grinning, I stepped over and carefully sealed the air around my wrist as I pulled on two gloves. Air whispered and complained and I had to offer yet another quarter inch of hair to my concern, but right then I pushed that worry to the side, wanting to focus on the refrigerator.

The gloves finally settled onto my hands and I carefully cracked open the fridge. Nothing jumped out at me as being weird or out of the usual, but maybe I shouldn't go by my experience. For me, a fridge full of beakers and petri dishes was relatively normal. Opening the fridge was pushing it, but if I started moving things around, it would be crossing lines.

With a sigh I closed the door. There was no freezer. That left only the wine fridge to look in. I crouched to open it and peer in. I blinked and had to look again. There, neatly labeled, was rack after rack of vials. I had to peer closely, the light not being the best, but I recognized the names as those of different viruses. Anthrax, variola minor-smallpox, even varicella-chicken pox.

"Merlin's balls, how did these get here?" I rose slowly. It didn't really matter. What did matter was they needed to be contained and dealt with. And that wasn't anything I could do. Well, I could, but setting the entire place on fire probably wasn't the best idea.

"Who are you? Why are you here? This is my place!" The voice came from right behind me.

SIXTEEN

Always mysterious, the AIN still occupy much of the United States government's attention. Though the BIA lost the ability to govern their lands over a century ago, the government still offers a reward to anyone who will provide access to the AIN land or bring them information about it. To this day they are one of the few nations the OMO knows almost nothing about. This needs to change. ~ OMO Internal memo

CHAOS

I spun, glancing at the shut door as I did. A man stood there, late twenties with lanky brown hair that reminded me of the cows I'd seen on the farm. He had a wiry build, but more from not eating than working out. What had my heart beating triple time was the rage in his eyes.

"This is my place. Who are you?" he repeated, his voice promising retribution.

I pulled Air and Earth together, creating a low wall between us. While not visually solid, it would serve to create a barrier if he moved toward me. The cost stunned me after years of barely paying anything. I ignored it as I called for Carelian and got my Stunner spell ready.

~Carelian, I need you!~ I didn't have to try to add panic to my mental voice. How had he gotten in here?

"My name is Cori Munroe. I'm an agent with SIU. The FBI and local authorities asked me to come out and investigate the occurrence of various poxes in the local area." I paused and waved my hand around the area. "From what I can see, you are involved in that. What is your name?"

He snarled. "They all deserved it. I'll prove to them exactly what I can do. Chaos will help me get revenge on everyone. But I'm not ready, not yet. You need to die."

Out of habit I'd checked his temple—no tattoo, which meant hedgemage worst case. What I didn't expect was the KO that headed right for me at merlin level. My wall was mostly Air above the knee-high Earth barrier. That dampened the KO, so rather than laying me out, or even killing me, I just felt woozy for a moment.

I jumped back, my heart racing and my hand covering my stomach in fear. This wasn't supposed to be a rogue mage case. Just an investigation. Right now I didn't care how expensive magic was, I grabbed and sent a Disrupt and a KO in quick succession, ignoring the two inches of hair it ate up.

But somehow, and I wasted too much time being surprised at this, he avoided both of them. He moved, not a sidestep but something else, and disappeared from my reality and reappeared on the other side of the room.

He's a plane walker.

My mind stopped on that thought and I just stared. Humans weren't able to walk the planes. Not like that. The denizens were plane walkers, the ones they were attuned to they could step in and out of with ease without any risk to their psyche.

Long ago, Esmere had mentioned plane walkers to me. Humans either adopted by a Lord, such as Tirsane or even herself, or those so out of touch with physical reality that they could move across the planes with no ill effects. The question was which one was he and which would be the better option?

He stood there in the corner of the room, the rip creating a halo over him. "You will die for violating my sanctum, like all the others. *!#$@# will see to it!"

My knees threatened to buckle and a shudder at the cellular level washed over me. I managed not to fall to the floor, but that didn't mean I didn't want to. It hadn't been Bob's name, I didn't think. The pain was different, but it was still a name of Chaos.

"How do you know that name?" I gasped out as I straightened. A warm trickle tickled my nose. I reached up to wipe at it. A smear of red graced my hand.

"My mentor, my lord. I shall follow the orders of the great one. You will make a suitable sacrifice!" He lunged at me and I moved to the side.

He seemed to be made of spite and power, as I barely darted out of his way. My mind spasmed as just how much danger I was in registered. My heart pounded as I increased the strength of air shield. Normally I'd have grabbed dirt, dust, anything loose in the room, but in here I didn't dare. It might still have living organisms in it, and after seeing the labels in the fridge, some of them would be deadly.

My shield rang as he cast entropy at it, but I knew how to make one that would hold against magic, even if it ate another huge offering from me. I cycled through options and tried a narrow KO again, aiming right at him. He plane walked away before it struck. I didn't know you could move that fast or avoid something like that. Tearing apart the building was bad. That would leave Soul magic residue everywhere. I was getting desperate enough, I was willing to take the chance.

"You killed someone," I said, trying to distract him. If I had to kill him, that paperwork would suck. This entire thing was going to be a mess, but it never occurred to me anyone would walk out of a rip. Where was Carelian?

"Excellent. I plan on watching many more die once I start spreading my vectors. Then my lord will have all the sacrifices needed to enter this plane on a whim. The world will be laid at my lord's feet like a carpet of gold."

Asking if he was nuts would be redundant at this point. If he wasn't insane, then maybe I was.

"I don't think so."

I reached out at the same time he did and my Soul pull hit a beam of entropy that made me scream in pain as it tore apart the magic I had cast, the inch of hair it had taken vaporizing with no result to show for it.

"Balls," I hissed as I staggered. At least he looked like my attack had staggered him, but he was recovering faster than I was. How in the world when he didn't have hair longer than his shoulders?

"You will be mine. You can help me finalize the last information I need to make my virus a true super strain."

He smiled as he spoke, walking toward me, and my lungs froze at the malice on his face. How had he not been caught before now? I pulled on Fire, more than willing to sear him where he stood. To my shock, Fire fought me and in the seconds it took to convince Fire to cooperate, his hands were scrabbling at my shield.

Even when Bob, Salistra, and Tirsane had come out in the football stadium, I don't think my entire being had been so gripped with terror. Maybe at that point I'd already hit numb or maybe when tens of thousands were going to die, I didn't have time to worry about myself.

Now I had me and a child who had barely had time to exist. Did cells count? Was it even more than a few cells?

~Leave my quean alone!~ The snarled words tore through my mind. From the way my attacker flinched and his shoulders sagged I figured Carelian's snarl had hurt him also. That didn't upset me.

A streak of ruby red appeared out of the rip in the corner and slammed into the man, all claws and teeth.

"Don't kill him if you can avoid it," I blurted out, even if I rather preferred him dead. There was too much information we needed from him.

~Spoilsport,~ he snarled and the blur of motion ceased. He stood on top of the man, jaws around his throat, one claw placed at his groin, the other beside the man's head. ~If you move, I rip your throat out and drink your blood. Please move,~ he purred.

It worried me that the man just glared, enraged and trying to talk. Anyone sane would have peed their pants. I would have peed my pants. This was a very, very dangerous man. Or an insane one. I moved over beside him slowly and touched his forehead, sending a KO spell directly into his mind. He slumped and went lax.

Carelian carefully pulled back, his eyes not moving from his prey. ~He is not right.~

"I figured that out." I pulled my phone out and hit the sheriff's number. "What took you so long?" I said to Carelian while the phone rang.

~I was waylaid. That area of Chaos is… unwell.~ His voice sounded odd, but before I could follow up on that, the sheriff picked up. "Sheriff Taliance."

I figured he had to know it was me. Caller id was a ubiquitous thing, which meant he was probably trying to make a point. But to whom I had no clue. Either way, I responded in kind with his answer, though I wanted to run away screaming at this point.

"Sheriff, Cori Munroe here. I have someone I believe is behind the pox outbreaks and possibly more. You might want to bring Dr.

Reardon with you. This place is something else. And let the Rogue Team know. I have him unconscious for now, but I don't know how to control him while he's awake. He is dangerous."

A year or two ago, I might have felt guilt or reluctance at saying those words. They pretty much guaranteed a mage would be killed. My guilt had vanished the more I saw. Choices had consequences, and I'd been learning that the hard way sometimes. There wasn't an easy answer, no matter how powerful you were.

"I see. And where are you?" His voice had no tells in it, so I didn't know if he was curious, furious, or apathetic.

I provided the address.

"And what led you there?"

"I'll explain when you are here. But hurry. I can keep him unconscious. I can force him to tell the truth, but you're going to need drugs to keep him from leaving."

A long pause, then a soft mutter from him. "I see. I will be there shortly. Dr. Reardon has been dispatched." He hung up after that and I slipped my phone away, looking at the young man.

"What exactly do you mean by weird and did you know he was a plane walker?"

Carelian jerked his head up, though his paw contracted, and I saw claws sliding in through the man's jeans. I didn't say anything.

~I did not. Are you sure?~

I opened my mouth, then shut it. I wasn't sure. At this point, the only thing I knew for sure was I wanted to go home. "He moved, the rip flickered, then he appeared on the other side of the room. After D.C. I know what a sidestep feels like and that wasn't it." When two mages had tried to take nuclear weapons to DC via sidestepping, I learned intimately what it felt like.

~Then yes, plane walker.~ He glared down at the unconscious man. ~They are never human. Humans don't take well to the planes without pockets. Or...~ He trailed off again, and I glanced at him.

"Or what? He kept talking about a mentor lord. It was a Chaos name. The pain from the name was different than someone saying Bob's name."

If Carelian knew how to pale to white, or if I could have seen his skin, I had the feeling it would have been ghost white.

~That is not good. For now, seal the rip. It does not need to corrupt anything more here.~

Part of me resisted that idea. You didn't touch things in a crime scene, but having the rip open created issues and raised risks. Besides, really, only Carelian could use it. I closed it with a thought, wincing at the offering. What was going on? I'd have to deal with it when I got home. Speaking of which, I raised the idea of sidestepping to Albany and the cost, while staggering compared to my normal cost, was payable. I'd worry about it when I was ready to leave. I didn't want to be here any longer than required.

We stood watching the unconscious man, me in the middle of the room, arms wrapped around my waist. Carelian above him, with a paw ready to gut him. I didn't move until I heard sirens approaching. At least the room wasn't sound proofed.

With a glance, I hit him with another KO. I was willing to go bald before I let him wake up. Then I headed out to flag down the reinforcements.

SEVENTEEN

We have records of some familiars exhibiting above animal level intelligence, and the monsters that live in the realms occasionally know how to talk to people, but we don't know much else about them. It could be anything from they live in the lost city of Atlantis to they are simply animals so steeped in magic they have changed. ~History of Magic.

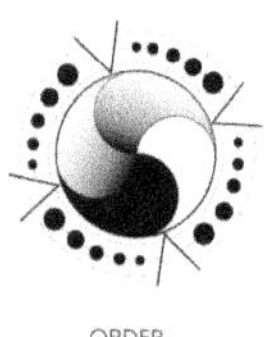

ORDER

I escorted the sheriff, his deputy, Amy Johansen, and Lizzie back to the room. Their expressions almost made the effort and terror worth it when they saw Carelian standing with one claw ready to eviscerate the man. He looked primal and amazing. I loved that Cath.

"He's a mage?"

"Yes. But not tattooed. I can tell you he's more than a hedgemage, but past that I can't say how powerful he is. Though I will tell you, I think he's a bit insane by any standard."

"Paul Goines insane?"

I jerked my head to the side to stare at Sheriff Taliance. Paul Goines had been the insane mage who had emerged a second time after the deaths of three mages. Then he tried to summon lords from the realms and enslave them. It hadn't gone over well. I was pretty sure Chaos ate him. I assumed it was Bob, but I could be wrong.

Few people followed that aspect of the story and even fewer remembered his name. I didn't know if this meant he'd been reading up on me or if he'd followed the story.

"Different." I paused and looked at the man. "Worse. I think he is a plane walker."

Taliance stiffened and narrowed his eyes at me. "And how do you know of them?"

I just glanced at Carelian. No need to lie or tell the truth when misdirection worked better.

"Hm. Lizzie, did you bring the Rohypnol?" He didn't take his eyes off me as he asked.

Lizzie sighed. "I did. But you really need to remember I'm a coroner. I might have my medical degree, but I'm not actively practicing on living people. The dead complain less." She pulled a syringe and a needle out of her bag, an honest to god old med bag. I figured it had probably been her father's and maybe even her grandfather's from its age.

"I authorize it, and you know my powers are more far-reaching than most." He jerked his head towards the man. "Hit him now before he comes awake enough to cause a problem."

All the hidden meanings in his comment fascinated me and if this situation hadn't been so fraught with danger, I would have been prying it all apart. The AIN were secretive and any chance to elicit information was something I would jump at. But right now I just wanted to go home.

Lizzie bent over, her multicolored hair so at odds with the staid persona of a county coroner. The needle slipped in and the man moaned softly. I hit him with another KO without thinking. I did not want this man to wake up. Not while I was anywhere near him.

Taliance raised one eyebrow at me and I shrugged. "Told you, dangerous." I didn't elaborate.

"Amy, get him out of here. We'll need to take him to Omaha for processing, but the KO and the Rohypnol should keep him out of it for a while. If it doesn't, kill him. We can figure out enough without him."

Amy nodded. She and the EMTs strapped the man to a gurney and wheeled him out. I turned to watch Lizzie. She had pulled on gloves and was moving around poking at things while a crime tech took pictures. I overheard a whisper that the tech was a Pattern hedgemage and very good at narrowing in on what was not right.

"The scary stuff is in the wine fridge," I offered as she peered into microscopes. My air shield was still as firm as I could make it and I'd even offered the blood from inside my mouth when I'd bitten the side of my cheek. The price was still too high, but Air wasn't fighting me as much. I didn't want to risk any of these diseases latching on to me. Maybe I should go dress up in the hazmat outfit.

"This is all scary stuff," she said, her voice colder and tighter than I'd heard. "What's your degree?"

"Doctorate in Biological Quantitative Sciences."

This had her lifting her head to look at me. "Huh, good grounding, no specialties. Makes sense if this is what you want to do with your life."

That stopped me. I had no idea if this was what I wanted to do with my life. Was that what happened to Steven? He'd fallen into something he loved and just never left? I put that concept on my

"Think About Later" pile and just shrugged. "Yes. Basically a good pre-med background."

"There are lots of viruses, most of them here in the dishes are inert." She waved at the counter covered with petri dishes. "I'd say he didn't have a good idea on how to grow them in a laboratory environment. Which is good for us, but I don't like the mutations I'm seeing. Maybe they are just variations—I don't know." She paused, her eyes hard, and I suspected she would have made a very dangerous mage. "What's in the fridge?"

I shook my head. "Not sure. I didn't want to move things around until they were catalogued and nothing was obviously labeled."

"Nice to know some merlins have common sense as well as power." Taliance stood in the center of the room, his eyes locked where the rip had been. His voice carried clearly and as I was the only merlin around, I had no doubt who the comment was meant for.

"Trust me, I still make stupid mistakes. Case in point, getting ambushed by that lunatic."

Lizzie had muttered at the photographer to get pictures of the inside of the fridge and wine fridge immediately. That was where the information she would need would be.

"Yes. Regarding that. I assume he came through the rip that was here in the corner?"

I turned my head to regard him and out of the corner of my eye, Carelian did the same. "I assume so."

"Closing it was smart. Having raw realm leaking in is rarely good."

"I closed another one about a mile from the house I'm renting," I said slowly. I knew he was AIN, but the lack of a tattoo kept me underestimating him.

He nodded, but I didn't see any surprise. "Chaos?"

~Yes. It is a section greatly influenced by a lord. It is twisted in ways that most Chaos creatures would not approve of.~ Carelian sounded disgruntled and I stared at him.

"You said that earlier. What do you mean wrong? I thought Chaos just meant Chaos."

His ears laid back and tail flicked. John had turned to stare at him also, though I caught a smile on his face. If Lizzie was paying attention, I couldn't tell. She stood behind the photographer, doing everything but tapping her foot.

~Chaos is Chaos, but there is a difference between the truth of entropy and decay, the wild randomness of the universe, and something that is twisted beyond what is natural. Chaos is the basis of existence, but it still has shape and form.~ He sounded frustrated as he finished, and I suspected he was trying to explain blue to a blind man. There were some things that didn't translate well.

"What your focus is saying, merlin, is that Chaos is wild and untamed and bounces against the limits of reality in all ways. It does not, however, warp or twist what does not naturally exist. Mutations are expected, gene splicing is not. Even Chaos has rules. It takes free will to create monsters." His voice was abstract as he stared at the now mundane space. Then he shook his head. "It is noted. Lizzie, what did you find?"

He spun and headed toward Lizzie, who finally had her head in the fridge. The crime scene tech moved over to the wine fridge. Everything would be cataloged and sent somewhere, I supposed. It was much more freewheeling than I was used to in Atlanta or other big cities, but then small towns didn't have that level of resources.

"Mostly vials of dead viruses, which is good. It looks like this was where he kept everything he was working on, but he didn't know how to keep them healthy. Lack of education for the win?" Her voice had a dry sarcasm to it that made me want to laugh.

"How can you tell?" he asked, moving a bit closer but not very. I wasn't letting down my air shield for anything. With my luck the fridge was trapped and it would explode, sending viruses flying everywhere.

"The mold growing on it and the rotting of the agar is a good sign," she said, straightening. "But that doesn't mean I don't want either an incinerator or a fire mage here to insure everything is disposed of completely. I don't want more than a few samples to get out of here intact." From the tone of her voice, you'd think she was talking about the worst filth you could ever find.

They both glanced at me and I was very happy that Fire was a null per my tattoo. I had no desire to stay here any longer and even less to explain the problem I was having with my magic.

"I'll contact the CDC and let them know. They can foot the bill for this." John turned to inspect me. "How much longer are you staying?"

"I'm gone as soon as you don't need me anymore. I'm more of a blunt instrument than a surgical knife." That wasn't exactly true and from the look both of them gave me, I suspect they didn't buy it, but it wasn't a lie exactly. I did get brought in as the "big gun" all too often.

They didn't have any more questions for me, so I waited outside until the rest of the people they called got there. Gave my story one more time for another group of people. At this point I didn't even care who they were. Nothing had been locked. I'd called out originally looking for someone, and I had been attacked after I identified myself. Not perfect and if it ever went to court, they might have an issue, but given it was someone with magic and access to the realms, I had no doubt he'd be dead by the time the week was out. It bugged me that it didn't bug me like it once would have.

I stood looking at the sky slowly deepening to purple, my emotions and thoughts twisted over all of this. But there wasn't anything I could do right now. This involved more than just me.

"You'll need to stay for a few more days. I already have the call in to the CDC for full containment. This entire place will be quarantined. Only the fact that it looks like all his samples were in the fridge saves us from a full decontamination procedure, but they'll need blood tests for the next few days. We are going to question your assailant. It is the son, Billy Jensen. They found his ID and matched him via fingerprints. Just want to clarify if anything comes out. We already have a judge coming by and some people from the OMO and the Draft board."

I blinked at that. If you had people like that coming out, it meant they were serious. And that I really wanted to go home. I guess I'd be here for a bit longer.

"Sure. Where do you want me to show up at?"

He pulled out his phone and started typing. "I'll text you the address." As he typed, he slipped in earphones and then dialed. "Amy? Got a job for you. Where you at?" She had left with the ambulance to escort the man to a secure location.

A spike of pain ripped through me and I whirled toward where it originated. A rip formed about 20 yards from us, near the cows, who started to moo and agitate toward the closed barn door.

I don't know if John felt it, or it was my reaction, but he spun with me, gun drawn as the portal sheared open the air between us and the cows. Most portals I've seen open have been gentle, like wavy cuts. This one felt like a tear in reality. The only one I've felt that was this violent was at the football game which seemed like eons ago.

~Carelian?~ Even in my mind, I whispered. He leaned against me, with his spine ruff bristled and his tail lashing back and forth hard enough I expected it to break the sound barrier.

~Something is coming.~

I didn't look at him, just left my hand on his head, waiting. What stepped out of the rip wasn't an amorphous blob like Bob, instead it was formed and solid, something out of Christian mythology or their nightmares. It stalked toward us almost ten feet tall, though after seeing how Tirsane could change her perceived height, that didn't impress me much anymore. Skin tightly pulled over human style musculature, except with goat knees and hooves, and midnight black horns twisting toward the blue sky. To cap the look was a long tail with a pointed end that looked sharp enough to pierce skin.

He, and the gender was blatantly obvious and about twelve inches long, stopped approximately five feet away and loomed over us. The devil smiled, revealing teeth made mostly of canines, and licked his lips with a forked tongue.

"You damaged my servant. You will pay," he said in a voice that vibrated my bones and sounded like it came from the depths of the earth.

EIGHTEEN

China institutes a mandatory six years of service for all mages, regardless of level, and offers bonuses to any mage who bears a child. This is an interesting change for a country that had an iron grip on its mages for years. What will be next? Tax bonuses or tax cuts? What is Cixi planning? ~ Magical Daily News

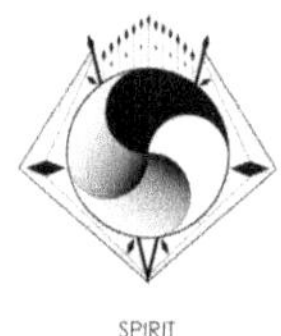

I blinked, even as Carelian was starting to sound like a chainsaw. A quick glance confirmed John was as dumbstruck as I was. I shifted my attention back to the thing in front of me.

"Really? Gorgons, dragons, elder gods, graboids? You could

have been any of those and you chose this? It isn't even practical. Why would you choose this form?" I couldn't keep the exasperation out of my voice. I knew that some of the Chaos lords could choose to take any form. Those like Esmere became Lords because of their skills and power. Some were born lords because of their power levels and they often chose what they wanted to be, at least in Chaos. The other realms seemed to vary, but I also didn't pay that much attention.

"Aren't you a scared tasty morsel?" It leered and leaned closer, its tongue flicking out toward my face. I didn't move away, but I did wave my hand in front of my face. The rancid breath made my eyes water.

"She sees through your tricks as I do. You might have scared a young man unsure of what the realms could spawn. We are not so gullible." John said all this in a bored voice and I had to resist glancing at him.

The creature actually sagged and appeared about six feet tall as it glared at us. "A Spirit Talker and a focus mage. Why couldn't you run screaming? You disrupted my plan. That is unacceptable."

Whereas before it came across as creepy and even dangerous, now it sounded more like a kid whining.

"Wait, you planned this?" I blurted, staring at him. "Why? What were you trying to do?"

He opened his mouth, then straightened up as if his mother had told him not to slouch. "You will regret ever interfering with my minions. Now I will take you back to my realm as toys. Humans will learn not to interfere in my plans."

Back in my hindbrain, part of me was gibbering at all of this. But most of me was lost in "What the fuck?" Because it made no sense.

"I don't think so." The words were uttered without me consciously choosing to speak. Carelian appeared next to me, his tail lashing as he sat down, looking for all the world bored with the entire situation.

The being lifted himself up more. I think he stood on his tiptoes. "Do you think you can withstand the might of Belcifer?" He boomed the last part, his voice coming out in a rumble of danger.

The door to the barn opened, there was the flash of a yellow vest, a squeak of terror, and then the door slammed back closed. I had no doubt panicked phone calls were going on. I didn't really think we'd need help. The lessons from Esmere and knowledge that Tirsane and Salistra had gifted me were about to come in very helpful.

"Well, maybe not me, but I bet I could give it a good try. But I don't think I need to." I crossed my arms and glared at him, beyond annoyed. It might be a good experiment to see if he had a soul I could yank out

To my right, John was just as calm. I'd ask questions as to why later. For now, I didn't want to get distracted.

"Oh, and what would one little mage, even with a focus, do against my might?" He lifted his hands and lightning cracked between them, arching across his broad chest with the snap and crack of ozone.

"I could yank out your soul, or pull all the water out of your body, or even just drop you into a hole in the ground. But those all sound so violent and frankly boring." I turned and focused on Carelian, making it look like I was ignoring Belcifer. "Carelian, do you think your mother and maybe our gorgon friend would like to know about this?"

~I think a unicorn and even a dragon might be more than a little annoyed by this. It is against the rules,~ he commented mildly as he extended the claws on his right paw and started to clean them.

I shuddered at the idea of putting anything that had been in contact with that room in my mouth, but trusted he knew his own limits.

Belcifer laughed, a loud mocking sound, and raised his hands as if to smite us. I did ground myself into the earth with Call

Mineral. No sense in letting myself get electrocuted. I silently blessed Jo for making sure I knew the basics of electricity. With a sigh I bid a goodbye to my phone. If I got hit and it fried, Steven was buying me a new one.

"And why should I care about a Cath's mother or even a Gorgon?" His sneer was impressive, but I kept my expression bland.

"Well, considering Esmere is a Chaos Lord, and Tirsane is a Spirit Lord, and Salistra is an Order Lord, and I know they have specifically said that creatures like you are not allowed to interact on Earth, it might matter. Zmaug would just enjoy testing out her flame on you."

"And I do believe Coyote and Raven would be most upset to have a creature like you operating so close to their territories on Earth. Not to mention my deputy has a sniper rifle aimed at your head, and Chaos lord or not, a .223 round will do a significant amount of damage." He held up his phone, and I realized he had kept his earbuds in and had been letting Amy hear what was going on.

Up until now, Belcifer had been a deep burgundy, with accents of black. As we spoke, his color drained away, like a chameleon trying to change to match the background. He went to a dusty rose with hints of gray outlining everything.

"You're her? The pet of Tirsane? And Esmere's get?" The words were said with the same horrified realization as if you'd just figured out you told the local police officer you were planning a bank heist.

"I don't think I am anyone's pet," I said, a touch offended. "But I do believe I could do extensive damage to you."

At least normally.

I kept that worry off my face.

~You do make an excellent pet, Cori. So well behaved, though I feel like I should get more salmon or maybe swordfish.~

I kicked Carelian, ignoring John's smirk.

"I do believe Coyote will want to know about this," John said.

"There have been way too many rips opening lately. Your doing, I take it?"

"I, well, I... I needed a summoner, someone to call me through. And Billy was so very willing. All I had to do was praise him and promise to help him create havoc. It was perfect." He was whining now and had lost at least a foot in height.

~Abner, what do you think you are doing?~ Esmere's voice cut across my mind loud enough that I had to double check I'd only heard her voice mentally, though her snarl was audible. Her emerald green fur flashed in the corner of my eye as she paced forward, looking like a cat on the hunt. Which she was. Part of me almost felt sorry for Belcifer, or Abner, as she called him.

He shrank back even further. "Esmere, you know my name is @!*#$&$."

I managed not to cry out, but sucked in a sharp breath as pain lashed through my brain. Next to me John rocked back on his heels, breathing deeply.

"I know that is what you want your name to be. Abner is much more accurate. Small and powerless. And Belcifer? Really? Your parents paid too much attention to the ravings of their lunatics. I thought you had more intelligence than that.~ Esmere shifted her golden gaze to me. ~Exactly what did he do?~

I wiggled my hand in a kind of gesture. "It is more who he manipulated. He got someone to play with viruses and set them loose on people. Luckily, they both didn't know what they were doing. If they had, there may have been a much higher death toll."

She blinked her golden eyes at me. They didn't have the same level of relaxation that blinking normally indicated. ~He what?~

"Add in the fact that this is skirting Adekagagwaa territory. They will not be happy." John sounded mild, but there was something in his voice that made me want to run and do research at the same time. I'd never heard it—the territory—called that before and I wanted to ask questions. But this wasn't the time.

Esmere hissed. The sound had me taking a step back, as the level of rage in it did not bode well. ~You dared to break the Pax, here? Near their territory? And then created rips to trap these lesser beings? That shall not be tolerated. Come.~

There was discomfort in knowing that we, humans, were regarded as lesser beings. That even Esmere thought of us like that. But I let it go. Belcifer or Abner looked like he was about to wet his pants with terror.

~Not only will your mother, Lilith, hear about this, I am dragging you to a tribunal right now. This is NOT acceptable.~

"No! Don't tell Mom. She'll be livid." Belcifer looked terrified, and I had zero sympathy.

~Your mother should be the least of your concerns. Bob is going to be most upset.~

Belcifer looked confused at the Bob reference until Esmere did the equivalent of whispering in his ear. I knew she was saying something, but it was more a feeling than hearing anything.

"No, don't tell him!" Sheer panic laced his voice, and he looked ready to run.

~Don't even think about it. March,~ she snapped out, and with his feet dragging, the two of them disappeared into the rip without a backwards glance. I had the distinct impression of a mom grabbing a kid's ear and dragging him out of the store.

I mentally reached out and closed the rip, ignoring the cost gleefully.

"Did you really have a sniper rifle aimed at his head?" I asked, my head tilted.

"Not yet. I was willing to stall as she was headed this way," he said as he slipped the phone back in his pocket. "You have interesting friends." It was a leading comment, but I just shrugged.

"Coyote and Raven?"

He quirked up one side of his mouth and looked at the barn. "We should probably go let them know the scary demon is gone."

"That wasn't answering my question." I pointed out as he walked away.

"Huh. Noticed that, did you?" he called back over his shoulder as he headed into the barn.

I shook my head and glanced down at Carelian. "You care to explain?"

He rose and stretched, then headed towards the rental car, leaving me standing there rolling my eyes.

"I'm starting to feel like a mushroom," I muttered as I headed to the car.

~Sauteed and good with salmon?~

"Fed bullshit and kept in the dark," I retorted.

He didn't say anything until we were in the car. ~You need to talk to Malkin about your magic. That is not normal. Even with me helping you, you had to offer too much. Something is wrong.~

His words chased away what good cheer dealing with Abner had left.

"Is it putting the baby at risk?" I sat there, my hand covering my abdomen with the sudden realization that if I'd put this child at risk because of my stubbornness, I'd never forgive myself.

Carelian's silence didn't help. I turned in my seat to peer at him sprawled across the back seat. "Well?"

He closed his eyes and laid his ears back. ~I do not know.~

Fear crept in and wrapped around my heart and mind. What was going on with my magic and how much danger was the child in?

CHAPTER

NINETEEN

The sole surviving civilian, a reputed "double" merlin, filled out an incident report on the SEC game, and is credited with saving the spectators, though that is highly improbable. The entirety of the report boiled down to "Scary monsters ate the human, we convinced them to go away". Anything else should be regarded as speculation and emotionally charged hysteria. ~ Portal Incident Reporting

---

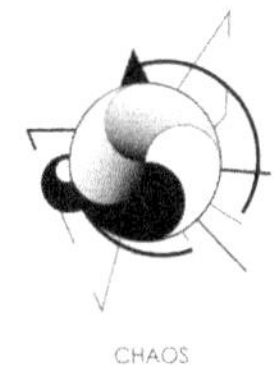

CHAOS

The next day I did some paperwork for the sheriff, but they hadn't needed me or my truth magic at all, which created a large amount of relief. The boy, Billy Jensen, had emerged as a wizard and started playing with opening rifts when his "lord" found him. He'd had an interest in pox's as one of his family's cows had come down with cowpox.

It went south from there. Abner, or Belcifer, taught him to use the rips he was creating to step into the Chaos plane. The Chaos plane helped destabilize him even more and by the time Abner was done, his mind had been twisted and broken and he'd become a very dangerous loose cannon.

CDC swept in, locked everything down, took blood from us and asked us to stay relatively isolated. They had zero sense of humor but I couldn't blame them. All the samples were logged and taken away, hopefully to be burned in a very hot furnace.

Taliance didn't have much to tell me other than he'd been thoroughly questioned by the Feds and they had no doubt as to the boy's guilt. They would be following up with me about Belcifer, but he thought I had dealt with it better than most would have been able to. They did ask some questions, but there really wasn't much more I could tell them as I purposely didn't ask Esmere any questions.

It seemed an odd series of events, but then my entire existence was like that—a sequence of events that created yet another one.

Four days later, Taliance and the CDC confirmed I was free to go. The sheriff gently implied a "please don't come back" message. I'd heard that one before. Carelian rode with me in the car to the rental car return in Omaha. We stood there, my bag at my feet, including the hazmat stuff I'd never used. I really should have when going into that lab, but I didn't expect to find what I did, or maybe I just thought I could protect myself. The significant amount of hair I'd lost made me rethink that arrogance.

I wanted to be home. The idea of another flight, then to the apartment, then either stepping or getting another flight to Albany made me want to cry. I just wanted to be home. But I had to follow process and rules.

Grumbling, Carelian stepped home and I headed to the airport. By the time I landed in Atlanta I didn't know if I wanted to cry or scream I was so exhausted. But I was picked up, the gear returned to the office, and I was dropped off at my apartment. Climbing the stairs took a mountain of effort. With my suitcase in hand I asked magic the price to step home and sighed in both exasperation and relief. A full inch of hair across the bottom. Normally, that would have cost me an inch or two of a few hairs, like five, not thousands. This was insane, but right now I'd pay the price to go home.

~Carelian, I'm stepping home,~ I told him, knowing he was already there.

His voice echoed with overtones of relief. ~Good. I worried about you in the metal tube for hours. Jo cooked. I will be there shortly, I am with Esmere.~

That intrigued and worried me, but I let it go. My exhaustion and worry were snapping at me and it was still another week before my first doctor visit. What if the baby had been hurt this time? The draft wouldn't let me hide at home for the next nine months. I pushed it all away, made the offering and stepped. The familiar space and scents in the air stripped off some of the weight I had not realized I carried.

"I'm home," I called out. I'd sent the occasional text message, so they knew I'd been working a case, though I'd not mentioned the cost of magic or what the case involved.

"Cori, in the living room, come join us. We have snacks." Jo's voice rang out through the house. I pushed my bags out of the way food sounding so good. The thought that if I lost the ability to sidestep I'd have to stay in Atlanta flashed to the front of my brain and I just cast it aside with all my other worries. There were so many things to be concerned about and I just couldn't deal with it right now.

I followed the sound of the TV to the living room. This had been the formal parlor, but with Hamiada's permission we'd turned it into a much more comfortable room with a loveseat recliner, full couch recliner, standalone recliner, expandable coffee table for card games and a large bean bag for Carelian, plus two club chairs tucked into one corner if people came over. My favorite was the loveseat recliner. I walked in to see them with the TV on and playing a movie, but they were both poking at the laptop on Jo's lap.

"I think we need that crib. I won't want it stupid fancy, and that one converts to a toddler bed, then a single. When the kid is sixteen, we can get a new bedroom set." Sable was pointing at something. "It's much more practical and reduces the amount of crap we need to buy. Besides, if we ever have more kids, this will work for them too."

"But that's the point of kids, buying them neat things. I want this child spoiled. Cori, what do you thin—" Jo broke off as her eyes met mine. "Merlin's beard, Cori. What happened?"

Sable jerked her head to look at me and her eyes widened. "Your hair. Are you okay? Is the baby okay?" She was scrambling off the couch as I reached up to touch my hair, a bit self-conscious. With all the magic and trouble, I'd lost almost four inches. Previously in a super busy week, I might lose half an inch.

Sable ran her hands over my body, checking me for injuries. "What were you doing? Were you in danger?"

~That is exactly what I would like to know,~ Esmere's voice whispered in my head as she stalked into the room from behind me, trailed by Carelian. ~Why were you messing with the likes of Abner, much less dangerous biologicals? Anyone with a nose could smell you were pregnant the second they stepped through, even through the awful methane gas those beasts put out.~ She paused canting an ear. ~Though they do taste good. Anyway, what were you thinking?~ Her voice was sharp and caustic as she sat in front of the TV staring at me with amber eyes.

By this time Jo had risen also, her worry and anger radiating off of her.

Guilt, defensiveness, and shame made me snap back. There were some days I failed as a human being. "My job. You know? The one I don't have a choice about doing? You knew I had to still work when you asked. Maybe this was a bad idea." I spun, ready to race to my room, when strong arms wrapped around me and pulled me tight.

"Cori, *mi corazón*. Don't you know you can't chase us away? We love you and right now we are both having panic attacks over the idea of you being hurt. The baby is important, yes, but you are just as important. Come, sit down, and tell us everything."

I turned in Jo's arms and looked up at her. She dropped a kiss on my forehead. "You don't get out of this issue by storming off. Sorry."

A laugh-sob slipped out, and I sniffed. "It's been a weird week."

Sable walked back into the room, carrying tea and snacks. I hadn't even seen her leave. Jo ensconced me into my chair as Carelian flopped in front of me, ensuring I couldn't get up unless he moved.

"Now spill. Tell us about the case. What happened? And explain why you had to use so much magic." Jo leveled her dark eyes on me, nipping any resentment in the bud.

I touched my hair, oddly self-conscious, then took a sip of the tea. The chamomile scent helped as much as the liquid heat. I started out, explaining the favor for Alixant, the search, the planar rips, the being, and Esmere scolding it like a truant pre-teen. That would go down in my memories as one of my favorites.

Sable nodded, but pointed at my hair. "Nothing you said sounded like world ending magic, or even anything super power-ful. Why does it look like your hair got caught in a lawn mower?"

I wrinkled my nose. The Cosmetics Offering class had been valuable, and I'd earned an A, but I'd never taken any of the higher-level classes, nor did I have any level of creativity in it. That meant that while my offerings were normally somewhat smooth, this time out I'd had to pay a lot fast, and my keeping the offerings in a cosmetically pleasing manner had failed.

"That is what I needed to talk to Esmere about." The Cath in question leaned forward, peering at me.

~What exactly?~ she asked, though she had said nothing

during my retelling of the events except to clarify once that Abner, or Belcifer, was not a lord, only a wanna-be lord. I didn't follow up on that right then, but added it to my growing pile of information about life in the realms.

I gripped my mug tighter and focused on the warmth. "Magic is asking for huge offerings," I admitted, an odd sense of failure washing through me.

Jo perched on the edge of her seat, watching me with brows furrowed. "Huge how?"

I shook my head as her worry radiated out. "Not that huge. I'd never give up the baby. Before we joined, I could use Fire. The offering was a few hairs for me to heat something up. Since I was a null in that branch it should have been huge. It never was. After our joining I could use Fire as if I was a strong. Sidestepping took a few millimeters of hair, nothing more." I fell silent and looked at my tea, trying to figure out how to explain the gut churning fear in my stomach and the back of my mind.

"And now?" Sable prompted softly.

"If I would have sidestepped home from Nebraska it would have been a quarter inch from of all of my hair. Even from the apartment it was more than normal. I've stepped from China to here for a fraction of an inch." My voice sounded numb. "And I'm terrified that if I continue to work it will put the baby at risk. How do women do this? Live with this responsibility?"

Sable and Jo exchanged scared looks, licking their lips.

~Really. You humans over dramatize everything. And people call Cath drama queens.~ Esmere's acerbic comment cut through my melancholy like a squirt of lemon.

"What do you mean?"

~It means you have an issue. We should talk to experts. Not act like the world is ending. This is life. Bearing a child is something you adapt to. Your magic should not react to your pregnancy, but I am not human, thank Magic. Humans are not as well designed as Cath. I will find someone for you to talk to. What seems life shaking rarely is. Eat, rest, and gestate the child. I am looking forward to human development. It should be interesting.~ Before anyone could say anything, she was gone.

Jo darted a look at Carelian, who kept his eyes closed, though his rapid tail flicks had slowed. "I guess we wait for her input, but meanwhile, I want to know why you didn't explain to us exactly where you were going and why." Her voice was neutral, but I flushed as guilt washed through me.

Head bowed; I spoke to my mug. "I didn't want to give up my life. I kept telling myself that other women do this all the time. They work and still have a life."

"Not usually with class five viruses. And they also take a lot more precautions than you did," Sable pointed out. It was the quaver in her voice that caused my protest to die on my lips.

I wanted to rail that I was barely pregnant, that someone who was pregnant wasn't an invalid, but the idea of what was in my body stopped me. "I thought magic would protect me. Isn't that why I'm so powerful? It didn't work that way. I'm sorry." My eyes burned, and I just wanted to scream, mad mostly at myself more than anyone else.

"Cori, you are our life, someone we love. We can't lose you. No one is so powerful they can afford to take unnecessary risks."

The warm understanding of Jo's tone made my guilt worse. I hated feeling guilty.

TWENTY

Pregnancy Facts: Pregnant women are more prone to broken bones because of a hormone called relaxin. The hormone allows your joints to soften so that your hips and pelvis can open up for birth. Without this change in bodies, even a mage can have difficultly recovering. ~ The Pregnant Mage

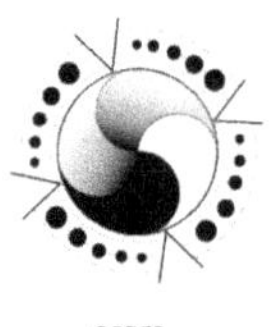
ORDER

T he doctor's appointment was in a few days, and I was unaccountably nervous. I didn't have any reason to believe I might have miscarried, but I knew the numbers. Carelian assured me I was still pregnant, saying he could smell my fertility, which was more than a little creepy.

Esmere passed a message every few days saying she was still

working on things, and I let Carelian take me to work. Sidestepping was easier.

The morning of the appointment, I should have been six weeks along. I paced around the house unable to settle down. My hands played with everything, needing to keep myself occupied.

"And here I thought I'd be the nervous one," Sable said behind me. I almost shrieked. My attention had been on the toast with cream cheese that I was supposed to eat. I wasn't morning sick, just anxious. Even coffee didn't smell good this morning, so I was downing water.

"What if my body won't do this? What if I can't work? Will the draft let me? What if my magic hurts the child?" I clenched my hands, a tidal wave of ridiculous fears battering at me.

What if the baby is born with fur?

"Cori, breathe!" Sable's eyes were wide as she stared at me. "I have seen you face down dragons with more aplomb. What is going on?"

"Dragons could only kill me. What if, what… what if I hurt your baby?" What was wrong with me? My hands were twitching as I tried to come up with something to do. Something constructive.

Sable pulled me into a hug, holding me tight. "Cori, breathe. This is something women do all the time. Marisol used magic while she was pregnant and there is no reason for this to not work. I'd like you to avoid gun fights or class five viruses, but this is normal. You'll see."

Sable chivvied us into the car and then we headed into Albany proper. Dr. Anna Lobdell had a private practice a mile from where I'd give birth, Albany Hospital. Jo kept up an argument about names all the way down, making me laugh. She was rooting for Merlin if it was a boy and Gwenhwyfar if it was a girl. Sable shot down both of them hard, to my relief.

The waiting room was done in cool green but it did nothing to calm me. I was dragged off for blood work and other vitals measuring. At this rate I'd have no blood left in my body. Then there was more waiting.

Finally, a nurse called us all into an office, pointing out my blood pressure was a bit high, then left so we could wait for the doctor.

"At this rate I'm going to spend more time in the doctor's office than at work. And have we thought about the fact that if I can't sidestep, me coming to these appointments is going to get expensive?"

Jo shrugged. "We'll figure it out. You said sidestepping still wasn't a huge price, and you only come in every three months. I can try to arrange it on Fridays, so maybe you can fly home? Or we ask Carelian?"

I shrugged, avoiding the question. Magic was getting more and more expensive. The normal vitamins I took for hair growth were all that kept me from stressing out. If this kept up, I'd have to offer blood. But if I cut back on everything else, maybe I could make it for nine months. The knowledge of how much it would cost without Carelian made my heart race. I'd been so wrapped up in what if possibilities that I didn't know what else to do.

There was a knock on the door and a woman stepped in, a friendly smile gracing her face. Her hair was brown with hints of red, though I couldn't tell if it was natural or added. Green hazel eyes crinkled at the creases, and I was struck by the pie wedge of brown in her iris. It gave her an otherworld air that made me feel comfortable. With wide hips and shoulders, she radiated calm strength.

"Cori. I'm glad to finally get to meet you. I was starting to think you were a figment of Sable and Jo's imagination." Her friendly voice and manner went a long way to dispelling my nerves. Part of me had expected her to walk in and yell at me. "I'm Dr. Anna Lobdell."

"Nice to meet you." I looked around. "So now what?"

Anna laughed, brown eyes sparkling. "Well, you are pregnant. About six weeks, but then you knew that. We can do an ultrasound, but at this point you'll just see a cluster of cells, not much else. Normally I don't perform one until about twelve weeks unless there is a reason to. By then, your body should be adapting to what is going on and your hormones will have kicked in. For most people, I'd advise you to start taking pre-natal vitamins, but you noted that you already do. So keep that up." She handed me the folder. "In there is all the information about diet changes you need to make, no alcohol and cut back on caffeine. There are recommendations about weight and exer-cise, but the three of you look like you have that under control." She grinned and waved at her own body, which showed a sturdy European frame. "And I am well aware of the fact that I could stand to lose another forty pounds. Too bad food tastes so good."

She checked her notes. "I see you had three implanted. You do realize the odds are only one child survived. You aren't expecting triplets, are you?"

"No," we chorused together and she laughed, a contagious laugh that pulled us in to share it. I was glad this woman would be with me through the process, she felt like someone I could trust.

"So, do you have any questions?"

I opened my mouth and my brain stopped. I had no idea what to ask. Everything or nothing? How could she tell me what was going to happen?

"Caffeine? Cut back on? What does that mean?" I grabbed for the one thing that seemed to have any clarity to it. No coffee, that would be very bad.

"Ah, coffee drinker, are you?"

"Yes. My coffee is my life blood in the mornings," I replied as both Jo and Sable suddenly had worried looks on their faces.

"Hmm. Okay, here is the rough truth. Caffeine increases the activity of you and the baby as it crosses the placental barrier." She sat, perfectly at ease, while Jo and Sable each had a hand touching me, their stress all but radiating down from them. "But, if you have been drinking coffee for a long time, we can work at reducing how much you drink."

All three of us nodded and I kept my fingers crossed.

"How much do you drink a day?"

"About 32 oz. The real stuff, not the half water stuff."

"Okay. That might be a bit much as the baby gets bigger. Why don't we do this; first let's cut back to 24 oz, then every week, cut the strength of the coffee by a teaspoon. You're healthy and your body is used to it, but trust me, by the time the baby starts to kick you will want to enjoy the occasional afternoon nap. Doing it this way will wean you down. And you'll want to watch the coffee intake while you are breast feeding." We'd already talked about that and the health benefits meant I'd breast feed as long as feasible.

I took a deep breath. That sounded doable, but I gave Jo and Sable looks. "My birthing present had better be chocolate covered espresso beans. The good ones."

"For after she is done nursing. The last thing you want is a wired infant. Trust me."

Jo snickered and dropped a kiss on my forehead. "How about as a weaning gift I get you the super fancy home espresso machine you wanted?"

"Deal," I said without flinching. That monster cost a fortune, and she'd have to beg Hamiada to make it fit. But it would be so worth it. True espresso. "I can do that. I'll start immediately." If I upped my water intake and lowered my coffee amount slowly, the caffeine headache wouldn't be too bad. But I would miss my morning routine.

"Then no alcohol, up your fish intake, and basically don't do anything stupid. If you have a craving as you get further along, note it for me and give in to it. At least ninety percent of the time, a craving is something your body needs."

"And the other ten percent?" Sable asked, her hand more relaxed on my back now.

Anna laughed. "Per my husband, it means I want to demand

something completely unreasonable from him at 3 A.M. just to prove he still loves me, even when fat." She winked at the three of us. "Somehow I don't think that will be the same reason for you ladies."

I snorted. "No, it will be 'Do it or I swear to god I'm going to be the aunt who spoils the kid rotten non-stop.'"

Jo and Sable laughed. "You do realize that threat only works if you don't live with us or at least next door," Jo said. "Thank you, Cori, for this."

I shrugged, trying not to flush. "Hey, I want kids to spoil, too. I just never thought they would be from my body."

We went over the checkup plan and what I could expect as well as some links to websites that had accurate information, not the horror story stuff I kept finding.

"I think that covers it. Cori, I'll see you in about six weeks. The front office will set up the appointment for you. But mostly just live your life. Your body might be making lots of adjustments, but that is the wonder of the female body. It is meant to do this. Anything else for me?"

"Oh, Carelian!" I exclaimed, just as I was getting up.

"And Esmere," Jo said with a wry smile. "I wouldn't put anything past her. She finds this whole process overly fascinating."

Anna glanced back and forth between us. "Mother-in-law?"

Jo and Sable grinned. "My mother," Jo said, tapping her heart, "is in the Atlanta area and would be here in a heartbeat. But other than excited grandma babbling, you won't need to worry about her."

"And my mother died giving birth to me, so other than a ghost, you should be fine." Sable leaned against Jo. "My dad and aunt are there for me, but neither has expressed any interest in being intimately involved in this aspect. They are happy with the kid to spoil aspect."

Falling into the pattern, I laughed. "And my mother walked away from me a long time ago. No, Carelian is my familiar. He doesn't like doctors' offices as they always yell at him about shedding. But he will be very aware of everything we are doing."

"And Esmere is his mother. She is both excited and curious, as she's never known a pregnant human. How much of it is grandbaby fever and how much is scientific interest we aren't sure," Sable finished, the three of us grinning like loons.

"But if they pop in, don't be worried about sharing anything with them. They are beings I trust with my life," I assured her. "Quite literally."

"Ah. So authorized people with HIPAA. I can work with that." She paused with an odd look on her face. "They don't have IDs or anything, do they?"

I covered my face with my hand, fighting laughter at the idea of convincing Esmere to get an identification card. Though Carelian had multiple badges, so he wouldn't care. I'd never broach the idea of him driving. He'd never let go of it. And I wasn't sure the world could handle a Cath with a driver's license.

"I could introduce you really quick? If it's short, he doesn't shed that much. Trust me, I don't think you'll have any problems recognizing them." I tried really hard not to snicker. I'd never met another Cath familiar and I suspected Esmere was one of a kind.

Anna had a puzzled look on her face, but nodded. "Sure."

~Carelian? Want to pop in for a minute and meet my doctor?~

~I thought you would never ask. I wish to inspect the person who will help my quean through her pregnancy. ~ The stab of pain sliced through me, then was gone as Carelian stepped through. In the white beige of the room, his red fur all but glowed in contrast.

"Ah," Anna sucked in a harsh gasp of air as she fell back against the door. Her eyes were wide and face pale as she stared at the apex predator who was too lazy to fish for his own dinner.

~You are the healer who will ensure my quean has healthy kits?~ He stuck his nose toward her, sniffing. ~You smell healthy. Are you a good healer? Experienced with squalling ones?~

Anna licked her lips, her voice higher pitched than previously.

"I've delivered a lot of children, yes. You are Carelian?" she squeaked as he licked her hand.

~You will do. Take care of my queans. They are precious.~ He turned and grazed past all of us, seeming to stroke us, in reality marking us as his. Then he was gone. The room seemed much bigger when he stepped back into the realms.

Anna sagged, looking at us with wide eyes. "And his mother is like him?"

"Oh, much worse. She is much bigger and way more professor like. And bright green," Jo said with a grin. "On the bright side, if you can handle those two, my mother won't be an issue."

"Oh my," Anna whispered.

TWENTY-ONE

Twins come in more than two types. We are all familiar with fraternal (two separate placentas) and identical (same placenta, same genetic structure) but there are also mirror-image twins where they are exactly what they seem. ~The Pregnant Mage

SPIRIT

We got home and decided to wait before telling anyone until we knew for sure I'd kept at least one of the embryos. After that point I'd tell work and we would tell our families. Carelian spent too much time being smug that his family already knew until I threatened to have Jo dump ice water on him if he didn't quit being a pain. He sulked for a day, then let it go. Jo wanted to tell Marisol so badly I could taste it. But with my magic being wonky, no one wanted to get anyone's hopes up. Miscarriages were common.

From my perspective time dragged and flew by at the same time. It seemed like things were happening super-fast and slower than ice melting simultaneously. Esmere sent back messages via Carelian that she had not found anything about magic being an issue while pregnant so far and I stressed over every millimeter of hair I spent. The only saving grace was that the next month's work was busy, but boring and in the office. I spent the majority of my time in the lab and doing paperwork and research. I still went home to Albany from Atlanta daily, but most days, I let Carelian take me via rips. Let's just say that I vastly preferred sidestepping home.

I still didn't feel different, and that worried me. Almost as much as my magic refusing to cooperate. I'd almost quit using it. Jo and Sable had faith it would straighten out, I just avoided thinking about it since I didn't know what I was supposed to do. Should I tell the draft board? Tell Naomi? Should I talk to Indira and Steven about it? In the end I didn't do anything. I just made sure I took all my vitamins and when I did use magic, I tried to be very specific. I dove back into James Well's research just to see if he'd ever looked at pregnancies. But the man had been a prolific writer and even with me reading a few pages a night I had barely managed to get through the journals he wrote during his draft since I started.

~I must admit failure,~ Esmere said in my brain. I jerked, spilling some of my precious limited coffee on the floor of the kitchen. I stared at it, wanting to cry. Caffeine lost to me. I took a deep breath and looked around. I was still alone.

"Esmere?"

~Out in your sunroom. The warmth feels good. ~

I checked my watch, twenty minutes until I needed to be headed to Atlanta. Oh well. Me being late wouldn't really matter. I just hated it. She was sprawled out on the floor, the sunrise casting golden light over her emerald fur. I had a flash of her laying on a pharaoh's throne, enjoying the adoration. It seemed all too fitting.

"And how have you failed?" I took a seat, savoring every sip of my coffee. I didn't drink it mindlessly anymore. I got too little to waste it.

~All the females I have spoken with who gave birth have never noticed magic issues. But...~ She paused, only her lashing tail giving me any hint as to her mood.

I waited—hurrying her didn't work.

~The majority of my contacts are not humanoid. And only a few used magic regularly enough to notice what the demand was.~ She mentally hissed at that and I wrinkled my nose. It felt like insects running over my brain. Most discomfiting. ~So I fear I am not much help. And it is worrying me.~

I didn't try to deny the tightening in my body. I had hoped this was normal, but in my very careful web searches, no one was talking about it. And it made me nervous. Did it mean the child was in danger? And for Esmere to be worried added extra stress.

~So I asked Tirsane to stop by and talk to you.~

"What?" I blurted out the word, sloshing my coffee again. Tirsane was still intimidating and powerful, even if I regarded her as an almost friend. She'd never lost the boost I'd inadvertently given her, and Salistra, the unicorn Order Lord, still hadn't forgiven me. I tried to remember the last time I'd seen Tirsane, at least a year ago. We invited her to things, more like you invite the powerful fairy because you don't want to offend her, but most of the time she declined. I liked her, but she still scared the willies out of me when I really thought about what she was.

~She is more humanoid than I am, and Spirit tends to have more beings that are humanoid than Chaos. We lean towards more animalistic natures. You saw Abner. That is about as humanoid as we get without conscious choice, and who would want to be human?~

She said it the way I would mention a pile of dog crap on my shoe. I might have taken offense, but I knew what her next words would be.

~After all, when you are Cath, why would you want to be anything else? Even canines are preferable to the blindness of humans.~

I shook my head. All Cath were convinced they were the best of any beings, and I didn't have the energy or centuries to try to convince them otherwise. Besides, I wasn't always sure they were wrong; opposable thumbs and grace and magic. They might be right.

"And what did Tirsane say?" I asked that with no small amount of trepidation. Tirsane wasn't as whiplash in her moods with me as Salistra was, but still.

~Nothing. She hmmmed a lot, nodded and slithered away. That gorgon does inscrutable better than most statues.~ Esmere sounded annoyed, and I hid my laugh by taking another sip of the dwindling coffee.

"Well then, I shall wait to hear what she has to say. Thank you for your efforts, Esmere." I rose, staring sadly at my empty mug. Water or juice for me for the rest of the day. Maybe I'd splurge on a smoothie with peanut butter in it. It was going to be a long eight months. Well, less than that, but still.

Her tail flicked in a dismissive gesture. ~I should have found better. It highlights how little I know about the vagaries of human reproduction. I shall be following your gestation closely.~ Esmere stared at me, amber eyes unblinking.

I rolled my eyes, then shrugged. This pregnancy was starting to feel like a class project. Jo and Sable were planning on sending regular updates to relatives when it was confirmed after the twelve-week appointment. I still didn't know how I felt. So I wasn't worrying about it, just watching it happen.

"I'm off to work. Carelian should be back after he helps me get to work if you want him."

~No. I shall enjoy the sun a bit longer, Earth sun has a heat to it I love, then I have work to do.~ She laid her head back down, eyes closed as she absorbed the sun.

I put my empty mug in the sink, then filled my water bottle with a glum look. Even the water flavorings didn't help. I missed my coffee. Five minutes before I was late. Making sure I had everything ready to go, I headed upstairs and crouched next to Carelian sprawled out on his bed. The colors still clashed, but he looked so cute against the brown and neon yellow.

"Hey," I said, rubbing his ear. He purred and rolled over to give me access to his chin. "You willing to take me to work? I should really be there, oh, now?" I said, looking at my watch. This magic issue already was making me understand why people didn't use magic. If it cost so much to use it, you never dared, just in case you really needed it later. I had more sympathy for other mages now.

~Yes. But sleeping once there.~ He yawned as he spoke to me, his long fangs driving home that I really didn't ever want him or Esmere to get mad at me. They could rip off an arm without trying. That may have been why I liked them so much. Death in cute fur.

I hefted my stuff as he opened a portal. I put my hand on his collar and walked in. It was a mostly empty gray space, with a scraggly bush, and dry dirt. The rip to the house closed and he opened a new one and we stepped out onto the sidewalk next to my building.

"Why is it always that space?" I asked. The few times he'd helped me travel, it was always that same location.

~Neutral space. Nothing to attack or be attacked by. Lot of us use it as a transport point. It is boring. Boring in the realms is safe.~

I gave him a look as we badged into the building. I'd clipped his badge to his collar after we stepped out.

"Someday I'd like to see the realms, your realms with you. I've only ever gone to safe places." Or at least mostly safe.

~Maybe. Someday. But absolutely not until your magic

responds correctly.~ He almost hissed. I got the feeling sometimes his offense at my magic not working was personal. Like how dare magic betray his quean. It was amusing and cute, if not a bit worrisome. I knew he wasn't an all-powerful being, but the fact that neither him nor Esmere knew why my magic was behaving this way didn't make me feel better.

I logged in as he sprawled under my desk, instantly asleep. I dealt with paperwork. The results were finally back from the CDC, as well as the full details of what the boy had been up to. Linking that into my existing case notes and filing everything as complete took most of the day.

An hour later I was pulling up the next research assignment when I heard familiar footsteps.

"I'm concerned about this aspect of your report." Naomi spoke before she had even rounded the corner of my cubical, holding her tablet in her hands.

"And which part would that be?" I leaned back, stretching—maybe I'd take a bath tonight.

"You said you found two rips while there? Both small?" She lifted her head to stare at me, light brown eyes like spotlights of focus.

"Both were small, not micro, and apparently still big enough for someone to step into, though I do realize that the ability to travel into portal openings usually has little to do with physical size, more the state of mind of the traveler. Humans like things to be human sized." I paused, then shrugged. "Well, normally."

"What?" Naomi gave me a curious look, and I gave her a lopsided grin.

"The kid, Ben Jensen, was a plane walker. That meant any rip, no matter how tiny, he could use it to step in and out of the planes. It's rare and rather creepy. Most of the time, and especially with physical things, it needs to be the right size. For example, if I want to drag a car through a rip, it had better be big enough for the car, or bad things happen."

"To the car or the person? And worse than you teleporting?" Her voice dry, as she stood hip-cocked, watching me.

"I step through the planet and time, not really through the planes. It's different and the cost is much, much higher to teleport." I wasn't trying to be difficult, but it was two separate things. And I wasn't going to mention what the cost difference was for me.

"Explain." Her voice was flat, but I knew she was serious. She wanted to understand.

I muttered to myself for a minute, trying to figure out how to explain. "Okay, you've been camping and have been in a tent, right?" She nodded. "So, if I'm on the outside of one side of the tent and need to get to the other side, traveling via the planes is like taking a knife and slitting open the side of the tent nearest me and ducking inside. I then walk to the other side of the tent and slit that side and step out. The tent is always the size of a pup tent, but I can step in and out on other sides of the planet."

Naomi narrowed her eyes as she thought, but finally nodded. "Okay, I get that. But don't you do the same thing when you teleport?"

I shook my head. "When I teleport, I take that same tent and instead of cutting it, I pull it to one side and step across where it was. But again, it can be to the other side of the room or across the world. You go someplace else when you plane walk or use the planes as a passage. Teleporting moves the distance you want to go out of the way."

She stood there for a long time, and I shifted under the weight of her gaze. "Magic is nowhere near logical enough for me. Let me know if you close any other portals, regardless of size. I've got a case or two coming down next week. Please have your workload cleared to deal with it." A brisk nod and she was gone. I sagged in relief. I liked Naomi, but sometimes she was a bit too laser focused for my comfort.

Co-workers stopped by and chatted for a bit, but soon left as they had their own work stacking up. It made me long to be out doing something, even while I was very glad to be doing nothing except filing reports.

Smirking at myself and my inconsistencies, I settled in to deal with work and see what other cases I might be called into, all while stress about my pregnancy and my magic bubbled at the back of my brain.

TWENTY-TWO

Pregnancy Fact: The average number of calories needed to support twins is around 4000 calories. If you are a mage plan on more. Mages generally spend more calories every day replacing the genetic material used casting magic. Keep in mind that healthy food options are best as supplying this calorie need via fast food is harmful to your health. ~ The Pregnant Mage

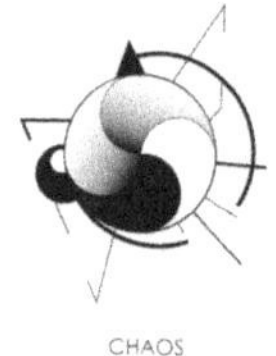

CHAOS

The next two weeks went by with nothing happening. A few investigations in Atlanta, one where a bridge was set on fire and collapsed, and they wanted to see if magic had been used. There hadn't been any, but I did find a micro rip. I closed it and noted it in my notes when I filed the report. The culprits weren't mages. That I checked with both Pattern and Recreate and checked for any magic remnants, but neither Carelian nor I could find anything.

My magic still responded like molasses to anything I wanted and it was easier to not use it, at least when I didn't have to. It scared me how easy it was to just not use magic. My loss of side-stepping was the worst, but Carelian helped with that, or at least made it more of an annoyance than crippling.

The number of days pregnant ticked in my head like a metronome, even as the problems with magic caused me stress.

I pulled out clothes for the morning, started getting dressed, had to suck in my stomach to button my pants and froze. I couldn't remember the last time my clothes hadn't fit. Gaining weight had never been an issue for me. Putting on muscle was, but I rarely gained weight.

"My pants are too tight," I muttered, staring at the tug of the waistband against the button.

~I thought your ass looked larger than normal, but I wasn't sure.~

I turned and threw my wadded up socks at Carelian.

~It is true. Weight gain is good. Mothers need fat to feed young ones. Skinny mothers don't have enough fat to keep their kits healthy.~

This time I threw a shirt at him. "That isn't helping."

Carelian closed his eyes and rolled over. ~Humans.~

I narrowed my eyes at him and grabbed a stretchy pair of leggings and a long shirt. If I spent the day in the lab with a lab coat on, it was doubtful anyone would notice. But no matter what, it meant shopping. A sigh slipped out as I contemplated that process. Shopping almost always sucked, and almost always meant Indira, Jo, and Sable would have a blast. I'd put off mentioning it for another two weeks. I could just wear longer tops until then.

"Morning momma to be," Jo sang out as I entered the kitchen.

She handed me a small cup of coffee. "Your allotted coffee for the day, perfectly fixed."

I narrowed my eyes at her and sat down, inhaling the aroma. Jo loved me being pregnant, and while we were all trying to figure out this new dynamic, I still didn't know how I felt about it. But I couldn't deny being waited on was a bit addictive.

"What do you want for breakfast?"

This was new, and I shrugged. "Just a bagel with cream cheese. I have a lot to do in the lab today. Dirt samples and then we are waiting to see if I get called in on a missing kid. Though I'm not sure if they want Carelian or me more."

Jo nodded as Sable came in. Sable stopped and gave Jo a deep kiss, then came and dropped a kiss on my head. "Morning, Cori."

"Sable," I murmured, trying not to smile at their sweetness.

"Okay, but remember you need protein at lunch, and no raw fish." Jo made me a bagel the way I liked it, half an inch of cream cheese and a sprinkle of paprika. "Your 12-week ultrasound appointment is next week. Are you excited?"

I could hear that she was, but I'd actually forgotten and panic gripped me; what if it showed nothing? Then I remembered the clothes that didn't fit this morning, I was definitely pregnant. "Curious might be a better word." I finished off my coffee and grabbed my water bottle.

Sable grinned as she fired up the blender. "I'm making you a smoothie. You aren't getting enough vitamins right now. Your eating habits have always been iffy. So drink this and eat the bagel. I know you don't want a full meal in the morning, but this will taste good and be good for you."

I narrowed my eyes as I watched her put spinach, red powder, and berries into the blender. "Uh huh."

They both grinned at me. "Deal," they chimed out as I made a face.

"Yes, dears," I muttered and sipped my tiny cup of coffee. They both gave me unrepentant grins and I just hid my own smile, feeling rather loved.

A sharp spike of transient pain lashed through me and I raised my head as Esmere slipped in.

~Good morning, queans. I trust the morn has found you well.~ She tilted her head, looking at me. ~Carelian is correct. You have started putting on weight.~

I groaned as both Jo and Sable's eyes snapped to me. They assessed me and grins spread over their faces. "Shopping time," they chorused, and I let my head hit the table with a dull thud.

"I hate shopping," I whined, knowing it would do me no good.

"Too bad. We are going to get you some cute maternity clothes this weekend. But you know you'll have to tell your boss soon."

I tried not to cringe at the idea of hours of trying on clothes, and I wouldn't even be able to get a mocha. Fine. But I was getting a coffee ice cream. Maybe even a coffee flavored milkshake.

~Humans. Your natural skin is functional, your dependence on extra fur is confusing. But that is not why I came.~ Esmere moved over to where Sable was still blending, her ears laying back each time Sable pressed the button. ~What is that?~

"Food for Cori. She needs to get more vitamins."

Esmere watched, her lips pulling back as she scented the air. She gave me a sidelong look, ears twitching. ~You will eat that?~ The disgust and outrage in her voice amused me.

"I would agree with you, but I've seen what Carelian eats," I responded, shuddering as his joy in eating fish heads flashed through my mind.

~You do not understand how good flesh tastes,~ he commented as he sauntered into the kitchen.

"Your taste buds and ours do not work the same," Sable commented as she brought the smoothie to me. "Try it," she said, this time looking at me. Wary of the taste, I took a sip and blinked. "Not bad. It doesn't taste like spinach at all." I took another sip. This would actually make mornings easier. She had it in a travel cup with a straw, meaning I could nibble as I moved.

"Good. I included ginger which should help with any morning sickness later."

I rolled my eyes at the reminder, but didn't follow up on it. "So why did you come if not to see how fat I am?"

~You are nowhere near fat enough, I don't believe. Humans are different from Cath. But that is part of the problem. Most of those I know are not humanoid. It is such an inefficient form.~ This time I did roll my eyes. Cath were horribly predictable when it came to some things. ~Nevertheless, Tirsane asked me to tell you she would be by next Friday evening with someone you can speak with regarding your pregnancy issues.~

"She found someone? Who?" Jo and Sable looked as eager as I felt.

~I am unsure. But she sounded assured, though that does not imply anything. Tirsane does not lack for confidence.~ She licked her paw as if that was somehow a crime. Maybe it was if you weren't Cath.

"We'll be back from the ultrasound appointment by then, so we should know the status of the baby," Jo volunteered.

I swallowed, but nodded. "That sounds great. Do you want to come? We can have a dinner party and tell people?" I offered. It had been a while since we'd had anyone over.

Esmere tilted her head, then darted a quick groom at her shoulder. ~If you serve fish, I shall attend regardless. It might be wise to invite Tirsane.~ She said it casually, but all of us caught the suggestion.

~Fish. The rest is their problem.~ Carelian yawned. ~I believe we are going to be late.~

I jerked my head down to glance at my watch.

"Crap." I downed the rest of my coffee and grabbed the smoothie. "Talk to these two about the dinner. I'll see you then." I headed to work with Carelian leading me through the planes and got to my office only five minutes late. My life would be so much easier if I could still sidestep. At least cheaply.

I settled down at my computer, called up my email and worked on drinking the smoothie Sable made. It wasn't anywhere near as bad as I expected. There were some benefits to this whole thing. The phone rang next to me as I dug through computer emails and research options. "Morning, Naomi," I said answering as I filed emails.

"Cori. I've got a new assignment for you. We have an accident in a chemical factory that the first responders need some help with. The fumes are so strong they can't get in without respirators, but they are trying to find unconscious people and they are worried they are missing things with lack of visibility and trouble hearing. I've got a helicopter coming in and should be here in twenty minutes. I need you to go see if you can clear the air and locate anyone?"

The request rocked me back. My magic was so iffy. But I knew that if she was calling me it was because they needed someone who could manage air and help with wounded. I looked at my hair. The doubling of vitamins meant it was growing well and with Carelian I should be able to do it.

Forcing my doubts down, I nodded. "Yep. Let me grab my bag and change clothes. I'll meet them at the helicopter."

"Excellent. Keep in touch. They said they have a wizard and a magician there, but neither are Order, so they are having trouble with Air. Use them as you need to."

"Got it." I hung up and stared at my fingers, then shook my head. I had a job to do and magic would have to deal. "Come on Carelian, we have work to do."

~Are you sure?~

I looked over at him. He stared at me, green eyes all but glowing in the office lights.

"It's my job. I'll do it and make the offerings as necessary. I can still use blood and cells. But with your help, it shouldn't be too bad."

He tilted his head, then nodded, brushing his cheek along mine. ~Then we shall go save the day.~

I quirked one side of my mouth at that. With sidestepping being an issue, I'd created a hefty Go Bag and kept it stored under my desk. Before I would have stepped home and changed, but it struck me even that took time. This was already proving valuable. I changed into jeans, cringing as I had to suck in my stomach to get them to fit. Purchasing some larger jeans with elastic waistbands would be important. I pulled on and laced up my hiking boots, grabbed my med bag from the other side of the desk, and we headed to the helicopter pad. Time to do what they paid me for.

As I stood on the roof waiting, another idea filtered through my head. Maybe the House of Emrys had some info about the weird fading effect of my magic? If Tirsane's contact didn't know, once we made my status public, I'd ask there as well as cornering Indira and Steven. My hand drifted to my stomach. In a bit over a week, I'd know for sure. I had no idea if that was exciting or terrifying.

Either way, right now I had a job to do.

CHAPTER

TWENTY-THREE

Pregnancy Facts: Babies in utero develop hair all over their bodies called lanugo. It looks like a fur coat! They usually shed this hair before they are born. But sometimes they may be born with a downy coat of hair. ~ The Pregnant Mage

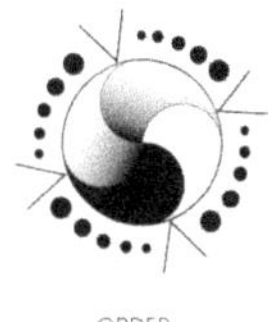

ORDER

It was my second helicopter ride, and I didn't know if it would be my last. Could I sidestep out of a helicopter? What about while falling to my doom? My hands were wrapped so tight on my seat belt it had cut into my palm. The Life Flight I'd been in had been calm and boring compared this one. The pilot flew like a hummingbird. I'd been jerked around so much I thought I might have whiplash.

I can't die like this. What about the baby?

Pounding heart and cotton mouth plagued me as I kept my eyes closed so tight my face ached.

"Coming in now. Mind the smoke when you get out."

Mind the smoke? When I got out, I might be kissing the ground. The fire was in a suburb of Atlanta and there were people trapped and no hazmat crews around because of a major traffic jam on 285, the freeway that circled Atlanta. Naomi had mentioned something else, but it didn't register. All I knew was that they needed me and I'd die before I got on a helicopter with that pilot again.

"Landing," the pilot said over the headset just as the helicopter rocked. "You can get out now, ma'am."

I unscrunched my eyes and then fumbled with the belt. Out sounded very good. My feet hit ground, and I stumbled forward, my bag pulling me down, and I didn't resist. My head spun as I gulped in the smokey air.

"Never again," I muttered as I pushed myself to my feet and headed further away from the flying death trap. "I'll walk. He's insane."

Smoke plumed up from three buildings and fire from a fourth.

The scent of smoke, sulfur, and some other chemicals I couldn't name wrapped around my lungs like a wet towel. I couldn't avoid it and then nausea plowed into me. My stomach lurched up. I almost went to my knees again, trying not to toss what I'd eaten everywhere.

A hand touched my shoulder. I jerked upright, still trying to convince my stomach that expelling its contents wouldn't change anything.

"Agent Munroe?" A large man with skin the color of Hamiada's bark stood nearby looking at me. The firefighter suit proclaimed him as Lt. Kerns.

I managed a nod, my mouth still firmly pressed together. Ginger ale right now would have made me cry in relief.

"Good. We need help. They are still trying to figure out what chemicals are in there. The computer records were destroyed by the explosions. And someone misfiled them at the fire station. We contacted the local hospital, but they said they were sent to the new hospital and the new hospital says they never received them." The way he said that made me think someone might get fired over that. "The smell is getting worse and you aren't the only one having issues with nausea."

Relief hit with a gut punch, and I managed a wobbly smile. I would gladly put the blame on the chemicals in the smoke and not my treacherous body.

He looked around, the smoke blanketing the area and his figure with ominous darkness. "Aren't you supposed to have a cat with you? They warned us a lot about that."

"Oh, yeah. Carelian?" My heart leapt at that idea. Leaning against him would be nice, because the world still spun. Helicopters were evil. The need to control my roiling stomach masked the expected stab of pain. The squeak and stutter step backward by the lieutenant told me Carelian was here.

~This smells like Chaos,~ he muttered pressing up against me. My hand found his head and part of me, the part that found the helicopter ride the most terrifying thing I'd ever done, unwound.

"It is. You ready?" I opened my eyes to look at him. His ears were laid back and whiskers tight against his muzzle, tail lashing.

~I do not know that I can find much in this environment. Even the dragons' sulfur springs are not as caustic as this.~

I had to agree, but it didn't change the job I needed to do.

"Is any of the smoke hazardous to health?" I looked at the lieutenant, who still had his eyes locked on Carelian.

"Not that we have any reason to believe. But that is part of the problem. We need a good chemical person to id what to use. Some of the products the employees have told us about reacts to water, others to sand, and yet others to our dry chemical agents. Some of it doesn't need oxygen to burn, so we aren't positive how to smother it yet without making it worse. That's why you're here."

"And the managers for this site?" We'd started walking and my brain had pushed past the primal terror of the helicopter ride. I started cataloging chemical reactions. Most of the time with chemicals, you either snuffed them or used a halogen-like system to put them out. But if they really had this volatile of a mix, it could be much more difficult. I ducked involuntarily as a nearby transformer exploded in a shower of sparks. "What about the power?" I said dryly. Getting electrocuted wasn't high on my list of fun things.

"Working on that, too. The manager is on vacation in the Caribbean with no service. The people he left here don't have access to the systems, and their MSDS sheets were stored near the tanks." He sounded more than a bit annoyed at that, and I understood. Per OSHA, copies of MSDS (Material Safety and Data Sheets) should have been stored in an area easily accessed by employees. By the tanks didn't qualify.

"Okay, so what would you like me to do? Please tell me you don't need me to do an S&R in there?" I pointed at the buildings of which two now were fully engulfed and fire danced around the edges of a third.

"We need to tamp the flames down and smothering is the easiest. We need to lower the heat so my men can get close enough to spray foam. If you can do the first two, we can do the spraying."

I bit my lip and nodded. "You don't have any mages?" There were lots of wizards and magicians that went into fire departments, so it almost surprised me that I was here. Almost. I could all but guarantee there was something weird going on.

"One is out pregnant, the other broke his leg two weeks ago. The wizards I have left aren't strong enough to compete with the fire at this stage. If they'd called us when the first building went up, we could have done something. Now it's too powerful for him to affect."

Swallowing, I nodded. "I see. Let me try."

His shoulders relaxed a bit, magnified by the thick coat he wore. We'd stopped walking near the trucks and the heat beat at my face, making me want water to cool down as well as push back the nausea.

"Here are my two mages. Katy Giordano and Rufus Benton." He nodded at the two people looking exhausted by the truck.

"Hey. Can you tell me what you tried?" I didn't bother to introduce myself. Either they would recognize me because of the tattoos or they wouldn't. Either way, I had quit caring about the double merlin status a long time ago.

"Blowing away the smoke, suppressing the air, neutralizing the chemicals," Katy responded dully. Her hair was in a pony tail, but I could tell chunks were gone.

"We can't figure out what is burning, so we can't neutralize. The storm coming in makes it so we can't snuff it out before we lose our control over the air. With all the corners in the building we keep getting pockets of fumes that turn volatile, making it worse."

Rufus spoke this time, and he seemed just as exhausted, his head even showing bald patches. "We kept trying to get a clear way for the firefighters to get in, but the air changes so much we can't manage to do even that."

"We still don't know if all the employees got out or not." His voice sounded like forming syllables was too much work. "Anything we do can make it worse. If we spray water on the roof and there are water flammable chemicals we'll get explosions. If we use flame retardant that high in the air with this wind, it goes everywhere. I need to know what's in there."

"I keep thinking I can hear screams," Katy said in a voice that sent chills up my spine.

I swallowed. Of all the times for my magic to be acting up. Oh well, I had offerings available. I'd use them.

"My chemistry is pretty strong, but I agree that not knowing the chemicals makes it hard. Break it down for me what needs to be done in what order."

Katy took a deep breath and faced me. "We need to get the structures under control so the fire doesn't spread. Then we can get in and get the internal fires under control and try to stop anything else from blowing up."

"Which building first? And will sand or dirt cause any issues?"

Frowning, but with a bit of life back in her eyes, she shook her head. "The one fully engulfed. We've had two muffled explosions in there so far. If we can get the building under control, we can get in with spray to control the internal fires."

~Ready to help, Carelian?~ I scanned the area looking for material I could work with to get the fire under control.

~As ever, my quean.~ He pressed against me, his heat reassuring as I went to work.

I nodded and leveraged Air and Earth. The torn-up area around us, the tankers coming in and out kicking up, even the ash that lay everywhere would work. Air fought me, though Earth felt amused. They asked more than they had ever wanted before, but still two inches of hair was easy enough to pay. I offered it up and pulled. Everything depended on Air, and that was Sable's power not mine. Which meant I wasn't a null anymore, but pale might be stretching it. And being so low translated into higher costs, larger offerings, in general.

Air swirled hard, creating dust cyclones so thick you couldn't see through them. They bounced around like a child playing hopscotch, collecting fine silt and sand. People exclaimed around me, but I focused on what I was trying to do. Air was never easy to control and with the storm riding in, it had a powerful urge to blow how it wanted, not in the direction I asked. But when my three dust cyclones were all but solid dirt, I pushed them up to the top of the building and released them.

With a subtle "whomomph" that sent dust flying everywhere, the dirt blanketed the buildings, snuffing most of the fires almost instantly. I'd focused on the fires near the doors and already firefighters were scrambling to pull open the doors and aim the retardant inside. The white foam sprayed out of the nozzles into the building.

"That work?" I asked, my throat screaming for water. The smoke and concentration drained me.

"Merlin's balls, it did. The next one we need the smoke to get contained. It's so thick we can't see and there is a good chance it is toxic, but with what we don't know." Katy sounded excited.

I shuddered. Had I been breathing that? The frantic thought had me looking around, but no one seemed worried and we were all well away from the building. The first one had been mostly flames, so when they opened the doors, the hot spots had been clear of smoke. The next one they didn't know what was burning or smoking. Which made it difficult to decide.

"Okay, pull open a door and I'll push the smoke back, but they'll need to figure it out quick. I can't hold that for very long. There is too much atmospheric activity out here." I pointed up to the clouds, and they nodded.

Orders were shouted, and I pulled on Air while they got someone with something that looked like a scope ready about 20 feet from the door. I figured they would need light too, so I added that complexity to my mind. Refraction wasn't something I'd spent a lot of time studying, but I figured I could pull this off.

The two mages gave me the go sign, and I pulled, cringing at an inch of hair vaporizing, but I sank my hand into Carelian's fur and concentrated. This was both complex and something I didn't do often, which meant it took a lot of mental calculations to get the effect I needed.

I had Air grab the smoke, creating a wall of force that no particle could get through, and pushed the wall toward the back. At the same time I got Air to refract light, combining Air and Water to create clouds. If it did it right there would be enough to brighten the building. With any luck they'd be able to see what they needed to.

"Oh shit." The words were loud enough that I could hear them, but it was the tone that cut through everything. It was the tone that said we were all screwed.

The lieutenant stormed toward the man. "What?"

The firefighter dropped the scope from his eye, and even through the soot, I could see his face pale. "There's a fire going strong under the liquid amatol tank. Looks like it is being fed from a gas line with storage inside the building, not an external line. If it blows, we're all dead. Because it will start a chain explosion that would be one for the record books."

"Uh, how do I stop that?" I blurted, moving over to them.

They whirled to look at me. "Can you snuff out the flames?"

I grimaced. "Sure for a few seconds, but you have a constant fuel supply, things sparking, and Air won't hold still for long. Even now it wants to move and the smoke is starting to seep out." I gestured toward the building. "So, meh?"

"Can you cool it down?"

A slow smile appeared. "Now that I can do. If I get it cold enough, it will take a while for the flames to heat it back up. But I need somewhere to dump the heat." I looked around and then sighed. "I'm going to dump it straight up into the atmosphere. I apologize now for any funky weather changes." I wasn't too worried about drastic weather changes. It took a lot of energy to affect the weather on anything more than a local scale. It was a cool day, and I just hoped the heat didn't make the storm worse.

I convinced Fire to listen to me, and I basically sweet talked it into sending all the heat up in a column. I had my eyes closed, concentrating on what I needed it to do: remembering the science behind heat conversions and sweet-talking to convince Fire that dumping it into Air was way more fun than keeping that tank hot. My world narrowed down to Carelian at my side and the Fire in the building.

"Merlin Munroe? Cori? I think you can stop now."

The voice came from my side and I turned, blinking my eyes open as I focused back on the real world. Carelian was my anchor as he rumbled a purr and pressed in at my side.

"I think it's good now," he said slowly and pointed into the building. I followed the line of his finger and blinked. The entire warehouse had frozen. The only flame was the one being fed by gas.

"Oh. Think you can shut it off now?" I asked, a bit shocked. It had cost more than I liked, but that level of response hadn't been what I expected.

"Already on it." He gave me a puzzled look, then shook his head. The rest of the day cost me two more inches, but we left happy. I refused to get in the helicopter and waited for a car. The ride back to my Atlanta apartment was quiet and sedate. I was more than happy with sedate. A quick shower there, and then I let Carelian take me back to Albany with my dirty clothes in my hands, and a mission in my mind.

TWENTY-FOUR

Pregnancy Fact: Chimera – most people think you mean a creature from mythology, and maybe from Chaos. It is said to be a lion with the head of a goat coming out of its back with a snake for a tail. But it is also what someone who absorbs a twin in utero and retains two sets of DNA in them is called. While rare, it has proven to cause issues for those so affected.

~ The Pregnant Mage

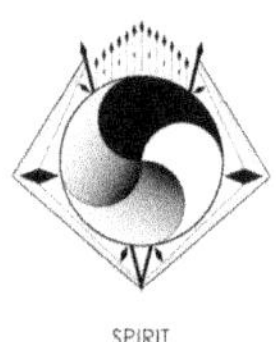

SPIRIT

I'd explained everything about the chemical plant to Jo and Sable. Well, not the nausea. That they didn't need to know. Ginger and crackers were helping that, but still why couldn't it be morning sickness instead of random all-day sickness? It would make everything much easier.

I got grumpy when my body refused to follow my suggestions.

"I know you don't use your society affiliation much, but I've been talking to mine more," Sable said, her brows furrowed.

That prompted a snarl of annoyance from me. I still didn't see what the outrageous amount of money I was spending each month and the even worse amount that I'd be paying when the draft was done was worth. "Okay, and?"

She smirked at me. "And they are a resource. While ours has weekly get togethers it also has nanny vetting, contractor recommendations, and multiple season tickets to various venues. So they might have information about this weird fading of your magic."

"Nanny? You aren't planning on getting a nanny are you?" I placed my hand on my belly, the idea of a stranger taking care of this child worse than the nausea had ever been.

"Or a contractor?" Hamiada burst into view, a panicked look on her face. "They'll tear up my walls, my branches, my roots!" She was all but wailing in panic and the interior walls went slightly orange.

Sable groaned and put her head in her hands. Jo patted her back. "The selective hearing you two exhibit is even more impressive than what my brothers can do. These were just examples of what our society Elementals offers. Each society offers different things and I doubt you've even thought about Emrys since you joined."

"I think about the money every month," I muttered.

"You will not bring a contractor in here?" Hamiada prodded, still a touch of orange around her eyes.

"No contractor without talking to you. You can do your own stuff pretty easily," Sable reassured her.

"Good. This is my body." Hamiada took two steps back into nothingness and faded.

Jo rolled her eyes and stared at me. "That leaves you. Emrys is a society of merlins. Merlins, who like James Wells, research and study and know things. Weird esoteric things." She narrowed her eyes staring at me. "So ask them."

"I've been reading James' journals. Surely it would be in there," I protested, shrinking a little. Going to the House of Emrys would mean admitting they might have some redeeming qualities.

"And James knew everything in the world? Besides would it have occurred to him to investigate something that is related only to women? Ask them. Worst case, they don't know anything," Jo said, reaching for her coffee. I watched her drink it with lust in my heart. Minimal coffee sucked. The no booze was simple comparatively.

"No, worst case is they'll start asking me to come to meetings," I muttered, but I pulled up my phone and started searching for a name.

"Oh no. The great Cori Munroe might have to go socialize with other people," Sable mocked, smiling at me. "You might find someone you like. Just because we are joined doesn't mean you can't have other friends too."

"I have other friends."

They both looked at me with arched brows. It was eerily like looking at Marisol and Henri. It made me squirm. "I have Charles, Esmere, Indira, Steven, Zmaug, Arachena, Hamiada, even Tirsane. And maybe Tiantang, though if anything he's like an annoying little cousin."

Sable rubbed her head, looking like she might need some pain killers. "Cori, at least half of those people aren't. And you only sometimes tolerate Steven and Indira. Charles is the only other human on that list and when was the last time we had him over or went out to do something?"

I opened my mouth to refute that, but I couldn't remember. Before we moved, absolutely. But after that. We'd had a housewarming, but had I hung out with him since?

"Oh," I muttered, staring at the phone.

"Go to some of the meetings. Eventually, the draft will be done. What are you going to do then? One of the problems of your job is it doesn't really translate into something you can do on a daily basis. Someday you'll have to get a real job. Then what?"

"I really prefer it when you don't rupture my delusions quite so aggressively," I stated with my nose in the air.

They both snickered. "We're just saying. The kids will forcibly expand our network, and you are always welcome to be part of that, but I can't really see you enjoying talk of baby formulas or what certain cries mean."

A cold shudder went down my back. "No. I don't think so."

"So get a life, Cori. And if it is going to be one with lots of denizens, great. But you need to think past the draft and how the government is trying to sabotage you."

I started to demand what she meant by that, but it became all too clear as I thought about it. A job that no private agency could support. I hadn't been developing a network for after the draft like I saw so many others doing. Mostly I leaned on them and Carelian. Wasn't that enough?

I didn't know the answer to that. I laid my hand on my belly, frowning and thinking. I still wanted to go into medicine and figure out what happened to Stevie, but to do that I'd have to finish pre-med and apply for an internship. That meant more college out of my pocket, but I'd be able to afford it. The question was, did I want to go through that at, what, thirty-seven? It didn't sound appealing. Going back to being a paramedic and specializing in Search and Rescue sounded much better, but then I'd never make the money that most merlins did. Which meant I couldn't afford the dues for the House of Emrys.

The dominos kept falling in my brain, research, discoveries, stuff that James had left me, investments. When I started to think about it that way, there were a lot of reasons to contact the House of Emrys and see what they had to offer.

"Point taken. I'm sending her an email now." Her being Joanna Snowden, the House of Emrys regional director for the Southeast.

"Excellent. Then I'd say work on using magic as little as you can and ask Esmere if she knows of any way to replace offerings faster. And don't forget, you'll be putting on baby weight soon." Jo grinned at me while Sable's face lit up.

"Ooh, that means shopping. Can't wait. You will be the cutest mommy to be."

"And I'm leaving now." I rose from the table, typing on my phone as I walked into the kitchen. I grabbed an apple then bit into it, holding it in my mouth as I headed back up the stairs.

~Are you trying to make me hungry?~

I looked up to see Carelian watching me from the top of the stairs. He loomed as I finished the email, took a bite of the apple and stepped onto the landing. "No, why?"

~You reminded me of all the pictures of a roasted swine with an apple in its mouth. I think we should do that for Christmas this year.~

I snorted. "Roasted pig, I hope you mean, not roasted human."

~I would have to try a roasted human to know if there is a taste difference. So I am open to either.~

I rolled my eyes and headed into James' study, determined to see if he had any more information about this strange magic behavior than I did.

~Cori, are you available to talk to Baneyarl and me?~ Tirsane's ping felt like snakes crawling through my mind, and I bit my tongue so I didn't screech, my hand instantly rubbing my left forearm where her last snake had crawled under my skin.

After a hard swallow, I replied with a mental smile. ~Always. I am in my office.~

I turned the chair around and waited. A minute later, a door materialized in the middle of the study and opened as Tirsane slithered out. As always, she was gorgeous, perfect alabaster skin, perky full breasts, silvery green scales, and her snakes writhing around her head in hello to me. Behind her Baneyarl stepped in, his wings hugged tight to his body. His white feathers seemed almost dingy in this dark office and I suddenly knew I needed to add more lights. If his feathers looked drab, this study was too dark. The two of them took up the office, making it feel tiny.

"That was different," I said, looking at the door as it closed and disappeared. Normally it was tears in reality, this time it had been an actual door.

"I asked Hamiada. This way it is opening into her realm and there is no alert that I have entered your realm." Her voice slid through the air like silk and I fought a smile. Even when not trying, she managed to seduce and bewitch. It literally was part of who she was.

I moved the club chair out into the hall, opening up the space for Baneyarl and leaving the footstool for Tirsane. It was the same leather as the chair, and I figured it would be more comfortable for her. I hoped. "Please take a seat. How may I help you?"

They exchanged glances, then looked back at me. ~Actually, we are here to assist you. Esmere mentioned that you were having issues with magic?~ Baneyarl took the lead, which made sense. He had been my teacher for years and was part of the reason I used magic by talking to the elements as opposed to sheer brute force and science. But I still didn't know what I wanted them to do. At least in some areas.

I wrinkled my nose. But I had asked her for help. "It is more that it seems since I got pregnant, I'm having to offer much more than I ever would have before."

~Clarify,~ Baneyarl said, shifting a bit. Human studies were not made for gryphons.

I blew air through my lips, then grinned. "Here." I grabbed a candle that was sitting on the window sill. This one smelled like lavender. Though Carelian hated it, I enjoyed the soothing scent. "Before when I was null, for me to light it, I want to say it took fifteen strands of hair." It had been a long time ago and I thought that was correct. "After joining when I was able to leverage the connections Jo and Sable had to those branches, it took me maybe two inches from three strands of hair." It was a good way to measure it.

I looked at the candle and asked for it to light. It did, but I cringed a bit. Their eyes were intent on me and for a second, I almost expected a pat on my head. It was a problem with dealing with creatures who had seen centuries. Sometimes you felt like such a child.

"Well?" Tirsane demanded, watching me.

"The equivalent of thirty twenty-six-inch-long strands of hair." It felt like I was admitting failure. But that would be why I had curtailed my magic use so strongly. I needed to save my offerings for work. Somehow I didn't think Naomi would be at all impressed that her power house was now a magical wimp.

Oh, I knew that wasn't quite accurate. From what I could see, I was still as powerful as most merlins, but compared to where I had been, it was a drastic change.

They both frowned, and frowning on a gryphon looks really odd. His brow ridges furrowed , and the corners of his beak lips drew down. It looked very similar to his "I'm about to attack" expression.

"Baneyarl?" Tirsane asked, and I watched her snakes wind back away from her head as if they were upset too.

~I want to say I have heard of this, but it is a memory that tickles. Something I might have read or heard of once. But I am not sure.~

The tiny amount of hope that had bubbled up in my chest drained away. "So, it is just me being a weird magnet?"

They both just stared at me and I curled up a little. Their stares were intimidating.

~It means something odd is going on. I shall research, but be aware I have little on the vagaries of human physiology. Esmere is more knowledgeable than I.~ Baneyarl nibbled on a claw as he talked.

"And she knows nothing. I've asked," I admitted, feeling like the world was shooting arrows at me. And hitting all too often.

~Then I shall research.~ He paused, looking around, his eyes on the journals. ~I do not suppose you would allow me to read these?~ The hint of avarice in his voice made me smile.

"Sure. Contrary to what Jeorgaz thought, most of them are just experiments which failed horribly and lots of whining about the politics involved in being a merlin." Which was yet another reason I'd been so reluctant to deal with the House of Emrys. "But here, I've finished these. They are best read in order, as he does refer to previous experiments quite often."

I got up and gave him the first three journals. "Here you go. Return them when you are done, and I'll give you some more."

He carefully picked up the journals with his front arms. Gryphon paws looked like three three fingers and a thumb but with sharp claws. He could manipulate objects as easily I could. With a no he slipped them into the cross-torso bag he wore. ~Thank you. I will take care of these.~

Of that I had no doubt. They rose and Tirsane paused as a door formed.

"You will be attending the council meeting?"

"I said I would, but I still think it has little to do with me. Is there a date yet?"

"No. But I think it is good humans finally have a representative there, even if you believe you have little power over humans."

"We have seven billion humans on this planet. Even the most powerful human today only controls about two billion, and she feels powerless most of the time." That I knew intimately. Cixi would give a lot to go back to being a lowly court mage.

"Perhaps, but I suspect that is because of the choices you made. Until later." She slithered through the door before I could figure out what she meant. I wasn't sure I really wanted to know which of my choices she thought should have been different.

TWENTY-FIVE

If women laid dragon eggs, unicorns would hate kittens. This is a direct quote from the obstetrician to the reality stars Merlin Mike and Merlin Joanna after a drunken rampage following their fight with pregnant Archmage Gloria Markes.
~ Daily Magical News

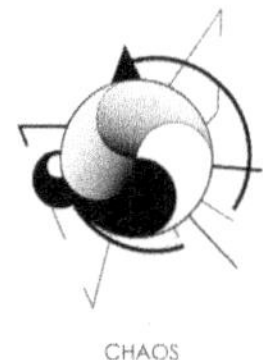

CHAOS

Time flew by and days melded tighter into a seamless blur. The next thing I knew, I was working from home, or more accurately answering emails from home prior to leaving for the doctor appointment.

"Come on, Cori. We need to go," Jo yelled up the stairs. I

sighed and hit send on the last reports, then headed down to meet them.

I didn't look obviously pregnant, but I was very glad to have stretchy pants to wear. I wasn't so sure about the other maternity clothes Jo and Sable had filled my closet with, but for now I kept my mouth shut. Worst case, I'd have a lot of stuff to donate.

The ride was spent with them babbling over names, baby supplies, and joy at the whole idea. Just watching them made me smile as they babbled. There were no people I loved more than those two. But I still couldn't help the nervous feeling about the appointment. What if the pregnancy hadn't taken? What if I'd lost them all? Or if they were deformed?

Fears washed through me, to the extent that by the time we got to the doctor's office I was almost twitchy.

So much rode on this and all I wanted to do was run away screaming.

"Breathe, Cori," Sable said, and I jerked my attention to her as she twisted in the front passenger seat to look at me. "It will all be fine. Millions of women get pregnant every year."

"Yes, and millions have complications and miscarriages."

She shrugged. "Yep. But you won't. You'll be fine, really. And if something goes wrong, we'll face it then. But borrowing trouble and worrying about things you can't change won't help anyone."

The words helped, but even as we entered the office for the ultrasound, I was worried about what it would show.

"Morning, ladies. Cori, how are you feeling today?" the doctor asked, staring at her chart where I knew all the information about my weight, blood pressure, and every little private detail was recorded.

"Fat?" I said, trying to smile.

Dr. Anna Lobdell looked at me and laughed. "You're only up five pounds. It will get worse, so embrace the curves. Doing anything else just adds extra stress. And regardless of what the world thinks, no one needs extra stress. You ready for your examination?"

I wasn't, but I sat up on the table, the gown doing its best to make me expose everything. Really, sitting here naked would have been easier and less annoying. She did all the normal, embarrassing checks, with Jo and Sable standing by my head, but the one we were all waiting for was the ultrasound.

"Anxious, are we? Well, I can tell you that you are pregnant. Magic and the urine test verify that, but let's take a look at the jellybean and see what it looks like." Her smile warmed me as she flipped on the ultrasound and spread the warm gel on my belly. "See, I'm not a complete monster. We even keep the jelly warm."

"It is greatly appreciated."

Anna glanced around. "Where is your familiar? Carelian I believe?"

"He said he'd wait at home for us. That he didn't need any more people to call him dirty," Jo said with a snicker. "It offends him."

The doctor snorted. "I can imagine it would, but still let him know to be careful. Regular cat scratches can infect, but I don't know about his. And don't change the litter box."

I looked at her in surprise. "Interesting. He's bitten me a few times, but always to protect me," I said in a rush as she glanced at me with widened eyes. "It's complicated," I muttered lamely, "but they've always healed without any issue. And he uses the toilet like the rest of us."

She blinked surprised. "It's okay. I don't understand, but merlins have different lives than the rest of us. And I wish I could get my dog to use the toilet." Dr. Lobdell's eyes flicked up to my temple, and she shrugged. "But take a look." She nodded at the ultra sound screen. "Here are your first pictures."

My eyes locked on the screen, both hungry and scared at what I would see. "Where is it?"

Her finger reached up to trace a kidney shaped blob on the screen. "Right there is your baby."

My heart leaped and I felt Jo and Sable lean forward, their bodies brushing mine as their hands tightened on my shoulder.

A baby.

"What is that other blob over there?" Sable asked, and I managed to move my gaze to snag on that bit of darkness.

Anna's smile widened. "That is your second baby. Congratulations, it looks like you are having twins."

I blinked, looking at her. Twins.

"Twins. We're having twins," Sable whisper-squealed.

The possibility really hadn't registered, but her saying the words kicked my mind into gear.

"Where is the third?" I blurted out, staring at the screen.

Dr. Lobdell shrugged. "Absorbed or rejected or even just dissolved. The human body can manage marvelous things. But for right now, you seem to have two healthy children."

"Do we know the genders yet?"

"Unfortunately, I only have a 2D ultrasound. That means you need to wait until your next checkup at eighteen weeks to know for sure." All of our faces must have fallen.

Anna laughed. "Does it really matter?"

Jo and Sable glanced at each other and then at me. "No, I guess not. We just wanted to know," Jo admitted. "But two. We will need to make some changes."

"Yes, twins require a bit more prep."

I stared at the two beans again in wonder. All of this seemed crazy to me.

"Here is your checklist for the next few weeks. You might start seeing some morning sickness and some weight gain is good, but swelling of your feet or other body parts can be an area of concern. But mostly eat healthy food and don't stress too much."

"I can still work?"

Dr. Lobdell nodded. "Yes, you can. Even firefighters and police don't quit working, usually until well into the third trimester and you're not in anything that strenuous. But if it feels unsafe, don't do it. You're pregnant, not sick."

We all laughed, and she printed out a picture for us. The first picture of our babies.

The drive home was spent with Jo and Sable babbling about names and what they wanted to ask Hamiada regarding the nursery. I just stared at the black and white lines, squiggles, and blobs that represented life inside me. The idea tugged and pulled and didn't seem so illusionary anymore.

"I think we need to tell people now," Jo suggested. "I know Mami has been pinging me regularly and I've just avoided answering. I'm sure your father and aunt would like to know, Sable."

Sable grinned and cast a look at me as we climbed out of the car, the drive home having vanished in rapt fixation on the picture. "Yes, and you need to tell Steven and Indira, and I bet Naomi and others at work would like to know."

A funny smile flickered over my face. "Can we have people over for dinner Saturday? The magic issues are still giving me fits, but I bet Carelian would help." All of that was true, but mostly I wanted to let people know all at once so I could watch Jo and Sable glow. They would be great parents.

"Oh, that sounds fun. We can invite everyone. I need to remind Esmere to not tell Marisol until the dinner. I think they still talk regularly." Sable grinned as we headed into the house, a spring in her step.

"Easily done, but there is someone we do need to let know now," I reminded them with a smile. They both looked at me blankly. "Hamiada, we have news for you," I called out as we stepped into the house, the warmth of it enveloping us.

"You do?" She materialized from wherever, floating on her toes. Her head tilted at an angle a human head would never succeed at. "That is?"

Jo and Sable looked at me. I shrugged looking at them. "Your news?"

"Your body," they countered.

"You're changing the diapers," I said, snickering. "So you can tell the fun stuff."

Jo rolled her eyes, but Sable just leaned into her. "Changing diapers will be worth it. We get to watch them grow up. Small price to pay."

"I do not understand, what news?" Hamiada asked, floating up and down as if bouncing on her toes.

Jo moved over and wrapped one arm around my shoulder, kissing the top of my head. "We are having twins."

The words hung in the hall of our home, full of import and power.

"Ahhh," Hamiada murmured, the sound ringing like a bell through the house. "There will need to be changes to the nursery. For there are two to care for, not one." Unusually for her, she turned and walked to their bedroom and the nursery that was accessible from there. "I shall need more wood. Something pretty, a zebra wood or purple heart."

Sable's eyes lit up. "We can do that."

I just laughed, leaving them to their art. I had paperwork to finish, and a familiar to inform. Climbing the stairs made me really want a nap, though. I entered my bedroom to find Carelian sprawled out on my bed.

"Don't you have your own bed?"

~Yours is better and smells of you. Why should I sleep there when this was vacant?~ He lifted his head and looked at me, yawning as he tried to wake up. ~You brim of secrets.~

That struck me as odd. Normally he would have heard everything I said as we walked in, but this time he hadn't? "Carelian, are you okay?"

~I am fine. You were barely gone at all.~

A quick glance at my watch gave lie to that statement. "We've been gone about three hours. And we've been back long enough to tell Hamiada." His tail lashed at that and I sat next to him, petting him. "And you didn't hear us."

His tail stilled, and sharp green eyes looked at me. ~Truly?~

I nodded and petted him, suddenly worried. "Is your mother coming tomorrow with Tirsane?"

He nodded, his eyes not focused on me, but elsewhere. ~She is now, why?~

"We need to ask her about this. This is not normal." Fear rippled through me. "Are you sure you are well? How old are you?"

He burst out in mental laughter even as he gently licked my cheek. ~Esmere was born before magic washed over your world. You need not fear me dying of old age like your Earth-born pets. I will probably outlive you all.~ There was a tinge of sadness there, but he stretched. ~But this overwhelming tiredness needs to be dealt with. You said you had news that I have not heard? I am rather put out that Hamiada knows before I do.~

As if summoned by saying her name, Hamiada stepped into the room from the nursery door. It startled me, as I still wasn't expecting the door to be there.

"Yessss, wonderful news. There shall be much laughter and chaos here. Putting it to order will be delightful."

Carelian's tail lashed back and forth as he stared at the dryad. ~And the news?~ he hissed it at me and I was tempted to let Hamiada tell him, but I gave in and scratched his ears with my right hand as my left cupped my stomach. "We are having twins."

His ears flicked back and forth and he sniffed my stomach. ~Only two? Is everything well? It is not good to only have two kits. Esmere's last litter had four.~

I blinked at him, then started to laugh. "Hey Jo!" I yelled out, trusting the house to carry the words. "Carelian needs to talk to you." I'd let her explain the mysteries of human reproduction to the cat and I'd escape. I left still giggling. There was no way in the world I wanted to be carrying four.

TWENTY-SIX

Beware the pregnant mage, for her temper is short, and magic strong. A wise man treats a pregnant mage like an angry dragon, bringing gifts and tender morsels. ~ Qia Hang Proverb

---

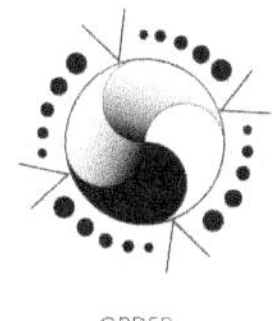

We spent Friday evening grocery shopping and sending out invites. The invites simply said "Family dinner at Hamiada's House for big news". Everyone got one; the Guzman's, John Lancet and his sister, Steven and Indira, Charles and Arachena, Tirsane, Esmere, Baneyarl, even Tiantang. To my relief, Tiantang had another commitment, but asked to be told the news. I left that up to Carelian. Their relationship was odd, and I didn't have the energy to try to figure it out.

Baneyarl bowed out, saying indoor interactions were too limiting, but hoped the news would be shared when appropriate. Sable's dad, John, and her aunt were both overseas traveling and had work-based conflicts. Carelian offered to take Jo and Sable after dinner to share the news. I'd do that rather than sidestep. I didn't want to waste the offering material, besides I wasn't sure where they were.

Only Sanchez could attend as Marco and Paulo had other commitments, but they sent their good wishes and demanded phone calls as soon as the news was spilled. Hamiada was delighted and subtly enlarged the dining room, creating more elbow room when the table was fully expanded. All in all, we expected to need twelve seats. Arachena would just share with Charles.

We'd asked Hamiada, but while she was okay with Tirsane and Esmere being there, she didn't want to "break bread" with them, so we let it be. She would hear everything anyhow if she wanted, and we made very sure she knew she was welcome.

As we set places, including Carelian and Esmere, I thought about our constant food bill. There were days when I envied Charles the smaller familiar. She was certainly cheaper and easier to feed. But I would never give up Carelian for anything. Or his incredible mother. Even if they had expensive food tastes. By one p.m. we were ready, and we went to take quick showers.

Jo's phone rang as we gathered in the kitchen, and I wondered what we had forgotten or missed. I wasn't as worried about it as they were. Both of them were fussing more than they had over their wedding reception.

For me it was dinner with friends and family. For them it was the announcement of new family members. I couldn't see why it was a big deal, but honored that it was to them.

"*Hola, mami,*" Jo said, picking up her cell. She chattered in Spanish for a minute, then hung up. "Carelian, Mami and the others are ready for you to go get them." She hollered that loud enough he could have heard her down the block.

"Jo, he's a cat. He heard you." I rubbed my ears as I frowned at her. She could be very loud when she wanted to be.

"He would be more than content to ignore me, saying he didn't hear me," she refuted, as she fussed with the table setting one more time.

~I would never ignore a request to assist Marisol. She makes the most wonderful treats,~ Carelian said as he strolled into the kitchen. ~Of course I will go get them.~

My phone pinged, so I pulled it out. "Steven and Indira are about ten minutes out."

"Charles? How is Charles getting here?" Sable blurted, looking around frantically.

~Arachena asked my Malkin to bring them. They should be here in a bit,~ Carelian said before he leapt through a rip he'd created and was gone.

"And I know Tirsane knows how to show up, so I don't think that's an issue. It'll be fine. I swear, why are you two so freaked out?" A wave of nausea hit me and I shoved a ginger candy in my mouth. This random nausea was annoying as all get out.

They looked at each other, then away, then at me. I crossed my arms and waited.

"This makes it real. We're starting a family. We aren't young adults playing. At this point, we are all grown up and I want them to be proud of us." The worry in Jo's voice took me by surprise and I glanced at Sable only to see her arms wrapped around herself leaning against Jo.

I covered my face with my hands, head bowed, and tried to control my laughter. When I thought I had it under control, I raised my head to be met with two very anxious sets of eyes. "Loves," I heard their twin intakes of air, I was rarely so demonstrative. "You are adults and have been for a long time. Your parents see it. The denizens see it. Esmere treats you with more respect than Carelian. You don't have anything to prove. The only thing you need to do today is share some really joyous news." I moved over to them, my arms open. "You are the people I love and that is all that matters."

We wrapped in a group hug and I could feel the stress release from their bodies as their arms tightened around me. "I love you. We will love these children. And no one is more proud of you than your families." I said the words softly, and they tightened their arms, then pulled away.

Sable carefully wiped under her eyes. Smearing her makeup was never acceptable. "You are a wonder, Cori."

A slash of pain told me guests had started arriving, and I turned to see Marisol, Henri, and Sanchez stepping out of a rip. They all were smiling, though Marisol looked a bit gray at the edges.

"I love how quick it is to get here with Carelian, but I don't know that I'll ever get used to the weird feeling of the realms," she murmured as she pulled me into a tight hug.

"They say the same thing about sidestepping," I said with a smile.

Sanchez hugged Sable, then punched Jo's arm lightly, then walked over to me. His face had a half pensive, half worried look. "So it's done?" he asked softly.

I laughed, his nerves washing mine away. Wrapping my arms around him, I hugged him first and held him until he relaxed enough to hug me back. "It's done. Don't worry about it." His arms tightened briefly, then a knock at the door interrupted us.

Sable headed off to greet Indira and Steven, while I headed to greet Tirsane, who had pinged me from the backyard. I stepped out into the cold evening to find Tirsane there. A beautiful Grecian style green dress set off her snakes and her eyes. But what threw me were the two legs and feet encased in Grecian sandals. I stumbled to a halt, staring at her. "You have legs?"

She glanced down at them with a contemptuous look. "I can change my shape enough to create legs as awkward and useless as they are."

"Then why change into them?" I rubbed my arms. The house was much warmer than out here.

"Because you have human guests," she said and brought out a scarf, wrapping it around protesting snakes.

"Ummm… no." I wasn't just cold. I was annoyed and a bit sad. Here was this demigod worried about scaring my guests. And changing because of them. Not happening.

She paused and looked up at me. I swallowed. "You are a friend. You were invited to share in our joyous news. Not a facsimile of you, but you, Tirsane, gorgon, Lord of Spirit. That is who I want at dinner. My friends and family will deal, or they aren't worthy of knowing you."

She stared at me for a long time, my skin and hers turning blue, but I didn't flinch. The smile that crossed her face was blinding in its beauty and joy, and for a moment, I feared I might turn to stone.

"Then we should go in." She slithered past me, two sandals laying in her wake, and the scarf nothing more than a shawl around her shoulders, the snakes bubbling up and down.

"Yes we should. It is cold out here," I said and led her into my house, terrified at my own temerity. I'd basically told a Lord of Spirit I thought of her as a friend. It was official. I'd lost my mind. Being pregnant was obviously dangerous. But I did cast a quick thought of gratitude that her breasts were covered. Even for me, having naked breasts in your face was distracting.

We arrived as Esmere stepped, Charles right behind her, with Arachena poking out of the hood of his jacket.

~Tirsane, you came as you are?~ Esmere sounded amused and proud, as if she had done something. I swear the Cath were so much the center of their universe it was amusing.

"It is the best way to be, I believe," she said, flashing a smile that had more than a hint of fangs, even if her snakes were twisting around with pleasure as they admired the house.

"Charles!" I headed over and hugged him tight. Jo and Sable were right, it had been too long. His long hair was in a thick braid down his back, and his ubiquitous hoodie had been upgraded to something that almost looked like a suit. He'd muscled up since college and the satisfaction of having a job he enjoyed had made him much more self-assured.

"Cori," he said, hugging me back. "It is good to see you. So what is all this about? Not that I would ever refuse dinner with three beautiful women."

I laughed. "You can wait like everyone else. Arachena, good afternoon."

Arachena, Charles' Chittarian familiar, waved a leg at me, but didn't emerge from the safety of his hood. I couldn't blame her. While she was a huge ten-legged spider, and when spread out was the size of a dinner plate, she was horribly out classed compared to Carelian, Esmere, and Tirsane.

"Come on. Ladies, Charles, this way," I gestured to the enlarged dining room where the Guzman's, Steven, and Indira were already. Everyone stopped and stared as I entered, with Tirsane and Esmere, Charles trailing behind us.

"Tirsane, Esmere, I believe you know everyone?" Everyone here had been at our Joining ceremony, even if Tirsane and Esmere had faded into the background.

I snickered as Sanchez had to fight not to drool over Tirsane's beauty, but Steven and Henri were much more circumspect. Charles, I couldn't tell, but then he was as much an odd duck as me.

"Everyone come on, eat," Jo said and shooed everyone to the table. There were place cards for everyone, and it only took a minute for them to find their seats. Jo was at one end, Henri the other. Carelian sat between Jo and me, while Sable was across from us. We'd placed Indira, Tirsane, and Marisol all next to each other, with Esmere at Henri's left. She could hear anything and reply without needing to worry about shouting, so it seemed the best option. That left Charles across from me, and Sanchez to my right. I squeezed his hand as we sat down. He had an expression on his face torn between stress and joy.

"Relax. There is beer for the men and Jo, everyone else opted for wine. " I shrugged. A cider would have been nice, but if I could give up coffee for these tiny things, booze would be cast to the side also.

"You're a miracle, Cori," Sanchez said in a soft voice.

I wrinkled my nose at him.

"Go on, eat up everyone," Jo said from her end of the table. "We'll share the news later."

Jo had really pulled out all the stops. She had pasta salad in a vinaigrette, beef wellington individual servings, bacon wrapped scallops, sautéed broccolini and mushrooms, olives, bites of smoked salmon, fresh bread, and a fruit salad. It was a lot of food.

Carelian and Esmere were in rapture over the bacon wrapped scallops, while Tirsane was fascinated by the beef wellington and the olives. Jo had even grabbed some fresh meal worms for Arachena, who grabbed two and slid back into the hoodie.

Tirsane, Indira, and Marisol all chattered away, while Steven and Henri talked around Esmere, who I didn't think did anything but savor the food. I was still pretty sure food delivery with actual flavor could be a good inter-realm business.

I caught up with Charles and Sanchez, and the two of them discovered they still played a lot of the same online computer games. Their conversation quickly left me in the dust as they got into game mechanics.

Between the food and everyone's enjoyment, I sat back and reveled in my family. Nothing could undermine my faith in them. This was a good environment to bring up kids. They would be loved and never left behind.

Jo glowed as everyone praised the food, but only a self-obsessed teen could have missed the glances and speculation in most of the looks. When most everyone had finished, or at least significantly slowed down in their inhalation of food, Jo spoke. "Dessert is waiting, but I thought we'd share the news," her voice shook and I glanced at her, but it was excitement not worry that shook her.

Sable reached across the table to grab my hand, as Jo did the same for my left hand and Sable's right. Carelian moved to put his head on my shoulder and I laughed, fighting almost euphoric joy.

"We set the process in motion about three months ago and we are pleased to announce that Sable, Cori, and I are having twins!" Jo's last word came out as a jubilant shout and the room exploded in celebration. Tirsane laughed and even her snakes seemed to hiss with laughter while Esmere and Carelian's purrs rumbled through the room with the power of a bass. It created a solid hum of love.

It was one of the best evenings of my life, and not even the worry about my magic managed to dampen my happiness.

TWENTY-SEVEN

Pregnancy Facts: Twins are often born early, but while a full-term pregnancy is 40 weeks, most children are viable at 37 weeks. Often twins will push the premature date range to before 36 weeks. The longest pregnancy on record (a non-mage) was 375 days, normal is 280. But don't worry, most mages have normal length pregnancies. ~ The Pregnant Mage

---

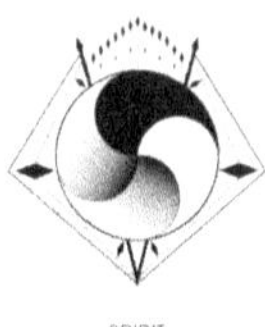

Monday came like a hangover of reality after a weekend of laughter. We had stayed up until the wee hours of the morning talking and celebrating. With the big question of the day being: what would we name them? The

suggestions abounded, from normal to absurd, but until we had a better idea of the genders, we were just coming up with ideas.

I caught a ride from the Atlanta apartment to work. Carelian had transported me there from Albany, but it was just as easy to use mundane methods and less costly. My body was changing, and it felt weird. The support from this weekend left me buoyant, if not secure in our choices. I headed to my office and dropped off my lunch, then I went to hunt down Naomi.

So far I always seemed to get early bird bosses and sure enough, Naomi was already in her office even though it was still quarter to eight in the morning. I had my travel mug in my hand, with only ginger tea in it unfortunately, and knocked on her door.

She lifted her head, arching a brow at me, her tight braids in a zigzag pattern on her head this month. Red strands had been braided in and she wore a suit that sheathed her lean body in blood red. She'd have matched Onyx, Zmaugs' mate, perfectly.

"Cori. To what do I owe this visit?" As always, Naomi was direct and to the point. But she waved me to a chair, and I sank into it. Carelian took up his position laying at the base of the door. I couldn't decide if that was so he could sleep without worrying about anyone coming in without waking him up or to guard my back. Probably both.

"I needed to inform you about a couple of things." I'd been avoiding it, but I needed to let her know about my magic. She wouldn't be happy about it, but at this point I was thinking it had something to do with the pregnancy, though why I didn't know.

Her eyes narrowed, and she leaned back in her chair, focusing completely on me. For a person who wasn't a mage, she could be intimidating. I cleared my throat. "I wanted to let you know that I'm pregnant, and the due date is in early June."

Her face shuttered harder than I'd seen since I'd started to work there. "You know the Draft Board doesn't like merlins getting pregnant."

It hurt. Part of me had thought she'd be supportive, but it didn't matter, I'd read up on the relevant laws and provisions. It was always best to know what I could and couldn't do. The laws were there for a reason.

"I know, but they also can't prevent or punish me for it. The repercussions are that any time I am off not covered by vacation time or sick leave is added onto my draft term." I kept my voice cool and a placid smile on my face. All draftees received 20 vacation days a year and 10 sick days. The sick days could also be used for doctor appointments. And then everyone was granted six weeks of maternity leave. "I estimate I will need the basic six weeks off, then another 2 to make sure the babies have transitioned well. I think the Draft Board and you will live with me missing eight weeks and having it added onto my Draft."

Naomi slid her eyes to the side as she pulled up an application on her computer, calendar most likely, and made some entries. "Yes, but it also means you will be on a light work load the closer you get to your due date."

"Oh well," I said, my voice flat, and more than a bit annoyed.

"Come off it, Cori. You know that is going to throw a huge crimp our workload and I'm going to get criticized about not convincing you to wait until after the draft or to not get pregnant at all." She sighed, looking more put out than annoyed at me.

"Well, you're about to be more annoyed." The elation from the weekend was dribbling out of me like a constant leak. "Something is going on with my magic. We have reason to believe it is related to my pregnancy, but until I give birth, I won't know for sure."

"And what exactly does that mean?"

I explained everything to her. "Bottom line, I'm about at magician power right now, at least by offering and effect levels."

The entire time I'd talked, she'd sat there with her arms crossed, her brows drawn down, and mouth pursed. "That does create a concern. I'll keep it in mind." She looked at my hair. "It is shorter. Using magic doesn't hurt the baby, right?"

"From what everyone says, no. I'm fine casting magic without any concerns. And it's babies. I'm having twins."

For a second she smiled, and the boss I'd known the last few months peeked through. Then she nodded. "I'll make a note. Is there anything else?"

I rose, holding my tea. "I think that is enough for today. I'll be in my cubicle, then back to the lab to work on some of the samples."

"Good, I have three more cold cases coming your way. They are at least a decade old, but no one has had the time to spend looking at them."

I turned and walked toward the door, tilting my head as I saw Carelian sitting up and staring at Naomi. Frowning, I turned to look at her and saw her pale under her dark skin, making the red almost garish. Her head jerked down like someone had yanked it.

"Understood." The words were clearly said to Carelian. Then she turned to look at me. "Congratulations, Cori. Sorry. You're watched more than you know. And I get pressure more than you realize. Please invite me to the baby shower. I'll attend if possible." She focused on her computer and didn't look back up at me.

I walked out of her office sliding looks at Carelian. "What exactly did you say to her?"

~Nothing much. I just reminded her that you had friends who were dragons that ate sentient beings on a regular basis, and none of them would have any issues with having an extra snack as a favor to you"

My knees almost gave as I tried to turn and stop at the same time. "You didn't!"

He cast a green gaze back at me. ~Yes I did. She was rude. Rude is deadly. You humans need to relearn that.~

I turned back to go apologize, then stopped. They wanted the double merlin, wanted to control me. Screw it, there was a price for screwing with me, so let them chew on it. "Don't be too mean. She's a decent boss."

~That doesn't always mean she's a good person, or that she shouldn't understand who my quean is.~ He seemed not to care.

I pondered the issues as I settled into my chair. ~Carelian, what would you do if they killed me?~ Even asking the question seemed dangerous, but at least via mindspeak no one else could hear.

He paused in his circling under the desk to look up at me, ears laid back. ~I would destroy them all if they purposefully got you killed. Remember that Tirsane would come down on them also.~ With a flick of his tail he finished curling up and closed his eyes, though I doubted he would actually sleep.

I had forgotten about that. Tirsane had threatened consequences if they killed me, but not if I was executed for breaking the laws governing mages. That would then be justified. I cautiously regarded her as a friend, but still, she was scary. And if I got killed on a job, well, neither she nor Esmere would do a single thing. I didn't think.

It didn't matter. I pulled out my phone to see if Joanna Snowden had responded to my email. She was the president of the House of Emrys, or at least she had been last time I talked to her. But that had been three or more years ago. Time passed faster than I realized sometimes. I had asked if we could get together for lunch, as I thought she still lived in Atlanta. It would give me a chance to feel her out about my magic issue.

No response, so I pulled up the next cold case, something from fifteen years ago, and started working. This involved three groups of murders, all escalating in body count and ritual markings. The victims had been found in Denver, but they never found the perp. The last crime scene implied something had happened to the killer. There were 27 people laid out in a circle, they had all been mages, though none above a magician. The center of the circle had blood and scuff marks, but there was no indication anyone left the circle.

The more I stared at it, the more familiar it seemed. I pulled up the VICAP system and logged in. I knew the case number I wanted by heart and typed it in. Paul Goines. The killer Jo and I had helped stop, though really Bob had been the ultimate arbitrator of that sentence. Bob was the human-compatible name for the Lord of Chaos. I still didn't understand why Esmere and that being had the same title, but I wasn't going to ask. The odds were she had abilities that I knew nothing about and a much darker side of her. But then she was a Cath, her morals and human morals didn't align exactly.

This killer had started with three, then nine, then twenty-seven, so multiplying by three each time. Paul had done something similar. I compared the symbols, and they had a lot in common. All trying to point towards a doubling of power. What was different here was that everyone was an Order mage. Paul had grabbed anyone with magic.

But if an Order mage had tried to emerge again it might be the start of a pattern. I logged into the OMO database and started to search. The Draft Board and the OMO linked data, and I suspected anyone trying to emerge would have been after their draft, as you were too closely monitored during your draft service. I filtered by Order and ranking of magician. The OMO noted the current statuses of all mages. From what I'd learned when I worked for the FBI under Steven Alixant, it was why mages had their driver's licenses updated every three years here in the US. It let them check our current address and that we were still alive.

I made the assumption the killer had to be born in the US, which might be wrong, but otherwise I'd need a better clue. Then I filtered by US and Missing. This narrowed the list down significantly, but still left too many people. From what I could see in the OMO data after your draft, they verified your existence via driver's licenses, bank accounts, or credit card applications. I filtered it so the person had been active prior to the murders, but no activity after the last one.

It took the computer a bit, but if nothing else I was sure it would come up with a list of names. I looked and almost everyone was from Denver, where the murders had happened and the places they had been staged weren't obvious. All of them were out of the way locations that you'd either have spent a lot of time with a map researching, or had to be local.

Waiting for something that I was pretty sure I already knew was torture. And I couldn't go get coffee to distract me. Decaf wasn't the same.

The list popped up on my screen and I started looking. The information there did surprise me. It never occurred to me so many mages went "unaccounted for". The confirmed deaths didn't surprise me, though with Cixi taking over, Charles had confirmed that the death rate of mages in the last year had fallen by 34.5%. Which was nice.

There were twenty-two mages on the list who had gone missing roughly around the time of the last murders. But only one had tested out as a magician—barely. I pulled up the file on him. Lewis Arnett. The OMO just noted when he'd entered the draft and not much else. I pulled up the Draft Board website and logged in. There I pulled up his draft assignment and reviews. While I couldn't access mine and would get in trouble for pulling up Jo or Sable's, I could look at other people just fine.

It read eerily like Goines. Angry at placement, complained constantly, shifted from position to position. But the catch for me was he and four mages had been digging out survivors from an earthquake in Mexico when an aftershock hit and the other three had died when the building collapsed. There were notes that he seemed different afterwards, but nothing concrete. He'd last shown up to work a month before his draft was over, then the next day nothing. There were no signs he had run. His possessions were still in his home, even notes as to plans for the weekend, but he was never seen again.

I pinged Esmere. ~Esmere, do you have a moment for a few questions?~

~Are they boring questions?~ she responded instantly.

My smirk reflected back at me from my computer monitor. ~They aren't to me.~

~Ask and then I'll decide.~ I could all but see her in my mind's eye, sprawled out, emerald coat gleaming, tail lashing lazily.

~About fifteen years ago, do you remember a mage opening

rips large enough to summon someone? They would have been Order, I think.~

She yawned in my mind and I couldn't stop the matching yawn. ~That happens about three or four times in one of your decades. Do you have a likeness?~

I looked at the picture of him carefully and sent the image to Esmere.

~Ah, yes, he ripped open a portal to Order and got Salistra. I believe he lasted a year before she broke him. Or more accurately, he tried to break free. She drank his magic. Nothing like how powerful yours is, but she was insufferable for a month.~

I shook my head. ~Thanks. That was the information I needed.~

~Not horribly boring, but not interesting either.~

~Thank you regardless. I shall attempt to ask more interesting questions in the future.~

~See that you do.~

I snickered, pulled up the case, and stared at it for a minute. Finally, I marked it closed. In the resolution I typed - "Confirmed dead. Death as a result of interaction with the planes." But it still left me with more questions than answers. How often did people re-emerge and did they always become murderers?

CHAPTER
TWENTY-EIGHT

Mage Anna Lobdell looks to have won the prime job of being the doctor for Merlin Munroe's baby. The two women spied with her are the ones she had a Joining ceremony with. So are they support, lovers, or maybe her servants? Wouldn't you like to be the focus of that trio? But the big question of the day is who is lucky man? Inquiring minds want to know.~ Daily Magical News

CHAOS

I had started a cold case search for any missing mages, but it was taking a while to get all the information from one database to match up with another. Until the last few years, the cold cases didn't have flags to indicate if they were a mage or not.

The easiest way seemed to be to log into the OMO and get a list of all missing mages in the last fifty years. That was about how far their records went back.

There were many more than I had thought. I'd expected a few, but not as many as I saw. It made me want to know more, but that meant asking permission. Sticking my nose into some of this without permission was a good way to get in trouble. I pulled up my work email and decided to take a moment to check my personal email as well. Checking my email wasn't something I did often, mainly because the people I wanted to hear from were a part of my life, so it meant I sometimes went days without remembering to check.

In my in box was an email from Joanna Snowden. I clicked open, my heart thudding in my chest. Would she even remember me? Could the House of Emrys even help or want to? A quick scan verified she agreed to meet for lunch. She suggested tomorrow at a restaurant a quick rideshare away. I replied with my agreement, trying not to get my hopes up. After hitting send I went back to my search for missing mages and placed a request for permission to match up all missing mages to files in the FBI and other law enforcement systems.

As I waited for permission or refusal, I focused on a different pile of work; writing up lab findings and after-action reports for the last few weeks. I usually wrote them all immediately after, but then I had to log them in different systems and then answer questions when they filtered back from all the various agencies. But the upcoming lunch never left my mind.

The next day I let Naomi know I was headed out to lunch and would be back late, something unusual for me, and headed down to catch my scheduled rideshare. Carelian tagged along, not really remembering the woman much. He'd only been a kitten when I'd met her and I didn't think he'd paid much attention to her then.

Walking into the restaurant, I saw her sitting there and was forcibly reminded that time had passed. Her hair had a few streaks of silver in it, but she still had the same calm smile and sharp eyes that saw everything. She nodded at the other chair as I walked up.

"Corisande, it is good to see you." Her gaze shifted to Carelian. "Carelian. I asked for this table. There is space to lie in front of the window if you wish."

The fact that she had thought about him, and that he would want to be nearby was considerate.

~The sun is warm through the window,~ he commented as he stretched out in front of it. Her blink made me try to remember if Carelian had ever spoken to her, but nothing leaped to mind. I didn't know how well known his penchant was for ignoring the normal behaviors of most familiars.

"Joanna, thank you for being willing to talk to me," I said as I settled into my chair, glancing around the restaurant. It was an upper scale American restaurant, and I fought a round of nausea as the odor of sizzling onions hit me.

She arched a brow at me, the corners of her lips quirking up a touch. "You are one of the most powerful mages in the country, and never use your benefits. Why wouldn't I talk to you?"

I repressed a snort. "Not at the moment, I'm not."

Before she could say anything, a waiter appeared. We took a few minutes to order. I was good and got a chef salad with dressing on the side. The foods I liked seemed to change every day, sometimes every hour, so having all the ingredients in little rows seemed safe. It made it easier to pick off what I couldn't handle eating that day.

She kept the smile on, but there was the tiniest hint of a frown. When the waiter had left, she looked at me. "Your email hinted something was wrong? Are you in trouble? Do you need research help?"

That made me blink, and I thought back to my email. All I'd asked was if the House of Emrys did any research on magic problems or knew people researching it. Then if we could meet to talk. I snorted to myself a bit. That might have been a bit vague, but at the same time the idea of exposing myself, that my magic was so wonky, didn't feel right either.

I sighed, all too aware of her intense look. Hiding information would get me nothing and maybe if people didn't see me as powerful, it would help? That seemed unlikely, and it felt way too much like I was exposing myself to predators. Or maybe I was being influenced by Carelian way too much.

"I'm trying to find out if there is any research on evidence of mages losing power while pregnant." I managed to keep my voice level and matter of fact.

Her eyes flicked down to my stomach, then narrowed a bit. "You're pregnant?"

"Yes, about three months." I didn't want to get into specifics, that wasn't why I had come here.

I could see the questions in her eyes. I sipped my water, trying not to rush to any conclusions. But really, was it that strange I was pregnant? My mental snark mocked me. Yes, yes it was.

"So, what do you mean by losing power?" She had leaned forward, focused on me. I swallowed to try to keep my voice from cracking.

"I mean, any offering I make needs to be ten times what it used to be, if not more. Even with Carelian my offerings are more than what I had to do to cast spells in my null branches."

Her face paled, and we both went quiet as our food was delivered. I grabbed one of the rolls and nibbled at it while she stared at her plate. She'd gotten French onion soup and a small salad. The smell of the onion made my stomach roil, and I swallowed the bread, hoping my stomach would settle.

"That is unexpected. Have you posted on the boards?" she asked after the waiter had drifted away. Carelian busied himself with some chunks of lightly seared chicken.

"Boards?"

She frowned at me. "Have you even visited the website or gone to any of the local meetings?"

I focused on my bread and wracked my mind. Now that she

mentioned it, I remembered her mentioning something about the website. I'd honestly had it in my head as an old 1800s sort of club and anything modern never occurred to me.

"I swear. Why do so many of the newer merlins think we are still stagnated in the early 1900s?"

I jerked my head up, wondering if she'd been reading my mind, but she was viciously stabbing at her salad and muttering. "We're a resource and if you don't use us all the money everyone pays just gets used up in expensive booze for the old fogies to drink." Joanna shot me a look. "Use your benefits, dang it."

My expression must have been as panicked as I felt and she sighed, taking a mouthful of soup. I had to fight to swallow the bile that rose in my throat. It was official: pregnancy mind was stupid.

"We have secure message boards for people looking for information or research. Most merlins spend a lot of their time doing research or just playing with what magic can do, but never in a way that attracts the attention of the Draft Board or the OMO. They are both regulatory agencies that are best avoided at all costs." The contempt in her voice about them made me smile. It rather relieved me that they weren't worshiping at the feet of either group.

"Okay. I can do that. Does that mean you think they've seen this before?"

"I have no clue. I know I was fine with my pregnancies, both of them." She snickered at me and I fought to still my face. "Most mages do have lives outside of college and the draft. Merlins are generally the only ones to get pregnant during their draft. With a decade of service required, that puts most of us in our late thirties and that gets a bit risky, even if you are a mage with medical training. Not to mention it's harder to keep up with toddlers in your forties." Her eyes sharpened, and she gave me a direct stare. "Do not let them convince you to not have the child. They like to mutter about how the Draft looks down on it and everything else, but a lot of people worked very hard to make sure mages got maternity leave like everyone else. Waiting until their forties has too much of a mortality rate increase for lawmakers to fight it too much. And merlins often have merlin children. It only makes sense."

"Oh." I thought back to Naomi's reaction and nodded. "I didn't. Besides, I'm a surrogate, so I don't want them to have to wait. And my age now is a good age for it."

Joanna nodded as she finished the soup. I almost sighed in relief as the scent also started to fade. I stabbed at my salad, glad I'd gone with the creamy ranch, but the first taste of egg convinced me not today. The bacon, however, made me happy.

"As for the rest. This makes me concerned. Are the magic issues something new that might happen to more pregnant women, or is it something related specifically to you? I don't know of any reports about that, but I can see how many women would never mention it and female merlins are only about 25% of all merlins. Usually we see male merlins and a greater percentage of female archmages."

That surprised me, but if I thought about it, she was the only other female merlin I could think of.

"But you don't know the answer," I said, feeling myself sag as what little hope I'd held onto seeped out of my being. What if my magic never came back? A lick on my hand grabbed my attention, and I looked at Carelian, who had moved to sit near me.

~You worry too much. There will be an answer, and even if there isn't, you are still my quean.~

I smiled as I rubbed his head. Some truths were self-evident. That I was Carelian's quean was one of them. There were worse things in this world to be.

"No I don't," she said. "But that means very little." I stopped petting Carelian to look at her, he was not impressed. "Cori, there are thousands of merlins. They all have their little hobbies, things to look at. Once you get out of the Draft people will hire you for projects. Especially with your degrees. You'd be excellent in a lab situation or even for private research. That is what people want.

Merlins who don't have something that excites them tend to die young and we don't know why."

My mind flitted to Stevie. I suspected that would drive me for the rest of my life, trying to figure out what happened to him.

"What are you suggesting?"

"Make a request on the research board," she said with a duh tone to her voice.

I fought not to look embarrassed, but I had no idea what she was talking about.

Joanna sighed and finished up her salad before pushing the plate away. "Give me a minute." She dug in her bag and pulled out a tablet. A minute later, she handed it to me. "I have the website up. On the top, you should see a menu link called Tomes of Wonder. I didn't set up the website and they like to make it look mystical. But click on that."

It was a very mystical looking website. In fact, if I had stumbled across it, I would have thought it was a fan site for Merlin or maybe merlins. I clicked on the Tomes of Wonder link and was brought to a much plainer looking forum. It was broken into sections, but I ignored most of them and clicked on research requests. There were thousands. I randomly clicked on one labeled Learning Stones.

Requesting information on learning stones. I have three in my possession and want to talk to mages who have used them and/or know how they are created. Paper forthcoming, shared credits and grant money for up to 50k offered for detailed information. Please contact.

I sat stunned and clicked on more. Many of them I had the information they requested or James did in his journals and research tomes. Now the name of the forum made sense. There was an entire market of information trading going on that I had no idea about.

I lifted my gaze to find Joanna torn between exasperation and amusement. "You really only joined for the legal protection, didn't you?"

"Yes. My life was crazy at that point. It seemed like I had no choice. Personally, I'm leaning towards buying out."

She groaned. "I swear, give it a try, Cori. There are meetings in most places, discussions, and you might find the information you are looking for. Post it. Make it slightly vague and trade some of what James left you as payment. You'll be amazed at how many offers you'll get."

I sat looking at the forum for a long time. I could have used this for the last few years to get information about Stevie's death. There might have been someone with information for me.

I was an idiot.

Starting a political action group. It is unconscionable that mages are drafted, yet we have no representation in Congress or the Senate. I am looking for mages willing to work to get the laws changed so there is no block to office for a mage. This year local, next year the presidency! ~ Tomes of Magic Post

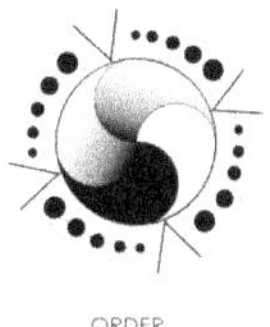

ORDER

Lunch with Joanna spurred me into action and I posted two requests for information, offering access to selected journals James had left for me and some of his research. While there were aspects I'd never hand out, other parts weren't that worrisome.

Then I dealt with waiting and trying to work. Tirsane said she had an idea, but it might take some time and favors. I wanted to tell her not to bother, but the need to know overrode any fear I had of incurring commitments. And being pregnant.

I hated it.

Maybe not hated it, but I could feel myself getting fatter and I'd rarely had any issues with my weight. My breasts were starting to increase in size. All of that made sense to me. But why in the world were my gums bleeding when I brushed them and why was I having random nosebleeds? The only advantage of that was that I could use that blood in my offerings. On the bright side, my morning, really it was all day, sickness started to fade. Which made life much easier.

I headed to my doctor's appointment alone. It was time to get an amniocentesis done. Jo and Sable both needed to work, and I had scheduled it at lunchtime. With my bloody nose as an offering I just sidestepped there. The blood, plus an eighth of an inch of hair, let me step out in the parking deck. I headed toward the office, still slightly nervous. I'd almost refused, as Esmere assured me the babies were healthy, and there was just something about the idea of shoving a needle into my stomach that creeped me out. But I had no idea if genetic issues were anything Esmere could detect, so I'd agreed.

I waited in the procedure room for Doctor Lobdell and stared at my stomach. In just the last few days it seemed to have increased in size, which made no sense. Babies didn't grow that fast. I knew all the "facts" about pregnancy, but none of them addressed my magic issues and I wondered what else no one talked about.

A knock at the door as Anna Lobdell came in pulled me out of my retrospective thoughts, though the nurse following her with a tray and a ginormous, though thin, needle on it did nothing to calm me down.

"Afternoon, Cori. How are you feeling?"

I glanced at her temple and realized I'd forgotten to ask

someone obvious about my magic. Was I always this dense, or was this the "pregnancy brain" people talked about?

"Physically, I think I'm fine. The body changes are weird and frustrating, but expected." I cleared my throat as she looked at me. It must have been obvious there was something else I wanted to ask. "Have you ever heard of anyone having trouble with their magic while pregnant?"

She settled on the chair and nodded at the nurse to just leave the needle. I resolutely tried not to think about that. "What sort of trouble?"

"That their magic gets harder to use or requires much larger offerings?" I bit my lip and tried to remember to breathe as I waited for an answer.

She closed her eyes, brow furrowed. "Not that anyone has mentioned, though maybe I should include it in my standard questions. I remember at least one woman commenting that every time the baby kicked she had air blowing in her face, but she was an Air mage. Many of my patients only use their magic sparingly or for little things constantly, like cooling or heating a drink."

The number of magicians who hoarded their magic that way used to surprise me. But if most people's costs were like mine were now, I could understand it. The glimmer of a research idea tickled at the back of my mind, but was gone before I could fully articulate it.

"Okay. I was wondering. Mine has been a bit wonky lately," I muttered, not wanting to explain just how difficult it had become.

"I've only occasionally had patients who were still serving the draft here. So many didn't lean on their magic much more than what was required at work." She sounded sad. "I use mine to check on my patients' health, work with hard deliveries, and if a baby goes really wrong, I can use two or three inches of hair to keep both mother and child healthy. This means I tend to reserve it for either practicing techniques or when I really need it." She pointed at her brown hair wrapped up in a thick bun. Assuming she wasn't using a filler, and few mages would, her hair probably hit past her waist. But she was right: two or three bad deliveries in a month could yank her hair all the way up to her shoulders.

"Okay. I thought I'd ask."

She kept that thoughtful look on her face as we went through the whole examination, then came time for the amniocentesis. I laid back as they started prepping me and moving the ultrasound over. A nurse came in and prepped the ultra sound, setting up the screen as Dr. Lobdell swabbed my belly with what looked like iodine. "You know if it gets too bad, I can write a medical waiver for you to not work until after you deliver the babies."

I looked at her. "But I'm in the draft," I countered, confused.

"Yes. And that means you're covered by the Family Medical Leave Act. In your case, it means your time is tacked on at the end. But you can take time off if you feel your health and the health of the babies requires you to not be working or at least not using magic."

The screen showing the blobs that were the kids distracted me. "I'll need to keep that in mind." The sharp pain in my belly had me jerking my eyes to the needle sliding in.

Medical, this is medical stuff. Think about the stuff you can learn.

The thought helped, but it still seemed weird to see the needle, then glance at the screen and watch that long thin piece of needle piercing me. I couldn't decide if it was the coolest thing I'd ever seen or if I was going to start screaming.

It was done before I made up my mind. I focused on the two blobs again. "Are they okay?"

Anna Lobdell listened to my stomach with her stethoscope, eyes closed for a moment, and I sensed her offering more than saw it. "They are fine. We'll run the genetic tests, but I am not expecting anything. Don't worry. They are two healthy kids."

"Can you see the genders yet?

"Hmmm, let's see." She moved the wand back and forth over my belly. "It looks like they are determined to not let us know just yet. Don't worry, odds are when you come in for your 21-week checkup we will be able to tell. I know I don't need to ask if you're taking vitamins, most mages do anyhow. Just try to keep your stress level manageable."

I repressed a snort. Between my magic malfunctions and work, I wasn't sure if I knew what a manageable stress level was. We finished up, and I headed out. Focusing very carefully, which did reduce the offering required, I stepped to my Atlanta apartment. I looked around—it needed to be cleaned, dust was piling up. I also really should empty out the mail. I stopped downstairs, opened it, and there was a flood of ads, political campaign stuff, and credit card offers. I just grabbed them all and tossed them. If it was anything important they could call me or send me an email. That taken care of, I caught a ride back to work.

There was a message flashing on my computer as I walked in and I groaned. I clicked and could almost hear Naomi's voice in my ear. "My office, asap."

I didn't bother to sit down, just dropped off my bag. ~Carelian? Drama about to go down.~ I was making the assumption it was work drama, not personal, but either way I preferred to go in with backup. And what better back up than my huge, loveable, ruby red familiar? Between one step and the next, a jab of pain, then his heat seeping through my slacks.

~The children are well?~ His voice rumbled in my head and I rubbed his ears as we went down the corridor.

"The doctor didn't seem worried, and they had good heartbeats, so yes." I was finding out there was a world of difference between knowing about the medical aspects of pregnancy and being pregnant. Even knowing everything was textbook, there was still the niggling fear of hurting the babies. That fear helped a lot against the coffee cravings.

~Excellent, you shall have strong kits.~ His purr of pride made me snicker. You'd think he had something to do with the entire thing.

I stuck my head in Naomi's office, but she wasn't there. I looked down the hall.

~Conference room. I can smell and hear her from here. ~

A quick pivot and I headed to the conference room. There were the two agents who had tried to chew me out a few months ago, Naomi and a few other people I knew enough to smile and wave at, but nothing else.

"Good, you're here." Her eyes quickly dropped to my stomach, then to my face in a lightning-fast move. She'd been oddly interested in my pregnancy and I wasn't sure why, but I decided to roll with it. "Everything okay?"

"All good." I nodded and flipped my attention to the screen in the room that showed footage from either a helicopter or a drone. Probably a drone, as I didn't see a shadow or hear rotors. There had better be no need for me to go on a helicopter again. I was too worried it would be that same crazy pilot and I didn't think my heart could handle it. "What is the situation?"

"Are you sure we can trust her? Last time she and her pet almost killed our perp." I turned to look at the red headed jackass talking, but Naomi took care of it.

"Agent O'Malley, I am delighted that you think you can comment about my agents. Rest assured that I have never known either Carelian or Agent Munroe to make a bad call. Your record, however, is not so pristine. I am sure that as long as we are given all of the information, our decisions will be above reproach." Her eyes got even narrower as she leaned forward. "Because I can guarantee you that if you keep anything back, there will never be anything for the missing persons department to find."

My eyes were wide as she said that. I saw the men puff up, ready to blast into her.

~I have always wondered what human tastes like. My quean has never allowed me to eat those she has defeated. But if I hunt and take my own kill, there would be plenty of time to savor the flesh in my own realm.~ Carelian's silky voice slid though my mind like a sharp knife. The effect on the agents was stark as they stared at him and backed up, hands on their guns. ~Oh please. If I want you dead, you will never know I am there. If you do anything to endanger my quean you will never see what takes your life.~

Everyone in the room swallowed except Naomi. Her smile grew teeth and if I didn't know better, I might have thought they actually got sharper. "Do we understand each other, agents?"

They nodded as she stared at them for three heartbeats; I was counting. "Good. Cori," she spun to me and pointed at the video footage still playing. "We have someone who just set off three bombs at a shopping mall and is now on the run. We have dogs coming in, but he has a motorbike and is moving fast."

The footage showed the heavily forested foothills of the Appalachians, and I couldn't see much but trees, shadows and flickers of light. The shadow of the drone didn't help to see what might be on the ground.

"We don't know that he isn't running to a shelter, but we have very good reason to believe that he has bombs in multiple other places with remote detonators. We are working with the cell phone companies to shut down the towers in that area, but we have four providers and if he has Wi-Fi calling and a land line, it won't stop him. What can you do?"

And that question right there was one of the reasons I trusted Naomi. I still needed to figure out what the pregnancy issues were, but she actually asked me questions rather than snapping out orders. I looked at the problem and started to think.

"Where is this exactly?"

She typed rapidly on the computer and a map pulled up. "We think he is here." She tapped on an area on the map. "But then, we think a lot of things we shouldn't." Naomi shot a look at the two agents, who backed up a step. "So, what do you want to do?"

I leaned in to look at the map, thinking furiously. I couldn't reveal my stepping ability, and leaning too much on Carelian let others think they could leverage that ability. And my magic was crap right now, so what could I do? A slow smile spread across my face. "I know exactly what to do."

CHAPTER

THIRTY

Pregnancy Fact: While twins are not common, yet they are not as rare as many expect. 32 out of every 1000 births are twins. Parents who are twins are more likely to have twins themselves. But twins can put more stress on the mother as supporting three lives is a significant change. ~ The Pregnant Mage

---

SPIRIT

Everyone turned to look at me, but I looked at Carelian. "Can you use plane rips to get yourself ahead of where he could possibly be?"

Carelian tilted his head and nodded.

"Can you then get a rough idea of where he will be by triangulating?"

His ears perked up as his head tilted. ~You want me to create rips to different places to triangulate his location and communicate back to you.~ His pink tongue licked his shoulder.

~Yes.~ His mental voice hummed with excitement. This was advanced hunting we rarely did. Normally I'd sidestep with him, but right now I couldn't afford that. We had tested extensively while out hiking and found out that Carelian always knew where he was respective to me. Which meant if he could find the suspect, he could direct me toward him.

"Carelian will need something of his to get a scent." It wasn't perfect, but he could use that to find traces in the air. Animals just followed a scent. Carelian could extrapolate and make a decision about which way to go. Plus, the sound of a motorbike would be much more audible to his sensitive ears.

Agent Jorges from Border Patrol nodded, a sharp, jerky movement that looked uncomfortable. "We have a glove he left at the scene. We couldn't get fingerprints, but it should have the scent."

"You have it here?"

He nodded again and picked up the phone. "I'll get it up here."

I shifted my gaze to Naomi. "Can you get me in a small plane with binoculars? If Carelian can tell me where he is, I can direct the pilot there and I can cast a very directed KO spell and take him out. Granted, if you want him alive, we should probably wait until he's slowed down or stopped." It wouldn't be a KO spell, those wouldn't reach that far, but a Soul Yank would. I'd created or discovered that spell years ago and rarely used it, but so far I didn't know of a limit if I had something to latch on to: the path of a bullet, line of sight, a phone conversation. I didn't talk about that spell ever and most people just thought I had an incredible KO distance.

"A helicopter would be faster," the O'Malley agent growled. "Trap him like a dog."

"No," I snapped, my guts twisting like Tirsane's snakes at the thought. Never would be too soon for a helicopter. It occurred to me I might have PTSD from that last flight. So be it. At least with the Life Flight choppers they were nice and steady. "It's noisy and he'll know we are coming and hide somewhere that I can't reach him. The small light plane will be easier to pass off as normal activity." I saw him get ready to protest, and I glared at him. "I think I know best how to use my abilities, don't you?" I narrowed my eyes as I stared at him. He shrank back the tiniest bit, though he still had a mutinous look on his face.

"Fine. Then what?"

I shrugged. "He falls where he is, and if he isn't going too fast, he'll probably still be alive." That aspect worried me a bit, but as long as I could see him, the least a Soul Yank would do was make him stumble and fall. At that point Carelian could get to him and keep him down until others showed up. "You are welcome to have helicopters on standby to get there quickly when we have him subdued."

There was a bit more grumbling, and I just waited, though I smirked as Naomi typed on her phone like a telegraph operator. No wonder she went through so many phones.

"Cori, the plane is getting prepped and there is a car waiting for you downstairs. Do you need to stop and get anything?" She looked at me as she asked, her eyes making a quick flick to my stomach.

"Nope. Got a bag at my desk. I'm on the way."

"Wait, the glove should be here in a minute." The sound of rapid footsteps matched his words and a man burst into the room with an evidence bag in his hand.

"Carelian?" I nodded at the junior agent holding the bag.

He walked over to the agent, who swallowed, but opened the bag. We all stood there for what seemed like an eternity watching him huff in and out.

~I have it. Lots of other scents too.~

"Then we are out of here." I turned and headed out of the room.

"Gentlemen, let me be very clear here," Naomi's words followed Carelian and me out of the room as we raced to my desk. I grabbed my boots, vest, and flashlight out of my bag and took a minute to change from my flats to my boots. Then I slipped on the vest, stashing the flashlight and my phone in its secured pockets. A quick double check, then I ran to the entrance of the building, bag in hand.

A black vehicle idled there, and I slid in. It was the same driver as before. "You again," I said.

He flashed me a smile. "At your service. Buckle up."

~Oh great, the insane driver.~ Carelian sank his claws into the upholstery and spread out. I buckled up and focused on my breathing. I had a plan, but there were so many ways it could go wrong. I went through my bag, trying to see if there was anything else I wanted to stuff in my vest.

"They going to have binoculars there?" I asked as he weaved through traffic, lights and siren blaring.

"As far as I know, ma'am." He didn't take his eyes off the road, for which I was very grateful.

"Ugh. Cori is fine." His lips curved the slightest bit.

"I can do that. Name's Ryan." That concluded our conversation until we reached the airport, still in one piece, though Carelian was vowing to never ride with him again. Carelian preferred a much more sedate pace with a large window for him to look out as we traveled. Planes were out. Maybe I should take him on another train trip?

I filed that idea as a possible present one day and scrambled out of the car. "Thanks," I said. I'd thrown a scrunchy, a small med kit, and a battery pack into my vest. "I'm leaving my bag here. Can you get it back to the office for me?"

"You got it. It'll be in your cube. See ya, Cori." His grin made me pause and frown, but I didn't have time to figure it out now as Carelian and I sprinted to the plane.

I didn't have the breath to talk out loud, so I settled for mind-speak. ~You know roughly where he is. If you hit where they last had him, there should be a scent. Can you do a bunch of hopping around while we get up in the air and head towards that vicinity? From the notes Naomi is sending me, it will take the plane about 15 minutes to get to that general area.~

~I am not pleased with you going on another flying contraption without me. But yes. I will.~ He paused at the foot of the stairs to the plane, the tarmac wet in the Atlanta drizzle. ~Be careful, my quean.~

I rubbed his head and dropped a kiss on his forehead. ~Always. I have way too much to live for.~ He licked my nose and turned. Between one spring and the next, he was gone. I lingered for a second, then headed over to the open door. It was a small plane and from here I could see the seats in the cockpits and a bit of room behind them, like a bench seat. There was someone in the other seat flipping switches and marking things off on a clipboard.

"You Munroe?" The voice was muffled and hard to hear over the engine.

"Yes. I assume I'm up here?" I asked staring at the plane, trying to figure out how to climb in semi gracefully. "And did they get me some binoculars?"

"That's what the seat is there for. Besides, it's the only way to have good visibility. They're in the seat. Don't sit on them." I climbed in and buckled up, not sitting on the glasses, then took the headset the pilot handed to me. After I slipped it on, the ambient noise dropped dramatically. The pilot looked at me. Mid-thirties, with close cropped hair, light brown skin and eyes, she would have fit in at any Guzman family reunion.

"Call me Kincade. They told me you're going to tell me where to go and I should listen to you. Fine. But don't touch the controls, and when I say we are done, we go back." Her voice was brisk and no nonsense, but that was fine with me.

"Works for me."

"Good. Latch your door and we'll get going."

I did as she told me and watched with fascination as she spoke with the tower, moved the little plane down the runway and then took off. It seemed both more and less terrifying than the big jumbo jets. I didn't know how I felt about it. But no matter what, it was better than the helicopter.

"Where to?" she asked, her voice in the headset echoey.

"Umm…" I said, looking around. ~Carelian, which way should we head?~

~I have not found him yet. He moves fast, and the trees are thick and pungent in this area. But I know he has been through here. Here.~ For a minute I could feel where Carelian was. Nothing as exact as latitude or longitude, but more that I knew he was far away to my left. We'd never been able to put anything as quantitative as a measurement on it, but when he was in China, I could feel which direction he was in even if it was so faint as to be unnoticeable. If only I could sidestep right now. This would all be much easier and less risky. One more thing to keep secret.

"That way. Towards the foothills. We have information the suspect is on a bike headed that way." I pointed to my left and to the north.

Kincade arched a brow but nodded and the plane tilted, much to my stomach's discomfort, to the left.

While we flew, I familiarized myself with the binoculars. They were very high powered, and it felt like I could see the leaves on the trees.

~I have a lead on him. Come my direction.~

I focused. "To the north more. We should be getting close."

"You're the boss," she said in a flat voice that I almost laughed at. Blaming her for not believing me would be a waste of effort. Even with people who were used to magic, Carelian and I were unique. Oh well, there were worse things.

~I hear a motor. But I can't tell if it is him. Your machines stink too much.~ Carelian's snarl of annoyance rippled as we flew over trees similar to the drone footage.

~Be careful, there might be people who have nothing to do with this out there.~ I waited for a response as I texted Naomi.

Status of the cavalry?

It seemed like my fingers had barely hit send when she was replying. *Headed that way, but other than the motorbike trail, we aren't sure where he is headed. Witnesses not reliable.*

That didn't sound good. ~Carelian, you sure you have his scent?~ The worry we were chasing the wrong rabbit grabbed me.

~Yes. I just saw him. We are headed into the mountains, where there are too many lake rivulets for the motorbike. He is slowing. I can hear your noisy flying machine in the distance.~

I focused and found him, closer than he had been. ~Tell me when there is a clearing.~

~Hurry. I am not made for all this running. I am a hunter, not prey.~ His grousing made me smile.

"There to the east." Kincade nodded, and the plane dipped that direction as Carelian's presence got stronger.

~Clearing ahead. It looks like a parking lot. He is still driving, though slowly.~

~Be careful. Let me knock him out first.~

~I can take live prey. Humans are soft.~

"Merlins Balls," I growled. "We are almost there. Get closer." I pointed down and at an angle, the lake sparkling back at us.

"You're the boss, but I'm not wrecking my baby."

I didn't respond, instead I used the binoculars to scan, looking for ruby red, or a motorbike.

~He's stopping. You are very close.~

"There should be a parking lot ahead. Slow over that. It's near some water, inlets."

We had flown over Helen, Georgia, the Bavarian style houses giving me an idea of where we were.

"Lake Burton. There are a few." She lowered even more, the tops of the trees looking too close for my comfort, but I focused past them and on the ground. They had to be here.

~He has stopped. Prey,~ Carelian purred in my head.

~Wait,~ I ordered, but he didn't respond. I peered around desperately. A huge explosion fireballed up into the sky not three miles from where we were. "There!" The word burst out as I reached for Carelian.

~Carelian?~ Nothing. We got closer. ~Carelian?~ Panic edged my thoughts. Kincade flew over the parking lot, smoke still rising from the air. A motorbike lay discarded next to a prone figure and a brilliant red cat.

"CARELIAN!"

THIRTY-ONE

The idea that the creatures that inhabit the other realms would regard humans as anything other than predators to fear is ludicrous. Even dragons would be wary when faced with a tank. The idea that they might have information that has any bearing on our lives is ridiculous. Someday, when access to the realms has been codified the way we have codified magic, we will tame and control that area too. ~ Merlin Ysing during an Emrys talk.

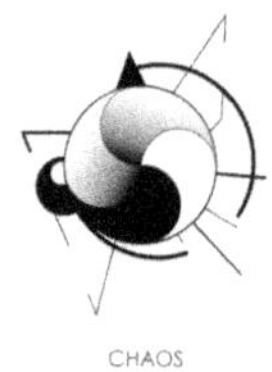

CHAOS

We were already over the spot before his name quit ringing in my ears. "Turn around," I ordered, my voice icy and hard as I unbuckled.

"What do you think you're going to do?" The mix of consternation and amusement in her voice rolled off me like a drop of oil.

"Get to my familiar," I snapped, but the rest of the sentence continued in my head.

My best friend. My companion. My family.

The thought of him being dead ripped at me and nothing else mattered. I grabbed the door and forced it open.

"What the fuck? Where the hell are you going?" Her voice was panicked, but it cut off as I ripped the headphones off and jumped.

Out of a plane.

Into the air.

I probably should have panicked or screamed, but all that mattered was that flash of red fur with streaks of darker red on it. I didn't call Air. I ordered, I demanded, and compelled. It came, though reluctantly, but it came. I repeated the long-ago trick Jo had done of flying, gathering the force of the wind underneath me and slowing my descent. My hair vaporized by inches, but I didn't care.

I hit the ground with a jarring thump, but no worse than if I'd jumped off the porch. I turned seeking him, having spun too much in the air. I wasn't sure where he was now. The glint of red had me sprinting to him, cursing at not grabbing my bag.

"Carelian?" I yelled the word, waiting for a snarky remark in my mind. The silence was as cold as my despair.

The smoke was clearing, and I saw a man, obviously dead, sprawled out on the other side of a still smoldering motorbike. Then Carelian lay about ten feet away, a rivulet of red seeping from him. My slacks shredded along with skin as I hit the pavement next to him. I didn't care. I wanted to pull him to me so badly, cradle him, but I let my training kick in.

The blood ran from his ears. There were deep gouges on the right side of his body, and his fur was singed along his chest and paws.

Focus, Cori. You can't fuck this up.

I held onto that thought as I pulled all my training to the forefront and ruthlessly shoved my emotions down so deep that it might take me time to access them again. With no supplies I was limited, but first step was always to assess. I laid my head on his chest, ignoring the flickering flames and drone of the plane.

I could hear his heartbeat, it was stuttering, which indicated problems. He was breathing, but his breaths were raspy and shallow. I ran my hands down his spine, but nothing seemed squishy or out of place. Taking a deep breath, my emotions screaming in that dark hole of nothing, I grabbed both his fore and hind legs and rolled him. My heart lurched, almost breaking through my analytical mind at the risk I might really hurt him. I needed to see his other side.

His left side had a jagged piece of metal through it, his face had a laceration that barely missed his eye but tore through his ear. Burns crawled across his fur, marring his ruby perfection.

My mind created an image of the scenario: he'd leaped, then realized something was going to happen and twisted trying to avoid, but ended up being broadsided by the explosion and obviously hit by shrapnel. His chest stuttered under my hand and my breath caught. They never let me study for pre-med. I knew cells and bacteria, not how to heal or operate. There was so much that had to be fixed on him and I didn't know how. I knew how to stabilize, not how to fix more than the basics.

~ESMERE!~ My mental shout was loud enough and with enough magic behind it that I felt rips open. My nails vaporized to the quick, and the world went still as I waited. I tried to figure out how to stop the blood seeping out of him at a rate that wasn't sustainable. I needed help. Or he'd die.

~Cori? What's wrong?~ Her voice was sharp, alert, predatory. And I needed all of it.

~Carelian is hurt. Help.~ I might doubt if she'd help me. I never doubted she'd help him.

There was a spike of pain so sharp I cried out. The sound had barely left my lips before her paws had landed next to me.

~What happened?~ Her growl reverberated through my mind as her nose ran over his wounds. Her front claws cut through the pavement, and I wanted to be able to do the same.

"We were bringing down a perp. He didn't wait. He did something. Then there was an explosion and fire. I jumped out of a plane to get to him, but he was already hurt." The words tumbled out over each other, not because I was nervous, but because I was trying not to cry.

~Cori. He lives. We will keep him alive. Your magic is still fighting you?~ Her mental voice lilted up in a question, even as her nose never quit going over his wounds. Wounds I didn't know how to heal.

"Yesssss," I hissed the word, never so angry as I had been at magic that didn't respond to me when I needed it.

~Then we will work together. She will not deny my need.~ There was steel in the voice that surprised me, and I leaned into it. I wished Jo and Sable were here. I needed my partners, but I'd survive.

"Ask and it is yours." I didn't hold back, even if I feared for the life of the babies in my body.

~I do not need their lives. We are not that grievously injured. Lend me your connection to Magic and a favor from Tirsane.~

Tirsane. I glanced at the snake on my arm. Four sections, only the last was solid. Somewhere deep inside I knew I had three favors left, but I'd never allowed myself to dwell on it. That way lay madness. But for Carelian, I'd sacrifice my arm.

"Always." I held my arm out to her and she licked it lingering on the last empty square on my arm. It tingled, then burned, then I wanted to scream as the snake wiggled and pulled out of my skin to look up at me, then it sighed and wiggled back under while I resisted the urge to claw my skin off. The space for the section filled up as the snake settled back down and my brain exploded.

"You called Cori?" Her words filled the air, and I forced myself to look at her, my hands still buried in Carelian's fur.

"I need help. Save him." I don't know if it was an order, a plea, or a prayer. And I didn't care.

Her aloof posture changed, and she looked around, frowning. "Oh, I thought," she broke off and shook her head, snakes hissing. Then her eyes alighted on Esmere and Carelian. "Oh." That seemed to rip out all the arrogance from her. She slithered over to us and crouched.

~Finally. We will talk later. I need your and Cori's help. I have the knowledge of Cath, but her magic is too volatile right now. He is grievously injured and we do not have time to do it the slow way.~

As she spoke, I could feel him struggling to breathe, my hand still on his body. I couldn't lose him.

~Heal him Tirsane, as your favor to her.~ There was command in Esmere's voice, but an odd note of pleading.

Tirsane turned her inhumanly beautiful gaze on me and my hind brain gibbered that I should run or cower. I did neither, just kept petting Carelian, trying to reassure him the best I could. Swearing in my mind to go into veterinary school after the draft. I would never be caught in this position again. Or I'd learn how to heal him myself.

"Is that what you wish, Corisande? To give up one of the favors I bestowed upon you to save this creature?" Her voice seemed odd, distant from the Tirsane I'd come to know over the last year. This wasn't my friend; this was the demigod.

"Merlin's balls, yes. I would give them all to have him healed," I babbled, the words nowhere near as fast as my mind wanted them to be.

She tilted her head, staring at me, then her face changed. For a beat of my heart, I thought I was about to become a statue for all eternity. Instead, joy spread across her face. "As you wish," she murmured and whirled toward Esmere and Carelian.

Esmere's tail was cracking through the air like a whip and her hackles were a solid ridge of green spikes.

~We will be having words about your games,~ she snarled at Tirsane. ~Heal him.~

"Soothe thy fur, Esmere. You know the forms." That comment meant nothing to me, but all I cared about was Tirsane leaning close to Carelian's limp form. Her snakes formed a corona around her head as they stretched out, seeming more filaments of power than snakes.

Carelian's breathing became more ragged, and I bit back the urge to beg. I would beg in a heartbeat, but for now I didn't want to distract them.

"Ah, three bites I think, then milk one, and your grooming," Tirsane murmured. I knew it wasn't addressed to me, but the bites comments made me tense.

~Agreed, but time is of the essence.~

"Mortals, always in such a rush," Tirsane teased as she pulled back.

~Immortals, always so sure they know best,~ Esmere countered, her tail cracking close to a snake, who snapped at it.

Tirsane laughed as she leaned closer to Carelian. "Delta, Nu, and Iota, if you please," she said, her voice soft as she cast a dark shadow over Carelian, turning his ruby fur dark and flat. Three snakes flashed out, their fangs sinking into Carelian, his body seized at the impacts.

"What by Merlin's balls are you doing?" I lunged forward, terror at losing him driving all other considerations out of my mind.

Before I could tackle Tirsane, Esmere moved and blocked me with feline speed. ~Cori, peace. It is okay.~

I stared in horror as Carelian frothed at the mouth.

"Ah, she has never seen me heal, has she?" Tirsane said mildly, but the hurt in her tone slipped through.

~I do not believe so, but you are wasting time.~ Esmere's tone had a bit of a bite in it, but her still tail worried me. Their tails were rarely still.

"So little faith?"

~Too much love,~ Esmere countered as I resisted the need to crawl over her and stop Tirsane.

Tirsane laughed, something full of joy, and it seemed so out of sync that I just stared at her. Her shoulders shook as she leaned down and one of her snakes stretched out and extended its fangs. She squeezed, still giggling, and drops of venom dripped into Carelian's mouth.

"What are you doing?" The words hissed out of me and I started to pull in my desires, figuring out how to kill them all. There was enough nitrogen in the air I could make nitrous oxide and then pull the water out of their blood. They'd be dead before they could fight off the effects of laughing gas.

"Pax, Cori. Truly." Tirsane looked at me. "My snakes have venom that is very similar to your chemicals. One helped blood production, the other helped him breathe by over oxygenating the blood, the third was a clotting factor for his wounds. The venom dripped into his mouth will activate healing receptors so Esmere can work."

At her words, Esmere went over and started licking his wounds. I watched; my hands buried in his fur. Magic didn't heal the way it did in stories. I had to know what I was doing, what I needed cells to do. This is why mages who were doctors were so prized, they could dismantle a tumor cell by cell. But often the cost was so high you had to find someone willing to spend that much of an offering on you.

With each lick, the blood cleared and healthy pink flesh was revealed. While it didn't close in front of me like a time lapse of healing, it still healed. As Esmere licked along his ribs where he had huge gashes, they looked less devastating. When she moved up to his face, her tongue tracing along the slice that just missed his eye, each lick brought improvement.

"Is he suffering any internal injuries?" I kept petting him and trying to figure out how to create a magical ultrasound so I could see internal damage.

~No. He has what you would call a concussion, but no other damage than what you see indicated externally. One of his major arteries was damaged. But it is clotted and healing. He will be okay.~ Esmere spoke as she licked. I looked at the wound on his face, the blood was gone and I could see the muscle and tendon, but even as I watched it faded from bright red to a healing pink and the gash seemed smaller.

"Carelian?" I whispered

~Cori?~ I started to weep as his voice echoed in my head. ~That might have been a mistake.~

The world faded as I put my head on his body and cried in relief until the cavalry arrived.

THIRTY-TWO

Seeking information on magical offering spike while pregnant. Specifically, almost immediately after conception. Payment would be access to the journals of Merlin James Wells. Contact Corisande Munroe at cori@magicuser.com - Tomes of Magic

ORDER

We both got chewed out by the Feds, Naomi, Esmere, then Jo and Sable. Tirsane left before the cavalry arrived, but Esmere remained. It turned out that the bomber had the equivalent of a deadman's switch on his bike. So when Carelian pounced, it went off, killing the suspect and seriously injuring Carelian. He was actually remorseful for a full month as everything healed. The scar on his face was the only reminder, but even that was something I felt when I petted him, more than saw.

I started taking veterinary basics classes and focused on cats. Esmere promised to let me know where the differences lay between domestic cats and Cath. When I asked how she knew Cath biology so well, she flicked her tail at me and murmured something about swift kills being as important as healing.

The Feds muttered, but the final report admitted it could have been a lot worse if the bomb had gone off in a more populated area. My little plane stunt received too much attention and more than one newspaper had a "Super Merlin" caption, but that disappeared quickly enough.

The calls from reporters were insane. I finally just changed my number, told the important people in my life, and Naomi, the new number and forgot about it. Charles updated the routing and the sheer volume of phone calls stopped.

I'd put an ad up on the bulletin board for the House of Emrys, offering access to James' Journals in payment for information on the reduction of magic during pregnancy, though I didn't mention his research. That got me lots of hits, but none of them had any information about pregnancy magic issues. Though the amount of offers to help me research it "personally" creeped me out.

Jumping out of the plane had used up a chunk of hair. For the first time in a very long time, mine only hit past my shoulder blades, and it made me nervous. If something bad happened, I wanted to be able to call on my magic, so this cost issue was driving me crazy. As were my clothes. All of them were too tight. My bras didn't fit, I'd started to live in leggings, and I kept falling into fits of giggles or tears with no warning. It annoyed me. How did women deal with this all the time?

Tirsane had reminded me the day before she'd be here tonight, as she had found a resource. I couldn't help but get excited at that and it made Friday fly by.

"I'm home," I called out as Carelian pulled me into the house from a planar rip. Only silence greeted me. I must have beaten Jo and Sable home. They had to drive in from Albany, and there were days when traffic was a bit more than normal. Okay, most days, but we were still trying to be positive about the commute. Otherwise Carelian might get begged to do more transport duty.

I changed into leggings and a t-shirt, then headed downstairs. The scent of chili told me Jo had set up our dinner before she left. We'd never serve guests her chili. It might melt their tongues. I'd managed to grab a glass of water with a squirt of lemon juice when Esmere pinged me.

~Yes?~ I sent the words back while I looked for something that wouldn't ruin my appetite.

~We will be there in fifteen minutes.~ Something about her voice sounded odd.

~Okay.~ I sent back and stared at the fridge. We had nothing in there to serve guests. A bit frantic, I pulled out my phone. *Jo, Tirsane, Esmere and whomever will be here in 15. I can't see anything in the fridge. There is stuff in the freezer but it'll take too long to thaw.*

I stared at my phone willing a miracle to happen.

At store now. Getting trays. Be there in about 20. Serve drinks. Porch. <3

Relief made my knees sag. *Thanks, see you soon.* I added a hug emoji to the end of that.

It didn't take long to get the electric kettle out, with tea, coffee, chocolate, and bottles of lemonade on the buffet we had put in the sunroom just for this reason. I set both glasses and bowls out. You never knew the type of mouth that a being would have. I double checked there were chairs and two ottomans to support almost anyone. Dragons would have to stay in the snow. While there was an inch of snow in the back yard as it was early January, Hamiada had created a fireplace in the sunroom and we had replaced the screens with glass windows that could slide down. This made the room much warmer than it would have been, as long as I remembered to start the fire. A chill encouraged me to get it going.

Five minutes later, I had it going, but it would take a bit longer to heat everything up.

"Hamiada?" I called out as I skipped my snack, trying to wait until Jo got here.

"Yes?" she said behind my back. I twisted in the chair to look at her. "I wanted to let you know that Tirsane, Esmere, and a guest are coming, just so you know they are here."

Hamiada nodded. Esmere and she had reached a stalemate and agreed to mutually ignore each other. There was something about the predator and the plant that just didn't get along, though neither of them had been able to explain it any more than "incompatible existences."

"Enjoy. I have leafing to do." She was gone with those words, which left me more confused than enlightened.

Pushing it to the side, I settled down in the seat closest to the fireplace, watching the crackling and sipping my water while I waited. Carelian traipsed in a minute later and threw himself in front of the fire.

~Best addition ever.~

"And here I thought your cat door was."

~No. This is best. Heat on a cold day. Family, my queans, food. How could anything be better?~

I smiled and rubbed my toes over his back. This was pretty good. Even if Tirsane still awed me, I'd kind of missed her.

A pain stabbed through my head then faded. I looked up to see figures moving on the back lawn, well a snowy expanse of yard. I got up to open the door to the back as Esmere bounded on through, trailed by Tirsane and a woman I didn't recognize. The fact that it was a human surprised me greatly.

~Snow is evil. Why do you allow such a thing to fall?~ Esmere snarled as she shook clumps of snow off her paws. ~Next time I will arrive in the house. Family doesn't need to suffer so.~

My brows drew together as I watched Tirsane come through the snow. I moved over to the buffet and grabbed the cinnamon tea I already knew she enjoyed. By the time I had filled the mug with boiling water, Tirsane and her companion were coming up the steps.

Gorgons did not tolerate snow well. Tirsane had a blue tinge and her snakes were coiled tight. She slithered in and headed directly to the fireplace, her lower body all but curling around it. "Snow is evil. Why do you tolerate it?" She managed to hiss the words as she shivered, her breasts bare and blue with the cold.

I tried not to laugh at the almost identical comments from Esmere and Tirsane. "Humans tend to wear more clothes than you do. Here." I handed her the hot mug. "Do you want a sweater?"

She cupped the mug in both hands, lowering her face to breathe in the steam. "Normally I would refuse. It amuses me to watch the human discomfort with nudity. But today I think I will say yes for my own comfort."

I smothered a smile and headed out of the sunroom, and up the stairs. A minute later I was back with a fleece, zip up hoodie in dark green. "Try this." I took the tea while she slipped it on and the snakes started to uncoil as she zipped it up, rubbing her hands along the fleece.

"This is most comfortable. Thank you." She took back the tea, and I shifted my attention to the other person. I'd seen her walking in, but I'd been so worried about Tirsane and the cold that I hadn't noted more than female, gorgeous, strong. Now I actually looked at her and introduced myself.

"Hi, I'm Cori." She had long honey blond hair in a French braid that went to the middle of her back, icy blue eyes that were as cold as the snow outside, and a short sword at her hip. The clothes weren't human normal, at least nothing outside the movies. But at the same time the leather pants, tunic, and light mail vest wouldn't have gotten too many double takes. At WyrmCon it would have gotten compliments.

"Yes. I am aware." Her voice was smooth and deep, and she looked tight with tension.

I slid a sideways glance over to Tirsane, who looked adorable with the green hoodie on. Her snakes had pulled the hood up and were hiding in it, avoiding sticking their heads out, even though the sunroom was a comfortable temperature, at least for me.

"Frej, be nice. I brought you here to help. She has questions and while rare, Valkyries do bear children and you have millennia of records to refer to."

The woman, Valkyrie, sighed, raising her eyes to the heavens. "What I do for Odin and his favors."

"Freya actually," Tirsane said mildly, but I heard the rebuke.

The woman sighed and looked at me. "Frej Anjadatter, holder of Kvel, I accept your hospitality." She cast a side glare at Tirsane, who ignored her.

I forced a smile. "May I get you some tea?" I offered in an attempt to distract. The last thing I needed was a fight to start inside Hamiada. She would not be impressed if the house, her body, was damaged.

Frej sniffed. "Do you not have mead? Beer?"

"Sure. One second." Most of the denizens I had met so far had little use for alcohol, but we had some. I returned from the kitchen with a bottle of hard cider and two different micro brews. I had no doubt that Jo's Coronas would be looked on as water. "Here you go, this is a fermented apple drink, and this is made from grains and hops."

I offered her all three. She considered the options for a moment. "Apple first," Freja said, though the words came out wary. I popped off the top and handed it to her.

She took a cautious sip, then nodded. "It will do, though I would be interested in trying the others."

"Sure. My partners will be here shortly. Sable is the one who can tell you about the beers and argue their worth. I normally drink the ciders." I stood there trying to figure out what to do next as I had no idea what the social etiquette was.

"Cori, tell Freja about your issue and see if she has any insight." Tirsane hadn't moved from in front of the fireplace, but she had quit shivering.

I took my seat, picking up my tea. "I'm what they call a double merlin," I said, waving Freja to sit down. She took the chair opposite me as Esmere started grooming Carelian, much to his delight. "It means I have access to multiple classes of magic." I touched my temple and the tattoo that hung there, my brand and badge. "Until recently, right after I got pregnant as a matter of fact, I had no issue doing large amounts of magic easily. With my familiar helping I could do even more." I nodded toward Carelian at this, who thumped his tail, Esmere working on his forehead.

"And now?" Frej prompted, swigging down more cider, though I sensed no concern from her. If I had to put a name to her tone, it would be annoyance and apathy.

"Now even doing something simple like making a drink cold takes triple the amount of offering it once did. And I don't know why." I paused for a moment, then blurted. "Plus, Carelian is really tired lately, even for a Cath. I came home yesterday and talked to Jo, Sable, and Hamiada in the entryway and he didn't hear us." That was bugging me more than my magic. I'd been living with my magic being wonky for more than three months. I'd figure it out. But Carelian was everything and if he was sick I didn't know what I would do.

~He what?~ Esmere had jerked her head up to stare first at me, then at Carelian. ~Why was I not notified of this? That is not normal behavior. Cath are always aware of what is going on around them unless sick.~

"We just realized it yesterday. That is why he asked you to attend today. I don't know what is going on with everything. I'm worried about him, and-" I broke off as Jo yelled through the house.

"We're here. And we have food."

Everyone perked up and turned to the entrance into the rest of the house, and I swear they all tracked the footsteps that were bringing the promised food. It seemed to take forever, surrounded as I was with a room full of predators. Sable pushed open the door, holding a tray, with Jo behind her with another tray.

"Behold, we arrive bearing food. Even some treats for the

picky Cath," Sable teased, setting a tray of sashimi, minus the rice, down. Jo followed it with a tray of cheese, antipasto, and salami.

"Tirsane, good to see you again." Jo cast a curious glance at the Valkyrie, who had already stood and was inspecting the trays.

"That is Frej. She's a Valkyrie," I said. I didn't whisper, but I didn't shout either.

"Really?" Sable's eyes widened. "I thought they had wings."

"We do. But they are awkward in buildings. I only display them when on a battlefield or when they will up my standing. Here, what I am is enough." The confidence in her voice made me giggle. Esmere snapped her tail at the fireplace in annoyance, but that didn't stop her from filling a plate with raw, glistening fish.

I wrinkled my nose at all of it and grabbed a cracker. Stupid nausea. If anything, I wanted more ginger tea or maybe a ginger ale and bread.

Tirsane had grabbed her own plate of munchies and was alternating feeding the snakes tidbits of fish and herself the salami. "So what were you about to finish saying, Cori?"

I had to think for a minute. There was so much going on lately. "Oh. Yeah. I'm worried about Carelian and the babies. I don't want to endanger them."

Both Tirsane and Esmere cast oddly proprietary glances toward my stomach, the baby bump still mostly invisible. I narrowed my eyes at them. "These are our babies. No poaching."

Jo and Sable had just settled down onto the couch when Frej snorted after swallowing a piece of sashimi.

We looked at her and she shook her head, contempt written on her face. "No wonder you are having issues. Are all human mages this stupid?"

CHAPTER

THIRTY-THREE

Pregnancy Facts: Identical twins will have different finger-prints. Remember to make sure their fingerprints are included on the birth certificate in this case. As a new mother you should prepare yourself for the twins to develop their own language and it will belong only to them. IVF is the most common way for twins to form, but if a mother is a twin the odds are they will have a pregnancy with a twin. ~ The Pregnant Mage

SPIRIT

The mood in the room shattered. My outrage at her comment reflected on Jo's and Sable's faces as we stared at Frej.

It took me a moment to get my shock under control, but all the time I'd been spending reading James' diaries came in helpful. While he had not met Valkyries, or at least I hadn't reached a book where he talked about them, he had written a lot about Norse mythology and the traditions of the Vikings, which had talked about their gods and other beings.

"We may be ignorant, but we are not rude enough to insult hospitality," I responded tightly, glaring at her.

A flush rushed up her neck to her cheekbones and for a second I thought she might rise and attack with her sword. I heard a soft hiss, though I didn't turn to look to see who had hissed. With resistance she dipped her head.

"You are correct. I am abusing your hospitality." She glared at the cider she had all but finished and sighed. "Very well." Frej focused her eyes on me. "While we do not have children often, we do have them. The use of magic is not normally affected by pregnancy, but the linking of your familiar being exhausted should have been a clue. Are you not yourself a twin?"

I frowned and nodded. "Yes, so?"

~Chaos spit,~ Esmere swore. Tirsane for her part flushed green, the snakes suddenly silent, hiding in the hood.

I exchanged a frantic look with Jo and Sable. "What? What's wrong?" I asked, looking at them. A cold feeling wrapped around my stomach.

The three denizens just exchanged looks that I couldn't read. Then Frej sighed and rose, placing more food on her plate. "I'll explain, but remember, I am the messenger, not the message."

My eyes narrowed, and I clenched my fingers around the mug, nausea burning the back of my throat. Carelian rose and put his head on my knee, tail lashing. The room had the same tense quiet

I could feel in the air before a lightning strike. The question was, where or who would it hit?

Frej settled down into the chair and popped off the lid of the beer I'd given her. The jittery angst from Jo felt like a pot about to bubble over, but I waited. Frej already had issues being here, and the odds were her cost to come here was higher than I wanted to think about, but she was here and I needed answers.

"Magic and babies are an odd pair," she said finally, and the tension in the room dropped. "Remember what I am telling you is from our knowledge of pregnancies among Valkyries, but as human women can become them, I have no reason to suspect the logic is any different."

I shot a warning glare at Jo because I knew she wanted to ask how they got pregnant. She caught my "I will kill you look" and clamped her mouth shut.

"Magic split between two people isn't as noticeable, and most Valkyries while pregnant don't use magic much. Our day-to-day lives aren't as magic heavy as some. But when there are twins," she paused and took a bite. I narrowed my eyes at her and she smirked.

The wench was enjoying this. I forced myself to relax. As much as I wanted to know the answer, waiting a few minutes wouldn't make any difference. Instead, I focused on my drink and watched her.

"Frej, my patience is waning," Tirsane said mildly. The Valkyrie had enough sense to flinch and set the plate down on her lap, dropping her smirk.

"Let me rephrase. The magic of any one person is enough to surround and nurture the child and allow the woman to do magic. Most mages do not use magic to the extent you do. Nor are they trying to change the world. When you are pregnant your magic surrounds and seeps into the child, much like how nutrients do, protecting, changing, nurturing them. But when the woman carries twins, magic is much more interested in the pair growing inside you. It resists being pulled away from the sparkling new lives and demands a higher price for having to leave its new toy. You should have noticed little things that make your life easier are cheaper than big things that have nothing to do with you."

I shrugged. It wasn't anything I'd thought about much as I had rarely done the cooling things off or heating them up and even when I did the cost was still low enough that while it was much greater, it wasn't obvious.

"What does all that mean? And what does it have to do with Carelian?" Sable asked. She and Jo were on a love seat together and the twin frowns they wore worried me. I wanted to go soothe their brows and tell them it would all be fine. But Frej had me worried.

She sighed, as if this should all be obvious. "Do you not read your own history? Remus and Romulus, Apollo and Artemis, Castor and Pollux, Heracles and Iphicles, Freyr and Freyja, Hahgwehdiyu and Hahgwehdaetgah, Nut and Geb, Osiris and Isis, Jukihú and Juracán, Izanagi and Izanami, Inanna and Utu. Twins are always mystical in nature, but when born of a mage, the magic is magnified. Why do you think the lives of Osiris and Isis were so tragic? They were twins of a twin."

"If I had known you were a twin, I would have advised against the pregnancy or at least advised to only have one ," Tirsane murmured. "I was never told."

I shrugged. "I don't go around telling people about Stevie. But I thought you knew I had two brothers?" I racked my brain, but I couldn't remember if I had ever mentioned my twin. "Why is it important? We knew the odds of having twins were much higher as they put three embryos in me. They aren't my biological children."

Frej opened her mouth, but Esmere's tail slapped her hand hard enough to leave a welt, and the Valkyrie hissed at the Cath.

~Shush. I have much to say first.~ Esmere turned to look at me. ~Cath are not human and we have litters not twins. Gorgons lay eggs. Twin stories are old stories for us but almost never have any bearing on our lives.~

"Truth. There are very rarely two children in one egg. The only ones I know of never developed. So we do not think in siblings, but in litters or clutches and hatchlings. And when I asked around, most were like us. Litters, hatches, clutches, spawn, not babies or twins. We thought there was something going wrong with your magic and it concerned me as Magic has favored you so greatly. I did not think of legends." Her snakes peeked out of the hoodie below her chin and I could have sworn they looked sad.

~And while I think Carelian might have mentioned your brother, Stefanos I believe, he just said brother, not twin. So I never thought about his death. Humans die so easily as younglings, I just assumed...~ Her mental voice trailed off, and she attacked her tail with her tongue grooming hard and fierce.

"Back up. I think I'm missing something. Are the babies in danger?" My voice was calm, but I'd put my tea down, too worried I was going to throw things if I didn't.

"No." Frej spoke in clear tones. "You should have a normal if low magic pregnancy."

I felt my insides untwist a bit at that. "Is Carelian okay? Why is he so tired of late?"

~My son is an over-achiever,~ Esmere said, her tail now wrapped around her. ~He chose you, and accepted two more queans as alternate focuses. Now he is trying to boost the magical focus of three queans, as well as the babies in your womb. Even as strong as he is, he is supporting five mages. That is a bit much, especially when two of them aren't even active yet.~

"What?" The word burst out of Jo and Sable.

I laid my hands across the baby bump and stared at the Valkyrie. "But we don't emerge until after puberty."

"Normally that is correct for humanoids. But twins tend to attract magic. They won't emerge until they are older, but they are very interesting to Magic right now. Think untapped potential."

"But what does that mean?" A part of me wondered if I'd have to fight the entire world for these babies, and the realization that I would be willing to do that shook me to the core. They were ours. I would do anything to keep them safe.

Carelian rumbled a purr, his head still on my knee. ~Fear not. The kits will be okay.~ I concentrated on petting him as a calming mantra as I looked at the doom speaker.

Freja looked frustrated, as if trying to explain something she knew because everyone knew it. "Even if they are not your children, it is your magic, twin magic, that surrounds and cradles them. It means that your twins will be very powerful magically, and should they survive, they will most likely be full users of magic."

Jo, Sable, and I all burst out in words: "Survive? Full Users?" Even I wasn't sure what I said or they said as the words and fear seemed to burst out of me.

Frej looked confused as she stared at us. "Mages are decided at birth, magic marks them. While she may not call them until adulthood, twin mages are different. They are already exposed to magic by virtue of being twins. Living to adulthood is the challenge."

I nodded a bit. My doctoral research had indicated that mages had a different genetic marker after emergence. What Frej said implied Magic knew but it wasn't anything we could see. But the difference of living or dying made zero sense.

"What do you mean?" I asked. Jo and Sable had quit cuddling and were on the edge of the loveseat leaning forward, their bodies trembling with the same tension as me.

"Do you not have records of mages? There are very few twins where both are loved by magic." She broke off and looked at me strangely.

Before I could follow up on that, Jo spoke. "So what does that mean for the babies? Are we going to lose one?"

Freja frowned, looking between us all. The sinking feeling in my stomach intensified and the desire to throw up burned at the back of my mouth. I fought the temptation to curl into a ball to protect myself and them.

"No. There is no reason to believe they won't be born healthy. That isn't an issue, as far as I am aware."

There was a collective sigh of relief from the three humans, but my relief was short lived as I noted Esmere and Tirsane were still tense.

"Then what does should they survive mean?"

Frej looked at the two denizens. "Do they truly not know?"

"Why would they?" asked Tirsane. "It isn't in their stories and if no one lives to talk about it, they would never link the two things. Twins are not that common and twin mages even less so, I believe." She shrugged. "Even I had forgotten about the risks. I do not know of any human that has ever known this."

"There is a very good chance I might lose my patience and attack both of you if you don't explain what you are talking about RIGHT NOW!" The last words came out in a snarl and I realized I was standing, shaking, with my fists clenched. Carelian stood near my right side, tail bristled and still.

Some of the arrogance had bled out of Freja and now she just looked sad and tense. If we had been in a coffee shop, I would have expected her to be about to throw coffee or something at me.

"I did not realize you were looking for explanations. Normally, when I am called, it is to kill the less desired child. I thought you already knew all of this since you were half of a twin."

"What?" The word burst from my mouth as I placed my hands protectively over my belly. "And how did you know that?"

She sighed, shrinking back into the chair. "Because the wounds left over from the fight where you defeated your twin screams out to my magic."

CHAPTER

THIRTY-FOUR

Research Assistance Requested: Tracking down dragon shells from those with dragon or lizard familiars. Most reptile familiars are found as eggs and hatch, imprinting to the mage they are a familiar for. I am doing a study on the chemical and magical properties of eggs from this offshoot and would like various samples to experiment on. ~ Tomes of Wonder

---

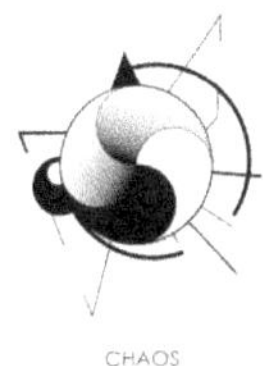

A very small part of me wondered about how her magic could see wounds from so long ago. But most of me got caught on her words. Everything around me went silent. The pain from that long ago day had become worn and

familiar. Something that I would live with, but nothing that slammed into me daily anymore.

It now burst to life in sharp, raw spikes that shredded my heart.

"I what?" The words were so soft they didn't qualify as a whisper, but they rang with power and need.

Freja gave me a flat look. "You must know this. You did defeat him and he is dead. Is he not?"

Pain hammered at me, and I turned and walked outside into the snow. The reminder that the house was Hamiada and Hamiada was the house kept everything I felt wrapped up tight inside me.

There were noises behind me, but I couldn't be bothered to interpret them. I stopped out in the backyard, the snow falling pristine around me, and I let my control go. Rage, sorrow, grief, shock, all of them, none of them swirled in me. I didn't have names for the feelings that lanced up and through me. All I could do was remember. I lost myself in the memories as I lost my hold on sanity.

Red burned my nose as I screamed blue light. Ash coated my mouth with bitter need and regret. Time stopped and skipped as the elements danced around me, known by their heat and the offerings they took with greedy joy. Earth and sound mixed as I pulled against gravity, wanting to bury myself, wanting to fly into space. I wanted to sunder the universe and trade my life for his. But all I could do was express my guilt through every pore in my body.

I sweated and shivered as fire and air wrapped me in their embrace, water streamed down my face. I gulped in mouthfuls of air trying to breathe, wanting to drown.

Sparks burst from my fingers and seared the ground as my offering became more strident, begging magic to undo what I had done. But they weren't accepted.

I'd killed Stevie. The guilt lashed at me. The vague memories of pulling on something resurfaced. My heart contracted as the knowledge I'd pulled his life into me registered. I needed to die. I should have died. It was all my fault.

My parents were right to hate me.

I lashed out, needing to not be. To not exist. Magic crackled around me in time to my guilt. My sightless eyes only saw his face, accusing me, blaming me for what I had, in fact, done.

~Cori. You need to stop.~

Yes, I needed to stop. Stop existing. It was all my fault. The sound wouldn't quit. My throat ached, and the sound cracked. My screaming cracked. The pain didn't become less, it just changed, warping, stabbing, reminding me I lived while he hadn't.

~Cori. Stop.~

The words circled me over and over again, worming their way into my mind. I needed to stop everything. I tried to side-step to flee into the darkness, but something prevented me. Stabbing pain sliced through my head and I welcomed it. I should hurt. I needed to pay for what I'd done. I'd murdered my brother. There was a name for that, for killing your family. Wasn't there?

~Cori. Stop.~

Warm, silky fur pressed against my skin. Pinpoints of pain sank into my being at my thighs. Cold points dug into my rear and thighs.

~Cori.~ A familiar head butted under my hand and I reflexively scratched. ~You're back.~

I blinked and looked down. I was naked, sitting on the ground. A ring of yard visible around me. About ten feet away the snow started back up. Standing there, just outside the ring of bare ground, were Jo and Sable. They looked at me, tears brimming in their eyes, hands over their mouths. I shied away, fearing their revulsion and curled in tighter.

~Cori,~ Carelian's voice sank into my mind and heart, reassuring, loving me. I started as Jo and Sable grabbed me, wrapping me in their arms, bodies pressed tight against mine.

"Cori, it was not your fault." Jo's voice. She always knew how I felt. Knew the guilt and the question I had never been able to answer.

"I killed him. By definition, it is my fault." My voice came out hoarse and my throat burned as I spoke.

"No. You were protecting yourself. You didn't know." Sable kissed my temple.

"You should hate me. Why don't you hate me?" The words came out in a whimper and I wanted to cry and scream, but my energy had fled.

"I will never hate you. I will love you until the stars die and we join again in the next life. Cori, you are my best friend, my soul, and the person I can't imagine not having in my life." Jo's words were quiet, but they rang in my heart.

Sable ran her fingers through my hair. "You are my soul sister and I love you. You make our life better and you did nothing to be guilty of."

We sat there, their arms around me, Carelian all but curled up in my lap, his purrs vibrating through my body. We sat like that as my breathing slowed and reality started to register.

"Why am I naked?" It had taken a while for me to realize that, but the cold wet ground under my butt, and Carelian's fur against my belly reinforced it.

~You burned away your clothes when you snapped.~ Esmere didn't sound snide, simply worried. ~That was a terrifying display of uncontrolled magic. Are you better now?~

Cold wriggled up my spine as I realized that if anyone from law enforcement had witnessed that, putting a bullet in my head would have been a valid response.

"I don't know that I am better, but I am aware of things now." I shivered. "Like the fact that I am freezing and would like some clothes."

Jo and Sable pulled away and pulled me up, giving me a chance to see what I'd done. I swallowed hard as I looked around. The area where I'd been sitting didn't just have the snow melted, it looked like something had impacted here, and the ground had been melted in a circle, a ring of glistening stones jabbing up at the edge. Furthest from the house a spring bubbled away at the edge of the circle I'd created, where previously there had been nothing but grass. My hand reached up to brush my hair that was only just past my shoulders where before it had grown out to brush my shoulder blades. As I turned towards the house I saw Tirsane, Esmere, Frej, and Hamiada all staring at me from the edge of the circle of snow.

Esmere stood there tail lashing, but her ears were perked forward. ~You seem fine. I am getting out of this horrible white stuff.~ She spun and in a few leaps stood on the steps to the sun room.

Hamiada floated to one side of the others, a tiny tendril of green pushing past her toe through the snow. "You are more powerful than I realized. Thank you for not damaging my body. The yard has possibilities. If I can't be a tree, being the house of a scary Lord is a good substitute." She spun, a whirl of green and brown, then was gone, the green tendril still poking up through the snow.

My eyes locked with Frej, who stood legs shoulder width apart, wings flaring out, and a sword in her hand. The expression on her face prevented me from examining her wings. It was dark and her eyes had gone to a midnight blue where previously they had been icy pale.

I gritted my teeth, meeting her eyes. There was enough self-doubt and guilt in my soul that I didn't need anyone else judging me. Especially not this arrogant Valkyrie. I straightened, letting my nakedness be inconsequential.

"What?" The word snapped out harder than I expected. Jo and Sable tensed next to me.

Freja tilted her head, her eyes still unmoving. "I misjudged you. You have the soul of a healer, not a warrior. You grieve too hard for what is done, yet I would not refuse you at my back."

"I will not let these children die," I warned, my hand possessively over my belly. There were matching growls from Jo, Sable, and Carelian. My vanguard, my family.

"I would not expect that. It is easy enough to prevent, if you know it is possible. Your world needs to let the little truths spread further." She sounded dismissive, but the sword disappeared. "I should go. I believe my favor has been fulfilled."

"Wait. How do we prevent it?" Jo said the words that wouldn't come out of my mouth. I wanted to ask, beg, scream, and yet I didn't want to know. What if the answer was too horrible to contemplate?

Freja shrugged. "When it comes time for their emergence, separate them. A few thousand miles and magic won't try to choose one or the other. Or you can put them on different planes, that would work too. Twins only self-destruct when magic wants the most powerful and creates a battle between them. Don't let it start a competition." She said all this with the same attitude I'd have trying to explain how you watched a movie on a streaming service as if it was self-evident.

"Wait, we don't need to let them kill each other?" Sable sounded like her knees might buckle and I didn't blame her. I felt the same.

"Of course not. Magic is like a Valkyrie with multiple heroes—she wants them all. But if she can only see one hero at a time, it doesn't require any choice. She just takes or emerges the one who is there. You humans overcomplicate things." Frej flared her wings and my eyes locked on them for a moment. Part of me had expected brilliant white, but they were more accurate to what she was, a collector of souls. The arches of her wings were a dark smokey gray, the same gray that made you feel like you were in someplace elegant and rich, but in ombre style they went lighter, then to an oddly dusky pink and continued until they were blood red at the ends of her feathers. They actually looked like they had been dipped in blood to the point I almost expected them to drip drops of red as she opened and closed them.

"Oh," I muttered, yanking my gaze away from her wings. "Like a boarding school?" My insides rebelled at that, but to save the children, I would.

"If you desire. Boarding school is possible. My people tend to do fostering as a means to send them away from each other. The cat should be able to tell you when they are close, but it will always be after the girls first moon cycle with twins. It is not complicated. If there is nothing else, I have my own business to attend to." She turned, then paused and looked back at me. "I thank you for your hospitality and offer up my home to you should you ever need it." It didn't sound sincere, yet that wasn't a typical offer.

"I thank thee," I managed.

Her head jerked down in a nod and she beat her wings, lifting into the sky, then she was gone. I was starting to understand why James Wells had owned this entire street if this was going to happen with any regularity.

I wanted to curl up in a ball and cry or not exist, but Tirsane slid forward, her hoodie still on, though her lips looked a bit bluer than healthy.

With an effort I swallowed and opened my mouth. "I..." I started but didn't know how to continue, unsure of what I needed to say or how to say it.

"No words are necessary. I would not expect anything else in your situation." Her eyes were soft on mine and I resisted the urge to lean in for a hug.

"Finding out I killed my best friend, my brother?" I couldn't hide my bitterness, my guilt.

"Finding out the truth hurt more than most would guess. But blaming yourself is counterproductive and in the end will hurt you and the babies you care for, more than help."

Tirsane sounded remarkably sanguine about all of this, and I didn't know if that was a good or a bad thing.

"I just...," I didn't know what to say. The first round of agony was over, but I had not begun to come to terms with this new truth, not to mention I didn't know what it would mean.

She smiled. "I believe I will keep this hoodie. It is most pleasant, and the girls love it." Several heads stuck out of the hoodie, hissing in agreement.

"Enjoy," I said, even as I tried to fake a smile. But all I wanted was to go cry some more and adjust.

"There is one more thing. I believe these are for the children. They fell out when you ripped open paths to the realms." Her words had me jerking my head up, and I realized there were rips there. The spikes of pain I had felt but hadn't cared about. With a sigh, I closed the rips, noting they opened to Order and Chaos. I looked back down to see Tirsane holding out two round objects.

"What?" Again I sounded like an idiot, but my mind couldn't parse what she held. They were about the size of mangos and round, and they couldn't possibly be what my mind thought they could be.

"Dragon eggs, or at least a type of dragon. I suspect they are familiars for the babies," Tirsane said with a smile.

She didn't have to sound so blasted smug.

THIRTY-FIVE

Placental eating is a tradition in many countries, but in most civilized areas it has faded into something very few do. There have been no significant studies that there is any magical boost in eating it nor any significant harm. For the most part, hospitals dispose of it as biowaste and move on. ~ The Pregnant Mage

---

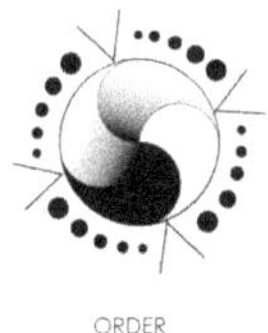

ORDER

J o and Sable got me inside and worked with Hamiada to create a safe place for the eggs. I'd contact Zmaug in a while. But frankly, if the eggs had survived my temper tantrum, they would be fine for a few days. I ran a bath and curled up in my bathtub, longing for a large glass of something very hard, instead I had hot tea and tears. All of this felt like too much.

I sat there twisting and turning over the new knowledge while I sipped the ginger lemon tea and battled nausea. It might have been morning sickness, or it might have been guilt. It didn't matter.

~You are… still my quean.~ Carelian laid his head on the tub and gazed at me, emerald eyes glowing. The cut in his fur haunted me. I'd almost failed him. What if I failed them too?

"You think I'm silly or stupid." I stared at my stomach and the slight swelling there.

~No. I think you are a powerful and caring quean. If you were silly, you'd not care so much about this.~

"It makes me a murderer," I murmured as I sank back, eyes locked on the ceiling.

~No more than I would be if I had killed Mi'Kal when he attacked me. You defended yourself. All beings have that right.~

"But he's dead."

~Yes. You aren't. Even Tirsane or Esmere can not bring him back.~ I started to cry again, but this time it was simply tears. ~You lived, Cori. There is nothing wrong with that. We have so much to celebrate. You carry life in you. If that isn't magic, then nothing is. Grieve, but don't let your grief still the life that is around you.~

He padded away and left me thinking in the bathtub. I didn't get out until the water was almost cold. I knew Jo and Sable wanted to talk to me, but I didn't have the energy. I crawled into bed and fell asleep, the weight pulling me down into dreams.

I couldn't remember my dreams, but the pain I held tight inside me had changed. Instead of being dark, heavy, and smooth, the silent burden of all these years, it was bright, jagged, and all but vibrated. The mystery as to what had happened to Stevie had been unveiled, and it altered my grief, my anger, my guilt. But it also meant it was done. I couldn't change anything and if I went insane and suicidal, it would kill the lives I carried inside me, leave Jo and Sable bereft, and I couldn't imagine what that would do to Carelian.

I emerged from my bedroom the next morning, sad and guilty, but inside the pain had morphed. There were things I could do, things to make sure no one else ever lived with this. And first and foremost would be informing the societies.

"Cori," Jo blurted as I walked into the kitchen. Before I could say anything, she'd yanked the pan off the stove and had me pulled into her arms. Amazingly, the tears didn't come, but I sank into her embrace and hugged her tight. "Are you okay?"

"Nope. But I might get there." She let me go and pulled back to look at me. I offered a wan smile, and she kissed my forehead.

"So, what do you want to do?" Jo bit her lip as she searched my face, her brows drawn together.

I shrugged. "Live." She arched a brow and Sable came in, taking a seat at the counter and watching us, her face hidden by her coffee cup.

"I'm very glad about that. Is there anything else you need to do? Do you want to tell your parents?"

I flinched at that thought. "No. They've always blamed me. Now I know it was accurate. I probably should tell Laurel." That thought hurt. Laurel Amosen was the police chief back in Rockway, Georgia. She'd found us both that day. Could they try me for this? Did it even count as murder?

"Okay. I'd like to tell *Mami*, though." Jo's voice was soft, hesitant almost. But I couldn't blame her. Her parents needed to know that I really was a monster.

"Of course." I hid my fear. "I think I'm going to get some tea and go think. We need to make sure these children never need to be faced with this choice." I rubbed my stomach gently, already wondering how we could protect them until they emerged.

"Agreed. We've been talking about it. I'd like to talk to Tirsane again, but we have some ideas," Sable said, setting down the defensive shield of her cup.

"Good," I said with a smile. I took a cup of tea, coffee didn't even smell good right now, and headed to look at the babies' room.

Walking into the nursery, the warmth and the diffused light relieved some of the stress. The place screamed magic, but it also all but glowed with love. It took me a minute to see it, but there in the corner of the room was a large covered basin about three feet off the ground. As I approached it, I noted the warmth radiating off of it. Peering down, I touched the lip, and the lid slid back like a roll-top desk.

Nestled in what looked like fine black sand or salt were two eggs. Yesterday I'd barely looked at them, still reeling from the revelations. Today I took the chance to examine them. They were about the size of large mangos, but more spherical in shape. Their color was a deep metallic brown that faded to almost gold on either side. They sat in the sand and I didn't see any cracks or other distinguishing marks.

"They are neat. I've never seen dragon eggs up close." I bit back the scream that wanted to jump out of me at Hamiada's voice.

"They are dragon eggs?" I thought Tirsane had said that, but then everything past Frej telling me I'd killed my brother had turned into a blur of pain and magic. My hair barely touching my shoulders was the biggest proof I had of the magic I'd done last night. Of magic fighting my attempts to do magic or damage while I was going insane.

"Yes, though I have no idea what type." She peered over my shoulder. "But all of them like heat and sand. That should keep them safe until they hatch."

"We need to return them," I said, a touch of sorrow in my voice.

"Give them back? But I just built this for them. They seem happy. Why do we need to give them back?" She seemed overly disappointed. Did the desire to have dragons as pets extend to dryads?

I smiled, just a quirk of my lips, but more than I had expected. "They might be dragons and from Zmaug's comments I know she searched for her baby. I can't take the risk that someone isn't searching for them." I let one finger drift over an egg, taking in the rough surface. Then I pinged Zmaug.

I let it ring and when she didn't respond, I let it be. I'd ping again in a bit.

"You did a beautiful job. And I like the dual cradles." I let my hands drift over the wood.

"I wish I had more ideas," she said, her leaves drooping as she patted the walls.

A mischievous thought flashed through my mind. "Would you like more magazines with articles?"

"You mean paper pictures? That would be neat."

This time, my smile almost encompassed both sides of my face. "I can do that." I pulled out my phone and subscribed to Architectural Digest, wincing a bit at the price. "It will take a week or two, but you'll have ideas, I promise."

She looked uncertain, but nodded. "Okay. Eggs?"

Before I could answer, a ping rang off my skull and I winced. I could taste Zmaug in that ping and she knocked hard. "I'll let you know."

I replied to Zmaug as I opened the door that led to my room. I didn't have the energy to have a public discussion, and part of me still wanted to slit my wrists. But it was a small part and growing smaller.

~Good morning, Zmaug. I needed to let you know that two eggs seem to have shown up here. I believe they are dragon eggs.~ I kept my thoughts clear and tight, focusing on the words. I stepped into my room then headed towards my study.

~Why would you think that?~ She sounded curious, not upset, which I took as a positive thing.

~Tirsane said they were.~

~Ah, she should know. Well then, why are you pinging me?~

I blinked and stumbled mentally. ~Umm. 'Cause we have the eggs and I remember what you said about looking for Tiantang after he disappeared. I didn't want another set of parents to have to do that.~

~Ah.~ There was a strangeness to that word that made me uncomfortable, but that seemed to be how I existed of late, in a world of strangeness, so I let it be. ~Image?~

Closing my eyes, I took the impression of the way the eggs had looked, felt, seemed to me, and I pushed it towards her. A three-dimensional image of them in the bowl.

~Nice nest. You are fine. They are not mine. But then I didn't think so as I haven't clutched in a while. That might be something I should think about.~

~But whose are they? I should let them know,~ I protested thinking of the eggs being lost.

~They are not a full dragon, probably wyvern or a quezto. They will not care. If magic sent them to you there was a reason. Just like Tiantang was sent there. I was mostly mad because I didn't realize Magic had sent him and thought him stolen. But I will let others know that you have the eggs. Most mothers are more than happy to have someone else care for the young. They are much work.~

I rubbed my temples at this. Motherhood seemed fraught with complications.

~Thank you.~

~Don't forget the council meeting. It is in three weeks.~

I cringed. I'd completely forgotten the meeting. ~When?~

~Esmere will have details. She will be your transport. See you then.~

Even groaning felt like too much effort, so I just nodded. Then remembered she couldn't see me. ~I'll follow up with her.~

I felt a snort, then the connection dropped. I sank down into the club chair in my study. My next item was to figure out which family and friends I should tell about this. I didn't know if I could deal with their rejection of me, but I needed to decide if they should be told. They deserved to know who I was, what I had done. I shied away from the thought of telling my parents though. Now, in the cold light of morning without coffee, even I didn't think Stevie's death had been my fault. The memories of that day had grown hazier, but I remembered pulling back at something tugging on me. No anger, no hate, and I definitely remembered the grief.

I curled up in the comfortable chair in the office, staring out the window. Snow started to fall, and I sat there, numb. Soon it would be a new year. Did I start it out with sorrow or joy?

~Cori, are you okay?,~ Carelian said in my head. He wasn't in the study so I figure he must be with Jo and Sable. Probably in the kitchen sneaking bacon. The falling snow had gotten heavier while I sat and stared. I should get up and get more hot tea, but that involved moving.

"I'm alive," I murmured, believing he would hear me. Dealing with other people just sounded like too much effort. Guilt still wracked me and I had no idea what to do. There were two eggs in my nursery, two babies in my womb, and a past I couldn't change.

The next thing I was aware of was Marisol sitting down on the ottoman in front of me. She cupped my cheek, a grave look on her face.

"Killing by accident when you tried to save your own life isn't anything to punish yourself for, *mi hija*." Her voice was soft and full of understanding. "The desire to live is pervasive and should not be treated as reprehensible."

"You know already?" I asked, a bit shocked. Who had told her? I know we were going to, but Jo would have waited. Why was she here, and why wasn't she railing at me?

"Carelian came and got me. He said we needed to know. He told all of us, actually. Henri and Sanchez are downstairs checking in with Jo. Are you okay?" Her hand wrapped around mine and I focused on it, her dark skin making mine seem even more washed out and sad.

I was still trying to wrap my mind around the fact that they were here, even as I tried to answer her question. "No? Yes? I don't know." And I didn't. How long could I cry about something that some part of me had always known? There had been no malice on my part. I hadn't even realized what I was doing.

"Good." My head jerked up at that and she smiled. "You shouldn't know how you feel. This is probably both a shock and a relief. Everything is up in the air. All I can say is let yourself be. There isn't anything you can change, and you are surrounded by people who love you, who know you. And the person we know would never have killed their beloved sibling. From what Carelian said, magic forced a choice, and you fought harder. For all we know, Stevie wanted you to win more than he wanted to." Marisol shrugged. "But you are alive, you have people who love you, and" she paused to touch my stomach, " and you have two lives in here depending on you."

That made me smile, and I squeezed back. "Yes, I do. And we'll do everything possible to protect them."

A slow smile spread across her face, chasing away the shadows and pain that were reflected on my own. "I would expect nothing less from my three daughters." Marisol pulled me into a hug and I sank into it, letting her warmth and strength act as a balm for my scarred heart. "You will be a great mother, and the three of you will be the best parents ever."

"Only because of you. My parents aren't exactly the role models I want for these kids," I murmured, leaning into her warmth, her love.

"Ah Cori, they will never know what they lost when they shut down their hearts."

And I will never do that to these children. We will always be there for them.

The words formed a vow so deep and strong that I felt it vibrate inside me. We would never let them go through what I had. Ever.

"Now come on. Henri and Sanchez are down there worried about you. You are loved, Cori, though I feel you should let Laurel know. Stevie's death has eaten at her for years." She rose and pulled me with her. With Marisol's arm around my waist, I went downstairs to explain what happened and be surrounded by people who loved me, even knowing what stained my heart. Maybe I could ask Laurel to be my confessor. I needed something to balance me out.

THIRTY-SIX

The fascination with twins has been with our cultures for a very long time, but few talk about the stress having twins can put on a body. Your calorie needs skyrocket, you'll need even more vitamins, and you are more susceptible to anemia as twins will suck the iron away from you. Remember this if you try using blood as an offering for magic, make sure you can afford to lose that offering. ~The Pregnant Mage

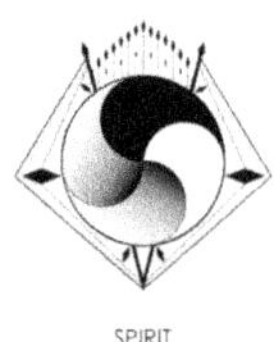

SPIRIT

Sunday I spent the day processing, but I did call Laurel and explain everything to her. "Does that change how you feel?" I asked after an extended silence on the line. The chief of police in my hometown was many things, but a laid-back woman was not one of them.

"About you?" She couldn't hear me nodding my head, but I think she knew anyhow. "Of course." My heart and breath seized up. "I'm even more in awe of your strength and I'm sure you are racked with grief and guilt right now. But it wasn't your fault. Though I do need to figure out how to write this up in the hopes it might solve a few cold cases."

That comment brought me up short. I hadn't thought of that. "I'll see what I can find as well. If it has happened before, there might be more than a few cold cases that can be resolved," I said, my voice distant as I filtered through my memories for any cases like that.

"Do that. But Cori, I'm glad you are alive. I'm just sad the price was your brother's life. Make sure your children don't need to make the same choice."

"Oh, I will. That much I can promise." The fervent tone of my voice should have convinced anyone. Laurel muttered my name with affection. "What about my brother Kris?" This I was hesitant about. Would he want to know his sister?

"What about him? That is your story to tell, not mine. My friend will contact him when he turns eighteen. Then he can decide." I looked at my phone, his birthday was very close to my due date. Maybe these kids would have an uncle? Or at least another one. I brushed it away. There wasn't anything I could do until he showed up.

"Thanks, Chief Amosen."

"Laurel, Cori. At this point, it's silly for you to still call me by my rank. Besides, I'm retiring soon. Time to go and enjoy sleeping in." Her huffing annoyance made me laugh, and we ended the call on a good note.

I spent the rest of the day with Jo and Sable checking on me, me checking on the eggs, and Carelian fretting about all of us. It meant by the time I headed to work, I was relieved to be somewhere different, somewhere I didn't need to think about the revelations of the weekend.

I walked in to find Naomi waiting for me at my cubical. "Morning," I said with an arch of my brow. My fist tightened around my mug of tea, and I knew I was going to be regretting the lack of coffee almost immediately.

"Morning Cori, Carelian. We have some people here who want to talk to you."

"Over?" The explosion had happened four weeks ago at the beginning of December and everything had already been gleaned from us. It was the one time my expensive offerings came in handy. If the "double merlin" had to spend that much to fly, it was probably out of range for any other normal mage. Mostly, I was glad it hadn't been caught on camera. That might have been more traumatic and spawned too many copycats.

"They have some questions about China and Cixi." Her flat tone and crossed arms had me looking at her funny.

"And you have issues with that?"

"You are my merlin and my department rarely gets mages at all. I wish all the other departments would quit poaching," she ground out.

I tried not to laugh. All this and she was more upset with office politics than anything. If only my life was always so banal.

The momentary humor fled as memory crushed me again. I shook it off and looked at her. "So where are they?"

"Same conference room. I swear I'm about to label it the "Munroe Conference Room" and just dedicate it to you and your complications."

I shrugged, setting my bag down but keeping my herbal tea in my hand. "If you do, remember a bed for Carelian. Up about table level would be best, so they can't ignore him." She was still chortling at the idea as I headed down to the conference room.

~That is an excellent idea, but it should be much higher, so I can lurk and decide who I will pounce.~ Carelian walked beside me, his tail bouncing in excitement.

"Are you trying to winnow out the people who annoy me by causing them heart attacks?" I could just imagine him springing on someone. They'd die of fright before his claws ever punctured their clothes.

~You will not let me hunt them, which makes this a valid option. I think you would have much more productive gatherings if this was permitted.~

I snorted at the idea of Carelian in the ceiling tiles peering down at them, licking his chops. Yes, all the meetings would finish very quickly.

Daydreams, I swear.

The door was open, so I walked in, and saw two people I'd never met before and one I did know. "Pearl. How are you? I didn't know you were here."

Working for her had irked me. Honestly, she'd been a decent boss, and we'd parted on good, if relieved, terms. The position had not been a good fit for my skills, more than anything being about her.

"Cori, it is good to see you." Pearl smiled at me and nodded her head, but neither of us made any move towards each other. We were former coworkers, not friends.

I turned my attention to the men and decided I'd rather sit. The small of my back had been hurting more lately and there was no need to try to wow them. I had the tattoos, they didn't.

I walked to the head of the table, my back to the wall and TV screen and took a seat. "So what's this all about?"

They all looked confused at my skipping the social niceties, but I was finding that between my clothes not fitting and the mood swings, I cared very little. Besides, they came to see me which meant I had the power.

"Merlin Munroe, my name is Joseph Bellwether. Ms. Chen suggested we come to see you."

I resisted sighing. "And you are? And about what?" People frustrated me. Thinking of that, we needed to see about having

Charles over. I had an idea I wanted to run by him and my partners.

Pearl hid a grin behind her hand while pretending to rub her nose.

The speaker, a man in a suit that cost way too much, with brown hair and a supercilious expression sniffed. "I am the aide-de-camp to the Ambassador to China and we are here to request your assistance."

It took a great deal of effort not to groan. Tiantang. I just knew he was behind this somehow. "And why exactly is that?"

"The Empress of China," he stumbled over that a bit, but I pretended not to notice, "is most perplexing. She isn't following any of the normal rules and has expressed interest in you multiple times. We are trying to figure out how to handle her. We knew how to deal with the former Emperor, but she is an unknown variable and that makes us nervous."

"And?" I stared at them. Did they think we were besties or something? I like the woman, sure, but I didn't really know her, though I hoped to someday.

"We are hoping to elicit your assistance in dealing with her." The word had a vaguely ominous tone that gave me the creeps.

Carelian had jerked up and was no longer laying behind me, but sitting up peering over the table. The idea of him having a high perch sounded much more comforting than it had a few minutes ago.

"And you are?" I stared at the other man. He wasn't a mage, so I assumed State Department like Pearl, but my assumptions were biting me on the ass too much.

"I am one of the liaisons with China, Reginald Jones. I believe you spoke with my cohort, Gloria?"

"Um, sure." The name didn't ring a bell but that didn't mean much. Names and faces were a constant blur lately. "But what does this have to do with me?"

"The ceremony will be an excellent time for you to communicate some of our concerns with her and maybe pass on some thoughts we would like her to entertain."

Joseph's voice was smooth, but I didn't buy it for a moment. Besides, at this rate that ceremony wouldn't take place until next decade. I still hadn't heard any further details about it.

Oh, that Gloria. Okay. Whatever. I still don't know when it's happening.

I opened my mouth to ask the question if any decisions had been made about it, when Joseph kept talking.

"Cixi is turning out to be… unusual. Her behavior does not match the patterns we have observed in previous Chinese rulers and this is cause for concern. We are concerned that her actions will upset the balance of power in the East and want to see what she is thinking."

Every warning bell I had went off, and I almost sidestepped away. But I stayed still, with my entire body tense and ready to react. But they had not lied once, which perversely made me more worried.

"So, what are you asking?" I said, my voice very calm, almost meek.

Reginald and Joseph glanced at each other.

"She is saying you are the only mage she will deal with. We would like you to occasionally talk to her for us. Encourage her to stay in the lines that are drawn or at the very least work with us," Reginald said slowly.

"Us being?"

"The United States of course. We want to keep the friendly interaction such as we had with the last Emperor. If Cixi is wise she will make sure the status quo is maintainted." Joseph sounded very sure of himself and I noted that they used her first name constantly after the first time, as if she wasn't worthy of the title.

"And if she won't?" I kept flicking my gaze between all of them. Pearl had lost her amusement and I could almost see the train wreck that was about to occur.

"Then we would like you to leverage your connection with the beings in the planes and take her magic away." Reginald stated the words the same way someone orders their coffee black.

I looked at the three of them. They were idiots, and they were trying to catch me up in their sheer stupidity.

"I never realized so clearly how much you hate mages," I murmured. "Or how little you understand."

They reacted as if slapped. Joseph drew himself up with an affronted glare on his face. "You should think carefully about this. You are a citizen of the United States and we can make your draft most unpleasant and redraft both of your partners." The sneer in his voice was unmistakable.

I smiled. It seemed to shock them, because I wasn't snarling, though the temptation was there. It was a smile of true amusement.

"You're right. You could. But ask yourself how wise it is to threaten someone who is on good terms with these 'creatures' as you call them. Besides, I think you greatly misunderstand the balance of power in my relationship with them. They are not at my beck and call. If anything, I am their pet and he is my leash." I nodded at Carelian, still smiling.

I heard a low rumble and flicked my eyes toward him, not at all surprised to see a snarl on his face displaying very sharp teeth.

"Now, are you seriously suggesting I get close to the Empress of China, who doesn't speak much English, and try to convince her and her familiar to do as you think she should? You do remember her familiar is a dragon, right? A dragon that can show up anywhere he wants at any time?"

The temptation to ask Tiantang to pop in was almost overwhelming. But I wanted to get them to think, not get them to eliminate me no matter what the consequences were. I resisted the urge to put my hand over my stomach.

"If I were you, I'd actually talk to the woman and figure out her concerns instead of trying to manage her." I glared at them, then asked one final question. "If the successor had been an Emperor, would you still be trying this manipulation?"

"Yes," Reginald lied, and I arched an eyebrow. He gritted his teeth. "Probably not. There are other ways to manage men."

This made me blink, then groan. "This is why humans are so disregarded by the realm denizens, because of stuff like this. Merlins are powerful and dangerous, yet we seem to have our teeth pulled. The Empress of China is a powerful, smart woman who would like to chart her own path. If you are smart you will see how to further her goals, not bend them to what you think they should be. I would advise you to not treat her as a 'woman'." —I was very sardonic on the word woman—"It would be unwise to think of her as anything other than what she is, the Merlin Empress of China. Discount that at your risk." When this was done, I would be sharing all of it with Tiantang. As far as I could see, I wasn't doing anything other than warning another woman they were trying to drug her drink.

They all glared at me, except for Pearl, who had her inscrutable look firmly in place.

"You will regret this, Miss Munroe," ground out Reginald while Joseph just looked weary.

I tilted my head, looking at him. There was so much I could lose here, but if I became their whipping boy the cost to all of us would be even greater.

"It is Merlin Munroe, and I probably will. But a few things to remember. Carelian is independent and intelligent. His mother is more so. And the creatures you mentioned seem to like me and my partners. They have already promised to seek revenge if I am killed. I can only imagine what would happen if my children or my partners were killed, even accidentally." All of them looked at me, and then toward my stomach, currently hidden by the table. "And just to remind you, they helped me create a place to dump a nuclear weapon, otherwise a good chunk of D.C. wouldn't exist." They would know I was pregnant soon enough, so hiding it gained me nothing, but reminding them what they owed the other realms was always a good thing.

They didn't look at each other, but I swear I could hear the thoughts burning through the air.

I sighed. It worried me when I became the voice of reason. Most of the time I was the one who wanted to rush into things, but this was crazy. The last thing I wanted to be involved with was messing with other countries. Japan and China together were more of a headache than I wanted.

"You might want to actually talk to her, not lecture like I suspect you've been doing. See why she is making the changes and what she hopes to accomplish. And I'd also suggest maybe have a woman talk to her, not a man trying to control her? From what I know, she is practical." I closed my eyes, then snapped them open. "If I can comprehend the need to kill someone before they kill others, I have no doubt that a woman in the Imperial Court has zero illusions. I suspect she just lacks knowledge. Or even worse, she might be an idealist." I didn't bother to hide the sarcasm in that comment.

Their faces didn't change, but I was done. I'd added two new tasks to my to do list. Warn Jo and Sable and get them a way to get to the glades in an emergency, and ask Hamiada what we could do to increase security around her. Something I probably should have done years ago.

I nodded at all of them and stood. They did too, striding out, but Pearl hung back. I arched a brow at her, curious.

"So, you getting excited for the big day?"

A smile slipped out, I couldn't wait to not be pregnant anymore, but not sure I was looking forward to labor. "I guess. Mostly I'm looking forward to it being over, I think."

"I understand that. It seems like so much planning and ado for something that's usually over in hours. You figure out what you are going to wear?"

I wrinkled my brow but shrugged. "Yes. It's all set up in a bag. So when it's time I won't have to think much about it." The go bag kept getting repacked by Sable and Jo as they thought of something else we had to have with us. I just let them take care of it, I'd be happy with a long t-shirt and shoes.

"Good for you. I can't plan that far ahead. Good Luck, I'll see you then." She nodded at me and strode out, leaving me standing there a bit perplexed.

Finally I shook my head dismissing itit. I suspected they had brought her to "soften me" with a woman's presence. People really needed to do their research more. I walked out, Carelian guarding my back. Which now had a target on it. Why couldn't people just let me be?

THIRTY-SEVEN

The body will redirect energy to build the placenta causing unexpected fatigue. This is why in the first few months mages may find the cost of magic a bit higher than normal, but not excessively. ~ James Wells Journal Year 25

CHAOS

The rest of the week went by quietly, mostly research on cold cases. I was preoccupied with trying to stay limber. My body felt weird and out of balance and it made me even more uncomfortable than I actually was. The council meeting was tomorrow, Saturday, and I still didn't know what to expect. But between the not-so-subtle threats from the OMO, and probably others, I'm surprised Naomi didn't send me home after the fourth time I burst into tears.

"Next time lounge on the blasted table," I muttered to Carelian as he let me step into the house. It was silent, though never cold. Hamiada ensured that. I felt some of my stress drop as her welcome wrapped around me.

"I'm home, Hamiada," I called out. She didn't always respond, and I wasn't even sure if she heard me, but it was only polite. I headed upstairs and slipped into stretchy pants and a looser bra. I would have to give in and dig into the maternity clothes Jo and Sable had purchased. At least they hadn't gotten me muumuu's. I might have killed them. I pulled on neon fuchsia leggings and a tunic top in green and black abstract. It didn't go together at all, but it was comfortable and that was all I cared about. The finishing touch was fuzzy yellow socks.

As I was home first, I headed down to pull something out of the freezer and put it into the oven, set the cooking time for two hours, then grabbed my book on pregnancy to read. I'd learned to not look online for information. The stuff I found there was enough to make me run screaming for the hills. So a nice safe book was better.

~Cori, are you ready to go?~ Esmere's voice startled me out of my doze. I'd been falling asleep more often. That part was both nice and annoying. At least my chair at work was too uncomfortable to fall asleep in.

I looked around, not seeing her. Trying to shake the sleep out of my brain, I responded. "Go where?" I focused on the window. The outside was dark and lights were coming on. From what I could tell, Jo and Sable weren't home yet.

Exasperation filled her mental voice. ~The council meeting. It starts in ten minutes.~

That cleared the last fuzziness out of my brain. "What?" I jerked upright and checked my watch. It was only 7:30 in the evening. "You said the meeting was Saturday," I protested even as I levered myself out of the chair.

~Yes, it is Saturday,~ she replied as she stepped out. Amber gold eyes narrowed as she looked at me. ~I am not much of a judge of human attire, but is that really appropriate?~

"It is Friday night. Not Saturday," I protested. But I was already headed to my bedroom to change. "And no, I would never be seen in public in this."

She followed me into the bedroom. ~I am sure it is Saturday.~

"Maybe in China. Not here." I pulled off my clothes as she inspected my bedroom. "Give me a few minutes."

~Being late will not impress them,~ she warned, though I didn't hear any real worry.

"I didn't think Cath cared about being on time." I pulled on simple black leggings and a loose dark green dress that hit my knees, and matched it with some flat sandals. I wasn't too worried about being cold. Every glade I'd been in had always been between seventy and eighty degrees or hotter. Dragon sands were hotter.

~They don't, but you are not Cath.~

"No, I'm someone attending under protest and only because people I like have asked me to attend. I've got enough problems with human governments; I really don't need to be involved in yours."

Esmere snorted. ~Keep that attitude. It will serve you well.~ She flicked me with her tail. ~Are you ready?~

"Carelian, you coming?" I hadn't seen him since I curled up in the chair and had no clue where he was."

He came out of the bathroom, to my amusement. ~Of course.~

Esmere walked over and ran her tongue over the lingering scar on his face. ~You are well?~ There was a world of meaning in those words, and I wanted to hug her.

~Yes. I healed well. I would not recommend that experience, however.~ He leaned into her touch. ~But do we not have a boring council meeting to attend?~

~I suspect this time it will not be so boring.~

Her cryptic comment didn't do anything to reassure me. I took another minute to brush my hair and teeth. The second I was done, I called out. "Hamiada?"

"Yes, Cori?" She didn't appear, but I could feel her attention on me.

"Would you please let Jo and Sable know I'm at the council meeting with Esmere?"

She faded into view, her head tilting at an angle no human would replicate. "That sounds like it will be interesting."

"I hope not. I would like boring."

~Come Cori, we are late.~ Esmere had a rip floating in my bedroom and stood next to it, her tail swaying back and forth.

"Will you?" I directed the comment to Hamiada as I walked toward the rip.

"Yes. Enjoy your meeting." Her comment lingered in my ears as I stepped through. I never knew what to expect when I stepped in. Fire, water, desert, plains, but what greeted me was new. I'd seen a few structures in the realms, but I'd never been in one other than the temple.

This was a large room with chairs set in a rough circle, with largish gaps between them. Beings gathered in little clumps. I looked around and saw Tirsane, Salistra, and a shifting blob I assumed was Bob.

A chime sounded and a voice that I'd never heard before rang out through the room. "All members are here. Please take your seats."

It was like having a spotlight on me as the room turned to inspect me. My nerves bubbled up, and I pressed them down. They asked me here. I still didn't understand why.

~Follow me,~ Esmere whispered in my mind. I knew this was for me only, and I sank my right hand into the fur on her shoulder as my left hand sank into Carelian's. She was still larger than he was, but I suspected in another decade he'd bulk up and he'd be about her size. She'd mentioned once that most Cath easily lived into their eighth decade, and those with magic double that. The odds were Carelian would outlive me. When I thought about the children I carried, I rather liked that idea.

There were so many creatures, but as the voice faded, most of them settled into the gallery area, leaving only nine plus me and Carelian on the main floor.

"Sit everyone. I do not wish to be here overly long," Tirsane said in a voice that left no room for dissent. She was topless today, but she had a harder edge to her than normal. She stared as everyone took their seats, perches, or just occupied a space.

~Sit here Cori, I will be next to you.~ Esmere moved into the space next to a chair, taking her Egyptian cat pose with regal grace. Carelian settled down in front of me, looking like a loaf of red bread.

The beings were still settling in as I stared trying to take it all in. It took me a minute, but I figured it out. There were three lords for each of the realms.

Chaos had Esmere, a naga, and Bob, who just kinda oozed, with a tentacle coming out occasionally like a tongue. I really hoped he wasn't going to talk too much. Having blood run out of my nose and ears put most creatures off. And it hurt.

Order had Salistra, a Chitterian, and a Valkyrie—though it wasn't Frej.

Then Spirit had Tirsane, one of the dogs with wings I'd seen Carelian talking to—an Aralez if I remembered correctly—and a bird so bright gold it glowed. It looked nothing like Jeorgaz, so I had no idea if it was a phoenix or not. But where Jeorgaz had a beak implying he ate fruits and seeds, this hooked beak screamed carnivore. But it was so dang pretty I wanted to pet it.

~Stop it. It would not be wise to pet Xeztori.~ Esmere's voice stopped me and I realized I was half out of my chair. I plopped down with a wave of embarrassment flashing through me. Luckily, people were still settling into their chairs and no one else seemed to have noticed.

~What is that?~ I hissed in my mind to her, my eyes still captivated by the golden feathers.

~Xeztori. He is a Hypnohawk. He tends to hypnotize prey. Makes him lazy,~ she said dismissively.

The longer I watched, the more I actually saw him and the desire to pet wore off, but the first few glances at him were powerful.

I had so many questions, but everyone had settled down and I peered toward where they were looking. At one point in the circle of chairs was a perch similar to the one Xeztori sat on. We seemed to be waiting for something, and I was just about to ask when there was a flare of light and a something appeared in the center of the circle in an explosion of color. My eyes watered from the brightness of it and by the time I could see again a glorious creature rested on the perch. While I had no doubt it was a phoenix, the color scheme was drastically different from Jeorgaz. Where he was all the colors of fire, from white to blue to red fire, this bird was the colors of the rainbow. Yellows, greens, blues, purples, everything in just a swirl that should not have worked, yet it did. Peacocks would hide their tails in shame at the glory of this bird.

~Welcome to the meeting of the realms. This is a special session specifically designed to address the human realm. No other business will be accepted for this meeting.~

I sat up straight, fear locking my back straighter than a back brace.

~Who speaks for the human realm? Who is the representative for Earth?~

Oh this couldn't be happening. This is not what I signed up for.

~Cori, stand up and say you do.~ Esmere's voice prodded me.

I gave her a glare and the desire to call fire mingled with my fear. I tamped it down and slowly stood, hating every word that fell from my lips. "Cori Munroe. I do." I wasn't sure I could get any other words out of my mouth.

~You are recognized, Cori Munroe. Tirsane and Salistra speak highly of you.~

I slowly sank back down into the chair and shot Tirsane a

wide-eyed look. What did they want me to do or say? I hated being blindsided, and this was the worst.

~If I find out you knew anything about this, I swear to Merlin I'm going to have a new ruby rug for my bedroom.~ I whispered the words mentally in a fierce hiss at Carelian.

His ears were back and eyes narrowed. ~I swear on my fur I didn't know anything about this. I was told that you were needed to answer some questions. Nothing more.~

Oh questions. This I can handle. I hope.

"Thank you. How may I assist the council?" With luck, that was a neutral comment.

There was a shuffle through the room, but I couldn't identify why or what it was about.

~I am still not sure she is the best choice. But to be honest, she at least is not as objectionable as many who have talked to us. And at least she hasn't been turned to stone.~ Salistra's voice cut through my mind as always, but while it sliced, it wasn't as painful as I remembered.

~Are there any other comments about our choice?~ the phoenix said, its voice ringing in my head like a bell, louder than previously.

There was shuffling and a few looks around, but no one said anything.

~Then we shall begin. Cori Munroe, where does the human realm stand on the request to join the council?~

Every being in there shifted to look at me, and I just wanted to run away. What in the world were they talking about?

THIRTY-EIGHT

Pregnancy Fact: If you are sexually active you can get pregnant while already pregnant. It's incredibly rare, but it happens when your ovaries don't stop releasing eggs. It's called superfetation. Any pregnant woman should let her doctor know if she is still sexually active. ~ The Pregnant Mage

---

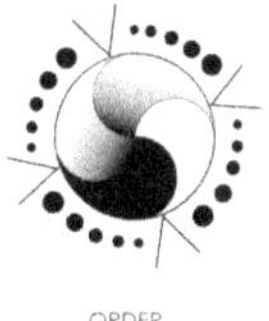

ORDER

I cleared my throat and stood feeling even more self-conscious. The pregnancy threw my balance off, which made me feel awkward. "I do not know what that question means or what you are asking."

The rush of whispers was like a trickle of water flowing over me.

~Did you not receive the precis of this discussion?~ The rainbow bird ruffled its feathers, a sense of agitation about the movements.

Resisting the urge to snark at all of them, I swallowed and tried to answer in a diplomatic manner. "There seems to be a bit of a mix-up. I was simply told that you wanted me at the council meeting. Nothing more. If there was something that I was supposed to read or have, I am unaware of it. I don't even know who you all are." That last part felt like a whine, but I hated not knowing people's names.

~What? Zmaug told me she'd given it to you when she told you.~ Esmere sat up straight, ears back.

I shook my head slowly, wondering if I should run now. The mood had changed from tense curiosity to annoyance. These were not creatures I wanted annoyed with me. Salistra was bad enough.

~Zmaug, your attendance is required.~ The ping ricocheted around in my mind, and I winced. I would not want to refuse that voice. There was a power to it that made me want to hide behind Esmere and under Carelian.

~What is it now?~ Zmaug's familiar voice rang through my mind and I clenched the sides of my chair trying to figure out the cost for an emergency sidestep back to Hamiada. Maybe her glade would be cheaper?

~ATTEND.~ The power made my teeth ache. A wall disappeared to my right and everyone subtly shifted to stare at the grassy stretch beyond. Part of me noted that it didn't end, just faded into gray like the other pockets I'd been in. The dark fading ray pulled the image of my nuclear pocket realm through my mind and I shuddered. It would be best if I never had to go there. Hopefully it would dissipate when I died.

A rip that hurt worse than any in a long time hit me as Zmaug stepped out into the glade. She was snarling and her tail lashed back and forth like a mace. And I thought maybe her throat was glowing.

~What do you want, Brix? I told you I had little patience for this nonsense. We are dragons and as long as you leave us alone, we will not protest what the council decides. Your rulings rarely affect us anyhow.~ The words came out as contemptuous snarls, leaving me with ruffles of pain in my mind.

~You agreed to pass on our message and give Cori the background information. You did not.~ The bird, Brix I guessed, had fluffed up all its feathers and seemed to all but sparkle. It reminded me of a glowing disco ball.

~I forgot. So? Is it that hard to talk to someone, or are you so used to having your feathers worshiped by the rest of these who beg for drops of your tears, that you don't know how to communicate?~ The scathing words had half of the room reacting as if she'd said something horrible about their mothers. Tirsane remained calm, but Esmere had bristled and her ears were laid back against her skull.

~Watch who you are calling tear suckers, lizard. You may find scales are not as much protection as you thought,~ Esmere hissed back.

I scooted my chair toward Carelian. ~Do we need to flee?~ He was alert and aware, but I was ready to run. There was no way I could survive a fight with these beings.

~You worry overmuch, Cori. This is council ground.~ His voice didn't sound upset, but he still was wary.

~Which means what?~ I was going to start beating people with golf clubs if someone didn't explain what was going on.

Other voices chimed in, in a cacophony of tones and pitches, both in my mind and audibly. It was creating a headache of massive proportions.

~Enough. We are scaring the human.~ Bob's voice cut through my mind with a spike of pain that elicited a whimper and I bent over, grabbing my head. That stab cut through my fear and snapped what little patience I had. Anger drove me, but even more so while I had these children growing in me, I wasn't about to be at ground zero for a fight between powerful denizens.

I stood letting pain and annoyance fuel me. "Yes, enough. Either explain exactly what you want or I'm leaving and you can suck the abyss." There was a rough intake of breath. I'd learned that phrase was worse than most human ones, but right now it fit. This entire situation was loaded with prima donnas and I wanted to go home.

"Her request is not unreasonable," someone said, but I didn't turn to figure out who. I kept glaring at Zmaug, Brix, and the staring match they had going on.

"So? I will leave. I have much better things to do tonight, like read a good book." My voice was icy, and I really wanted to strangle all of them right now. If it wasn't that I wanted to keep on good terms with a few of them, I would have already left.

Brix flipped tail feathers at Zmaug, who for her part just sneered, the glow in her throat slowly dying.

~Pretentious lizard. Memory problems, she must be getting old.~ Esmere's words rippled as a low growl through my mind and Zmaug mantled her wings in a flick.

~Lazy furball. You've become a house cat.~ Zmaug mimicked Esmere's favorite pose, wrapping her spiked tail around her.

If I wasn't so frustrated and tired, I might have laughed. They reminded me of frenemies I'd seen in high school. It was amusing and ridiculous at the same time.

"How old are they?" I said in a sotto voice to Carelian, knowing that every creature in the room would hear me. "Because I've seen teenagers act more maturely."

~A few hundred each at least. You'd think they would know better.~ The snickers that rippled around the room had both Esmere and Zmaug ignoring each other.

I let them be. It had reduced the tension in the room. Instead I focused on Brix. "Well? Am I going to get information or am I leaving?" The mix of amusement and outrage at my arrogance came through clearly via the audible and mental murmurs, but

Brix settled down on the perch, and spent a quick second preening breast feathers.

~Yes. You are quite correct. We have questions about the magic you still feed to Tirsane. It is creating a possible power imbalance. Please address.~

I snorted. "I'm not feeding her anything. I asked a favor, she granted it. If there is still magic being fed to her, I'm not doing it."

Brix fluffed up and turned his head to stare to Tirsane. ~You implied that she was feeding you magic.~

Tirsane looked back coolly. "No. I said that the favor had no constraints. You interpreted that to mean she was feeding me. I am still fulfilling her favor as many have magic they can not use in accordance with human laws. I take the magic from them to spare them."

The council murmured and stared at me.

~Tell her to end the favor,~ Salistra snapped out, her tail lashing. ~She doesn't need all that power.~

I groaned, my head and back hurting. I needed to pee, and I was craving sushi, which I couldn't have.

Breathe. You can do this. Breathe.

Every eye in the chamber was on me as I tried to come up with a solution. There were days when I wished no one had any magic or everyone did. It would make life simpler and more even handed.

"I am not quite sure why my request to remove magic from one girl, or at least that had been my intent, has become this. I do not control what Tirsane does or does not do." I firmly believed that, there was something about how they regarded magic and permission that controlled this and I wasn't about to try to point that out as they might figure out anyone could take a human's magic. "So as she has this ability, while don't you talk to her about sharing. Spread the magic out to everyone."

The attention shifted again and Tirsane stood up proud, the snakes coiled like springs on her head. "I would be delighted to talk trade agreements for a sharing of this excess magic."

Comments, shrieks, and growls rumbled around the chamber. I ignored them.

"So are we done? I would like to go home." I had to pitch my voice louder to carry over the noise.

Brix chimed, like a long perfect note, and the chamber fell quiet.

~You were also requested to come here as a representative of humanity. As this just proved, humans are involved in magic. We have tried multiple times to get humans on the council, but invariably they wanted to use it as a means to obtain power and not work for the betterment of all beings. Esmere and Tirsane have been impressed by your choices and your compassion. They felt you would be a good lead representative and able to find others to serve on the council. We wish for two mages from different countries and a member of the Chosen of the Beasts. You, of course, will be one of the mages.~

I blinked at them, trying to order my list of questions. "Chosen of the Beasts?"

Brix ruffled his feathers, his head peering around me to stare at Esmere. She vibrated lightly in something between a purr and a chuff.

~If I am right, they are referred to as the American Indian Nation of your species.~

Oh. It answered the question, but it tended to raise more questions. But I focused on the important ones right now, which meant not following up on my curiosity. "What does the council do exactly?" I couldn't see any of these beings being governed by another, much less a being from another realm. Why did they meet and what did they do were things I needed to know.

~Conspire to make my life miserable,~ Zmaug muttered. Or at least I think she meant to, but her voice rumbled through my mind like a slow earthquake. Everyone else managed to ignore her or at least not react in a manner that I noticed.

~Mostly we deal with changes in magic, rips opening between realms, summonings. It lets us all know of changes. For instance, when you created that pocket to dump radiation into, Jeorgaz came and let us know so we could avoid it. Many of us get overly curious at times. We only meet once each season or so, but there are reports to hear occasionally.~

The way that was phrased caught my attention. "Hear?"

~Writing is both annoying and you miss too many details. Whenever something interesting happens, we require a witness and a report. Jeorgaz's recitations of your exploits have been some of the most attended meetings in recent history. Report meetings are always held in public venues. It is almost like what you call a play, I believe.~

"Yes. Shakespeare was entertaining. I watched him many times via small windows before the major openings occurred. I wish there were more like him still."

I twisted my head to see who had spoken, as this rang in my ears. To my surprise it was the Aralez. With a shrug, I wrenched my attention back to my priorities. "And why do you want humans involved?"

~They are a part of Magic, are they not? They should be as involved as any of us.~ Brix ruffled feathers as if to say "duh".

"And you want me to decide? Why me?"

To my surprise Salistra spoke, her voice gentler than normal. ~As much as I find humans to be selfish and rather shortsighted, you have consistently risen above my admittedly low expectations. Given that, I am content to let you guide the human voice on this council.~

I blinked. That was close to effusive praise from Salistra.

"I see. There are a few things you need to be aware of. I will not be on the council." There was an instant uproar and protest from the various voices. It amused me to note Tirsane and Esmere stayed silent.

A headache built behind my eyes, and I rubbed my temples and fought back the sudden desire to drop to my knees and start bawling. The room quieted around me as I fought to get my emotions under control. Hormones sucked. I could hear the beings' breaths and I fought against the weight of their stares as I struggled to control my tears.

I don't want to cry.

I repeated those words over and over as I clenched my fists. It helped, as did breathing through my nose in harsh snorts.

"Okay. First, I am pregnant, which means in about four months, give or take, I will be giving birth to two babies. Two. And most humans only give birth to one. That means my life will be otherwise occupied until I am done with that and human children grow slowly. That is non-negotiable. Ask me in two decades and I might, MIGHT, have a different answer."

The sounds that rose in the chamber were a mix between laughter, disgruntled sounds, and commiserating. I ignored them all.

~I can see how that might be distracting to you. Especially as your young ones require nursing,~ said someone, I wasn't sure who, but I wasn't going to let any conversation devolve into a human sexuality conversation. Jo could handle that, not me.

~Shiarissa, enough.~ Brix snapped out the words, glaring at the naga. I shifted my attention to the naga for a moment, noting the similarity to Tirsane, minus the snake hair. ~Your objections are noted. However, we still need to find mages with your level of internal consistency. We want people who have your lack of desire for power.~

I laughed. "You are talking about mages and expect them to compete with you? Only mages with massive egos and who are very selfish yet aware of that, will be able to function against or with you. Anyone else would be too intimidated by this collection of beings. Ego is mandatory."

Tirsane, to my right, snorted, but I managed to not look at her.

Brix peered down from the perch, claws silvery against the dark material. ~Your words have validity. Are there ones who you feel would serve well on this council? We would weigh your opinions well regarding any who may be called to this burden. It would be best if they were at least what you call merlins. Anyone weaker would be at a disadvantage here.~

"I can't answer that. I've not even thought about it until now, but I will approach a few and see if I can find candidates for this. I believe you are right and that Earth realm should be involved matters of the council." Gritting my teeth, I forced out the polite words, even if I wanted to call them all Merlin's banished idiots. "I am honored by your trust in me."

They all bowed to me, which weirded me out to no end, and then Esmere's tail tapped my butt. ~It is time. We should leave. I have zero desire to listen to Zmaug excuse her lax adherence to duty.~

I fought back a laugh, and we walked through a portal back to the house, Carelian protecting my back.

CHAPTER
THIRTY-NINE

Employment offered: Looking for an Air mage with a degree in aeronautics to work with the NTSB investigating air crashes. Must be Archmage or higher with relevant degree, experience in crash investigation or criminal justice background preferred. ~ Magic Indeed Job listing

---

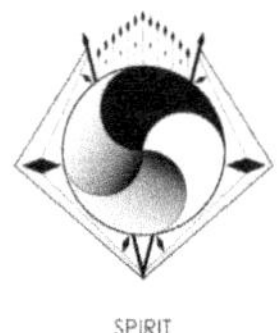

SPIRIT

I stepped out of the rip from the council chambers back into the house and sighed in relief. Voices filtered down the hall. "What? She didn't tell you any more than that? I swear I never realized how terrified I was of her getting hurt when she ran out the door until it was three people who could get hurt." Jo's voice echoed down the hall and I laughed, following it into the kitchen with Carelian and Esmere behind me.

"She'll be fine. With Esmere and Carelian with her? The world would have to end before she would get hurt. You're being overly paranoid." Sable soothed Jo as I stepped into the kitchen to see them working on dinner.

"Ah, you're worried about me?" I said, leaning against the door jamb, the scent of pasta and marinara sauce making me ravenous.

They jerked their heads up to stare at me, smiles crossing their faces as stress bled out of their postures.

~Humans. Did you think any harm would come to her? She carries babies who I have not met yet. Ones I wish to watch grow. There was no danger.~ Esmere pushed by me and lifted her head to sniff the pasta sauce on the stove. ~That is not blood. What is the red?~

"No danger if you don't count a pissy dragon, arrogant phoenix, and realm lords bickering like old ladies in a retirement home," I countered. For a few minutes, I had seriously considered running for cover. But the odds were half the denizens in the room would have taken it as an offer to chase me.

Jo and Sable glanced at the three of us, then Sable pointed at the table. "Sit. I want to hear every detail."

"Let me change clothes first and I'll be back." The next forty minutes were spent eating, telling my tale, watching Esmere try to decide if she liked pasta Bolognese or not, and catching up on their day. I ended with, "So I have no idea who to recommend or who might be suited. It scares me to think what someone unethical, which most people are when push comes to shove, would do in that situation."

Jo shrugged. "I think you are worrying about it too much. They aren't going to invade earth, and from what I've seen, most of the Lords don't have the same morals that we do. Their view on life is drastically different and I'm not sure anyone who was super ethical would be able to handle them. I think if anything you need a person who is good but with very flexible morals."

Sable nodded. "I think you'd be better off with good, not nice, as your guidelines."

"Maybe. I only have one person who might be able to get a message to the AIN and even then I have no idea if they will help or not. But your way of phrasing it, good not nice, makes me think of someone who might be the right fit. I would almost say Cixi, but she has a country to run."

"True," countered Jo, "but you don't want only people like us."

I motioned with my hand for her to go on as I popped a piece of salad in my mouth.

"We are worried about our own lives, maybe those of our friends, but we don't have to think about how other things affect the people or global economies. We don't think how what other people or countries do could affect our own. If you are going to recommend people, it needs to be people, or at least one person, who can think that way."

"Huh," I said, leaning back in my chair as I thought. She was right. And oddly, I didn't want it to be anyone I knew well. I wanted them to be what, acquaintances? Why? The realization slammed into me as I followed the thought. I wanted them to be people I wouldn't be devastated over if they were killed.

"Esmere, how often are council members killed?"

She had played with the pasta, licking off the sauce mostly, and was busy cleaning her claws. ~Caught that did you? Yes, there are deaths between the councilors, not common, but neither is it rare.~ Esmere flicked an ear at me. ~Does it matter?~

I managed to not start laughing, mainly because I didn't know if it would fall into hysterical laughter. "I would prefer to not send anyone to their death. It means I need to pick people who know both how to provoke and protect themselves. But why me? Why drag me into this?" There was a bit of whining in my voice, but dang it, why me?

~We have discussed it for a while, but we meet very few sane mages. And those who are sane, or mostly, are like James Wells—

hoarders.~ She sounded so matter of fact that I didn't know how to react.

"Hoarder?" Jo asked, grabbing for more bread before Sable ate it all.

~Some humans are like dragons. They find things they want to collect and keep those things to themselves. For James, it was knowledge. For others it is eggs, memory stones, plants. I have seen almost everything over the years.~ She retracted her claws a few times, checking to make sure all the red was off them. ~The others who find us are used as toys all too often, they get what they wanted. Access to the realms and the consequences that come with that.~

Sable frowned. "What do you mean 'toys'?"

I winced. Toys had all too real meaning for me. I liked the denizens I knew, but they weren't human and didn't have human reactions to things.

~We play with the lesser beings. Humans qualify as toys, food, even sexual perversions. Not all of us, but note that most of us only do it for those who invade our world seeking to destroy or control us. The few who enter honestly or with no ill intentions end up as the stars of your stories.~ She said all of this as if explaining how justice worked. I bowed my head, remembering the feeling from when I understood how law and justice worked around mages. The absolutes were stark and painful

Not my world. Not my consequences.

"That doesn't sound like you or Tirsane," Sable said slowly, and I couldn't look at her. She hadn't seen the way Salistra behaved. Or even how some of the other denizens acted.

Esmere sighed, a weird sound coming from a cat. It was more like a long low hiss. ~Chaos is not like Earth. Your world is constant—though people may choose to act weirdly, your world does not change.~ Jo looked ready to protest, but Esmere held up her tail. ~You have tides when the moon rises, your sun always comes up in the east, if dropped, objects fall at the same rate every time. Your world is constant. Ours is not. Most denizens do not become mages like me or even Carelian are. He is the only kit I keep in regular contact with. The rest have found their own lives or deaths wanting little to do with my choices. The life of a Lord is not simple.~ She huffed. ~I do not know how to explain. We are not animals, but we are not human. For many of us, even other Cath, families are only there if both sides choose that. I chose to keep in touch with my kits, even when they chose lives without active magic. We eat intelligent creatures that were too slow or too stupid. Life is what you make of it in the realms and you can not judge it or us by human definitions, otherwise you will be sorely disappointed.~

We all just stared at her and Sable sighed. "So you and Tirsane are oddballs?"

Esmere didn't say anything for a minute, then she looked up at us. ~Tirsane and I are choosing to try something different. So far Cori, and you two, have made that attempt worth it.~

A mountain of responsibility slammed onto my shoulders and I felt it take my breath away. One more thing to try to figure out.

Carelian huffed. ~You take this too seriously, all of you. We are no better or worse than humans from other cultures. Treat us, them, as you wish to be treated and you will be fine.~

I looked at Jo and Sable and they had the same serious look on their faces as I knew was on mine.

"You know they are right. We treat them as friends, so they treat us that way. I know Paul Goines saw them as pawns at best, disposable things at worst. Then why should they treat him any differently? I say don't worry about it, but it means I think I know who to suggest for the council, if they will accept."

Jo perked up at those words. "Oh? Who would that be? And do we know them?"

"I think providing multiple names might be best, so I'm going to suggest Shay and Hishatio Yamato. I'd like Scott Randolph but he isn't a merlin." I'd been thinking about this for a bit and they were really the only merlins I knew who might be flexible or arrogant enough to be on the council. I wasn't a hundred percent certain they would do it, but maybe I could convince them.

"Shay? What made you think of him?" Jo was a casual friend of Shay, though I wasn't sure if they'd kept in touch or not after the bomb incident. O'Shaughnessy Sato was a Japanese Irishman and even among the Merlins he was regarded as weird. I hadn't ever talked to him as another Merlin. Maybe I should.

"I don't know. Do you guys want to go to your mom's tomorrow for dinner? I think she'd let me borrow her car to go talk to him. "

"Sounds good." We made plans to do that and I headed up to find the number for John Taliance, the only idea I had to contact anyone from the AIN. He'd made comments and I suspected he had connections in the AIN. I changed my clothes and curled back up in the chair in the study. I loved that chair; it was comfortable and supportive. Even now when it felt like all of me was expanding.

"Merlin Munroe. Should I be worried you are calling me on a Friday night, late?" He answered on the first ring, speaking before I could say anything. Worried, I glanced at the clock then frowned.

"It is only seven p.m. for you, not exactly late."

"Aren't young mages supposed to be out partying on a Friday night?"

I had no idea if he was teasing or not, as his voice was completely serious. "Not when they are pregnant and deal with government bureaucracy on a daily basis. If that is their life, then hiding in the house sounds perfect. Too bad that rarely works."

"Ah. I take it that is why you are calling?" I heard creaking in the background and my mind created an image of him sitting on a porch in a rocker. It just seemed like what he'd be doing, a cup of coffee in his hand. And maybe I'd watched way too many westerns as a kid.

"Basically," I said, clearing my throat, trying to figure out how to phrase this.

"So what does the government want with me now? And why ask you? Normally these one-off requests come from up my chain of command."

I coughed, uncomfortable with this whole thing. The vicious mutter of "why me" floated in the back of my mind, but I ignored it. Though I took a second to check for Murphy's Cloak around me. Nothing. "That's the thing. It isn't our, or my, government."

His end went silent, but I knew he was listening with every fiber of his being.

"I was approached by the council ..." I floundered. I didn't even know what they were called, just the council. My life was ridiculous. I started over. "There is a council in the realms populated by the lords of each realm. It is moderated by a rainbow phoenix named Brix. They are asking to have three merlins representing Earth attend. They requested one of the mages be from the Chosen of the Beasts. I was told that was the AIN. I am hoping maybe you can send the AIN a message and see if there is someone who would be willing to be a representative on this council." I said the last part in a rush, worried he'd interrupt or ask questions.

Instead, he was silent so long I almost said something to see if he was still there.

"I knew I had said too much while you were here and that you would remember it." He sighed. "I will ask, but only because of what this implies and could mean long term. They will not want to be left out of anything of this magnitude. Who are the others?" His voice had a tone of exasperation in it, which seemed to be the default after people had known me for a while.

"I have a few others who I need to contact. But right now, no one. They wanted me and I refused."

"That makes sense. The pregnancy, I assume?"

"Partially, but mainly 'cause I really dislike being a pawn in their entertainment."

"Ah. I will let you know. Good evening, Merlin Munroe." With that, he hung up and I stared at the phone. Somehow I was either going to get blamed for or dragged into this whole mess.

"Cori?" Jo called up the stairs.

I didn't move, just lifted my voice. "Yeah?"

"Mom said yes. She'll see us tomorrow and you can borrow her car."

"Thanks!" Marisol still drove a serviceable mini-van. More protection around me was always a good thing.

I pulled up Shay's number. Laurel Amosen had given it to me a long time ago. I figured Shay's number was unlikely to change. This time I called him as it had been at least three years since I'd even seen him, much less said hello.

"What?" I repressed a snort as he answered the phone. It was oddly reassuring having him respond like that.

"Shay, this is Cori Munroe. I need to talk to you about something. Can I come over and see you tomorrow? I'll be in town."

Silence, then a grunt. "Why not? But the answer will be no. I'll text you." He hung up and my phone beeped with his address.

I shook my head. Shay hadn't changed at all.

FORTY

The rumors are true, the ice mage herself seems to be knocked up. Pictures of her leaving work with a defined baby bump have leaked. Who managed to get through the walls of her ice? No one has seen her date or look with favor on any of the eligible mages, no matter what they've done to get her attention. ~ Daily Magical News

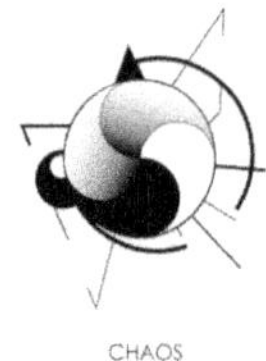

CHAOS

Carelian dropped us all off with Marisol. Travel via the portals seemed more exhausting for him each time, and it worried me. But he snoozed while I visited Marisol and let her in on all the details of the babies' development, told her I was already tired of doctors' visits, then I borrowed her van and set off.

~Are you sure about this?~ Carelian asked from the back seat where he sprawled like a red coat of fur.

"I'm sure I don't know enough to be involved in making any decisions. And it isn't like I know that many mages personally. Which I admit is my fault." Those words tasted bitter. I liked my life just fine with Jo and Sable and the friends I had. "After the babies are born, I'll think about going to more House of Emrys events. Okay?"

~That would be wise. You are too isolated. Though you have no desire for a mate, a strong clan is good for waging war.~

I looked at him in the rearview mirror. He looked relaxed, but his tail was stiff indicating worry. "Carelian, I'm not going to war. I'm not going to do anything too insane. They just want to have human opinions."

~You have never sat in on those sessions. There is a lot more to it, though I doubt the majority are worse than Tiantang's court.~ His answer did not reassure me.

I sighed and concentrated on where I was going. Carelian was right, but I certainly wasn't going to tell him that. We didn't talk the rest of the way, though his soft snore in the back made me drive extra carefully. He didn't wake up well when I slammed on the brakes—we'd learned this the hard way, and I didn't want to damage Marisol's van.

I pulled up to the address and saw two cars parked outside. It wasn't a huge house. It was on a short street with other houses, all in brick, and with lawns and trees. Nice if a bit boring, as all the houses had obviously been built by the same company.

We walked up the path and knocked. A minute later the door was opened by someone who wasn't Shay. He looked vaguely familiar, but I couldn't place him until a familiar green flying snake darted out and coiled around Carelian's neck in what I recognized as a hug. It surprised me, I didn't know he knew Elsba.

"Elsba!" I said with a smile. One of the first familiars I had ever met, she was still just as brilliant a green as I remembered. I looked at the man again and the tattoo on his temple and tried to dredge his name up out of my memory. I failed. "Sorry, I don't remember your name." I offered a smile to make up for my lack of memory. There had been a lot of customers at the coffee shop.

"I'd be surprised if you did. My girl is always more memorable." He gave his familiar a smile I recognized from my own image when I looked at Carelian. "Sloan Michaels at your service. Come on in. The others are in the living room."

"Others?" Honestly, I was surprised that he was here, but then that was Shay's business not mine.

"Yes. Shay asked for Scott to stop by." He spoke as he led us into the living room where I was stopped by the sight of a huge black dog.

"Dahli!" The not-dog was up and licking my face as soon as I stepped into the room. She blithely ignored Carelian growling behind me.

~That is my mage. Get your slobbery tongue off of her.~ Carelian's words were accompanied by a hiss and I felt his heat behind me.

~Doggy kisses always better,~ Dahli boomed in my mind and I winced.

"Sorry. She's gotten better about talking to people, but she still bellows everything."

I looked up at the voice, happy to see Scott Randolph sitting there. I gave Dahli one last scratch behind her ear, much to her pleasure and Carelian's annoyance, before I rose. "I take it her chosen mage didn't survive?"

Scott shook his head. "Nope. Never came back from the diabetic coma. He never managed it well and even with their best efforts it was still fatal. I was sure Dahli would disappear after he died, but I woke up one morning to find her sitting on my doorstep. I think her first words to me were, "Staying. Mine now." He lowered his voice to a rough growl, and I smiled. Even after all these years, Scott Randolph had a presence you couldn't ignore. He was someone who would fit into my family of misfits, but I was pretty sure he was in his sixties by now. He'd feel more at home with Marisol and Henri than us. Though I really wanted to introduce him to Tirsane.

I let that thought go and turned to see Shay hunched in a recliner staring at all of us morosely. "Shay. Good to see no one has killed you yet."

Scott and William barked out a laugh as Shay just gave me a flat, unamused look. "Glad to see you finally dealt with that Murphy's Cloak fetish you had."

I rolled my eyes. "Yeah, well."

Sloan glared at Shay. "Sit everyone. Cori, can I get you something to drink?" he offered, and I must have looked confused. "Shay stays here. This is my place. He's never set down roots long enough to buy a house. So he stays here when he passes through."

"Oh," I muttered, feeling unaccountably foolish.

"Plus, I'm too broke and too busy to deal with the foolishness involved in rent or mortgages. Easier to pay him money. Coffee with some bourbon in it," Shay said in his straightforward way, though he never took his eyes off of me. "The strands of probability around you are still insane."

I snorted and settled down. "Just water for me." My attention went over to Shay while Carelian and Dahli separated to opposite sides of the room to my amusement. "And yes, that seems to be constant." I didn't see probabilities the way Shay did, but then every mage was just a bit different.

"You're also pregnant," he pointed out.

"Really? Wow, who knew?" I said dryly. Scott snorted as Sloan came back into the room.

"Be nice, Shay. It's been a while since we've had people over and I'm enjoying this." He handed Shay his coffee, me my water and gave Randolph a Coke. He settled down and they turned to me expectantly.

"Guess I better get used to this. At least you three probably won't try to have me killed." They all frowned at that, but I ignored them. "I have been approached by the Council for the realms and they would like to have human mages on it for input on issues that affect all the realms. They are asking for three, as the other realms have three lords. I thought you might be a good person to have there." I stared at Shay. "Personally, I think Scott would be better, but they only want merlins." A cloud crossed Scott and Sloan's faces, but I shook my head. "I wouldn't take it as a slight, more that they want to make sure the representative would be powerful enough to keep themselves alive."

That set everyone back, though Shay looked interested. "What does that mean?"

I opened my mouth, stopped and thought. "Think of a meeting between nations where everyone is merlin-level arrogant, powerful, and is sure they are better than any other being at the meeting. Add in magic and the fact that it is not Earth, and you might have an idea."

"Then I'm more than glad to not be eligible," Scott said, raising his hand. "I've got enough problems. I don't need to add to them. It would be like running the BAM, but these people don't need to worry about breaking the rules."

I snorted. "I'm pretty sure the only rules are the ones that Brix is powerful enough to enforce." I had to take a minute to explain who Brix was or who I thought Brix was. Carelian stayed quiet oddly enough and when I glanced back at him, he and Dahli were engaged in a staring contest.

"And why should I do this?" Shay asked.

"I have no idea. I'm refusing. I don't need that sort of drama in my life and frankly, once the babies come, I doubt I'll have time."

Three sets of eyes darted to my belly.

"Huh, I thought you looked fatter than carrying just one child," Shay said.

"Shay!" both Scott and Sloan snapped out. I just rolled my eyes.

"You will fit right in. None of the denizens I know have any filter at all."

~We just don't see the need for your little white lies. Though even I know it is stupid to mention a woman's weight. There is no gain, only consequences.~ Carelian's voice almost sounded reproving, but he was busy cleaning his very sharp claws. Dahli was stretched out on her back, ignoring him.

I jerked my head toward the two familiars. "And there is a lot of that. You'd better get good at your one upmanship."

"Why not? It will give me something to do. I'm bored."

I arched a brow at that but he just took a drink of his coffee.

"You said they wanted three. Who else are you going to ask?" Scott asked.

At the same time Shay said, "And how and when do I get there?"

That was a very good question. Luckily Carelian answered it for me. ~A Lord of Chaos will appear and take you there. I trust you can get home after that?~

"Yes," he said and tapped his temple. "I am Chaos and while I might not use it as much as I use my Earth abilities, once I know where I am going, I can then go back and forth." Shay grinned. "Never let anyone know everything you can do."

I looked at Scott and shrugged. "It might sound crazy, but I was thinking Hishatio Yamato."

Scott and Sloan looked at me blankly, but Shay hissed out a long sigh. "I take it back. You are crazy."

"He owes me. Besides, I can't see the Emperor letting him turn it down, and he's got the arrogance down pat."

"Who is this Hishatio? I thought I knew everyone you deigned to slum with, Shay." Sloan's voice had a teasing quality to it and Shay tilted up his lip.

"He isn't exactly someone I know. He's the Majyutsu-shi for Japan. AKA the royal magician," Shay said dryly. "The last time he was big in the news, he tried to kill Cori here."

The two men looked at me, while Shay buried a smirk.

"Why would you ask someone to deal with this council who tried to kill you?" Sloan seemed outraged, but Scott had a thoughtful look on his face.

"Meh. He owes me and honestly, they need someone who looks at the bigger picture. I have never needed to look much beyond my friends and family. I think for this to be a worthwhile endeavor they need people from different backgrounds."

"That is two," Sloan pointed out. "Who's the third?"

"No clue. They specifically said they wanted someone from the AIN. So I've reached out to see if I can get someone." They all looked at me oddly. "What?"

"I used to think Shay was just playing up his weirdness vibe, but you really do attract the weirdness of life to you," Sloan said with a frown. Elsba darted over and wrapped around my arm, and I focused on petting her.

"It isn't like I ask for this. It just is what my life seems to be. Full of twisted luck."

"At least you aren't bored," Shay muttered, staring glumly at his coffee.

Scott and I stared at him. "You have no idea how nice being bored is. It generally means someone isn't trying to kill you." Scott's voice was dry and full of experience.

"What he said. I much prefer boredom. It means I have a steady, predictable life," I agreed.

~She whines. I quite like when things are going on. It gives me much currency among others,~ Carelian murmured, the echo telling me the other mages probably heard it also.

"What is he talking about?" Sloan asked. Both Dahli and Elsba had gone still, frozen as if a predator was nearby.

I snickered, amused to have something to tell these mages that they didn't know. "Familiars or focuses apparently have the equivalent of telling stories around the campfire, except they are stories about us. The more wild, dangerous, and stupid we are, the better they are rated. Think of it as bragging rights."

They all stared at Dahli and Elsba, who tried to disappear from their sight. I laughed, then flinched in surprise.

"Is something wrong?" Sloan had a worried look on his face as he rose.

I stared down at my stomach. "The baby or babies kicked." My hand rested gently on my stomach and there it was again, a kick. I started giggling in surprise. "They're kicking."

"Congratulations, Cori. I'm happy for you." Shay spoke with a rare moment of sincerity and I looked at him.

"Be happy for Jo and Sable, they are the parents. Or well, we all will be. But yeah. I can't wait to let them feel."

"That makes more sense," he said with a sniff, and I rolled my eyes at him.

"Just proof of one more thing I can do and you can't," I said sweetly, but I winked.

Scott and Sloan snickered as Shay held his hands up in protest. "Thank you, but no. I'm perfectly happy being child free. I'll just play the random weird uncle who sends gifts the parents hate. Drum sets, puppies, things like that."

"Hmm," Sloan murmured, and I narrowed my eyes at them.

"You go have your own life. I'm busy with mine. I'll let you know when the introductions are for the council and have you picked up. Be aware sometimes the warning is awfully short, but mainly because I still haven't figured out where on Earth they decide what day it is. But usually you'll know a week or so out. I think."

We exchanged a few more pleasantries before I headed back to the Guzman's hoping the baby would still be kicking when I got there.

CHAPTER

FORTY-ONE

Breaking News – The crash of a Bering 777 has just been reported. All passengers and crew are presumed dead as the plane disappeared mid-flight. This makes the third disappearance of this model and all others are being recalled. This is worrisome news for China who was expecting Merlin Cori Munroe to arrive for an awards ceremony on this flight.~ AP News

---

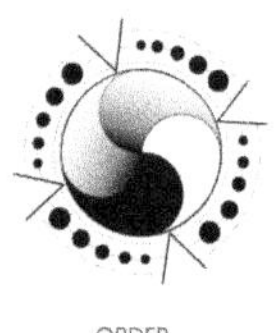

ORDER

John sent me a message saying that my request was being discussed. I passed that on to Esmere, who didn't seem worried. She let me know that the candidates would be needed in a few months, so there was no pressure. I sent an email to Hishatio that I wanted to talk to him, but I figured it would take a few weeks for him to decide how to respond, so I let it go and focused on being pregnant.

That took up way more energy than I would have expected. The amniocentesis test had shown nothing to worry about. We had two healthy babies. My next checkup was this week, and they wanted to talk about birthing classes and do a glucose test. Basically, I went in and I was miserable, but it was soon over and we set up the birthing classes. Some were online, and I cranked through those, but it still felt weird to accept that I was going to be going through all this. Jo and Sable were excited and took all the classes with me and I had to admit, given how much my body was changing, I was more than appreciative of the massages they were learning to do.

They had an in-depth birth plan laid out, and we had talked about me going on leave the week I was due. I'd already filed the paperwork, and Naomi hadn't said anything about it, though her worried glance stayed with me. I still felt oddly out of control of my life, like these beings inside me were more important than I was. That my existence was kind of just there. It didn't help that nothing fit, my back hurt, my breasts ached, and it seemed like all anyone could talk about was the babies.

Even Carelian got in on the act, laying his head on my stomach and purring. Though I didn't mind that too much. It soothed the babies, so they didn't kick as hard or as often. Which made my life more pleasant. They were both very active. Plus, I seemed to fall asleep every time I sat down. So far that was the biggest benefit I'd found. No one criticized my naps.

I was downstairs in the living room with Carelian cuddled up next to me on the couch. Jo and Sable were talking about baby names when Zmaug pinged me. I kept petting Carelian. He was very much in favor of my nap attacks, declaring I was learning to see the world the Cath way.

~Yes, Zmaug?~ I was still a bit snippy. She'd never apologized and the hissy fit she and Brix had thrown made me nervous. I understood most of them thought I was a pawn in their games. That didn't mean I needed to play by their rules.

~I found the parents of the eggs. They were a mixed breed killed by a predator. It is agreed that you and your hatchlings will be adequate for their raising.~ She sounded bored, but yet had taken the time to let me know.

~Thank you. Is there anything special we need to feed them or do for them?~

~Meat, eggs, anything the cat would eat. They won't get very big. And they will stay in the eggs for another few years, most likely. They just need warmth and magic to finish gestating.~

~Years?~

~There is much less magic on Earth than in the realms. It will take a while and the odds are they will imprint on the children as long as they are nearby. They would be excellent body-guards, though poor familiars compared to my child.~ Pride and arrogance rang through her voice and I fought back a laugh.

~Ah, that helps. Though I am perfectly happy not having a dragon the size of Tiantang here.~ I wasn't sure how to end the conversation.

~Your loss. Do you have your representatives selected yet?~ That surprised me. I hadn't thought she cared.

~Only one. The others are still undecided.~

~Hmmmm. Do let Brix know when you have them. They probably need more orientation than our people would, never having been around the council before. I may have to start attending again for the entertainment. Until then.~ She disconnected, and I laughed to myself. With the changes going on in my body, my life, even my job, it was oddly reassuring to have Zmaug still be so uniquely her.

~I love you,~ I whispered to Carelian.

~Of course you do. I am infinitely loveable. ~ He purred louder as I petted him. My gaze latched onto Jo and Sable, words of love and fear on my lips. They were leaning into each other talking quietly, the looks on their faces such perfect joy it stilled my tongue.

I didn't understand my own body. All the changes to it and the way everyone reacted to me seemed weird. Like I didn't exist. Part of me resented it, and I really resented my magic being wonky. But at the same time I wanted to meet the little ones who were growing inside me.

"Cori? What's wrong?" Jo was next to me on her knees, her hands touching my face. I realized I'd started crying. The words were there, I could tell her, tell them. But then she'd be worried and upset, which meant Sable would stress. Women did this every day. I got this. The result would be two beautiful children. I was being ridiculous.

"Hormones. The weight gain is bugging me, then mix in the mood swings, you get this." I smiled at her. "Nothing out of the ordinary. So where are we on names?" We knew we had one girl, but the other baby was avoiding letting us see what gender they were. So the names had been all over the place.

Sable came over and lifted up my legs, sat down on the other end of the couch, then put them on her lap as Jo wiped my tears. "Just know you are amazing. And hormones are stupid." Jo kissed my forehead and scooted Carelian over a bit to sit near my head. "We are agreed on Jasmine Corisande Guzman for the girl."

I rolled that over in my mind. I rather liked it. Sweet but not too weird. "And the other?"

Sable looked at her list. "If it is a boy, I'm leaning toward Charlemagne Jonathan Lancet."

"Charlemagne? Really? Won't he get nicknamed to Chuck? Which you know Charles hates," I pointed out, remembering how much Charles disliked the obvious nickname.

"I know, but if we mix it up, his name would be Magne as a nickname. That just sounds neat." She pronounced it as "mane". "Plus, it is linked to Magnus, so we can switch to that?"

"Or Charlie, or Mags, or Lee or Jon," I pointed out with a smile. It was an unusual name, but then so was mine.

"Oooh, I like Mags or Lee," Jo said. "They are shorter and fun."

Sable shrugged, a smile playing on the edges of her lips. "See, lots of options."

"And if it is a girl?" I smiled, wondering what they had come up with.

"Well, this is going to sound stupid." Sable chewed on her lip and I smothered a smile. We all just looked at her, even Carelian opened one eye. "I was thinking Sorsha Marisol Lancet. It does honor to your mom and Sanchez. He may never be her dad, but he is her father."

Jo smiled at Sable and nodded slowly. "I like it."

"I think you're right, but you know, they can have more than one middle name. What about Jasmine Sorsha Corisande Guzman if you only have one girl? That way she's a part of both of us." The brilliant smiles they threw me made me laugh and chased away the odd feeling of disconnect that haunted me some days. While my skin did glow, I was ready to be done with this but I still had at least fourteen weeks to go and that was if I was a week early.

The conversation fell to the baby shower and who to invite. I left it all up to them. Parties weren't really my thing, and I still had this odd ambivalence. But maybe the shower would make it more real. I'd participate, but I really hoped they didn't do some of the stupid games I'd seen in books and on TV. That would drive me insane.

~Cori?~ I flinched as Tiantang pinged me. He was always a bit excitable. For all of his age, he still acted like an oversized puppy.

~Yes?~ I nodded, Carelian giving me the evil eye as he lifted his head. I knew he could feel Tiantang talking. The dragon did tend to yell.

~I have someone here who wants to talk to you. Can I bring him through?~

That made no sense to me at all. ~Who?~ Tiantang wouldn't bring Cixi here and I couldn't imagine a random denizen approaching him as opposed to Tirsane.

~He says his name is Hishatio, and he needs to talk to you.~ He sounded confused, but proud at the same time.

I jolted upward at the name. ~Oh no. Don't bring him here. One minute.~ Carelian had his ears back as he stared at me, but seemed oddly resigned. Jo and Sable though, had been startled by my sudden movement. "Hamiada, can you make your glade accessible to Tiantang and a visitor? He is a merlin and I'm not willing to have him in my house."

There was a moment's pause. "It is done. You will need to access it through the attic stairs though."

"Thank you so much." I stood up, groaning as the weight in my belly shifted and both of the babies complained. They showed their displeasure by pummeling me with kicks and elbows. I swear there were days when I was sure they were ready to come out now.

"Everything okay?" Jo had risen too, a look on her face that told me she was about to go to war.

"It's fine, but I need to talk to Hishatio about council stuff and I'm not doing it here, and I can't afford to sidestep there, though it sounds like he's in China for some strange reason. The glade is easier."

"Need us to come?" She pulled fire and had it dancing on her fingertips.

"Nah. Hamiada will keep us safe."

~And I will be at your side,~ Carelian said as if he expected me to disagree.

"I know, dear. Come up. Let's get this over with." I gave Jo and Sable a reassuring smile and headed to the stairs. That last flight sucked, and I vowed to do more stairs. The last thing I need to do was get out of shape. It had been too much work to get into shape.

"Will you bring Tiantang and his visitor to the glade?" I glanced at Carelian as I walked through the attic door into the glade.

~Yes.~ He was gone between one step and the next, the prick

of pain so fast and subtle that if I didn't try to notice it, I wouldn't have.

Hamiada didn't appear, but she had created a little area with two comfy chairs and a table. I was still walking over to it when a rip formed and Carelian stepped out with Hishatio and Tiantang following him. Hishatio hadn't changed much over the last year or so, though the wrinkles seemed deeper. He still held himself upright, the sheet of liquid black hair brushing his knees.

He started to bow to me, then jerked up, eyes widening. "You're pregnant!"

"No, really?" I looked down at my burgeoning beach ball. "Now, how did that happen?"

He stiffened and completed the bow. "That was impolitic of me. It was unexpected."

I shrugged that off. The snark had slipped out, and I needed him to be at least polite to me. Which meant I needed to be polite to him. "I've received that response often." I turned my smile onto Tiantang who was romping around the glade while Carelian stayed near me. "How are you doing, Tiantang?"

~I am well. Cixi is excited to see you. The medal has been special made for you."

"Huh? Oh, the ceremony. I haven't seen any more information on it."

~Oh, it is soon. It will be fun.~ He paused in his romp, head cocked to one side. ~Cixi needs me. You will be okay with him?~ Tiantang focused on Hishatio with a fierce look.

Soon? Given he's a dragon, that could mean tomorrow or next century.

I put it out of my mind. They knew how to get a hold of me. "Yes. Thank you for letting me know."

Tiantang spun in a circle, then slipped away through the still open rip. I turned my attention back to Hishatio who had spent his time looking around the glade with an inscrutable expression. "You wanted to see me?"

Oddly, I didn't hate the man. I mostly felt sorry for him and even slightly guilty that I was adding another burden on him, but he was the best person I knew to fill this role. Regardless of what the other lords might think, Earth was huge, and I only knew a small fraction of the merlins on the planet.

"I received an email from you that made no sense. There was reason for me to travel to China, and I leveraged that opportunity to get a message to you that would not be easily intercepted." He said this while looking around the glade. "This reminds me of what Jeorgaz would create," he said softly.

"It is probably similar. Most of the glades have a familiar feel." I waved at the table and chairs. I waddled over and took a seat. "Thank you for taking my request seriously, and I can't say that being covert in this instance is a bad thing. Given my recent inter-actions with both the OMO and my government, I don't feel they always have the best interests in store for everyone."

He snorted and his mouth quirked up on one side. "Yes, I have run into issues with that myself. Please explain about, and I quote, "consider a unique position in magic". That does sound rather mysterious and vague, and to be honest, if it hadn't been from you, I might have ignored it as spam or phishing."

I explained what the council was, and finished with, "They asked me to bring candidates who are merlins and you are one of them. I felt someone who had experience with how policies and decisions can affect countries would be a wise choice."

"Are you going to be one of the three?"

"No. The other is O'Shaughnessy Sato and a third from the American Indian Nation. Though I don't know who yet."

"And if I had refused?" I noted how he phased that and I mentally checked off a box, leaving me only with the AIN candidate.

"Probably someone from the House of Emrys. I think most merlins are associated with them." He nodded, and I assumed that meant he was as well. "Otherwise I don't know. Fake it I guess."

"You said in your email the time is not that excessive?"

"I haven't been led to believe it is. Probably once a quarter, but for all I know, each meeting lasts three weeks." His eyes widened in worry and I sighed. "One minute."

~Esmere, how much time, Earth time, does an average council session last?~ I waited, regretting that I hadn't brought some water with me and realizing I needed to go pee soon. This was becoming annoying.

~The longest ever was fifteen Earth hours. Though that ended when Tirsane attacked Bob. He was being problematic. The average tends to be three or four hours depending on how quarrelsome the other lords are being.~ She sounded busy, so I shot her a quick thanks and relayed that information to Hishatio.

"Attacked?" he said, arching an eyebrow.

"That is part of the reason they want merlins. You need to be strong enough to kick asses if needed and arrogant enough to stand up to their egos." I smiled at his affronted yet understanding expression.

"When do I need to decide?" he asked. He'd never sat down, instead peering around the glade with an odd expression.

"Soonish?" I hazarded. "I don't know their schedule, but I'd assume they want to know before the next meeting."

He turned one more time, something hungry and sad in his gaze as he looked around. "I'll consider it. It would be interesting and provide my country an unexpected advantage." The way he said it sounded more question than statement. Either way, I decided to disabuse him.

"Don't expect too much. At best, it might shield Japan more from possible issues rather than give you any advantages. Though if you want to try bribes, fish is very popular among the carnivores. It is a rare delicacy there."

He looked shocked. "Are you suggesting I bribe them?"

"To keep your hide in one piece, to make friends, and convince them humans aren't all barbaric idiots? Absolutely." He blinked, his attention finally on me. "This isn't contract negotiations. It is powerful beings making decisions about how to deal with the myriad ways Magic can manifest and temper her impact. It will either be fascinating and something you'll enjoy your entire life or boring as all get out and you'll try to pawn it off the second you can. But that being said, if you take this, it's up to you to find a successor."

"I am finalizing the last few issues before I end my tenure as Majyutsu-shi. The emperor and I have decided it is time for me to retire, and I must admit I am tired." He cast me a sidelong look. "My views are no longer what they once were. This might be a new thing for me to try that is wholly mine, not my emperor's or my country's. I think I understand the situation."

I doubted he did, but this made it his problem. Not mine.

"Let me know if you decide to do it. But either way, I'd better get back before my partners start making baby decisions without my input." I rose, waggling my hips a bit to settle my balance. "Carelian will show you out."

All this time Carelian had been stretched out under the table at my feet, saying nothing as we talked. He rose and flicked a tail at Hishatio, a rip appearing behind him.

~This way. I will take you back to where you were.~ A moment later they were gone, and I headed downstairs, where the laughter from Jo and Sable engulfed me in love. It would be okay. Really.

CHAPTER
FORTY-TWO

A previous version of this book listed the largest rip made by a mage to be six inches. We apologize for the mistake. The actual length was six meters. During the transcription the measurement was inadvertently changed. ~ Magic Explained

---

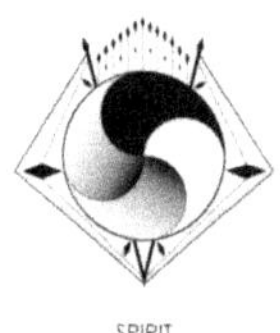

SPIRIT

"Everything is scheduled for the baby shower." Sable was bouncing as she put boxes in the closet.

"Okay. But I swear if there are stupid games, I'm leaving and hiding in my study," I warned as I sat down. The last month had flown by and there was no way anyone would mistake the beach ball in my stomach for anything but a baby.

"You can't hide. You're the guest of honor," Sable pointed out

reasonably, and I glared at her. My temper was super short of late and the kids inside me were trying out to be soccer players or maybe roller derby racers. It felt like they were all punches and elbows.

"No, the babies are the guests of honor, and they will not be showing up unattended." I snickered at that idea and Sable came over to kiss the top of my head.

"Not your favorite thing?" she said softly.

"Oh, I don't mind the having people over part, but being the center of attention for something I still am unsure about feels weird. Some days I'm excited and know these two kids will be joyful additions to my life. Then there are other days where I feel like a stranger took over my body and did something with it. It's exhausting. And I miss my jeans," I moped a bit. "The magic being even wonkier is upsetting and Naomi is about to strangle me. I'm leaning on Carelian so much he's as exhausted as I am, and…"

I bit off what I was about to say and took a deep breath. "Sorry. Yes, party. But are you sure?"

"About the guests? Absolutely. I like Tirsane and Esmere. I did invite Salistra due to the evil fairy precaution. And if people can't handle our friends, they don't need to be here." Sable finished putting the supplies away. "Besides, we decided only people that know about our weirdness are invited. They are planning a small shower for me at work, and it will be boring and normal. Anything you're involved with is never boring. I don't think you need to worry about pretending to be too normal. Though it might be nice to remind people that you aren't boring or average."

I rolled my eyes and tapped my temple. "Few people think that. There aren't enough women at my office to make it worth it, but I think Naomi said she had a gift for me and wanted to take me out to lunch. I do feel better not having to lie to anyone who will be here."

She shrugged. "I get that. But you don't act like a merlin, much less anyone powerful. You'd be surprised at how many people just think of you as average. I'll have mint tea for you and set out brushes for Carelian and Esmere. That way everyone can concentrate on spoiling them, too."

"How many people?" I asked, just trying to get my head wrapped around it and glad Jo and Sable were running the party.

"Fifteen? Maybe a few more? I really haven't worried about it. Marisol, Henri, and Sanchez are coming, bringing gifts from Marco and Paolo. Then my aunt and Dad. Since it is mixed gender Steven and Charles as well. I think Scott, Shay, and Sloan said they might come, but didn't commit. Plus Indira, Tirsane, Jeorgaz, Baneyarl. Whatever, it will be fine."

"Great, the three stooges or the three musketeers. I'm not sure which." I snickered at the image of them running around in tricorns. "Okay. If nothing else, Hamiada will be happy to have people here to show off for."

"Oh, she is. We've got the back yard ready too. Hamiada is still working on creating a fountain with the water. I'm glad spring is here." Sable looked around. "Okay, Jo and I are headed into town and going out to dinner. You sure you don't want to come?"

"No, you go. Enjoy. You aren't going to get much more peace once these show up." I patted my stomach. We still didn't know if it was another girl or a boy. So at least one would be a surprise, but that was fine.

Sable tossed me a compressed lip look. "Maybe, but remember we love you too, and you are welcome to come."

"I'm good. Go." I shooed them out and wandered over to the nursery. The two eggs were still warm, and I guessed happy in their basin of sand. Hamiada assured us they were healthy, just waiting to hatch, but that it wasn't time. I wasn't sure how long eggs could remain dormant like that, but Zmaug had told us to expect years. We were already planning on turning the guest room into a room for the kids. I still had about eight years until the final stage of the inheritance kicked in, so they would share a room until that time. Then we would decide what we wanted to do. Part of me suspected I'd be more than happy to have the place to myself by then, but maybe I was wrong and we would all move, though Hamiada had mentioned she could turn the third floor into real rooms if we wanted. That might be a consideration, but with Carelian and my sidestepping, we rarely needed to have guests sleep over unless they wanted to.

Assuming my magic comes back to normal after the birth.

The worries still plagued me up until the day of the baby shower. I didn't have an answer back from the AIN yet, and Esmere said they did want to meet the humans I'd selected as soon as possible. I'd promised to let them know, but so far I only had two confirmed. Hishatio had gotten back to me about a week after we'd spoken, saying yes. I was proud of myself for refraining from asking if he had decided to do it, or if the Emperor of Japan decided.

I awoke that Saturday, already exhausted. The children had decided to spend the night arguing about the lack of space in my belly, and one of them had the hiccups first thing that morning. But I could sense them better and found myself becoming more protective, less estranged from my own body.

Dr. Lobdell said the babies and I were doing fine, and Jo, Sable, and I had taken all the childbirth classes. I'd opted out of Lamaze, as our first choice was a birth at the center near the hospital. They would let Jo and Sable be there and didn't require all the gowns and medical equipment. Mages had a bad habit of zapping machines during labor as their magic went a bit wonky. We were really worried about what my magic would do. The center also agreed to allow Carelian to be there, though he was still on the fence about it. All of that made me much more relaxed about the idea.

Now if only the party wasn't stressing me out so much.

"You look adorable," Jo said from the door.

I wrinkled my nose at her and looked back at the mirror. I wore a bright green skater dress over leggings and slip-on shoes. I had not been impressed at the varicose veins that had shown up on my thighs—until after the birth I couldn't do anything about them with magic, but it was high on my list.

"I look like I'm about to burst." I still had about nine weeks to go, but Dr. Lobdell didn't think I'd last that long. Apparently, twins usually came early.

"Nah. Not yet." She came over and draped her arm over my shoulders, pressing a kiss into my temple. "You look pregnant and lovely. This will be fun."

"No baby food tasting contests," I warned. I'd tried a few to be prepared and decided there was no way in the world I would feed that to any kid. Blech.

"Promise. Mami is bringing food, as are LaShonda and John. Plus everything we ordered." That was Sable's dad and aunt. They'd taken vacation days to come celebrate and were both going to take a two-week vacation when the babies showed up to stay nearby and help out.

"You know, maybe we should make the garage into a guest house? We can just build an awning for the cars?" The suggestion burst out before I finished thinking as we went down the stairs. "Hamiada said it wasn't part of her. So we can get some contractors in to do it?"

"Huh. That might be a good idea. Especially with the kids. Let me talk to Sable and Hamiada later about it? I don't want to have people traipsing all over her and building without her okay."

"Of course, just a random thought. I seem to have no filter lately. I think it and out it comes."

Jo laughs. "Pregnancy. Marco's wife was just like you in the last few months."

"True." I remembered now, but still; it was disconcerting.

"Come on. Indira and Steve are already here. Carelian went to grab Mami, Papi, and Sanchez. The others had stuff planned with their kids this weekend. I have no idea when the denizens will be here, but Tiantang said he would try to come as did Jeorgaz and Baneyarl." I nodded, making it down the stairs. It would be fun to see everyone. Even though I already wanted a nap.

"Hi momma to be," chirped Sable. She was sparkling with joy, and I was sorry she couldn't carry kids. I had a suspicion she would have loved being pregnant.

"So where do I sit?"

The spring weather was gorgeous today, so we were in the sunroom and the yard, with all the doors opened and it felt even bigger than it was.

"Here," she waved at an Adirondack chair complete with a bench for my feet and a light blanket if a breeze came up.

I laughed. "I'm going to be spoiled, huh?"

"Yes you are. You have given us the best gift ever, so yes, we are going to spoil you. Now sit." Sable mock glared as I heard the doorbell ring. The next twenty minutes were spent saying hi to my family and friends and being vaguely surprised they all made time to come to celebrate this with us. The table they had set up for gifts overflowed onto the floor. I kept seeing glimpses of Hamiada beaming with joy at the life and magic filling her.

I got hugs from Steven and Indira, not to mention seeing Charles and Arachena. To my surprise and delight, Scott, Sloan, and Shay showed up courtesy of Dahli, much to Carelian's disgust. But Arachena seemed delighted from how she and Elsba chattered.

A ripple in the air and a spike of pain heralded the arrival of our other guests. I smiled as Tirsane slithered out of the rip, followed by Esmere, Baneyarl, and to my surprise Salistra. A moment later, Jeorgaz popped out over my chair and perched on the back. He bent over me, peering at my stomach.

~Humans clutch weird. Isn't it easier to have them in eggs?~

I laughed and petted his breastbone. All the animal shaped denizens loved to be petted and scratched. They didn't regard it as demeaning, simply leaned in and enjoyed. Deep down I admitted it made me feel better. They oozed contentment at such times.

"It might be easier, but you know very well mammals don't lay eggs."

~Platypus do. It seems a much wiser course of action.~ He preened my hair as Tirsane talked to Marisol and I watched everyone stare at Salistra. She was gleaming today, with flowers in her hair, and only about the size of a normal horse.

Suddenly every denizen in the area stopped and stared at the yard, at the empty area where I'd had my meltdown. The grass hadn't grown back over it and we had discussed building a fire pit there, though Hamiada had turned the spring into a small fountain. I still had slashes of guilt about Stevie, but all I could do at this point was try to get the information out there so no other mother or sibling ever suffered this way again.

Above that glazed area of ground a ripple appeared with the accompanying spike. The rip to a plane didn't worry me. It was the reaction of all my non-human guests that caused my heart rate to double.

The ripple expanded, then slid open. It was ponderous, and oddly painful. Even as I frowned against the pain, I did a quick count of everyone I'd expected. Tiantang was the only being not here that I might have expected. So it could be him.

Jo and Sable moved over toward me, standing in front of me, while Esmere and Carelian stood at my side. In subtle movements, I was now protected back and front as the rip stabilized.

"Are you expecting anyone unusual?" Sable murmured in a low voice. Everyone around me was focused on the rip and I was braced to run, attack, or greet them with a smile. But the production this entrance was making set my teeth on edge.

"Not that you didn't know about. Did Tiantang verify he was coming?" That was more to Carelian than anyone.

~Not yet.~

Hishatio doesn't have the ability to plane travel, does he? And why would he come here?

My phone rang, and I shunted the call away, not caring who might be trying to get ahold of me at this moment. Besides, near rips the phone tended to misbehave, dropping calls and more. Plus the fact that darn near everyone I cared about was right here.

Before I could let my imagination run away with me more, two people stepped out. Two tall men with flowing black hair, muscles for miles, and chiseled faces that could have been carved from granite. Their skin was a red brown that I'd only seen in terra cotta, while their clothes were bright colors of the earth, both strong and sharp at the same time. They carried between them a perch similar to what I'd seen in the council chamber, only three times as big.

All of that burned into my mind as I watched a third figure step out.

FORTY-THREE

China seems to be settling down, though more and more mages are being brought to the palace for training. But is it training or re-education, or could Empress Cixi be looking for a new consort? As the first single female ruler in over a century, men must be begging for her attention. The question is does she want a powerful mage at her side or will she marry for political power. ~ Magical Daily News

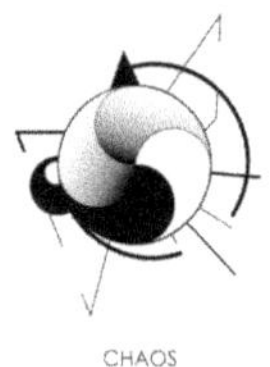

CHAOS

'd always thought of powerful women to be like Indira, beautiful, elegant, flawless. Something that I could never be. The only thing this woman had that I equated with power deep in my mind was long hair threaded with feathers and beads. But she wasn't tall and willowy.

Instead, she barely topped five feet. She was almost as wide as she was tall, with hair so gray I wasn't sure which strands were white and which were dark. Her face was wrinkled and drawn in to the point that a wizened apple came to mind. In her hand she held a staff covered with carvings, but so detailed I couldn't see what they were. At the top feathers hung from braids, waving in the soft breeze. She wore clothes that reminded me of Indira, loose, flowy, and elegant. But what caught me most of all was her companions' reaction to her. They checked to see if they had put the perch in the right spot. They moved out to flank her, yet when she stumbled just the slightest, they were there to steady her.

Liquid symbols that meant nothing to me came out from her in a soft undertone and out of the rip flew a giant bird. I'd seen eagles and a condor once at an animal park. This bird made them look like hummingbirds in comparison. It settled on the perch, his crown a dark brown that was almost black, but along the body the colors lightened down to the tail feathers that were a gleaming gold.

~Huh. A thunderbird. I haven't talked to one of those in, well, ever.~ Jeorgaz murmured the thought in my mind, but I couldn't take my eyes off the strange woman.

She pivoted around, looking at the gathered people. I followed her gaze, to see that the Guzman's were on the porch, looking worried and determined, but everyone else spread out around me. I didn't know if I was proud or terrified. I pushed it away and moved out through my friends, though I didn't go past Tirsane, who stood a bit off to one side to the left of Jo and Sable. She was coiled down, calling to mind a rattler about to strike. Most of her body was hidden behind one of the Adirondack benches we'd brought out, and she had on a wide-brimmed hat containing her snakes.

Salistra had been under the trees and she had faded back, invisible to the people standing there.

"May I help you?" I pitched my voice to carry out into the yard.

They all pivoted to look at me wearing my bright green dress and the crown of flowers one of Jo's co-workers had made for me.

"We seek audience with Corisande Munroe," one of the men boomed. It sounded formal and odd in this setting.

"That's me. Can I help you?"

The woman stepped forward, or more accurately shuffled, then the bird shifted its attention back to her and her steps became firmer. "Who are you to order one of the Nation to attend you in the realms?"

"Umm? What?" I stared at her, confused. "I was asked to gather human mages to represent the Earth on the council. They requested one mage from the AIN."

"Why? And do you serve them? Are they your masters? Do you expect one of mine to serve you?"

My temper spiked a bit, and I folded my arms across my chest, wincing at how much my breast size had increased. I could barely cross my arms. My arms dropped to my sides, uncomfortable with my body. It just made me more annoyed.

"I think the better question is, who are you? This is my house and a baby shower is being held here for me. And you are here making demands."

One of the men stiffened and glared at me. "You demanded we provide a person."

"Um, no." I didn't even try to prevent the sarcasm in my comment. "I talked to someone who I suspected had contacts in the AIN and asked if there was anyone I could talk to. I can call him if you in any way doubt that was what happened."

The men seemed to swell with outrage and I noted Esmere starting to bristle and Carelian sink down lower, his ears flat across his skull.

The bird raised his wings, and they extended past the men on each side, casting them in shadow even as the portal resealed behind them.

~Enough. I see others here. On the side of humans? Why?~

I figured it was the thunderbird speaking, and I gritted my teeth. At this rate people were going to come to parties I attended just to see drama.

"I have a better question. Who are you to be so rude to the Herald of Magic?" Tirsane rose to her full height, and I guessed put on a few inches or a foot. At the same time, she pulled off the hat that had kept her snakes corralled. "In fact, I believe Brix should be here."

The double takes from the representatives told me they had not noticed her, though Baneyarl and Esmere were impossible to miss. Even Elsba hung in the air in front of Sloan, her fangs bared.

From her tone I knew she was pissed, and I really didn't want statues on my lawn. "Tirsane, I've got this," I said mildly, walking out front. Having her fight any battle on Earth would be bad. I couldn't swear to it, but I knew it. Baneyarl stepped forward with me, as did Esmere, Carelian, Jo, and Sable.

I couldn't help it. I laughed and waved at the army I had at my side. "They are here because they are my friends, my family, and ones I love. Can the same be said about you? Do you value open requests for assistance so little?"

From how red the men turned, I feared they were in risk of imploding, as the bird glared at me, but a warning hiss from Tirsane had him lowering his wings. I'd never researched a thunderbird, so I had no idea what his abilities were.

"I see," the old woman spoke, and this time her words were hesitant. "It seems information has been twisted. Would you please tell me what message you meant to pass?"

"Merlin," I muttered as I tried to remember. "I called up John Taliance and told him that Brix had requested one of the human council mages invited to be a new council member be from the AIN. I asked if he could get a message to someone. That I needed to talk to someone and see if the AIN had a mage that was willing to serve on the council, per their request. That was it. Merlin's whiskers, I was hoping someone would call me and ask what I was talking about."

All three of them stood, staring at me.

"If you don't believe me, I'll call Taliance up and he can tell you what I said." I started to reach for my phone, but the woman held up a hand.

"I believe there has been a misunderstanding." She waved her fingers at the men and then looked up at the bird. He mantled and shuffled, but dipped his head down. She made an odd face and for a minute she looked like she would spit, but she walked out onto the lawn, away from her entourage, and used her staff to steady herself. "I am Amadahy of the Wakinyan. I am here to discuss this request with Corisande Munroe."

I sighed. This was not going to go well, I could tell. But I couldn't refuse the offer. "We are having a baby shower at the moment. If you would like to join us then I can talk to you after, that is fine. Otherwise, later?" That last part was offered weakly. I had no idea what it cost them to come here, and I didn't want to piss anyone off, but dang it, this was a party partially for me. And I wanted to try and enjoy it.

She tilted her head. "Baby shower?"

"A celebration of the new lives to come, a time for family to gather and help the new parents prepare for that life."

"Ah." She paused as if thinking. "We would be honored to participate in the celebration of new life yet to come." She tilted her head, then turned to look at the bird. I could almost hear the discussion between them, though not a sound was made. He, and I had zero doubt it was a male, clacked his beak hard, then turned and preened, pulling out one long golden black feather from one wing and dropped it in the hand of one of the men, then a matching feather from the other wing.

The man brought the feathers to the old woman, his face surprised, but more relaxed than when they first appeared.

She walked toward me slowly, not in a shuffle but a cautious movement as if testing the ground before her as she took each step.

She's blind.

I flicked my eyes toward the bird and his intent gaze on the woman, no, the area in front of her.

And the bird is her eyes. Wow.

She stopped a step or two away from me and lifted her head to face me. Her eyes were mismatched, something I knew was called heterochromia. One was blue, the other brown, but both had fixed pupils tight and small.

"I apologize for the rudeness we showed. As a gift for the babes you carry, I gift you with primary feathers from our Wakinyan, Kalihchiia. When they are older and wear these, they will gain passage into the Adekagagwaa."

I heard sharp intakes of breaths around me. What she had provided was almost priceless. And my government would do anything to get ahold of these.

"Your gifts will be cherished. Come and join us." I glanced at Jo and Sable, who nodded. "Be aware this house and land is that of the dryad Hamiada. Be kind to her."

As if my saying her name summoned her, Hamiada slowly faded into existence between me and Tirsane.

"Ah," Hamiada said. "Those who work with nature, not against her. I have heard of you. Be nice to Cori. I like her." She leaned close, her sharp pointy nose almost touching Amadahy. Hamiada's head twisted to an inhuman angle. "Interesting." Then Hamiada faded back out.

"I begin to see why you were approached. Go celebrate. We will talk later." Amadahy waved at me and I narrowed my eyes, feeling uncomfortably like I had just been given permission to attend my own party.

"Let me, Cori," Indira murmured in my ear. "I'll escort her."

I heard all the things contained in the word escort: guard, watch, protect, spy. Stress bled away slightly and I gave Indira a huge smile. "Thank you." My "I owe you" went unsaid, but understood.

Before getting involved in the festivities starting back up, I headed directly to the nursery, Jo and Sable close by, with Carelian standing at the door, his tail still lashing and hackles raised.

"Hamiada," I said softly in the nursery, Jo and Sable at the door, making sure they filled it as Carelian lay at the door to my room.

She stepped out of the trees painted on the wall as if she'd been waiting for me.

"Your parties are so interesting. Do you mind if I talk to the bird woman later? I have a sister that would like to be transplanted there."

I blinked at her. "No, you are always free to talk to anyone you wish."

Hamiada just bobbled on her toes. "Hmm?"

"This is a protected safe room, right? Your place? No one can get into it?" I pushed, needing to make sure. All of me was vibrating just a bit too much and the lemonade I'd had didn't sit well in my stomach.

"Unless I allow it, no. It is my space, part of my reality." Her voice was unconcerned as she spun slowly.

"Then I will trust that you can protect these from anyone," I said, holding out my hands with the feathers nestled in my palm.

She froze at my words, even as I felt the tensions from Jo and Sable fade a bit. "Put these someplace safe, where only the babies can get to them when they are ready."

Hamiada peered at the feathers, her green eyes widening a bit. "And how will I know when they are ready?"

I shrugged. "You'll know or they'll tell you, or maybe we will. But they need to be kept safe." If I wasn't worried it would be a slap in the face of Amadahy I would have burned them.

"Hmmmmm, oh yes." She reached out and gently picked up the feathers, then scaled a tree to the sketch of a bird I hadn't noticed before. As she touched it, it fleshed out, becoming more realistic and sharper. With care, she put one feather in one wing, and one in the other. A ripple ran through the bird, then it moved, flying through the trees to another limb. It reminded me of watching animation, the bird obviously a drawing, yet real too.

She jumped down and pointed. "There. They are safe until they ask for it."

I all but sagged in relief. "Thank you."

"My existence is much more interesting since you moved in. I have much to chatter with the other dryads about. They are very jealous. You may get your dryad for the second house. I have friends that are considering it."

I just nodded and headed back, keeping my mouth shut about the gossip between denizens.

We walked back outside to see Baneyarl and the two men talking, while Amadahy sat in a chair, her head tilted as she watched and listened. Indira sat next to her keeping up a light chatter. The thunderbird perched on the back of Amadahy's chair, his head twisting one way, then the other.

Jo slipped her arm around my waist and I laid my head on her shoulders. "Only you, Cori." Her voice amused as she hugged me to her. "Most people are going to do a shower, make diaper designs, have some cake, get baby clothes, but no, you have to have people from an almost mythical part of our world step out and give you gifts of immeasurable worth."

"Pfft," I muttered. "I just was hoping I wouldn't have to do anything too stupid. Instead, I end up in a political game, again. People need to learn to chill out."

"Good luck with that," Sable murmured, resting a chin on my shoulder while her arm snaked around to touch my belly. "When it comes to you, I think you're the only chill one."

~And you wonder why I love being your focus. You three are rarely boring.~

We snarled at Carelian, much to his amusement, and went to enjoy the rest of the party.

In the end, the conversation with Amadahy was a bit anticlimactic. She apologized again, and I foisted her off on Tirsane and Salistra. They could convince her. She'd barely flickered an eyelash at Salistra and Baneyarl, implying she'd seen or knew of unicorns and gryphons, so I left them to it. I wanted a nap.

FORTY-FOUR

Pregnancy Fact: Baby showers predate magic, America, and most existing civilizations. Believed to have originated in Ancient Rome or Egypt, they were originally women-only affairs. Over the years, as men have stepped into more pro-active child rearing, this has changed, becoming an event to celebrate the forthcoming birth. ~ The Pregnant Mage

---

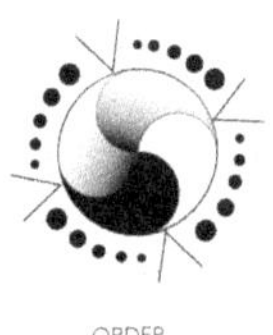

ORDER

The party was fun, and I think even the crashers had enjoyed themselves, though I noted that Scott Randolph and Charles kept a close eye on them. It amused me that Arachena did not like any of them, though Esmere didn't seem to mind. Carelian stayed near me and time went on.

I worked, prepped for the babies, did my checkups and basically existed, feeling fatter and more awkward all the time. We'd given up our hikes when I'd lost the sidestepping ability and I hated how out of shape and self-conscious I felt. I was at the 36-week mark and I wanted it to be over. It felt like I was constantly censoring myself because I wanted these parasites out. I might love these two kids, and Jo, and Sable, but right now the idea of going on a murder spree and killing them all was forefront in my mind.

~It's time,~ Esmere whispered in my mind.

~What?~ I said back. I'd just gotten comfortable after a long day at work on Wednesday, and wanted nothing more but to rest my feet until dinner. It would be nice if my feet weren't the size of watermelons, or at least would fit into my shoes. I had started to understand the allure of slippers all day. ~Time for what?~

~The others are here. You need to introduce them. They are your representatives.~

~Are you kidding?~ I groaned. The idea of getting up, finding a bra, good clothes, even brushing my hair sounded like a monumental effort.

~No. I will be there shortly. Be ready.~

"ARRGHGHGH!" I screamed at the top of my lungs, the small study ringing with my screech. Pounding feet, a sudden growl, and a poof of Hamiada all followed. In less time than it took me to pry myself out of the chair I had a Cath, a dryad, and two women staring at me with wide eyes and panicked looks. Panic on a dryad meant twigs jutting out everywhere with little thorns.

"What's wrong? Are the babies coming? Are you okay?" I was sure Carelian hadn't asked any of those questions as I brushed by them, grumping with each waddling step. But that was only because they were all audible.

"No. I have to go introduce the delegates, and Esmere is coming now." I snarled at Carelian, whose tail was starting to unpoof. "Your mother doesn't understand the words advance notice."

I made it to my bedroom, ripped off my top, fumbled a bra on, and another top. "So I'm headed to the council now." I winced and sighed as a ripple of pain went across my belly. "And I'm having Braxton-Hicks contractions and they suck."

Those had started a few days ago, but Dr. Anna Lobdell had assured me they were normal and I still had weeks to go. I swear I almost started crying in her office. Hormones sucked.

"Do you want us to go with you?" Jo looked worried, and she almost loomed with the need to help or protect me.

I took a deep breath and pushed down my annoyance and frustration. I walked over and pulled her head down to kiss her forehead. "I'm fine. Just cranky and tired. A few more weeks and you'll get to welcome these kids to the world. Sorry, I'm being such a bitch."

Sable snorted and kissed my temple. "You aren't. You're amazing and there is nothing we can ever do to thank you for this."

I laughed. "Be glad you're getting two this go around. Not sure I can do this again." Neither of them said anything, just squeezed me tighter.

A prick of pain, then Esmere arrived. ~Are you ready?~

From experience I knew that fussing at her would leave her unmoved. I pulled away from my family and slipped on some shoes. "Yes."

She opened the rip and the three of us stepped through into the unfortunately familiar stonework of the council chamber. I stared around the chamber and spotted Shay and Hishatio, who were very obviously not paying attention to each other. I didn't see Amadahy.

I walked over to them. "Merlins. Having fun yet?" I didn't even try to stop the snark. The pain had settled into my lower back and I didn't have time to pay attention.

They both looked at me, then at each other, and stiffened. "It is fine, Merlin Munroe," Hishatio said stiffly.

"I swear to Merlin, if you don't yank that stick out of your ass,

I'll have Carelian bite you. I don't care if you have issues, I don't care if one of you slept with the other's wife, I don't care if you stole something that was more precious to you than the world. Take a good look at these denizens. They regard humans as little more than cattle and often have humans as toys. Your entire job here is to prove that we aren't disposable and help keep Magic in check and maybe stop the number of rips appearing on Earth." They both looked at me like little boys who'd just had their hands caught in the cookie jar.

A shuffle and tapping behind me had me turning to see Amadahy walking up, her staff tapping on the stones. The thunderbird, I couldn't remember its name, was sitting on a perch at the edge of the stones looking fierce and protective.

"Hishatio and Shay, this is Amadahy from the Adekagagwaa territory, also known as the AIN." Both men blinked, but nodded to her. She gave them a blank stare followed by a sharp nod.

~Shall we begin?~ Brix's voice filled my brain and the room. I gestured to the chairs and the perch and they shuffled over, looking around at all the beings in the place. I think it finally began to dawn on them they weren't top dog as they took in the naga, gorgon, unicorn, Cath, and others I didn't even have names for. Outside on the grassy area where the wall had been before Brix vanished it, lounged Zmaug. She waved at me and I shook my head and waved back, before moving to stand in front of the three mages.

I didn't know for sure what was going to happen, but I had a very good idea.

~Who speaks for the mages from Earth?~ The abrupt launch into the meeting didn't surprise me this time, though I still wondered if there was a conversation I was missing, like not getting sign language or something. Either way, I'd do this and get out of here.

"Corisande Munroe wishes to introduce the council representatives for Earth." I projected my voice, making it as clear and loud as I could, even as another fake contraction wrapped around my body. Why did anyone do this pregnancy stuff? Figuring out how to create an external womb with magic moved higher on my to be researched list.

~Proceed.~

The eyes of everyone weighed heavy on me. Even Salistra, who still sneered a bit, had her full attention on us.

I went through and introduced each of them, playing up their power and rank. "They will serve as the representatives of Earth on the council." I nodded and waved at them.

~We welcome the Lords of Earth.~

I groaned a bit at that, especially as all three of them actually preened. Egos. Merlin, save me from egos.

~The first order of business,~ Brix started to drone, and I slipped backward. The stupid false contractions were annoying, and I wanted to get home.

~Cori, we need to go back. Naomi is on the phone; she needs to speak to you.~ Carelian's voice was both welcome and cringe worthy. The last thing I wanted to do was deal with Naomi, but it was an excuse to get out of here, and I'd take it.

~I have to leave,~ I sent to Esmere. ~Please make sure they get back to their homes.~

~Of course. This should be an interesting meeting.~ She had her amber eyes locked on the thunderbird and I just shook my head as Carelian opened a portal between here and the house.

Jo was standing there, phone to her ear, giving me a funny look. "Cori, did you have any plans for this week?"

I blinked at her, "Napping?"

"Umm… here, you better take this." She handed the phone to me. It was her phone not mine. With a puzzled look I took it.

"Hello?"

"Cori, where in Merlin's name are you?" It was Pearl Takahashi.

"Ummm, in my house?" I said warily, having no idea what she was talking about.

There was a hiss of exasperation. "Is there a reason you haven't responded to any of the emails, confirmed flight information, or followed up to make sure you knew what was expected of you?"

I stood there my mind racing. "Pearl, what are you talking about?"

"Cori, you are expected to be in Beijing for the ceremony tomorrow. Why are you still in the US?"

"Last I heard they were still arguing. I haven't even talked to anyone about it in months. I figured it would take another few months to even get agreements figured out."

A hiss of annoyance slipped through. "You have been sent multiple emails, all the calls have either gone to a non-working or disconnected number, they even sent you mail. Your personal emergency information still has the Atlanta numbers for Jo and Sable, and emails to your work have gone unanswered."

My mouth opened to refute everything then I paused. "Oh. I changed my number after the jumping out of a plane incident, and I guess I never updated anything when Jo and Sable moved up here. They got new local numbers. But email?"

I waddled upstairs, groaning a bit, being on the second floor now seemed like a huge mistake.

"Yes email and letters and calls!" Pearl hissed. "Then to make it worse Gloria got really sick and had you marked as verified. No one realized until two days ago when she was well enough to be taken off the ventilator that she had meant she needed to verify your plans."

My shoulders were hunched in guilt as I made it to my computer. "One minute, let me put you on speaker." My work phone was on the desk next to my personal computer. I pulled up both of them and there were no emails. Then I checked spam. "Oh."

"Oh what? The only reason I even knew how to get ahold of you without sending someone to your work was I remembered Jo's last name and looked her up."

"The emails all went to spam. Both work and personal. Sorry." I was sorry. I didn't mean to cause this much trouble. I checked my work phone and sure enough a bunch of numbers from DC had been marked as spam calls, so they never rang through and I hadn't thought to look. "I'm sorry."

"Cori. There is a flight leaving JFK in two hours. You will be on it, you will have clothes. I am telling you this as a friend, because there are state department people at your Atlanta apartment right now, and they have dispatched people to the Albany house. I'd get packing."

"I don't have anything to wear for a fancy ceremony!" I blurted, panic setting in. "And I'm eight months pregnant. Just tell them I can't come."

"That is not an option," Pearl gritted out through her teeth. "Pack. You have twenty minutes. Maybe. I'll get you something decent to wear." She hung up with a click that had restrained rage in it.

"Are you kidding me?" I stared at the phone. "Jo! Sable! Help!"

I explained everything to them, and after they quit laughing they got me packed, pulled out my rarely used make up, found flats that would go with most dresses, and got me into comfortable clothes for the flight.

"I'd like to say I'm not super happy about this," Jo commented as I stood on the front porch waiting for the car.

"If I didn't think it would cause an international incident, and I'm suspecting they would arrest me and throw me on the plane, I'd probably decline."

~Should I go with you?~ Carelian's ears were back and his tail cracked back and forth.

"No. You really don't like planes. Go hang with Tiantang and be there when I land." I smirked with a bit of sadistic pleasure. "You two can cause an incident by waiting for me at the gate. Get everyone up in arms."

His ears perked up a bit. ~That does sound amusing. I am sure Tiantang will enjoy being rebellious.~

"Good." I leaned down and rubbed his ears and kissed the top of his head. "I'll miss you, but I'll probably sleep most of the way.

And if I'm not sleeping, I'll knit." I held up my bag that had my knitting needles and the almost done baby blanket. I'd had to unravel and try again seven times so far, but this time I might have figured it out. It had almost become fun. Almost.

The car pulled up with two very official looking men. After verifying credentials and one last round of hugs and pets, I was whisked off to JFK. Oddly it was the best flying experience I'd ever had. I was granted priority first class, and because moving fast in my condition wasn't possible, I had a golf cart take me right to the gate. I don't know if they had been holding it for me, but the stewardess ushered me and my bag into a first-class seat and the door was locked.

I sank, exhausted into the seat, ecstatic that it was comfortable. The flight from JFK to Beijing was about twenty-one hours, including a three-hour layover in Taipei. I looked at the folder one of the men handed me, and sighed. The extensive itinerary, the promise someone would meet me in Taipei, and everything I needed to do while I was there at the ceremony looked exhausting. I shove it in my bag, pulled out the blanket and knitted until I fell asleep.

A shudder through the plane jolted me awake, and I sat there listening. Another violent shake, then an explosion from my left. I whipped around to peer out the window and saw the engine on the wing burst into flames. I pulled back surprised. Another explosion from the right had me flinching. I struggled to look out my window only to see the other engine with more fire licking out of it. The oxygen masks dropped onto my head, hanging above me.

What was going on?

"Flight attendants, prepare for a water landing," the captain's voice came over the speakers and I felt my heart seize as I looked at the oceans of water around us.

The attendants jumped into action. Talking on the announcement system, getting us into life vests. I sat there numb.

We were all going to die.

Around me people were freaking out and I could hear terror as people grabbed at the masks. My heart and throat locked as I looked out at black-as-night water. It rippled below us like the heart of chaos, hungry and unforgiving.

~Carelian, tell Jo and Sable I love them. I'm sorry.~

CHAPTER

CHAPTER
FORTY-FIVE

When written in Chinese, the word 'crisis' is composed of two characters. One represents danger and the other represents opportunity. ~ John F. Kennedy, 35th U.S. president.

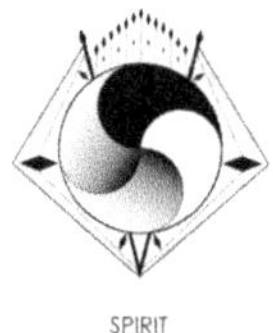

SPIRIT

~Cori? What is wrong? Cori!~ Carelian's voice was hard and desperate in my mind, but I couldn't even think enough to reply with all the chaos surrounding me.

The hard, unforgiving water reflected light, and I knew we would shatter. In theory, I should be able to control air to lift us, but for this far, to let us land? The display a few minutes ago had pointed out we were halfway through our journey and the nearest land was further than we could ever make with no engines. Even now I could feel the plane shuddering as we descended. There wasn't any place to even crash on, the Atlantic had few islands from what I knew.

There was still cabin pressure, though the masks dangled like a threat and promise in front of me. The attendants were moving back and forth getting everyone belted in and prepared for the water landing. I tried to think as I caught the hissed words between them as they passed.

"Someone did this. Either magic or a bomb. They want this plane to go down."

The muffled words wrapped around my soul. Was this a set up or someone taking advantage of the situation? Either way, someone on this plane was most likely involved. There were many people willing to die to achieve their goals.

What had I done? Had I put these children at risk? My hands curled over my belly. For the first time I felt the fierce connection with them. These were my kids too, and I'd face down Tirsane and Salistra for them. That final snap of connection motivated me, and I started to think.

How do I save us? Preferably everyone?

Most of my expertise was on small things, moving cells, starting fires, identifying patterns, not keeping planes from falling out of the sky. How in the world could I do anything to stop us from crashing?

I grabbed a breathing mask as I thought, forcing my mind to focus. If I had time and the chance to work with others, we could do that. But this? I assumed we only had minutes as the plane shuddered and jolted.

The bomb from D.C. and how I had dealt with it flashed into my mind. It was an idea. Crazy, insane, but an idea. And maybe it might work. If my friends, my family, could come through for me. I definitely couldn't do this by myself.

And I'd never have to.

~Carelian, can Hamiada create a huge pocket realm full of swamp to catch a plane?~

~TO WHAT?!~ His mental voice held so much terror I almost cried.

~I don't have time. Can she do it? And let me open a portal to it?~

Frantic seconds passed as the plane shook and people cried out. My fear just made it worse and I couldn't help but wonder what would someone gain by killing us? Because we would die if this plane went down. At least that was my fear. What did I know? I'd never been in a plane accident before and I'd like to avoid ever being in one again.

~I grabbed Malkin and Tirsane. They say with Hamiada they can do that. Tirsane says she needs to know how fast the plane is traveling and that you will need to make the rip big enough for it to fit. Cori, what is going on?~ His voice gave me hope.

~I'm trying to save myself and everyone else. Get it made, I'll get the speed.~ I struggled from my seat, the bouncing around making it hard. But I held onto the backs of the seats and started to force my way to the front. ~I love you all so much. Make sure they know. Carelian, make sure they know.~

~I'm with them now. Cori, come home.~ His frantic pleading broke my heart, but I couldn't do anything. Even if I could sidestep from something moving, at this speed I'd die slamming into something. We both knew it.

~I'm trying.~

"Ma'am, sit down. You have to brace for the emergency landing." One of the attendants yelled at me over the noise. She was belted in and her face was whiter than the uniform shirt she wore.

"I have to talk to the pilots. I have an idea." I reached the door between us and the pilots.

"You can't. Sit down!" She barked as she wrapped her arms over her head. "You're going to get killed. The door is locked. Sit!"

I pounded on the door, but realized I didn't have time to wait, even if they opened it. With a thought, I reached out and accelerated the decay of the molecules in the door, ignoring the inch of hair it cost. If I could get us to the pocket realm, get everyone isolated, we would all be safe. The authorities could deal with it then.

The attendant had been about to unbuckle and come after me when the door collapsed into a pile of dust, and the co-pilot on the right whirled to look at me. "If this is a hijacking, you're too late. We're in full water landing mode." Anger and fear lanced through his voice. The cockpit was full of flashing lights and sounds, which only cemented the feeling of certain doom. Healthy vehicles didn't make all those sounds.

"I'm hoping I can save us instead." I braced myself in the doorway, the freefall making my gorge and protruding stomach rise.

"What? Are you strong enough to make us fly?" His voice was sarcastic as the other pilot frantically pushed buttons and talked into his headset.

Maybe, before this, I might have been. But now there wasn't a chance, much less the time to learn enough about aerodynamics to be able to do anything.

"No. But I can give us someplace else to land that should be better than the middle of the ocean." Which was another thing that stuck out in my mind. We were crossing the largest stretch of water in our journey and now is when this happened? Was this on purpose? A terrorist threat?

Or are they trying to kill me?

I avoided thinking about that and asked the question. "How fast are we going, in land miles per hour, please?" I had no desire to try to translate the speed. At least in miles I could comprehend how fast we were going.

"You're crazy, and we don't have time for this."

"Do you have a better idea? Because I'm thinking that water looks like a death sentence." My voice was sarcastic, and I didn't care. Fear wrapped around me, and I wanted to hold my kids, but first I needed to make sure we lived through the next five minutes.

"Whatever, lady. We're going about 308 mph right now. I've got the nose so we can glide as long as possible. If we're going slow enough when we hit the water, maybe we won't shatter on contact." He kept looking at me, but I could only focus on the unforgiving ocean so far and yet too close below us.

~Did you hear that?~ I sent in my mind, my fingers aching from how hard I was grasping the door frame.

~Yes, giving her the information now. They are creating it.~ Carelian's voice was clipped, so tense with worry he could barely make words.

I watched the water shimmering ahead, so calm, peaceful, and deadly. This had to work.

"Whatever you're going to do lady, you better do it fast, because we've got about 3 minutes."

~Do you have the realm ready?~

~Yes, here.~ He sent me a feeling. It was kind of like how I would know where to sidestep by memorizing a place, but it was more than that, it was knowing and feeling the essence. He sent me that.

~Got it.~ I looked at the pilot who had an expression somewhere between "get the crazy woman out of here" and "can a merlin save us?" Hope was so damn insidious.

"This is going to sound insane." Another bump and I almost fell, but there was no other option. I had to do this. A double merlin or more and I didn't know how to fix this. Was I being arrogant thinking I was the only person who could come up with a solution?

I turned and looked, hoping for a mage with an aerospace degree, but everyone else had strapped in, heads down, crying, yelling. Ten minutes. If I had even ten minutes, I could find another mage or two on the plane and we could plan something. But I suspected no matter what, eventually we'd end up in the water.

"You need to fly this into a portal rip."

"Are you insane?" The other man turned to glare at me. "I can barely control this thing as it is, and crashing in the ocean is one thing. Into a portal sounds insane."

"Better than the ocean, where I suspect we'll die. On the other side of the rip I'll have friends waiting." I peered through the cockpit windows from my braced position in the doorway. I had to do this right. I would not die like this.

"Why not? The risk when we hit the water is not good. I don't know if we can slow the plane enough to keep from shattering upon impact, and that's if the water was completely calm. It isn't. I suppose being eaten by monsters will be better." He clicked something on the control panel. "New York Control, this is Kappa 324 we are descending through 6000 feet. Unable to restore engines. We are trying a Hail Mary. We have a merlin creating a rip to another realm for us. No other changes since last communication."

"Repeat Kappa 324. You are going to ditch into a planar rip, over?" The person on the other side of the radio sounded incredulous, and I couldn't blame them. The whole thing seemed unreal to me and I was creating it.

"Roger. We are going to try."

There was a long pause. "Roger Kappa 324. Good luck." The pilot let go of the toggle and looked at me. "Go for it lady, we have nothing left to lose."

The sound and jouncing got worse, and I was sure I was about to throw up the water I'd drank. "Here goes nothing or everything," I muttered and focused. I'd sacrifice all of my hair and everything else to pull this off.

The rip formed. I felt it, but it was too tiny to see from this distance. I needed time to get it large enough. In the past, just the offering for the rip was more than enough to make it human sized. This time I needed to make it big enough for an airplane. Hair vaporized like an invisible trimmer was cutting off lengths. The bigger I made it, the more it cost.

To complicate everything, the damn contractions were doubling down, and I was trying to breathe through them. I didn't have time for this, and each pulse of pain jarred my concentration.

"Merlin's balls," one of the men whispered. "She's doing it. Initiate fuel dump now."

The portal hung in the air, huger than anything I'd ever seen. If I'd had more time I'd have tried to make the opening horizontal instead of vertical, but habit had made it vertical, which meant trying to widen it also made it taller. If there'd been someone to measure it, I'd have to bet it was the largest portal ever recorded.

"Fuel dump initiated, but we lost a lot when the engine blew. Estimate another ten minutes to empty."

The rip hung there sparkling at us, impossibly close and far away.

"Fly into it. I've done what I can." I was panting, in agony, and covered with sweat. What was wrong with me?

"Lady, you've done enough. We've got this. Get in your seat and buckle in," one of them said, awe in his voice. But I was already staggering back to my seat, all but falling into it. I wanted to throw up so badly and my hair barely reached past my shoulders, whereas when I'd gotten on the plane it was to the middle of my back.

People were crying and muttering and from the odor in the cabin more than one person had given in to the urge to throw up. The belt secured, I curled up in a ball and reached for Carelian.

~I love you. We're coming in. Make sure everyone is clear. Soft mud is going to bake and be hot. Tell Hamiada to be safe. Don't let her get hurt.~ There was a large crack and groan and I glanced across the plane out the other window to see one of the wing tips get sheared off. The rip hadn't been big enough.

The plane fell, hitting something. I slammed forward, the seat groaning. My head impacted the wall, a lash of pain, and light exploded in my mind.

FORTY-SIX

Preparations are underway for the big ceremony in two days. Delegates from all over the world are arriving. Hishatio Yamamoto will be standing in for the Emperor of Japan as his last official act as Majyutsu-shi of Japan. ~ Magical Daily News

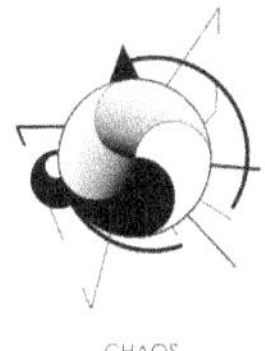

CHAOS

"Merlin Munroe, I need you to wake up now." The insistent words fought through the blackness in my mind and I managed to crack my eyes open, only to shut them instantly as my brain tried to implode.

My fingers quested over the side of my skull, lingering over

the large lump on my temple, and came away sticky. No wonder my head hurt.

"Merlin, you need to get up." The voice was male and desperate. I cracked my eyes, flinching as light sent razors through my brain.

"Did we make it?" I muttered, the words slurring more than I liked. I swallowed thickly and tried to think.

"The plane is damaged, but we're motionless, which means a lot." His voice quavered at the end.

I focused. I was in my seat in first class, the one next to me still empty. People were hovering in the aisle and leaning over the seats in front of me. I felt like a specimen on display. "But?" I asked, trying not to whimper in pain between my head and the contractions still ripping through me.

"We can't get the doors open and there are... creatures outside." He actually whispered the word creatures.

~Carelian?~

~CORI!~ There was a flash of pain that had me sobbing, then his head was in my lap, his body in the empty seat, his purr vibrating my body, and soothing my heart. ~Cori, you're okay.~

The people around me screamed, and I caught glimpses of them diving backward away from Carelian, but I didn't care. I buried my face in his fur and tried not to sob. Everything hurt. My head, my body, even my mind hurt. And why was I wet if we weren't in the ocean? I looked down at my leggings, and they were completely soaked, but I felt like I needed to pee. It took me a long moment to register what that meant when I added in the need to push.

"Ummm, I think my water broke," I muttered so softly that it didn't carry far over the noise people were making. The crash. I jerked my head up. ~We need to keep everyone isolated. I think someone, or more than one person, tried to kill us all.~

"Miss? Are you okay?" It was one of the pilots and I just looked at him blankly for a moment, then nodded.

"Out. Right. Door?" He led me to it, the floor of the plane slipping a bit. The plane was at an angle and I had to struggle to not slide down. I held onto Carelian for stability as the pulsing pain beat with my heart.

Contractions. I'm in labor.

That thought beat at me and I couldn't even find cuss words. My head still reeled, and I looked up to find various people staring at me. The expressions ranged from fear to panic to hope.

"Open the door," I said, my voice shaking. I bit back a groan as another contraction hit me.

"It's jammed," someone said, and I groaned. Though if that was due to stupidity or a contraction, I wasn't sure.

"Give me a second."

I could almost hear the shamefaced reactions as I moved to the door. A minute later the door dissolved, along with another inch of hair. A wet gray area with no sun, though it wasn't particularly dark, and no real scents appeared. A few others stepped out first, then they helped me out. I walked away from them a little ways, Carelian making it clear he didn't want anyone near me. It sounded like a stampede as people rushed out. I could hear lots of exclamations and hysterical yells, which had been constant, but I ignored everything.

How had someone sabotaged the plane? Magic? Mundane means? Who was in on it? Had they communicated with anyone?

Another contraction and most thoughts faded out of my brain. I wanted my family.

"Where are they?" I leaned on Carelian again as another contraction hit me, threatening to make my knees buckle.

~There.~ He nudged me, turning me a bit in the endless gray. There in the distance I saw the rip a gleam of blue back into our world. The path of the plane was easy to see. Steam, a furrow deeper than I was tall, and plane parts traced from the rip to where it had come to rest. They had created a realm of sand, mud and water, and I could see where parts had baked to glass, even as water started to fill in the gouges.

I turned further and saw Jo and Sable racing toward me.

Esmere easily kept pace with them, bounding along at their side. To my surprise, and relief, Tirsane following behind them, though a bit more sedately.

I fell into their arms sobbing with relief as I leaned on their strength. "This sucks. Why do women get pregnant?" I muttered as another contraction hit. Their arms wrapped around me and for the first time in hours I felt safe.

"Because it seems to be the only way to get children. Come on, let's get you to the hospital." Sable's logical words made sense. I tried to stand when everything else clicked into place.

"No, this was too well timed. I don't know if it was a terrorist or someone trying to kill me. If it is me they have to know I'm pregnant. We can't go to a hospital. If they try again how many would die?" I swallowed a gasp and tried to breathe.

Am I being paranoid?

Why hadn't anyone else figured out how to save the plane? Surely someone must have been an aeronautical engineer. Weren't there other mages on the plane? I couldn't have been the only one. If I was crazy, I was putting these babies at risk. If this was orchestrated, I was putting a hospital with babies and mothers at risk.

I can't.

"We can't. We can't go there." The sounds of people approaching behind us muttering and exclaiming increased my panic. Anyone among them could be a saboteur, or worse. "Stop them. They can't go anywhere until—" I broke off mid-sentence to moan.

"Enough." Jo, my strong take-no-nonsense Jo stepped in. "Stay back near the plane. We'll get to you in a bit. You're safe here." Her voice carried with it power and an unyielding tone.

"Who are you? We want to go home. You can't keep us here."

"Yeah. I need to call my boss and the airline. This is not how paying passengers should be treated."

"I want to go home and you aren't going to stop me."

The voices chimed in a cacophony of anger, fear, and arrogance. If I could have focused, I might have killed them all in a fit of pain and rage. If, of course, my magic and the pain wracking my body didn't disrupt me halfway through. My hand clamped down on Sable's hand as I fought to stand, to give a united front.

"I believe I can be of assistance here." Tirsane's melodic voice came from behind as she slithered up even with us. She was in full gorgon mode, her naked torso smooth and alabaster, her snakes writhing around her like a corona. There was a collective gasp, and I sensed more than saw her face go from beautiful to inhuman. The first line of people, about fifteen, stiffened as their skin hardened and went marble white, held in the pose they were when she looked at them.

"I suggest you go wait patiently until the Herald has figured out what to do with you." She smiled again. I could see it from the corner of my eye. There was nothing inviting about her smile.

Muffled screams and shuffling arose from where the passengers huddled. But I could feel magic rising again.

"Be aware I can change you all to stone and just keep you like that, or you can sit down, enjoy not being dead, and you will get to go home soon enough. Otherwise, I am more than happy to change you to stone permanently and have new statuary for my domicile." The fact that she sounded delighted about all the possibilities, plus the weaving of the snakes around her skull made her even more terrifying.

It occurred to me the majority of people in my life were rather powerful and terrible. What did that say about me?

The thought was chased away by another contraction, stronger than before.

"Carelian, Sable, go get Dr. Lobdell. She's giving birth here. Esmere, Tirsane, help me get her further away. Hamiada, I need a comfortable area to give birth." Jo snapped out of all of this. And I gladly gave myself over to her capable hands.

As we moved further away, Hamiada appeared, vines twisting up and down her legs as she bounced with agitation. "I do not know what is needed. I have never witnessed a human birth. The rabbit simply makes a nest."

Rather than screaming, which is what I wanted, I gasped out. "Just a chaise lounge for the moment. Dr. Lobdell will tell you what is needed."

"That I can do." A lounge covered in thick grass rose from the ground and I sank into it with relief.

Jo turned and took control of the situation, to my immense relief. "We need cradles. I need to grab blankets. Swaddling clothes. Hamiada, open a door to the nursery please. Then ensure no one else goes through it. Tirsane, can you close that rip? I'd like to keep everyone confined here. Feel free to turn them all into statues if they even look like they are thinking about being stupid."

Tirsane smiled. A smile I hoped she never gave me, as it was all teeth and venom. "They are human beings. I am certain stupid is their default condition."

Jo whitened, making her rich brown skin gray as I saw her realization of just who she was ordering around sink in. But she rallied. "Thank you. And don't forget the rip. You're better at it than I am."

This time Tirsane laughed. "And this is why I hang around you. The three of you are delightful." The rip snapped closed, and she glanced over her shoulder at the still cowed passengers.

Jo nodded with a smile, then raced through the door to the nursery that had appeared between two trees on the other side of the clearing.

They wouldn't stay cowed for long. A contraction ripped through me and I began to struggle out of my pants. "Hamiada," gasp, "can you create something where we can see them, but they can't see us? There are enough witnesses already."

Esmere had stayed by my side. She helped me get my pants and my underwear off. Opposable thumbs made everything easier, though she could have shredded them and I wouldn't have cared. I was glad my tunic covered me, but I could feel what little modesty I had vaporizing as pain and need drove me.

~Breathe child. This is a natural thing. Your body can deal with the changes. Your doctor will be here soon.~

While we had been stripping, a wall of mist appeared between us and the people from the plane. From the confusion I could see on people's faces, and how quickly the fear faded, I knew they couldn't see us. I relaxed. About then Jo came back, arms full of stuff, and she started to give Hamiada orders.

My bossy Jo.

My amusement and love lasted until the next contraction and then I decided that I was going to kill her for ever asking this of me. And twins? Was I insane?

"Breathe, Cori. You remember. Deep, even breaths. You need to wait until Sable gets back."

"She'd better get here fast," I gritted out. I couldn't concentrate. This was not the calm safe environment I'd imagined, but the very idea of going to a hospital made me want to scream in panic.

"Everything is good, Cori. I will keep you safe. No one can hurt you here. This is my place." Hamiada appeared next to me, her vines sprouting little flowers that winked vivid colors at me.

"It is true, Cori. To do anything here she did not allow, I would have to kill her and it is very difficult to kill a dryad when attached to her tree. You are safe." Tirsane's words helped a bit, but still. This was not the ideal birthplace.

Was I broadcasting thoughts now? The next contraction came, and I breathed through it, oddly thirsty. "Water?" I croaked. I felt like I was drenched, but my sweat was absorbed by the grass furniture I lay on, so it seemed like I wasn't sweating, yet I was parched.

"Here," Hamiada said, and I looked around for a glass. A vine reached down to me toward my mouth. A drop of water hung from the tip. My thirst overpowered any other thoughts, and I opened my mouth. A gentle stream of the clearest, coldest water I'd ever had poured into my mouth. Slowly enough I could swallow and I had to force myself to stop drinking, it tasted that good.

The next contraction hit and I tried not to scream. Screaming sounded like such a good idea.

"Where are they?" I asked, in a voice that implied certain death if the answer wasn't "they are here."

Jo moved over with a clean cloth in her hand. She let the vine get it wet, and she bathed my face. The cold felt good to the point the next question out of my mouth was almost polite. Almost.

"Dr. Lobdell?"

"They are coming. Carelian pinged me. They should be here in a few minutes." There was a level of worry in her voice that I didn't like, but the contractions seemed to take over everything in my brain each time.

"Breathe. You got this."

~We are coming back.~

I almost sobbed in relief. I wanted to see my doctor. I lifted my head to see Carelian snarling and hissing at a terrified Anna Lobdell stumbling backwards through the portal with a grim-faced Sable, arms full of supplies following them.

"What in the realms?" I managed before Anna started screaming as she looked around.

"Monsters! Monsters are going to kill me." With a terrified shriek, Dr. Lobdell collapsed to the ground, unconscious.

CHAPTER

FORTY-SEVEN

The ceremony has been planned for months and the royal palace is decked out like a bride waiting for her husband. The rumors of the feasts that will follow the ceremony is the talk among the gourmands. But what really has everyone wondering is the appearance of Corisande Munroe. She is notoriously media shy. But this will be a fete that will be covered by most major news agencies, and our fearless reporters. Just wait to hear the best gossip we can ferret out as Merlin Munroe receives the Chinese Friendship Medal and The Presidential Citizens Medal. ~Magical Daily News

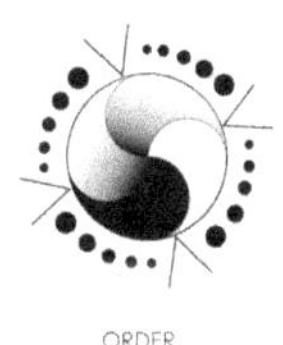

ORDER

I grunted through another contraction as I stared at Carelian and Sable. "What happened?"

Hamiada created a table which Sable dumped the supplies on.

"She said she didn't do house calls and couldn't work without her staff and a labor and delivery room. She wanted us to bring you there." Sable shrugged. That wasn't happening.

~Humans. You are all so excitable. I'll deal with her.~ Esmere stalked over to the doctor and a minute later, a vine dumped water on her face. Anna sat up, a look of terror on her face as Esmere leaned into her face and growled.

Whatever she said, it was only to Anna, but the woman nodded, then looked around, her eyes widening as she took in the glade, Hamiada, and Tirsane. Carelian had his head next to my stomach, purring like he was a motorcycle. But it helped.

Anna's eyes lingered on Tirsane, then Hamiada, then she closed them and breathed in deeply. Esmere sat in front of her, no longer growling, but still exuding an aura of menace. It looked like Anna's lips were moving, but I couldn't hear anything. Then she stood up. "I need to sterilize. Is there soap and warm water to wash in?"

Jo pointed silently to something off to the right, and I followed her gesture.

Over facing the wall of mist, with a clear view to the statutes Tirsane had created, was a basin and another vine with a ledge where Jo had piled towels. Anna nodded once, the sharp jerky movement I saw a lot when people got too far into my life. Maybe that should worry me. Right then, all I cared about was the pain that rippled through my body.

At this point, I was shaking with pain as the contractions came closer and closer together. The vine nudged my mouth, and I gratefully sucked down more icy water. Then almost choked on it as pain hit again.

"Okay, Cori, I'm going to need to look and see how dilated you are," Anna said from my feet.

It took me a minute to figure out what she was saying, then it registered. "Hamiada? Jo? Can you show Hamiada what we need?"

Jo conversed with her, and a minute or so later the chair bottom rose and split, creating support for my legs and letting me slip down a bit. The change in position helped. Everything hurt so much and the only male in the area was Carelian, assuming Hamiada even had a real gender. Though at this point I just didn't care.

It was a strange feeling to be so exposed, but each successive contraction pushed away any concerns.

"You are almost fully dilated, Cori. That means these babies are ready to come out soon. Do we have bassinets to put them in and clothes for the babies?" She looked around. Her trembling had stopped, and she seemed more at ease now that she was in her comfort zone.

"Yes to the clothes, and you've got four people here who can hold them," Jo said. I watched Anna frown and count people, and the widening of her eyes at Tirsane when she realized the gorgon was included. Somehow Tirsane had become a friend to all of us and it solidified some thoughts in my head.

"Okay. Then I think we are ready to do this. Cori, I know we'd talked about a block if the pain got too bad. I can't do that here. I don't have the equipment. So you're going to have to suck it up and push through it." Her gaze was direct, and I got lost for a second in those eyes. "I can help make sure you heal easily, but without machines to monitor your vitals, I'm not willing to apply a magic blockage, as I might not realize you are in trouble until too late."

I nodded shakily, but part of me wanted to cry. It had barely been an hour and already I wanted to wail with the pain and stress.

"If she is hurting too badly, I can assist. One of my snakes has something that resembles your narcotics, but it is not." Tirsane had moved over, gazing at me curiously. "Though I will never complain about laying eggs again. This looks very unpleasant."

Laughter burbled up, but was cut off by a moan as I was hit again by a contraction.

"We ready?" Anna looked around at everyone and the answer must have been an affirmative. "Then take your positions."

Jo moved to my right, Sable my left. The bed widened at my waist and Carelian jumped up to lie next to me. His head sat below my breasts and his purr vibrated through my bones.

~I will alert if her heart rate increases or decreases significantly.~

My sneaky bastard.

Anna seemed to take Carelian's comment in stride. "Excellent." Hamiada lingered over near the edge of the trees, both interested and freaked out. Tirsane hovered a bit with Esmere.

"Cori, do you mind if we watch this…birth?" Tirsane asked in an odd voice.

I was shaking with pain and I shook my head as Jo and Sable each held a hand. "Just stay out of Dr. Lobdell's way." If I was going to get snippy about beings who didn't even have these body parts seeing a baby come out, then I really needed to have a different life.

"Okay Cori, push."

The wave hit and I pushed with it, my voice rising with a scream at the sensation of my body focusing down to trying to expel the boarders who had been in my body for so long. For a moment the sensation of pushing blocked out the pain.

"Good. That is what we need. Listen to your body. It knows what to do," Anna said soothingly, and I almost kicked her. My body had no clue what it wanted to do. But I wanted this pain to stop. Again, I pushed while Jo and Sable murmured how strong I was.

I am going to kill them all.

A chuckle from Tirsane pulled my attention in between the ripples of eviction. I looked up at her and she was smiling.

"What?"

"You said that aloud, dear," Jo said with a smile. "No killing us, please. We're looking forward to these kids."

Any other time, I might have been horrified. Right now, all I wanted was them out. I screamed as I pushed again. Was it supposed to hurt this much?

"Tirsane, they are becoming dangerous," Hamiada's words cut across even my pain, laden with fear as it was.

My attention darted to the scene beyond the wall to see the statues had been set free and they had found a mage or two among the passengers who started casting magic at the wall, as well as beating on it, trying to get to us. To me.

"I have no time or patience for this nonsense. Excuse me."

Even my contractions seemed to freeze at those words. Tirsane turned to face the mob, not that the mages on the other side could see her. "Drop it," she said to Hamiada.

With her words, the wall dropped and Tirsane became Gorgon.

Over the years I'd seen her do her inhumanly beautiful look for a split second, though it had never been directed at me. Usually it was at a single person or a small group. I'd never seen the long-term petrification done in person. I had never realized the difference. This time she became–other.

Even seeing her only from the back, the change was awe inspiring and more terrifying than anything I'd ever felt. My body clenched down hard with strength I didn't know I had. I heard bones crack in Jo and Sable's hands, but I couldn't take my eyes off Tirsane. They squeezed me back just as hard.

The friendly snakes became serpents of nightmares, eyes glowing, hissing, venom dripping from fangs. Her alabaster skin went so white it glowed. Her scales, usually soft and supple, turned into razor sharp petals against her body. I don't know what her face looked like, and I'm not sure I ever will. But from the screams of terror that cut off as men and women became exquisite statues, I'm not sure I want to.

The whole process took less than 30 seconds, and the entire group of people were now a cluster of statues slowly toppling over on marshy ground.

Then she was herself, shaking her shoulders and head to work out kinks. "I haven't done that in a long time." A slow smile spread, holding wicked amusement. "Maybe I should do that to the council the next time they annoy me."

I blinked, and it felt like the glade did too. Then everything restarted, but something was different.

"Crap." Anna was reaching between my legs and pulling out a blood covered babe. "I might need to hire you for difficult pregnancies. That is the hardest I've ever seen someone contract."

"Ow," Jo and Sable said in unison, their grips slacking. "You broke bones in my hand, Cori." Jo gingerly pulled her hand out, moving over toward the doctor and the baby. Carelian jumped off the table and followed her, his eyes locked on the babe. "That hurt, Cori. No more strength tests for you."

Dr. Lobdell handed the baby to Jo, who walked out of my line of sight, Carelian on her heels.

I heard Sable muttering something, but she didn't pull her hand away, just squeezed mine gently. "One more to go, Cori."

I nodded, but my attention was back on my body. Which was loudly demanding the other squatter get out. And I completely agreed. My world narrowed to contract, breathe, contract. And then pressure and…a cry.

I lifted my head to see Dr. Lobdell lifting up another infant, smiling. "Congratulations, ladies. You have a boy and a girl." She stood up and turned and shrieked. "He's eating the baby!"

In a jackknife move, I was sitting up, pulling at my magic, that answered with full force, ready to kill whomever had dared to touch my children. I peered around to see Carelian, leaning over the baby, licking it clean of the blood and afterbirth.

~I do not eat the children of my queans. I would never.~ The affront in his voice made me snicker, even as each swipe of his tongue cleaned off blood and made the child squirm.

"That is not sanitary," Anna squawked, clutching the second baby to her.

~We are not cats, we are Cath. Our saliva has healing properties when we wish. Now let me see this baby, so I can clean him.~ Esmere poked her nose at the infant clutched in Anna's hands.

I collapsed back down. "Ewww, but I've seen their licks heal and clean. Just don't lick off their flesh, please," I muttered as I closed my eyes. Exhaustion draped over me like a limp cat. Sable squeezed my hand once, and went over to rescue the child from Dr. Lobdell. She presented it to Esmere, who began to lick it clean. I closed my eyes, too worn out to even be grossed out.

"You are the strangest group I've ever been involved with." Anna shook her head and came back over to me. "You need to push one more time. The placenta needs to come out."

If whining would have done me any good, I might have whined. As it was, I braced myself and squeezed. I'd never been more exhausted in my life. My body ached, my heart hurt, I was confused, and worried about the idiots Tirsane had turned to stone. That wasn't quite true. I was worried about the fallout from the idiots Tirsane had petrified. But my magic bubbled at me as I reached for it. All the requests even less than they had been before. I wanted to cry with relief, but that would have taken energy and I had none.

There was an odd feeling as the placenta slid out, and I sagged back, questing for the vine with the water. I managed to get a mouthful down, when Anna held up the slimy, bloody bag that had, until recently, protected our children.

"What would you like to do with this?"

I blinked. "Do?"

She shrugged. "Many cultures eat it, or bury it, or preserve it."

I fought down a shudder. "I'm good." The idea of treating it as a fetish made me slightly sick. It was a body part.

"May I have it?" Tirsane spoke from the side of me and I rolled my head over to look at her. Lifting my head sounded exhausting.

"All yours," I said, waving my hand. Then froze in something between horror and nausea as she lifted it into her mouth and slurped it down the way I'd eat an oyster.

Anna shrugged, and I looked at her with raised brows. "That actually qualifies as the most normal thing I've seen in the last hour. Well, humans tend to get it encapsulated, but whatever. I still have more issue with the cats," she said, turning to look.

"Cath," Tirsane and I corrected at the same time. I managed a weary smile. I wanted some clean clothes and a bath. I wanted time to play with my magic and get familiar with it again. It seemed so long ago I hadn't wanted to be a mage, but having it a pale shadow of itself had hurt in a way more than having it gone would have.

"If you say so," she said. "Here, let's get you healed up and cleaned up, then see to the babies." Jo and Sable had one each and were rocking and humming, so I made the assumption there was nothing wrong. I did want to see them, though.

Anna squatted back down and began to clean me up, making offerings as she did so. Just the warm water soothed and helped restore my spirits. Though I still wanted to sleep. Five minutes later, she was done. She brought me over a clean gown, and I stripped and gratefully pulled it on. Part of me relaxed with clothes on, though I was still sore and tender.

"I repaired the tear to your perineum, reduced swelling, and helped the blood flow to your skin. I'll send you an article on how to use your magic to help heal and tighten up your belly. You'll want to massage lotion into your belly daily, as it will help keep it supple and prevent stretch marks."

I nodded, looking at my oddly deflated belly. I'd been rubbing shea butter in regularly, and my skin was softer and healthier than it had ever been. But still it looked weird and sad.

"Give me a minute to run some checks and then—do you want to see your children?" Anna smiled at me, waiting for an answer.

A lump caught in my throat and I nodded. A hunger I never expected and didn't understand tickled at my heart as I watched her take each baby, check them then give them back to their mothers. Wrapped in swaddling clothes, they were quiet for the moment. The incandescent joy on Jo and Sable's faces was the next thing I focused on. The only memory that even came close was the day of their joining.

Tirsane stood back watching all of them, looking curiously complacent, but I only had the energy and caring for a quick glance. I flicked my eyes back and saw Jo and Sable walking toward me, Carelian and Esmere near them. Both Cath looked oddly smug. I so wasn't getting near his tongue until he'd brushed his teeth.

Eww.

Jo walked over to my right and Sable to my left. Jo spoke first. "May I present our first child, Jasmine Sorsha Corisande Guzman." Jo put the baby girl in my arms and I stared down at the child. Wide, dark brown eyes stared up at me out of a face that contained aspects of both Sable and Jo. Tufts of wispy black hair poufed out of her head. Her skin was a light caramel color that came across as golden in the diffused sunlight of the pocket realm.

Wonder filled me and a bit of relief. This beautiful baby was ours, and I was delighted to meet her, but that was it. There was no well of emotion or panic. Love yes, but no foreign emotion. I was still me.

~Told you,~ Esmere whispered smugly. I rolled my eyes, but the last bit of stress that doing this would make me into someone else faded away.

The baby fit neatly on one side of me as Sable presented the other baby. "And this is our son, Charlemagne Henri Jonathan Lancet."

Charlemagne already had tight black curls on his head, and skin the color of chocolate like Sable's. His eyes were so dark brown they looked black as he stared up at me, unblinking.

Two children. I had children.

"They are good? Healthy?" I asked, cradling both of them.

"Yes. I ran checks. They are healthy babies and probably getting hungry." Anna smiled and showed me how to nurse both of them at the same time, something that wouldn't be possible once they started to grow.

It was now or never. "Tirsane, Esmere?" The two females in question glanced at me, as did Jo and Sable. "Do you know the custom of godmothers for humans?" I asked, hoping Jo and Sable would go along with this. We had talked about it, but never settled on anyone. But I knew in my heart this was the right decision.

Esmere tilted her head. ~I believe so. One who will protect the child if the parent is unable to. Otherwise, a special relative that is theirs alone.~

"Basically. Someone they can turn to when all seems lost. Esmere will you be the godmother of Jasmine? Tirsane will you be the godmother of Charlemagne?"

The two beings looked stunned. They glanced at each other and then the three of us, as Jo and Sable had moved to either side of me, watching the two babes nurse.

"You are okay with this?" I glanced at the kids' moms, worried I'd overstepped.

"I think it is a wonderful idea. Cori, who did you want for the godfathers?" Jo asked, dropping a kiss on my head.

"Sanchez for Charlemagne and Charles for Jasmine. That way they both have contacts in all aspects of the world able to help and protect them regardless if they are merlin or mundane."

Tirsane laughed at that. "They will be merlins. Already I can feel them waiting to emerge. Your children will be full merlins, Cori, with full access to all of magic."

That didn't excite me, but it would wait until another day to be dealt with. For now, I'd try to enjoy having two kids and no longer being pregnant.

"I love that idea. Let Sanchez spoil him without anyone wondering why." Jo laughed and I looked up at her smiling face.

"And it gives Charles a reason to visit more often," Sable chimed in, one hand on Jasmine's head. "It's perfect, Cori."

I smiled and looked at the two beings. "So, will you?"

When Tirsane became Gorgon she was as beautiful as she was deadly, but right now she glowed with joy and excitement and she was the most beautiful woman I'd ever seen. "I would be honored."

~As would I. I shall teach my beautiful god-daughter how to make any Cath proud.~ Esmere glowed with pride.

Carelian licked Esmere's muzzle, then jumped up, curling next to me, purring like a freight train. There amid the trees, near the petrified passengers, a gorgon, a dryad, my life partners, two Cath, and one kidnapped doctor, I fed my children for the first time, basked in the love of my family, and delighted in feeling like myself with my magic again.

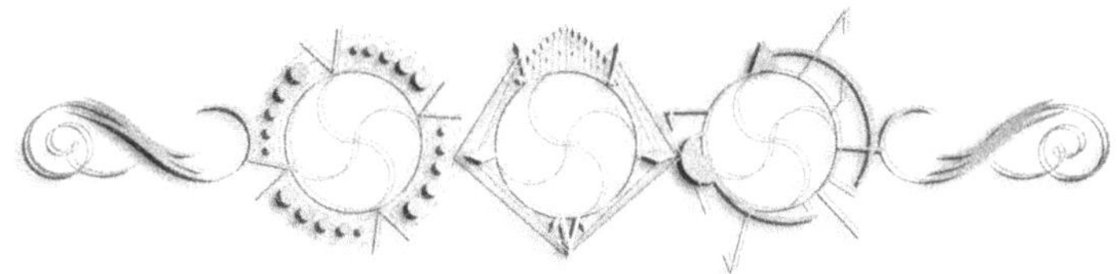

EPILOGUE

Information Request: Anyone who has any insight into the incident with Merlin Cori Munroe, the gorgon, and the plane crash is asked to contact Merlin Katilina Ivanisky. This is for an ongoing research study into the nature of the planes creatures. ~ Tomes of Wonder

---

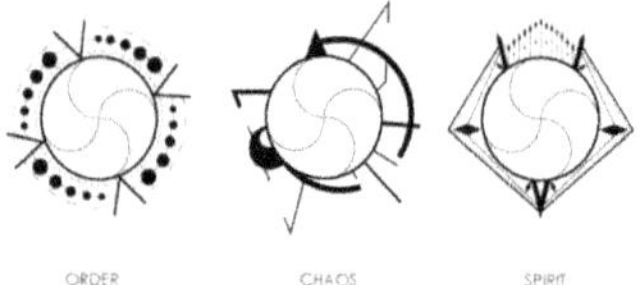

J uggling babies, investigators, statues, smug Cath, and an annoyed doctor made the next few weeks interesting and exhausting. Oddly, the babies were the easiest to deal with. They wanted food. Charlemagne preferred my left breast and

Jasmine my right for no reason I could figure out. They wanted to be held and changed. That covered their wants. Nobody else was quite that easy.

For all that she stepped up when we needed her, Anna Lobdell was not happy about being kidnapped. She read the three of us, plus Carelian, the riot act. After much groveling she agreed to not press charges, but only if we donated a hundred hours of community service, each, to the woman's shelter and be a silver level sponsor for the next birthing center fundraiser. As all of us agreed with the mission of the shelter and, well, we had kidnapped her, we willingly agreed. Then apologized again.

The outrage over the ceremony rattled around the world for a week, and we were telling government officials to go away as we dealt with newborns. It didn't stop until Cixi made a public statement that she was honored and horrified that I would try to live up to social expectations so close to giving birth. She publicly presented her birthing gift to Tiantang, who flashed away to deliver it to me. He had cleared coming to me, and I received him outside on the lawn with the babes, Jo, Sable, Esmere, and Carelian all there. I'd started to feel like I had an entourage. He inspected the babies, shook his head at their tiny frailness, then left the gift, the Friendship Medal, and popped back telling them I and the babies were happy and healthy. That finally managed to put an end to all the drama.

The gift was actually two. They had found or made two small jade dragons that were both beautiful and useful. If you chilled them, they were supposed to be good for babies to chew on when they started teething, with the rippled scales carved into the jade. They looked very much like Tiantang and were such works of art I hesitated to let babies abuse them. Cixi had sent a letter written in painstaking English apologizing and asking me to tea sometime after life had settled down. I sent her a formal reply graciously accepting. That was set up for some time in the next two months.

Indira got tagged to be the liaison between Tirsane, Hamiada, the FBI, and the NTSB. Mainly because I wasn't up to it. Tirsane refused to work with a man and she knew Indira. They'd bonded a bit at the dinner and baby shower. It took a solid week of negotiation between everyone for Hamiada to give investigators access to the aircraft. It took another week to figure out how to get the airplane back to Earth. Luckily Indira was good at opening rips, and when you weren't fighting a crashing plane and your own terror, it proved to be much easier to get it back to earth, if more swamped in bureaucracy.

The statues took even more time. Tirsane was annoyed. At least that was the feeling I got. I wasn't sure what the various government agencies thought, but either way I knew their files on us had tripled. Eventually she relented, after negotiating payment, or offerings, in snickerdoodles and balut, and turned them all back to humans.

At that point, the FBI, NTSB, Draft office, and I'm sure other agencies descended on the passengers like the second coming of Merlin. And I found out I was an idiot.

It turned out there was no saboteur, instead there was a catastrophic domino effect failure that had already taken down two planes with all people on board dead, and no idea why. This plane had been scheduled to be recalled and inspected, but the emergency had diverted it to JFK and our flight.

So many little things. If I'd been in Atlanta, they would have all died and I would have had a normal labor in a hospital. Less terror but more mysteries because no one doubted that the plane would have been lost with all lives on board and they may never have figured out what happened. I finally finished the blanket, though not before the babies were born. We couldn't decide who got it, so it draped over the eggs, wrapping them in us.

Shay, Hishatio, and Amadahy were terrorizing the council, or at least per Esmere's stories they were. I got a nice gift from Shay, a 100% cashmere blanket in burgundy, with a note saying–Thank you for the best job I've ever had. This is a blast.

I laughed and kept the blanket from Carelian. It was mine. He had rebounded back to normal the days after the twins were born. We hadn't realized how exhausted trying to support five beings had left him. He was almost okay with the idea of the twins having their own familiars. Almost.

Everything settled down, and I had three weeks of maternity leave left and I was almost ready to return to work. Our children were mostly perfect. The amount of drool, shit, and pee two creatures so tiny could produce stunned me. But holding them and nursing them was more enjoyable than I expected. My breasts were huge and just getting the milk out created enough relief that I remembered their feeding times better than they did. Though I'd already gotten in the habit of pumping milk and freezing it, just in case. Being able to do magic again made everything much easier, bottles were simple to heat, and more than once I used urine to do magic just so I didn't have to get up and disturb the kids.

Jo and Sable were over the moon and treated me like a princess. Everyone in the house loved Jaz and Magne, though we pronounced it mane. After two weeks I couldn't imagine my life without them. It was odd, I completely loved them, but while I didn't mind nursing them, Jo and Sable were the ones ga-ga over them. Already I could see our life; I would be the calm logical one unmoved by pleading or protests, and those two would lean on me to be the one to set the rules. It sounded like a good life.

My body responded to the yoga I did every day, with Carelian alongside. He refused to call it downward dog, it was cat stretch. But he flowed through most poses with a grace I tried to mimic. If nothing else, he made me laugh. With everything going on, I didn't have much room in my brain for anything else. Babies, healing, questions from Shay about various council members, returning to work, and government questions kept me busy.

"Someone's coming up the porch," Hamiada sang out seconds before the doorbell rang. I was feeding the kids. Sable had found a chair made to support a mom while nursing. I was feeding Magne. Jaz was already back in her crib and yawning. They both ate like Carelian and slept about as much.

Esmere peered at them from beneath the changing table. She'd rarely left, oddly fascinated by how helpless they were. But her purrs filled the room, and the children were comforted by the presence of the two Cath. I just hoped when they started demanding to ride her, she didn't hurt them too badly. Even I was tempted occasionally. It was hard not to live out cartoon dreams when you had a cat the size of a pony. Not to mention she made most of our rooms seem tiny.

I pried Magne off my breast—at three weeks he had suction that was insane—and wrapped him back up. A walk outside in the spring weather sounded wonderful. I wanted some sun.

"Hey, Cori. Up for a surprise visitor?" Jo had stuck her head around the door and was smiling.

I furrowed my brows in confusion. Most of our friends had already swung by to see the babies. Even Salistra had popped in while we were in the glade to snort and pronounce them tolerable. Charles had come to see them and hold his goddaughter. He admitted they were cute, then fled before anyone could see the tears in his eyes. Hamiada spilled the beans about that. Sanchez had been delighted and Magne already had custom onesies from him.

Even Jeorgaz and Baneyarl as well as family on both sides had already invaded us. Most of the drama regarding the plane was being held away from the house, and most of the human friends would have called or texted first.

"Sure," I said, double checking I'd fastened my top. At this point, I think I'd flashed everyone.

Jo smiled at me and stepped out of the way. A young man, he couldn't have been much over sixteen or seventeen, stepped in. Hazel eyes, a lanky body, brown hair pulled back in a low tail at the base of his neck, and a self-conscious smile that looked strangely familiar.

"Hey, Cori. Sorry it took me so long." His voice cracked as he spoke. At the same time my heart snapped a missing piece in place. Be it hormones, the active few weeks, or just a heart that needed more, whatever, I threw myself into my brothers' arms with a cry of joy.

"Kris, you're here!" I exclaimed as Jo watched with a smile, Sable appearing behind her.

He didn't say a word, just hugged me tight as I held him in a death grip.

All my family here.

Finally.

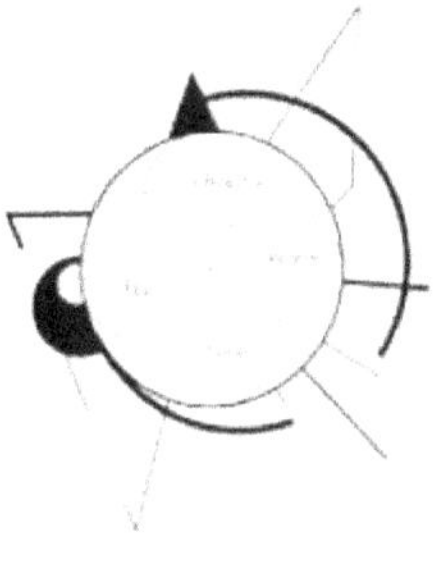

CHAOS

Chaos:

- Entropy
- Fire
- Water
- Time

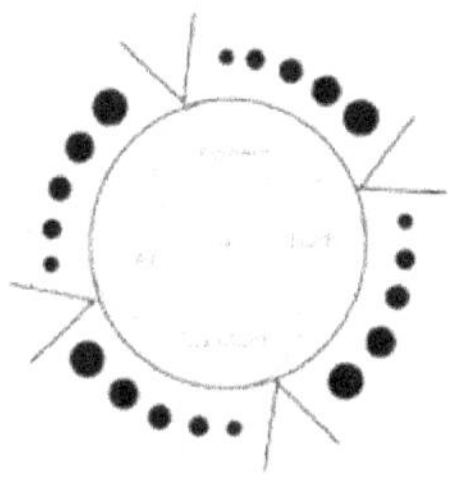

ORDER

Order:

- Pattern
- Air
- Earth
- Transform

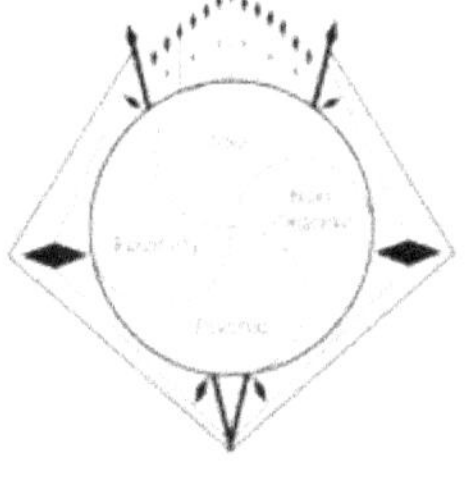

SPIRIT

Spirit:

- Soul
- Relativity
- Non-Organic
- Psychic

Author's Notes

This is book 6 in Twisted Luck, based in the Ternion universe. This series is just the first stories in what is a complicated and fascinating world. If you enjoyed Cori getting a taste of what life holds in store for her, wait until you see where she ends up. This is a long series and I hope you enjoy this world as much as I do.

If you loved this novel, please take the time to leave a review, you will be amazed at the difference it makes.

Book 7, Unbalanced Luck, is available now.

If you'd like to stay in touch, you can follow me on social media at the following places:

Website: https://www.badashpublishing.com/
Facebook: https://www.facebook.com/badashbooks/
Twitter: https://twitter.com/badashbooks
Instagram: https://www.instagram.com/badashbooks/
Bookbub: https://www.bookbub.com/profile/mel-todd

There is a Twisted Luck Fan Group. I can't wait to see you there - https://www.facebook.com/groups/1500124503671599

If you're interested in free books, keeping up with what is

going on in my life, as well as sales and launch announcements, you can sign up for my newsletter at my website. You never know what freebies might be in it

Mel Todd